Omnibus e(

# MURDER IN THE TITLE
## and

# NOT DEAD,
# ONLY RESTING

Simon Brett

Back-In-Print Books Ltd

Copyright © Simon Brett 1983, 1984, 2004

The right of Simon Brett to be identified as the Author of the
Work has been asserted by Simon Brett in accordance with the
Copyright, Designs and Patents Act 1988.

Published by Back-In-Print Books Ltd 2004
ISBN 1 903552 43 5
Previously published in Great Britain by
Victor Gollancz under ISBN 0 575 03266 9 and 0 575 03438 6

A CIP catalogue record is available from the British Library.

Printed and bound on demand by
Lightning Source.

Back-In-Print Books Ltd
P O Box 47057
London SW18 1YW
020 8637 0975

www.backinprint.co.uk
info@backinprint.co.uk

When Simon Brett studied at Oxford he became President of the OUDS, appeared in cabarets and directed the Oxford Theatre Group at the Edinburgh Festival Fringe in 1967.

Later he worked as a light entertainment producer for BBC radio and TV before taking up writing full time in 1979.

Simon created the Charles Paris and Mrs Pargeter detective series and, to his fans' relief, he is still writing more. He also made a name as the author of the radio and TV series *After Henry*. The radio series *No Commitments*, the best-selling *How to be a Little Sod* and the novel *Shock to the System* filmed starring Michael Caine are other fruits of his imaginative mind. He is married, has three children and lives in a village on the South Downs.

## This is a Back-In-Print Book.

# MURDER IN THE TITLE

To Little Fat Jack

## ACT ONE

## *Chapter One*

SUNLIGHT, FILTERED THROUGH the stained glass armorial bearings of the De Meaux family, splashed bloodstains on the painted flooring. The maid, Wilhelmina, pert in her black and white uniform, entered through the heavy oak door to answer the telephone's insistent summons.

'Good afternoon. Wrothley Grange,' she intoned, economically providing both temporal and spatial information for those unable to afford programmes.

'No, I'm afraid Sir Reginald De Meaux is not available at the moment. When he's working on his collection of duelling swords in the study he does not like to be disturbed,' she continued, thoughtfully revealing the name and a little of the character of her employer, as well as planting a useful murder weapon.

'I'm sorry, Mr Laurence, the butler, has just had to pop down to the village,' she apologized, raising comforting expectations that, when Something was Done, there would be at least one obvious suspect who might have Done It.

'No, I'm afraid Lady Hilda is in the rose garden and Master James is playing tennis with Miss Kershaw,' she responded, filling out the cast list a little.

'No, Professor Weintraub has gone for a walk with Miss Laycock-Manderley and Colonel Fripp,' she continued, mopping up most of the rest of the cast.

'What, me?' Coy giggle. 'Oh, sir, you don't want to know my name. Well, it's Wilhelmina,' she confessed readily, completing the dramatis personae (except for the policemen in Act Three).

'Oh yes, certainly sir, I'll take a message, just let me get a pencil and paper.'

This she did, and stood with the one poised over the other. 'Right. I'm ready. Yes, and the message is...? What? Did you say...Murder...?'

She looked at the receiver with eight-years-at-stage-school's worth of amazement.

'Who's there? Who's there?' she demanded jiggling the buttons of the telephone.

She replaced the receiver and looked out front. 'Well, I declare,' she said, momentarily perplexed.

But her confusion was short-lived. 'Must have been a crank,' she concluded with an easily satisfied shrug, and went over to the mantelpiece, her feather duster poised, to draw attention to another potential murder weapon, a heavy brass candlestick.

With her back thus conveniently to the French windows, she did not perceive the entrance of James De Meaux, dressed, for reasons of plot, in dazzling tennis whites and, for reasons of vanity, in a lot of body make-up. She did not see him deposit his racket on a leather armchair, nor apparently was she aware of his approach behind her until his arms were chastely round her waist.

'Oh, Mr James,' she protested, fluttering her feather duster without much conviction in order to evade his grasp.

'Come on, Willy. One little kiss,' James demanded roguishly.

'No, James, not here. Someone might come in. I must go.' She made for the door, but was prevented from reaching it.

'You weren't so coy at half-past eleven last night in the summerhouse,' James reminded her (at the same time setting up a useful point of reference for the untangling of alibis which lay ahead in Act Three).

'That's as maybe,' Wilhelmina reprimanded him primly. 'What a girl does when she's got her uniform on is very different from what she does when she's got it off.'

There had been considerable discussion during rehearsal as to whether this was a deliberately funny line and as to how it should be played. The final decision to play it straight was vindicated by total lack of reaction from the Rugland Spa audience, except for a dirty guffaw from a fourteen-year-old boy who hadn't wanted to come but been dragged along to the theatre by his parents.

'Oh, come on,' James pleaded.

'No, really, Mr James. There's you engaged to Miss Kershaw and –'

'She won't mind.'

'She'll be a pretty strange fiancée if she doesn't.'

'She won't mind, because she won't know. Look, Willy, you know the situation...'

In spite of Wilhelmina's rueful nod, James still proceeded with his explanation, because, although she might know the situation the audience did not. 'The old man's money only comes to me if I'm married when he pops off. Now, I know there's no chance of him dying in the near future...' (Tragic irony, this, if the audience did but realize it.) 'On the other hand, I don't want to get caught on the hop, so it'll be safer if I marry Felicity now just to be sure.'

'Huh. I thought you really loved me – but all you want is a bit of skirt.'

'I do really love you. But even if I did just want a bit of skirt, my father wouldn't wear it.'

This line, which no one had thought of as suspect during rehearsal, was greeted by huge laughter. Anxiety glinted in the eyes of James and Wilhelmina. It intensified as they heard an echoing giggle from behind the door of the tall cupboard by the fireplace.

'He's got this social thing about dangling with tomest – er, tangling with domestics,' James fluffed on desperately.

'But surely.'

Wilhelmina put a full stop after these two words (which were all that the author had supplied in the script), and the pair of them waited ten seconds until the door opened.

It admitted Lady Hilda De Meaux, who informed them that she had something of enormous importance to impart to her son. On his own.

Wilhelmina made for the door. But before she could reach it (and before Lady Hilda could reveal her secret), Felicity Kershaw appeared through the French windows in tennis whites, complaining that James was jolly lazy and that she was fed up with always looking for his balls in the long grass (another moment which made the recalcitrant fourteen-year-old think that he had perhaps hitherto underestimated the theatre as a medium of entertainment).

The cast all looked nervously at the cupboard door, from behind which another snort of laughter had been heard.

A little idle banter ensued between Lady Hilda and Felicity about how much they could do with a cup of tea, and Wilhelmina was despatched to make the necessary arrangements. She made for the door.

But her exit was again delayed, this time by the return from their walk of Professor Weintraub, Miss Laycock-Manderley and Colonel Fripp. The Professor, fuzzy in tweed and garlanded with binoculars, cameras and tape-recorder, expressed his hopes for good bird-watching during his stay in the area, stating the intention to try his luck the following day over beyond the pine forest.

Colonel Fripp, moustache and hackles bristling, advised caution. Surely the Professor knew that in the pine forest was a top-secret army research establishment.

No? Really? The Professor feigned surprise. How interesting.

In the ensuing pause Miss Laycock-Manderley suddenly announced that she had returned from their walk early because of a premonition. She was, she explained, psychic, and she was experiencing a strong sense of evil. Something awful was going to happen at Wrothley Grange. The feeling was very powerful. 'It's happened to me before,' she confided, 'in many different ways. But I've never had it like this.'

Here was another line to tickle the fourteen-year-old's sense of humour, and again the cast had cause to look with irritation at the cupboard door. Beneath its make-up, Lady Hilda's face set in an expression of annoyance as she laughed off her guests' fears and once again suggested-the cure-all of tea.

James thought this was a jolly good idea, Felicity confessed to being parched, and Professor Weintraub joked heavily about the way everything in England stopped for tea.

Wilhelmina (for whom the Act had now degenerated into a series of frustrated attempts to exit) was once again sent off to fetch tea. She made for the door. But before she reached it, Lady Hilda remembered that they would not have enough tables for so large a party. Would Wilhelmina mind getting one of the folding card-tables out of the cupboard by the fireplace?

'No, of course not, milady,' enthused Wilhelmina, glad perhaps of another door to make for.

In the front row of the Circle, the time-freckled hand of Leslie Blatt, the play's author, squeezed the knee of his eighteen-year-old companion. 'This bit's good,' he wheezed. 'Never fails.'

Wilhelmina turned the handle of the cupboard and the door swung outwards.

The body of an elderly man in tweeds fell out. It landed neatly on its back in the space between a sofa and an armchair.

Stuck in its chest was a duelling sword. The red light from the window intensified the glistening wet redness on his shirt-front.

The cast, disposed in a neat semicircle around the body, gasped as one.

'Oh no!' screamed Lady Hilda. And then, for purposes of identification, 'It's Reginald!' Finally, for those in the audience of particularly slow perception, she added, 'Killed by one of his own duelling swords!'

The duelling sword trembled and swayed as the body shook with suppressed giggles.

The curtain fell to a clacking of geriatric applause.

As soon as it was down, Lady Hilda's face lost its last vestige of benevolence. 'Bloody unprofessional!' she stormed. 'I will not work with people who behave like that. Either he goes or I go!'

And she made for her dressing-room.

In the stalls an old lady fumbled with the cellophane on her box of After-Dinner Mints. 'Not much of a part for that actor, the one who dies, is it?' she observed to her companion.

'No,' her companion agreed.

'I wonder if it's someone we know from the television.'

Her companion turned the pages of her programme with arthritic hands. 'No, the name doesn't mean anything to me.'

'What is it?'

'Charles Paris. You heard of him?'

'No, dear.'

## Chapter Two

AFTER THE CURTAIN-CALL Charles Paris tried again to ring his estranged wife Frances, but again there was no reply.

There were no spirits at the brief first night party, so Charles had to make do with a glass of bitter Spanish red. It was not what he needed, but it was better than nothing. It might dissipate the headache left from the day's earlier excesses. He knew he was weak-willed to react to stress by drinking, but stress had a very debilitating effect on his will. His resolutions to drink less always occurred when he was feeling strong-willed, and at such times he didn't need the support of excessive drinking anyway.

He didn't want to talk to anyone at the party, just to pickle his distress in private, but the theatre's General Manager, Donald Mason, dragged him across to a middle-aged couple who were introduced as Herbie and Velma Inchbald. Donald, who had the incisive manner and affected the pin-striped suits of corporate middle management, was difficult to refuse.

The Inchbalds were well-dressed – possibly over-dressed for the first night of a play at a provincial rep theatre. Herbie, who compensated for his stocky shortness with an Einstein mane of grey hair and a large cigar, wore a dark velvet suit and a velvet bow-tie, which at first sight gave the impression of evening dress. His wife's pudgy, powdered face was squarely framed by black hair which looked like (and quite possibly was) a wig. The precise definition of her curves was expensively obscured by a blue full-length dress in some ruched semi-transparent material, but the space it took up suggested they were ample. The fat of her neck and fingers was constricted by jewellery.

'Herbie is Chairman of the Theatre Board.' Donald Mason supplied this information and bustled off efficiently.

'Ah,' said Charles Paris.

'First time you've worked at the Regent, Mr Paris?'

Yes. If working is the word for what I'm doing, he thought savagely. Does being a dead body count as working? Though of course someone has to play it – can't have non-Equity stiffs crashing the union closed shop.

He contented himself with saying, 'Yes.'

'Grand little theatre,' Herbie Inchbald affirmed complacently. He pronounced the word 'thee-ettah', which made Charles' hackles rise. He knew it was mere snobbery, hut he could never believe that people who said 'thee-ettah' were true friends of the medium.

'Won't find a better little rep for a few hundred miles, I can tell you,' Herbie Inchbald continued. 'No, people come a long way to see our little shows.'

'From as far away as Leominster,' Velma Inchbald agreed. 'Even some from Worcester.'

'Ah.'

'Do you know Herefordshire well, Mr Paris?'

'Not very, no.'

'You'll find it's a lovely county.'

'Oh, good.'

The conversation seemed about to go under for the third time. Charles handed it a straw to clutch at. 'Did you enjoy the show tonight?'

Under normal circumstances modesty would have stopped him from asking the question, but he felt that the size of his contribution to this particular production absolved him from any charges of fishing for compliments.

'Oh, yes, grand show.'

'Grand,' Velma agreed.

Charles wondered whether his hearing was going, along with other waning faculties like hoping, coping and bladder control. Could it really be that they had enjoyed *The Message Is Murder*? He hadn't spent very long rehearsing the piece, because of the nature of his part, but it had been long enough to form the opinion that the play was the direst piece of codswallop ever to be exhumed from the mortuary of dead plays.

'You mean you thought it was well done?' This seemed marginally more likely than that they had actually enjoyed the writing.

'Well done, and a damned good little play.'

'Yes, a good little play,' echoed Velma.

Charles must have failed to disguise his disbelief, because he found himself being asked if he didn't like the piece.

'Well, erm, it's probably not my favourite sort of play. I mean, I often wonder how plays like that do get chosen. I mean, there are thousands of really good plays around and...'

'Herbie helped choose the play.'

'Oh. Did he?'

'Yes, I did. Well, credit where it's due, Donald first suggested it. But soon as I read it, I thought it was a grand little play.'

'And then you read it again when we were in Corsica in the summer.'

'That's right, I did. Still thought it was grand.'

'Ah.'

'You see, Mr Paris, in a local rep you have to give the public what they want. All right, maybe *The Message Is Murder* isn't experimental, hasn't got any arty-farty pretensions, but it's damned good entertainment. Nothing like a thriller to bring the crowds in – especially if it's got "murder" in the title. And you know, Leslie Blatt's a local author too – retired to Bromyard – so that's another attraction. Oh yes, a good thriller, a Shakespeare, the pantomime, of course – those are your bankers at a local rep. Those are the sort of things people in Rugland Spa want to see. Get those under your belt and then you can afford to be a bit experimental. I mean, do you know what our next production is...?'

'Yes, I heard.'

'*Shove It*, that's what it is. *Shove It*. Now there's a modern play, if you like. Going to raise a few eyebrows in Rugland Spa, isn't it, Velma?'

'I should say so.'

'But it's the sort of show we ought to do...every now and then. And with Kathy Kitson in it, the people'll come along.'

'Yes...'

'We're very proud of the Regent here in Rugland Spa, Mr Paris.'

'Yes, well, it's a lovely old theatre,' said Charles, trying to soften the accusation in Herbie Inchbald's tone.

'Certainly is. Built in 1894, you know. Chequered career, like most theatres. Kept opening and closing under different managements. Closed completely after the last war – sold and used as a repository for corn.'

'A tradition that is still maintained,' Charles joked ill-advisedly.

'What?'

'Nothing.'

'Anyway, virtually derelict in the early sixties, then some far-sighted lads on the council took it in hand – all refurbished – reopened in '62.'

'And has been going ever since?'

'More or less, yes. Nasty scare, what, three years back? Big offer for the whole Maugham Cross site – that's what this part of the town's called – from a property company. Don't know if you know them – Schlenter Estates?'

'No.'

'Oh well, they're big. Anyway, lot of the council wanted to sell, but we organized local opinion and held on. Close call, though. After that we reconstituted the Board, and I got in Lord Kitestone to be our Patron.'

'Oh,' said Charles in a way that he hoped sounded interested. The name had been delivered in a way that required reaction.

'Willie Kitestone owns Onscombe House, stately home out on the Ludlow road,' Velma added helpfully. 'Very large place.'

'Ah...'

Once again the conversation lay inert, and Charles tried a tentative kiss of life. 'So many provincial theatres these days seem to depend for their survival on the local council.'

'Oh yes.'

'And the Arts Council, of course.'

'Oh yes.'

'Still, we're all right here.' Velma Inchbald smiled sweetly. So long as Herbie's on the council. He's a real thee-ettah-lover.'

Charles couldn't think of anything to say. He didn't like the Inchbalds and that made him feel guilty. He should have liked them, he should have approved of their support for the theatre, his profession needed more people with their attitude. And yet...And yet they seemed to him just boring and slightly pompous.

No doubt a reflection of his own mood. But he felt cussedly disinclined to resuscitate the conversation yet again.

Herbie did it for him. 'Of course, it's not just me,' he said magnanimously, in a voice that seemed to invite contradiction. 'A lot of other people help make the Regent a going concern. I mean, you know Donald – he's a real firecracker. Full of ideas. Only been here a year, but he's really made some changes. Bright young man is Donald. I'm always ready to listen to his advice.'

'And of course Tony works so hard.' Charles felt he should mention the Artistic Director. Though Antony Wensleigh was somewhat vague and a bit of an old woman, there was no questioning his commitment to the Regent Theatre.

'Yes.' The word contained less than whole-hearted endorsement from Herbie Inchbald. 'Mind you, he'd be lost without Donald. And we have to be careful. This theatre's under constant threat you know. Prime position in the town. Good few developers like to snap it up. Only take a little bit of mismanagement for the place to cease to be economically viable. Then it closes, I get out-voted on the council – there's plenty of Philistines on that council, you know – and before you can say knife, the Regent's gone to make way for another supermarket, or hotel, or what-have-you. And that'd be terrible.'

'Terrible,' Velma concurred.

After *The Message Is Murder* Charles didn't feel so sure. And despised himself for the meanness of the thought.

He managed to escape the Inchbalds and get another glass of the Spanish red, which was tasting increasingly as if the bottle had been left open for a week. It matched the sourness of Charles' mood.

He knew its basic cause, but he also knew that it had been aggravated by the events of the evening. It really hurt him to have been described as unprofessional by Kathy Kitson at the end of the first act. And it hurt the more because he knew the charge was justified. No excuses about the state of emotional tension he was in could excuse his childish giggling at the idiocies of Leslie Blatt's dialogue.

As he thought of the playwright, he looked across to the old man, whose claw-like hands were pawing his eighteen-year-old companion, trying to dissuade her from her assertion that she really ought to be going home. Charles shuddered. For a man in his fifties with a taste for young actresses, the sight of Leslie Blatt prompted unwelcome comparisons.

Still, one thing he could do – indeed, should do – to regain some of the day's lost ground, was to make his peace with Kathy Kitson.

He looked across at her. She had changed out of her Lady Hilda De Meaux costume, but didn't look any different. Kathy Kitson never looked any different. She was an actress who lacked the humility Mahomet had shown to the mountain. She didn't go to her parts; they came to her. And if a few of the lines – or even the whole emphasis – of the play had to change to accommodate her performance, then that's the way it had to be.

Kathy Kitson's only performance consisted of Kathy Kitson, her hair set that afternoon, walking elegantly round stages in waisted silk dresses, and speaking with brittle elocution whatever lines she thought appropriate to Kathy Kitson. This she had done endearingly in West End comedies during the fifties, popularly in the television sit com, *Really, Darling?* during the late sixties, and with decreasing éclat in decreasingly prestigious provincial theatres during the seventies and into the eighties. This performance she had finally brought, with the desperation of the last dodo, to *The Message Is Murder* at the Regent Theatre, Rugland Spa.

And this performance, to judge from what she was saying to a young man in a leather jacket as Charles approached, was the one she intended to give in the forthcoming production of that searing indictment of contemporary society by one of Britain's most controversial young playwrights, *Shove It..*

'You see, darling,' she murmured huskily, 'I don't think all that...language is necessary.'

'But,' protested the young man in the leather jacket, 'Royston Everett's language is an authentic reflection of life on the streets of Liverpool.'

'I'm sure it is, darling, but one can't just present plays for the people of Liverpool.'

'It's not *for* the people of Liverpool, it's *about* the people of Liverpool. Everett was brought up in Toxteth. He knows what he's talking about.'

'I'm sure he does, but that is not really the point. You see, my feeling is that playwrights tend to fall back on bad language when their confidence is threatened.'

'Oh.'

'When they're afraid their points won't get across, they reinforce them with bad language.'

'Well –'

'In my young day that wasn't necessary. We used something else to reinforce the playwright's points – an old-fashioned little thing called *acting*.'

This left the young man in the leather jacket without speech, and gave Charles the opportunity to intervene. 'Kathy, I just wanted to apologize –'

'And another thing I think is unnecessary,' she went on, turning a deep-frozen, silk-clad shoulder to Charles, 'is all this nudity.'

'Oh, but sometimes,' the young man in the leather jacket protested, 'it's absolutely essential.'

'No, darling.' Kathy Kitson's put-down was gentle, but firm. 'Again, a good actress can give the impression of nudity while remaining dressed.'

In a waisted silk dress, no doubt, Charles thought vindictively. He couldn't really blame her for cutting him, but it didn't improve his mood. He drained his Spanish vinegar and went to replenish it. Ahead of him at the bar were two men, one crumpled, fat and unfamiliar, the other Gordon Tremlett, the actor who had played Colonel Fripp.

The crumpled fat man was persuading the girl behind the bar that it'd save time if she filled him a pint glass of wine rather than 'one of these piddling little things'. He succeeded, and moved away with the brim of the tankard already to his lips.

Charles could always recognize a professional drinker. 'Who is he?' he asked Gordon Tremlett.

'Frank Walby, love. Theatre Critic on the *Gazette*.'

'Ah. And what's he going to think of the show?'

'Oh, he'll adore it. Never given a bad notice in his life. Bit like a review in *Stage* – so nice it doesn't mean anything. Praise for all, my dear, including the lady who tore the tickets. No, I've lived in Rugland Spa fifteen years and never seen a harsh word from Frank.'

Gordon Tremlett had an unusual history for an actor. He had come into the business after taking an early retirement as, of all things, a bank manager. Always a keen (and talented) amateur actor, he had managed to get his Equity ticket, and worked at the Regent whenever there was a suitable small part for him. He had hardly ever worked anywhere else, but demonstrated the fanaticism of all converts and was far more theatrical than most lifetime actors.

His colleagues regarded him with amused tolerance and occasional resentment. The latter arose whenever he tried to identify too closely with the rest of the company. They could not treat as an equal in their own hazardous profession someone cushioned by a large pension from Barclays Bank.

Gordon Tremlett's talent was serviceable, but he was an example of Antony Wensleigh's tendency to surround himself with casts of friends rather than searching out excellence.

'Sorry, love,' Gordon apologized, picking up a tray of drinks and moving off. 'Got some people in.'

Gordon always had people in. His own little claque, all members of the amateur dramatic society he had formerly supported and now patronized, all still slightly breathless at the fact that one of their number was working in the 'real' theatre.

Charles was walking away from the bar with another glass of gall, when Donald Mason again busied up to him.

'Charles,' the General Manager whispered. 'Just a warning.'

'What?'

'Lad in the leather jacket – he's one of the Arts Council assessment team.'

'Really?'

'Yes. And our prospects of getting a grant for next season are dicey enough, so just be careful.'

'Sure. But you'd better detach him from Kathy. He seems to be a big fan of

Royston Everett's work, and she's calmly telling him how she plans to expurgate all her lines in *Shove It*.'

'Oh, that's not the sort of thing that's going to worry him. No, I'm more concerned that he doesn't hear about Tony's mismanagement.'

'What mismanagement?' It was news to Charles that the Artistic Director had been guilty of any.

'Oh, you know, cock-ups over the budget and all the other things. For God's sake don't let the Arts Council bloke hear about those.'

Charles raised his head and, over Kathy Kitson's shoulder, met the eyes of the young man in the leather jacket. There was no doubt that the Arts Council bloke had heard Donald Mason's words.

Mr Pang, owner of The Happy Friend Chinese Restaurant and Takeaway, watched impassively as Cherry Robson rose from the table, slapped Leslie Blatt round the head and swept out. Cherry, a former dancer now toying with the idea of becoming a straight actress (she was playing Wilhelmina in *The Message Is Murder*), was a tough girl who knew with great accuracy what she wanted from life. It didn't include being touched up by septuagenarian playwrights.

Leslie Blatt, totally unsquashed, leered at Charles. 'I'll get her, you know. Women are like that, always say no when they mean yes.'

Charles shuddered and returned to his congealing Number Forty-Three. He shouldn't have come on to the restaurant. He wasn't hungry. He knew he was only there because he didn't want to be alone yet, and also so that he'd get back too late to catch the appalling tea and curiosity of his landlady, Mimi.

He felt alienated and alone as he looked along the table. Rick Harmer, the young Assistant Stage Manager, appeared to be baiting Leslie Blatt. Rick was a bright boy, who had got the Rugland Spa job straight out of R.A.D.A.. When he'd served his forty weeks and got his full Equity ticket, there was no doubt that he would go far. His readings-in for other members of the cast at rehearsal had revealed considerable talent, and he was already signed up with one of the biggest London agencies, Creative Artists Ltd. He treated the Regent Theatre with a slight air of patronage but, since he did all the many duties required of him with more than the usual efficiency, it was difficult to find fault with him. But his certainty (probably quite justified) that he was going to be a lot more successful than the rest of the company had ever been didn't endear him to his colleagues.

He had also had some success as a writer of comedy sketches for radio and television, and it was with this that he was baiting Leslie Blatt.

'Yes, they're making a radio pilot of one of my scripts in a couple of weeks. Up at the Beeb.'

'Beeb?' asked Leslie Blatt, out of touch with such colloquialisms. 'BBC. No, I'll be going up to the recording-ooh, that reminds me, must tell Tony I'll need the time off. Only radio, of course, but that'll lead to telly. LWT have got one of my other scripts at the moment. My literary agent...' He left a little pause to ensure that the distinction between this figure and his performing agent was not missed '...says they're very keen. Think it might be a good vehicle for Christopher Milton.'

'Who?' asked Leslie Blatt, rather testily.

'Haven't you heard of him?' Rick Harmer did not comment further on this ignorance of the entertainment scene. 'Has all your work been tatty old thrillers, Leslie?'

The playwright bridled. 'What do you mean?'

'I mean, have you done much telly?'

'Not a lot, no,' the playwright replied, cautiously dressing up failure to its best advantage. 'I'm really a man of the theatre, you know. The theatre and the boudoir...'

Further down the table, Laurie Tichbourne, seen earlier in the evening in the tennis kit of James De Meaux, preened himself in the beams of adoration that emanated from the girl beside him. He was one of those people, many – though not all of whom are actors, who reckon that being born with exceptional good looks excuses them from all further effort in life. Laurie Tichbourne, now in his mid-thirties, had had a perfectly satisfactory career exposing his looks and moderate talent as juve leads in most of the reps in the country. He was well-liked (indeed, there was nothing about him to dislike, unless one wanted something positive, like a decision, out of him) and it was quite possible that one day a casting director would swoop down and carry him off to star in a television series or even a feature film. It was quite possible. So long as getting the job didn't involve any effort on his part, quite possible.

His current source of adoration was the Regent Theatre's other A.S.M., a girl of quite astonishing prettiness called Nella Lewis. In looks she was the perfect complement to Laurie Tichbourne though Charles suspected she rather outmatched her escort in seriousness of emotional intent (and intelligence).

'Thing was,' Laurie drawled, 'they wanted me to dye my hair blond for the part. Can you imagine that, Nella – me with blond hair?'

'No, I can't, Laurie.'

'Well, I'd had it done once before, for a day I did on a film, and I knew it made me look an absolute fright. Absolute fright. So I said, come on, I know I'm meant to be a German, but all Germans aren't blond. And if this girl's meant to fall for me, she's not going to fall for me with blond hair.'

'So what happened?'

'Oh, the director took my point.'

'Oh, good.'

Charles wondered how long Nella's intelligence could be curbed by infatuation. Then he became aware of a voice on his left.

'You see, every performance is a political statement. Don't you agree, Charles?'

The voice belonged to Gay Milner, the actress who had played Felicity Kershaw.

Charles gave his usual response to questions about politics in the theatre. 'Um...'

'No, I mean every part reflects some facet of society, and if you feel that society's got to change, then you can express that in the way you play the part.'

Unwisely, Charles decided to pursue this line of thought with her. 'But you can't apply that to every play. I mean, take tonight's little epic. *The Message Is Murder* has nothing to do with any society that's ever existed. It's set in its own little cloud-cuckoo-land of country houses and butlers and bodies in the library. You can't make political points when you're acting in something like that.'

'Oh, but you can, Charles. If you're committed, you must. I mean, it's more difficult. You know, I was in *Scrag End of Neck* at the Bus Depot.'

'Ah.' Charles nodded appreciatively, as if he'd heard of the play and the theatre. 'Really?'

'Yes. And there of course the political message is overt, so it's that much easier to play. *The Message Is Murder* is more of a challenge.'

'Hmm. So what is there in your playing of Felicity Kershaw that makes a political statement?'

'Ah well, you see, she is obviously a representative of the propertied classes.'

'Yes, I accept that.'

'The small percentage of the population who own a disproportionate amount of the country's wealth.'

'Okay.'

'So, by making her repellent and untrustworthy, I am sounding a warning to the audience to distrust people of that class.'

'Oh.' That was why she was doing it. And Charles had thought she was playing it repellent because that was the way Leslie Blatt had written the part, and untrustworthy because of her devious involvement in the murder that had to be revealed in Act Three.

'You see, Charles, the theatre has a vital educational function. It's one of the most persuasive forms of grass-roots agit prop that...'

Gay Milner droned on. She was not unattractive. Not sensational like Nella, but she had a certain sexy angularity. And seemed to be unattached. There was a time when Charles would have put up with the political claptrap in the hope of getting somewhere with her, when he'd have talked along, maybe gone back to her digs to pursue some complex crux of socialism, maybe moved aside the coffee cups and tested the reaction to a tentative hand laid on...But that time seemed long ago.

He felt desolately miserable.

'Charles, old man.'

Antony Wensleigh had come down the table to him and squatted on the floor beside him.

'Yes, Tony?' Charles looked at the Artistic Director. The most noticeable feature of Antony Wensleigh's face was his huge, liquid brown eyes, infinitely mournful, infinitely sensitive. They showed enduring sympathy to his casts through all the squabbles and hiccups of rehearsal. They were the reason that people liked working with him as a director.

And yet, it had to be faced, he wasn't in the front rank of his profession. Though passionately devoted to the theatre, there was about him a certain vagueness, a certain lack of push that deprived his productions of a West End finish. He lived to some extent in a world of his own, happiest in the rehearsal room, surrounded by casts he knew well, uneasy and occasionally by default inefficient in boardroom and administrative office. Herbie Inchbald had been right: someone as frequently abstracted as Antony Wensleigh needed the incisive support of a Donald Mason.

Perhaps part of Tony's trouble was that he had been at the Regent too long. Twelve years in the same job had set him apart from the square dance of movement from rep to rep, which is the only way by which theatrical directors rise in their profession. He was now in his early fifties, an age which made dramatic changes for the better unlikely. And he was cosily settled in Rugland Spa. He had come to regard the job as his for as long as he wanted it, the renewal of his annual contract a mere formality, almost as if he were in a normal job like the rest of humanity. And that attitude, in the world of the theatre, was a potentially dangerous one.

'Thing is, Charles...' The huge eyes looked more mournful than ever, as they did when they had something unpleasant to impart. 'Thing is, Kathy was a bit upset...'

'I know, Tony, it was unforgivable of me.' No point in making excuses. 'One of those ridiculous corpses, where something stupid just suddenly seems funny. And I'm afraid, stuck in that little cupboard, things seem disproportionately funny...'

'Yes, well, it's...'

'Won't happen again, Tony. Promise. Better tomorrow.'

'Good. Thanks.' Antony Wensleigh stood up with relief, and then articulated the prime motivation of his life. 'It's just, you know, I like everyone to be happy.'

'Yes. Sure.'

Mr Pang was not so indiscreet as to look pointedly at his watch, but he did come over and ask if anyone would like a sweet. Laurie Tichbourne asked what flavours the 'Ice Creams (Various)' on the menu were. Mr Pang said 'Vanilla', so they all agreed they'd just have the bill. Its arrival prompted the customary discussion as to how it should be divided. Gay Milner produced a calculator and worked it out. Charles reached into his pocket for his share.

He had just enough. He'd been to the bank that day. Where had it all gone? In the day's depressed drinking, he realized.

Up to his overdraft limit. Only Wednesday and not paid again until Friday. Then his agent, bloody Maurice Skellern, would get his customary ten per cent for doing his customary nothing – shit, no, Maurice had recently, after much argument, raised his commission to fifteen per cent.

Then he owed Mimi for the digs…Oh God, money, too. To add to his other problems.


He didn't want to, but back at Mimi's, in the brushed nylon sheets of his single bed, he reread the letter.

Dear Charles,

I don't know how I'm going to say this, but presumably by the end of the letter, I will have managed somehow, so here goes.

I have met someone else.

It sounds corny, but I can't think of any other way of putting it. His name is David. He is, of all things, a schools inspector. There are complications.

I am not in a state of bliss, I am in emotional turmoil. I know that feelings don't cut, they fray, and I am a tangle of fraying feelings.

I don't know what's going to happen. It's the first time since you left me that I've had this sort of problem (if problem's the right word).

I want to see you and talk, though I know that would only mix me up even more.

I'm sorry, Charles. I am very confused. But I wanted you to know.

Love,
Francis

SIMON BRETT

## *Chapter Three*

IN SPITE OF his promise to Antony Wensleigh, Charles Paris was not better the next day. He was worse.

Self-hatred takes many forms. One of the commonest involves publicly bad behaviour, as if the sufferer is willing the world's opinion of him to descend to the level of his own.

And that was the form it took that day with Charles. Not only did he again drink too much, he also drank too long, and was not in the theatre when the 'half' was called.

This was a serious professional crime. The 'half' is a magic moment, half an hour (plus five minutes for safety) before the curtain rises. All members of the company, except for those who have arranged special dispensations because of late entrances, must have checked in by then. If any haven't, then the Stage Management starts to panic and frantic reorganization of understudies begins.

But in a profession which has encompassed drunkards of the stature of George Frederick Cooke (whose life Lord Byron described as 'all green-room and tap-room, drains and the drama-brandy, whisky-punch, and *latterly*, toddy') and Edmund Kean, allowances have frequently been made. Young A.S.M.s quickly learn which pubs to check out for actors who have 'not noticed the time'.

But allowances that might be made for stars are less likely to be made for actors playing dead bodies in tatty thrillers. And Charles had compounded his felony by deliberately not drinking in the pub round the back of the Regent (so much an annexe that bells sounded there at the end of the intervals). Instead, he had sought to match his mood by searching out an hotel by the station, which was as seedy as anything could be in as genteel a place as Rugland Spa.

He knew what he was doing. It was part of a course in self-abasement, a need for some violent purgation, a flushing-out of all the pained confusion in his mind. There was no conviviality, just pointless, solitary drinking – a gesture which, even as he made it, he knew to be ineffective. Those for whom it was intended would not see it; and those who did see would misinterpret it.

And he hadn't even the courage to make the gesture total. Having guiltily braved out the half he found his resolve weakening. The show went up at seven forty-five. His hopes of being dramatically oblivious of time were not realized. At twenty past seven he decided not to have another drink. And twenty-five past found him lumbering uncomfortably through the quiet terraces of Rugland Spa towards the Regent Theatre.

He was lucky in that there was no one by the Stage Door when he lurched in. It was after twenty to eight, Act One Beginners would have been called and be waiting in the wings for the curtain to rise. The Stage Manager would be on the desk, ready to cue lights, and the A.S.M.s would also be busy. A furtive hope, worthy of a truant schoolboy, crept into Charles' mind, that he might yet get away with it. If he went up to his dressing room quickly, got into his costume and slipped into his cupboard, nobody might notice. After all, he was only the body; probably no one had bothered to check whether he was there or not.

He grasped the banister of the stairs to the dressing rooms and pulled himself upwards. The movement seemed bigger than he had expected; he swung round against the wall, which made him realize just how drunk he was.

As he swayed there, he heard the panicky clatter of shoes coming down the stairs. Round the corner of the flight Nella Lewis appeared at full speed. Her face was flushed and frightened. In her hand she clutched a duelling sword. It was the one produced as Sir Reginald De Meaux's murder weapon in Act Two.

'Oh!' she panted, screeching to an ungainly halt. 'Charles!'

'Yes,' Charles confirmed, though his tongue, suddenly too big for his mouth, seemed to distort the word.

'You're terribly late.'

A nod of the head to confirm this was easier than words.

'We've been in a terrible panic. All kinds of people were going to replace you.'

''Sall righ', though. I can do it now.'

'Are you sure?' Nella didn't sound convinced.

'Of course. I'm absolutely in control.' To emphasize this point, Charles — unwisely, as it turned out — let go of the banister and made an expansive gesture of insouciance. At the same moment the concrete steps seemed to be filched from under him, and he crumpled to an ungainly heap at the foot of the stairs.

'No,' said Nella decisively, skipping over him. 'You can't go on in that state'

'I've only got to be a dead body, for God's sake,' the heap on the floor complained.

But the young A.S.M. was adamant. 'No. We'd better stick to the plan we've made. He...he...' Her voice was strained with emotion. 'That bastard had better go on for you.'

'But I —'

'I've got to go. Curtain up in a second, and I'm on the book tonight.' Then, with surprising gentleness, she said, 'You need to get back to your digs. I'll organize a cab for you when I've got a moment.'

She scuttered off.

Charles lay there. Everything around him seemed to be moving; only the contempt he felt for himself remained immovable in his mind.

Had it really come to this? Fifty-five years of development reduced to an alcoholic mess on the stone floor. A career washed away by booze, a marriage – the thought of Frances stopped him short like a blow in the face.

Whatever their relationship, what he was doing now wasn't helping it. No, he must pick himself up, not succumb to self-pity and its attendant alcohol. He had a job to do and he would do it.

With great concentration he pulled himself to his feet and walked very carefully up to the first landing, where there was a men's lavatory. He filled the sink with cold water and splashed it copiously over his face.

It made him feel a very little better. He walked cautiously along to the next flight of stairs, and found himself confronted by Leslie Blatt.

The elderly playwright looked extremely guilty. Charles wondered what he had been doing. Most of the actresses had their dressing rooms on the floor above. Charles wouldn't put it past the old goat to have been doing a bit of keyhole-peeping.

But he was in no position to be censorious. As Leslie Blatt wasted no time in telling him.

'Oh, Charles, everyone's been looking for you.'

'I know,' Charles said wearily.

'I was going to go on for you.'

'You?'

'Yes. I used to be an actor and director, you know, before I started writing. Kept my card up. Always ready to do the odd little bit.' He sniggered, somehow infecting this remark with unwholesome innuendo.

'Yes. Well, as you see, I'm here now. So it won't be necessary for you to –'

'Oh, I'm not going to now,' said Leslie Blatt petulantly. 'No, I've just been told I mustn't, by young Mr Smartypants. Says it's his job. Huh.' The old man tossed his wrinkled head.

'Oh, well, I –'

'No, he's going to do it. He's arranged it all. So you'd just better go home and sober up.'

'And what are you going to do?'

'I'm going to watch my play from backstage. Always enjoy that. Get a completely different set of thrills backstage.' The playwright stalked off, once again giving an unpleasantly sexual overtone to his final remark.

Inside his dressing room Charles discovered who Leslie Blatt had meant by 'young Mr Smartypants'. Rick Harmer, dressed in the late Sir Reginald De Meaux's tweeds, was sitting in front of the mirror, about to apply make-up.

'Charles!' he said. 'You're terribly late.'

Charles was getting sick of people stating the obvious. 'Yes, I am.'

'And you're pissed.'

'Again, yes, I am.'

'You'd better go home. You can't act in that state.'

'Dead bodies don't have to act,' Charles argued belligerently.

'No, but they have to keep still. You can't have a dead body lying there with an attack of D.T.s.'

'I haven't got D.T.s. I'll be fine. Now please could I have my costume?'

'As A.S.M., Charles, I'm understudying all the male parts. And if someone isn't in by the half, then –'

'Rick, please.'

The appeal contained just enough dignity to prevent it from being abject, and Rick responded to its nakedness.

'Okay,' he said, as he started to unbutton the tweeds. 'I shouldn't really, but okay.'

'Thank you.' With great caution, uncertain of his balance, Charles started to take his clothes off.

He tried desperately to think of something to say, something that might make the situation seem normal, something that would remove the expression, half of pity, half contempt, from the young man's face. 'How are things going with your radio pilot?' he finally managed.

'Oh, okay. Got a good cast together. Toby Root, Anna Duncan...you worked with either of them?'

'Yes. Long time ago.' The second name stirred memories that Charles did not wish to exhume further.

'And George Birkitt's very keen. But his agent's shilly-shallying over money.'

'Ah.'

'Only trouble is, that bastard Wensleigh won't release me for the day to go up to the recording.'

'Really? That's most unlike Tony.'

'Don't you believe it,' said Rick bitterly. 'He likes to play the little Hitler. Jealousy, really. Typical of someone who's over the hill and knows it.'

The A.S.M. used that as an exit line, and Charles didn't feel he was being unduly sensitive in including himself in its application. Nor could he really feel that the aspersion was without justification.

He turned up the loudspeaker in the dressing room. On-stage James De Meaux was still reminiscing to Wilhelmina about what they had got up to in the summerhouse the previous evening, so he had plenty of time. Laboriously, he got into his costume and did his make-up. The latter took a depressingly short time; to look sixty-five all Charles had to do was grey his temples and stick on a grey moustache; to look dead all he had to do was powder his cheeks down to a horrid pallor (and the way he looked that evening even these minimal changes seemed superfluous).

Then he remembered he was meant to be impaled by a duelling sword. If he had omitted that, he would really have finished the evening. He imagined

Kathy Kitson bringing down the curtain on the First Act with the lines, 'Oh no! It's Reginald! Killed by some method that is not immediately apparent!'

The thought made him giggle weakly. No, no, mustn't do that. No corpsing tonight. He was already in enough trouble. With uncoordinated fingers, he started to remove his jacket and shirt.

The device for his apparent transfixion had been improvised by Nella Lewis in the props room, and was simple but effective. A broad elastic belt, of the type that used to be called 'waspee' (though that description was singularly inappropriate when it was buckled round Charles' chest), had a thin block of wood stapled to the front of it, and through this block a bolt had been fixed to stick out at right angles. The shirt was buttoned around this protuberance, and a foreshortened duelling sword with specially adapted end was screwed on to it. The area of the wound was then sprinkled liberally with stage blood (known in the business as 'Kensington Gore'), and the effect, even from close quarters, was surprisingly convincing.

With gloomy intimations of mortality, Charles surveyed his dead body in the mirror. Then he made his way unsteadily down on to the stage.

But before he could reach the sanctuary of his cupboard, he walked into Tony Wensleigh. Rick Harmer's description of a 'little Hitler' was most inappropriate; at that moment the anxiety on the Artistic Director's face made him look more like the White Rabbit.

Unfortunately, having bumped, Charles overcompensated to regain his balance, and again found himself on the floor. Tony Wensleigh bent down to pick him up.

'Charles,' he whispered sadly, 'you can't go on in that state.'

'I can, Tony. Be all right. Honestly.'

'No. Donald told me what had happened, and I've just seen Rick, who said you're completely pie-eyed.'

'I'm not, Tony. Just a bit pie-eyed. And I'm very sorry.'

'That's not the point now. Look, Charles, you know I don't like coming the heavy, but I've got to think of the play. You could ruin it.'

Charles bit back the retort that Leslie Blatt seemed to have done that already.

'No, I've decided. I've told Rick. I'm going to go on for you.'

'You?'

'Yes. Rick's needed backstage. Nella's not experienced enough to cope without him.'

'But, Tony...'

'No, Charles. Sorry, it's nothing personal, but I'm responsible for the show and I can't afford to take risks. I have my position as Artistic Director to think of.'

The drink was now making Charles belligerent. 'Oh, don't be so bloody pompous!'

'I am not being pompous. Listen, the Chairman of the Board's in the theatre tonight. I can't run the risk of you ruining the show.'

'But –'

'I'm sorry, Charles, but my mind's made up and nothing's going to shift me.'

'For God's sake, Tony...' The drink was also making him unusually pertinacious and eloquent. 'Look, what threat am I to you? What harm can one slightly drunken middle-aged actor do to your "position as Artistic Director"? What do you think I'm going to do – expose you, denounce you to the Board, reveal a long history of fraud and peculation?' He paused after this flight of rhetorical hyperbole. 'All I'm going to do is to go on stage and be a dead body. I haven't even got any lines to cock up. Please, Tony. Please let me do it.'

At this point Tony Wensleigh gave a classic demonstration of his qualities as a decision-maker. 'Okay, Charles,' he said. 'You go on. But don't show me up.'

What appeared from the auditorium to be the interior of a cupboard was a little niche made of two small flats. The third side, invisible from out front, was not there, allowing easy access for dead bodies. But space backstage was so cramped by the large box-set of Wrothley Grange that Charles had to spend most of the act in position. And once inside the cupboard, its miserly proportions offered him the alternatives of standing bolt upright against the back flat or sitting with his legs twisted through the cleats and stage weights that supported the set. Charles had always found standing preferable.

The flats of the cupboard were old and had been used many times. On the back of one was scribbled 'Uncle Vanya – Act Two', on the other 'When We Are Married – L. Fireplace', and these scrawls perhaps reflected their original provenance. But the stretched canvas had been repainted many times and many colours since then, and contributed to a wide variety of theatrical experiences.

The feel of the thick paint was comfortingly familiar against Charles' hands, as he stood against the back wall of his cupboard. Must stand, mustn't lean, he kept telling himself. His full weight could easily overtopple a flat and, since most of the others were nailed together with lathes at the top, might easily bring down more. He had already done enough wrong that evening; he didn't want to add the total collapse of Wrothley Grange to his misdemeanours.

But he did want to lean against something. The uncontrollable phase of his drunkenness had passed, to be replaced by a deep, deep tiredness. The heat of the stage lights through the canvas door before him, the familiar backstage smells of sawdust, size and dusty drapes, and the relentless banalities of Leslie Blatt's dialogue, all contributed to his fatigue. He just wanted to go to sleep.

If he just closed his eyes for a little...just for a little, he wouldn't miss his cue. He closed them, then opened them again with a start as he lurched against the back of his cupboard.

No, be safer if he sat down. Just for a minute. Professor Weintraub was still going on about bird-watching, so he'd be safe for a little doze. Just a little doze.

A noise very close woke him. A strange noise, a sudden ripping, a tearing of cloth. It seemed to come from just above his head.

He looked up, blinking in the darkness. But even as he did so, he heard Lady Hilda De Meaux asking her maid if she'd mind getting one of the folding card-tables out of the cupboard by the fireplace.

'No, of course not, milady,' Wilhelmina replied, and the door of Charles' sanctum swung open, flooding him with light.

And in that light he saw something sticking through the flat at the back of the cupboard.

Then he saw Wilhelmina's startled face looking down at him, and realized that his recumbent position was totally obscured from the audience with a large sofa.

Instinctively trying to save the act, he leapt up with a throttled cry, staggered forward to his correct dying position and fell with what he thought was not a bad death-rattle.

It was only as he lay still and heard the edge in Kathy Kitson's voice pronouncing the curtain-line that he realized he had completely buggered up the play's plot. Professor Weintraub was going to need a great deal of confidence to make his assertion in Act Two that, from his examination of the corpse, it was clear that Sir Reginald had been dead for at least eight hours. Oh dear, more recrimination.

There certainly was, plenty, as soon as the curtain fell. Kathy Kitson was the most vociferous, but none of the cast showed much charity to Charles.

He hardly noticed. He let the abuse wash over him. His mind was fixed elsewhere.

It was fixed on what he had seen at the back of his cupboard when the door opened. Clear in the light, before it was hastily withdrawn, he had seen the sharp blade of the prop duelling sword.

It had been thrust with some force through the canvas of the flat from backstage.

And, but for the drunken lapse which had moved Charles from his usual position, the sword would have gone straight through him.

# Chapter Four

'COURSE, I'VE HAD drunks before...' Mimi drew her pale green candlewick housecoat round her with the confidence of a woman for whom the world could hold no surprises. 'Oh yes, lot of my gentlemen been drunks.'

Charles grunted. At half-past nine in the morning the last thing he wanted to hear about was Mimi's 'gentlemen'.

'Mind you, real drunks they was, most of them. I mean, drunks on the grand scale.'

So even his drunkenness was to be disparaged. Mimi was capable of disparaging anything. Why, not for the first time Charles asked himself, did he never end up with the theatrical landladies one always heard about, the 'treasures', the motherly ones, the ones for whom no trouble was too great? They did exist, they must exist – too many actors talked about them for their existence to be complete fiction. There were even, if the stories were to be believed, sexy landladies, whose bed and breakfast were really worth having.

But Charles Paris never ended up with them; he always got the Mimis of this world, the censorious, the resentful, the mean, the...God, Mimi couldn't even cook. He looked down with distaste at waxy eggs which had brought half the frying pan with them, and wooden fried bread which had brought the other half. A pair of tomatoes shrivelled like used condoms. And her tea...Some vital ingredient seemed to have been omitted from its making. Tea, perhaps.

Granted, he was not in much of a state to appreciate any food. Nausea bobbed like an extra uvula in his throat. But even in that condition he could recognize the true horror of Mimi's culinary efforts.

'One drunk I had – Everard Austick. You met him?'

'Yes.'

'Now he was a drunk. Completely lost his senses when he'd had a skinful. Came home one night so drunk he told me I couldn't cook. Imagine that.'

'Yes.'

'Said I cooked like an Irish labourer mixing cement.'

'Ah.'

'Didn't mean it, of course. Ate up his scrambled eggs like a lamb the next morning.'

That's what made Mimi so difficult to deal with-her unassailable confidence. Whatever was said to her, whatever complaint about her sloppy housekeeping, she seemed impervious. Worse than that, she took everything as a compliment. Her self-image remained perfectly intact. She saw herself as the lovable figure of the theatrical landlady who always eluded Charles.

'Always comes back, Everard Austick, when he's working Rugland Spa. All my gentlemen always come back. It's like home from home with you, Mimi, that's what they all say.'

God, thought Charles, a lot of actors are supposed to have depressing home lives, but not many of them could be that bad.

And yet what she said seemed to be true. She kept a visitors' book, and Charles had not escaped scanning its pages. And there was the evidence – names, dates, comments – 'Just like being back with Mum', 'Ee, you spoil me, Mimi', 'Lovely as always'...Did she practise some mass sorcery on her victims? Or had her very first theatrical gentleman lost his nerve and, by putting something nice in the visitors' book, embarrassed all his successors into doing the same?

Charles was determined that, when his stay was up, he would write exactly what he really thought of Mimi's hospitality. But, even as he had the thought, he felt his conviction drain away and knew that he would succumb like all the others to smirking insincerity.

'Oh yes, I seen drunks,' she reiterated. 'All the famous ones stay with Mimi. Ask specially to stay with Mimi. Because, you see, they know I'll never pass judgement, never tell them how contemptible they are.' With this, she flashed Charles a look of withering judgement and total contempt.

'Oh yes, they all stay with Mimi. You name them, they've stayed with me.'

'George Frederick Cooke?' Charles hazarded maliciously.

'Oh yes, he always comes. Whenever he's in the area he pops in to see Mimi.'

Another of Mimi's little charms was name-dropping. Whoever was mentioned, she knew them; and if discussion ensued, she knew them better than the person she was talking to.

'What about Edmund Kean?' Charles continued recklessly. 'Has he stayed with you?'

'Just the once,' said Mimi tartly. Then she again looked sharply at her guest. 'Oh, did I say – there was a telephone message for you?'

'No, you didn't.'

'From the General Manager at the theatre.'

'Oh.'

'I didn't wake you. Told him you was sleeping it off.'

'Thank you very much, Mimi.'

'Think nothing of it. Anything for my gentlemen.' She gave a sickly smile, as usual obscuring whether she was aware or not of her own ironies. 'Anyway, he wants you to go and see him.'

No surprise, really, thought Charles. Long time since I've been sacked. The prospect gave him a perverse pleasure; it was the logical culmination of the previous day's kamikaze behaviour.

'When does he want to see me?'

'Soon as convenient, he said.'

'I'd better go straight away.' Charles rose.

'Oh no, you've got time to finish your eggs.'

Charles sank back into his chair.

The administrative office was at the top of the Regent Theatre, above the bar. When Charles entered, it was empty. The room, snatched out of storage space as an afterthought, was cramped but, compared to most of the theatre administrative offices he had seen, well organized. Its tidiness, he thought, probably reflected the mind of the General Manager. Donald Mason, it seemed, had been with the Regent less than a year, but had made a quick impression on the efficiency of the theatre. His predecessors, according to Gordon Tremlett who knew about such things, had been, to a man, creatures devoted to the principle of minimum effort.

An in-tray and an out-tray were neatly aligned on the desk, with a telephone and intercom placed exactly between them. The in-tray was empty, a commendable sign of industry at that time in the morning. The out-tray was fairly full, and on top of it was a hand-written note.

The writing was recognizably tiny. Charles had received a good-luck note in the same hand on the opening night of *The Message Is Murder*.

He couldn't read the note in the in-tray without crossing the room to peer at it. Which he knew he shouldn't do.

But which, with the recklessness of a man about to lose his job, he did.

The note read as follows:

SORRY ABOUT THE TOTAL COCK-UP OF EVERYTHING.
NO EXCUSES.
YOURS ABJECTLY,
TONY

Oh dear. What was the Artistic Director's latest feat of mismanagement?

Charles heard a movement outside the door and moved hastily across to the other side of the room. Donald Mason entered in another of his executive suits, looking grimly flustered.

'Sorry, Charles, won't keep you a minute. One important call I must make.' The General Manager dialled without disturbing the symmetry of the telephone's position on his desk. 'Ah, Mr Hughes. Donald Mason here, Regent Theatre. Just checking the position on the Drill Hall. Yes, yes, that's what I heard. Hmm. No, of course I can see your point of view.' The General Manager sighed. 'Oh yes, I did mention it to him, but it must have slipped his mind. Yes, well, he's got a lot on his plate, particularly when he's in rehearsal for a show. Yes, I agree, he always does seem to be in rehearsal for a show. Well, we must make allowances, mustn't we? The old artistic temperament, eh? What? Oh, yes. Anyway, no hard feelings on my side. Mr Hughes. You gave us plenty of warning and, if it's booked, it's booked. Okay, sorry again. 'Bye.'

He put the phone down and looked at Charles with a grim smile. 'Sometimes, you know. I feel like one of those men who follows a big parade with a shovel and cleans up after the horses. Except it's a one-man parade that goes by the name of Antony Wensleigh.'

'Ah.' Charles didn't feel he could comment on the Artistic Director's behaviour.

'Know what he's done now? Only lost us the Drill Hall for rehearsals. Caretaker told us weeks ago the Badminton Club wanted to book it, but he'd hold it for us so long as he got written confirmation. Which he didn't get – and guess who should have done it?' He sighed. 'So now we'll have to get somewhere else as of the week after next, and that's going to cost us more, and once again the budgeting all goes up the spout and...Still, I shouldn't burden you with my problems.'

'No.' Then Charles volunteered, 'I rather assume that I have problems of my own.'

'Yes. So you know why I've asked you to come here.'

Oh God. The interview was beginning to sound like something out of a Billy Bunter school story. Charles wondered whether he should have stuffed a newspaper down the back of his trousers.

Donald Mason looked at his out-tray. Seeing Tony Wensleigh's note, he casually picked it up, folded it and put it in his inside pocket. No need to advertise the Artistic Director's lapses. He then picked up the next piece of paper from the tray. 'I've had a report from the Stage Manager about your behaviour during last night's performance.'

'Yes.'

'You were late for the "half", and then, when it came to the moment – and I use the word advisedly – of your performance, you did not play your part as rehearsed, and the general opinion seems to have been that you were...'

Charles finished the sentence for him. 'Smashed out of my mind.'

'Yes.' The General Manager paused. 'A lot of people would regard such behaviour as grounds for dismissal.'

'Yes.'

'I've talked to Tony about it, and he says there's no question about it – you should go.'

'Yes.'

'You're just contracted for the one show?'

'That's right.' Oh, for God's sake, get on with it. 'And my role is hardly onerous. It won't be difficult to get someone else rehearsed up to take over.'

'No.'

Oh, get on with it. What else is there to say? But Donald seemed hesitant. It was unlikely that someone with his abrasive manner would have difficulty in sacking an actor, but maybe he was finding it awkward. Charles decided to help him out.

'Obviously I'm sorry for the trouble I caused, but I fully understand that you have no alternative but to show me out and –'

'Oh, I wouldn't say that.'

Donald Mason's words were so unexpected that Charles gaped at him.

'No, Charles, there are alternatives.' Then, with surprising gentleness, the General Manager continued, 'People usually have a reason for getting drunk. What is it – domestic problems?'

'Well...'

'Woman?'

For a second Charles felt tempted to spill it all out, to succumb to pathos, to plead for sympathy. But, hell, no. He couldn't define the situation with Frances to himself, let alone spell it out to a stranger. 'No, I just got drunk. I sometimes go on these benders. I know it's unprofessional and stupid, but...' He shrugged.

'Hmm. My inclination, Charles, is always to give people a second chance.' This again seemed inconsistent with Donald Mason's brusque image. 'If you want to stay, I'm prepared to ignore Tony's opinion and let you. What do you say?'

Charles felt embarrassingly emotional. 'Well, I ...er...'

'I mean I'm sure it's not the sort of thing that's going to happen again.'

This was once more back to the headmaster's study. I'm going to give you one more chance, Paris, and I'm going to trust you, because in my experience most chaps respond to trust.

'So tell me, do you want to stay in the show?'

'Well, yes, I would be very grateful if...' Mumble, mumble, grovel, grovel.

'Good, that's settled then.' The General Manager screwed up the Stage Manager's report and threw it into his waste paper basket. 'You know, I think part of the trouble for you is that you've got so little to do in this show.'

'Maybe. I think we should try to get you more involved in the company. Perhaps there'll be a part in another of our forthcoming productions.'

'Well, that'd be very...'

'I'll see what I can do.'

At that moment the intercom on Donald's desk buzzed and a female voice crackled, 'Mrs Feller in the foyer. She wants to come and see you about *Shove It.*'

'Oh God. Okay, send her up.' Donald Mason rose from his desk and straightened his tie. 'Have you come across the redoubtable Mrs Feller, Charles?'

'No.'

'You will. She's Rugland Spa's answer to Mrs Whitehouse. A one-woman Puritan Backlash, who only comes to the theatre to count the number of letters in the words.'

'So she isn't going to care for *Shove It.*'

'No. There'll be protest meetings, picketings, strong letters to the local paper...Honestly, what a bloody stupid choice of play for Rugland Spa. Over half the population's past retirement age – they're hardly going to lap up the Anglo-Saxon diatribes of Royston Everett.'

'The theatre's got to do some modern stuff.'

'Modern, yes, but it doesn't have to be obscene. I sometimes think Tony's judgement has gone completely. He's just lost touch with reality.' He shook his head ruefully. 'Still, again not your problem, Charles. Anyway, with regard to you, we'll leave things as they are – Okay?'

'Yes. Thank you very much.'

'And if Tony –'

Donald Mason was interrupted by a knock on the door. 'That'll be Mrs Feller. This is obviously the early stage of her campaign – she still bothers to knock. It'll get worse.'

He extended his hand to the actor. 'Thanks for coming in, Charles. I'm relying on you, so keep it up.'

Considering the circumstances, Charles reflected, the General Manager's final cliché was singularly inapposite.

Well-being flooded through Charles. Partly it was the first symptom of recovery from his hangover, that breakthrough moment when continuing existence first seems a possibility. When he had woken, three hours previously, the movement from horizontal to vertical had seemed insuperable, and yet here he was, on two feet, moving around, suffering from nothing worse than a light headache playing around his temples. He was even feeling hunger, a sensation which he thought had abandoned his body for ever.

He went into a little café near the theatre and tucked into an espresso coffee and two jam doughnuts.

Of course the euphoria wasn't just physical. The interview with Donald Mason had contributed enormously. Though he'd thought he'd wanted the catharsis of dismissal, he was deeply relieved to have been spared it. Basically he had a respect for his profession and was disgusted by his unprofessional behaviour.

And the surprise of how he had misjudged the General Manager's character added an extra glow.

All he had to do was to behave impeccably for the remainder of the run of *The Message Is Murder*.

And sort out where he stood with Frances.

There was a payphone in the café. But there was still no reply from his wife's number at her new flat in Highgate.

Still, she was unlikely to be there at twelve o'clock in the morning. If it was term-time, she'd be hard at work at the school where she was headmistress. And if it was half-term or holiday...oh God, he could never remember when they came. Frances' life was always sliced up into neat segments by these academic dividers, while his own remained a shifting morass without any demarcation.

He contemplated trying the school, but rejected the idea. Even if she was there, she was bound to be busy, and the circumstances wouldn't be ideal for the sort of conversation they needed to have. Instead he rang the Pangbourne number of his daughter, Juliet. She answered.

'It's me...Charles.' She never called him by his Christian name, but he couldn't bring himself to say 'Daddy'.

'Oh, hello. How are you?'

'Fine.' The conventional lie. 'And you?'

'Yes, fine. Busy, but fine.'

'Kids?'

'Twins are at school, thank God, but Sebastian's being a bit of a pain. He's teething.'

Charles had forgotten about his third grandson. Sebastian, born some eight months previously, 'a brother for Damian and Julian'. God, why did they choose those names? Probably because Juliet's husband, rising star of the insurance world, had discovered there were special reduced premiums for people whose names ended in I-A-N.

'How is Miles?'

'Oh, fine. He's just been promoted. He's now an Assistant Branch Manager.'

'Oh.' Then, because comment seemed appropriate, 'Good for him.'

'Yes, it is. It means we've been able to get a new dishwasher.'

'Oh, good.'

'Makes a big difference.'

'Yes.'

'And Miles has just bought me a food-processor, which is going to be a great help mashing up Sebastian's stuff.'

'I'm sure it is.' He had to change the subject before he was treated to a complete inventory of the Taylersons' kitchen. 'I've been trying to contact your mother.'

'Ah.' He was sure Juliet's tone changed with this syllable. It became more guarded. What was she hiding? Had she been given specific instructions from Frances as to how to deal with enquiries? Had Frances moved into some love-nest with her schools inspector and was Juliet the guardian of their secret address?

'Can't get any reply from her flat.'

'No. Well, it's half-term. She's away.'

'I thought you said your boys're at school,' said Charles with involuntary suspicion.

'Yes, but they have different half-terms from the State schools.'

My, oh my, Miles was doing well. Private education. No doubt paid for by a carefully selected insurance policy.

'Of course. When's Frances back?'

'Sunday afternoon, I think.' The 'I think' was mere dressing: Juliet obviously knew the exact hour of her mother's return.

'Where is she?'

'Paris.'

'Ah.'

Silence hung between them, the old silence of poor communication and ungainly love, but now shadowed by another awkwardness.

Charles couldn't just let the conversation drift to more kitchenalia and then goodbyes. He had to ask the questions hovering between them.

'Is she there on her own?'

'No.'

He must mention the name as if it were familiar, as if he were a man of the world accepting the *fait accompl*i. 'Is she there with David?' he asked, begging for a negative reply.

'Yes,' said Juliet.


In some ways it made things better. At least it introduced an element of definition. Like a condemned man who has heard his sentence, Charles could begin to plan, devise ways of coping with his situation. He ordered another cup of coffee.

It had been inevitable and he had no right to complain. He had left Frances twenty years before, and had been lucky to retain her as an emotional long-stop for so long. There had been rapprochements and reconciliations, but none had lasted. His character and his life were not compatible with the regularities of marriage. The only surprise was that she, still an attractive woman in her early fifties, had not met anyone else sooner.

So he reasoned it out.

But it still hurt.

It was by forcing his mind off the subject of Frances that he began to think about the events of the previous night. His worries about her, the haze and pains of alcohol, the threat of dismissal, had prevented him from concentrating on the rather significant fact that someone had tried to kill him.

Some of his recollections of the night were blurred, but the sight of the sword-blade stabbing through the flat above him was cinematically clear.


It had happened. There was no doubt about it. When he inspected the flat under the working lights of the stage, Charles could see the new gash in the canvas. He stood in his normal dead body position and confirmed that gash corresponded with the middle of his back. He shivered.

He went round the back of the flat and found that the tear had been repaired. A rectangular strip of canvas had been glued on to prevent the split from spreading. Someone had made that repair, but had it been just an act of routine maintenance or the cover-up of a failed crime?

The theatre appeared to be empty. It was lunchtime on the Friday of the first week of the run. The *Shove It* cast would be at their outside rehearsal room (the Drill Hall which, he had learned that morning, they were about to lose). Any stage staff who might be in the theatre were likely to be up in the bar. But Charles did a little backstage tour to see if he could find the mysterious flat-repairer.

He heard a voice as he approached the Green Room. It was Rick Harmer's. Charles stopped out of sight of the phone and listened.

'Yes, I know that's the situation at the moment, but don't worry, I'm going to be up for that recording. And the whole day's rehearsal. I'm going to see that cast says my lines *right*. Look, I know that, and I'm not going to risk losing the job here, but somehow I'm going to make the bastard change his mind and agree to release me. I don't know how, I'll think of something. He is not going to stand in my way. No, okay, leave it with me. Yes. Anything else come up? Any enquiries? Availability checks?'

These last questions identified Rick's interlocutor as his agent. And Charles gained unworthy pleasure from the fact that Rick obviously got the same answers as he did when making the same enquiries of Maurice Skellern.

He waited till the phone was down before proceeding casually round the corner.

'Oh, Rick. Hello.'

'Hi. Feeling better this morning?' the A.S.M. asked with a hint of malice.

'Yes, thank you.'

'Seen Donald?'

No secrets in a provincial theatre company.

'Yes. Yes, I have.' Charles deliberately delayed gratifying Rick's patent curiosity, before saying, 'I'm staying on.'

'Oh.' The A.S.M. was so surprised it was a moment before he managed to say, 'Good.'

'Yes. Oh, incidentally, Rick, I was just looking onstage...at the scene of my disgrace...'

'Yes?'

'And I noticed there was a tear in the flat at the back of my cupboard.'

'Oh yes, I noticed that. I just repaired it, so that it doesn't spread.'

The answer came quickly enough, and apparently without guile.

'Any idea how it happened?'

'What?'

'The tear. What I mean is – did I do it while I was thrashing around last night?'

'Oh, I don't think so. No, I imagine something fell against it or someone caught a prop on it in the dark.'

Which sounded reasonable enough – to anyone who hadn't seen the real cause.

Charles justified having a pint at lunchtime on medical grounds. It wasn't going to be the start of another heavy day; it was just a necessary compensation for the dehydration caused by his hangover.

And it did taste good.

As he sat over it, he concentrated his mind on the stabbing.

Two things seemed clear. First, that it had been a deliberate act. And, second, that he had not been the intended victim.

The second conclusion came from lack of motivation. He had hardly been in the company long enough for anyone to build up murderous resentment against him, and the one person who might harbour such thoughts, Kathy Kitson, had been onstage at the moment of the attack.

Leslie Blatt had been pretty furious with him the previous evening for 'making nonsense of my play' (no very difficult task, in Charles' view). But the unwitting sabotage of the plot of *The Message Is Murder* had come after the stabbing, so could not be claimed as motivation.

Nor were there any young ladies in the company who might (as in many other companies in which he had worked) have been offended by amorous advances from Charles Paris. His state of confusion over Frances had prevented him from even being aware of other women.

No, whoever had wielded the duelling sword was under the impression that someone else was playing the late Sir Reginald De Meaux. And there was no shortage of candidates for the corpse's job. Practically every male in the company who wasn't actually onstage at the end of Act One seemed to have been considered to take over Charles' role.

He thought them through in the order that he had met them the previous evening.

Lesley Blatt was the first. The repellent old playwright had offered himself for the job and reckoned he was going to do it, until told otherwise by Rick Harmer.

Rick had officiously taken over, even getting dressed and made up for the part, before giving way to Charles himself.

And then Tony Wensleigh had forbidden Charles to go on and said that he would go into the cupboard.

Leslie, Rick and Tony – each one of these at one time thought – and no doubt told others – that he was going on for Charles Paris. The pivotal issue then became: who had each of them told? Or, who did the potential murderer think he, or she, was stabbing?

Again Charles thought back. When he had met Nella Lewis on the stairs, she had been coming down from the floor where both Leslie Blatt and Rick Harmer were. And she had told Charles that his part was going to be taken by 'that bastard'. Since the two young A.S.M.s appeared to have a harmonious relationship, it was reasonable to assume that she referred to the old playwright. And since she was then occupied for the rest of the Act 'on the book', she could well have continued to think that Leslie Blatt was the occupant of the cupboard. And it might not be out of character for her to respond violently to some septuagenarian assault on her virtue (an action that would certainly be in character for the playwright).

What was more, Nella had actually been carrying the duelling sword when Charles met her.

But no jumping to conclusions. On to the next potential victim.

Rick Harmer had put a lot of backs up in the company by his cockiness and success, but the only person he had roused to real anger was Leslie Blatt. The younger man's taunts obviously got through to the raw nerves of the older. Leslie Blatt had certainly been under the impression that Charles' part was to be taken by 'young Mr Smartypants'. On top of that, he had intended to spend the Act backstage, which would have given him ample opportunity to choose his moment for a murderous stab through the canvas.

Then on to Antony Wensleigh. Who had arrived late on the scene, heard about Charles' condition from Rick Harmer, and announced the apparently firm decision that he was going to take over as Sir Reginald De Meaux (deceased).

Well, as Charles had just had confirmed by the telephone conversation, there was one person with a very substantial grudge against the Artistic Director. Rick Harmer was a very ambitious young man and Tony Wensleigh stood in the way of one of his ambitions.

It was like a game. Three sets of potential murderers and potential victims. And, in spite of all those permutations, the person who nearly got spitted was Charles Paris.

If he'd been standing up in his normal position when the lunge was made... The thought still gave him a nasty little frisson.

Drunkenness, he thought as he rose to buy himself another pint, does have its advantages.

## Chapter Five

*THE MESSAGE IS MURDER* moved into the second week of its run at the Regent Theatre, Rugland Spa, without further mishap. It was playing to over fifty per cent capacity, which was deemed to be very good business. Herbie Inchbald's words about anything 'with "murder" in the title' seemed to be being proved true. And the play was greeted with a few oohs and aahs and the modest applause which, regulars assured Charles, was the nearest the Rugland Spa audience got to enthusiasm.

Company life continued with its customary uneasy bickering. Kathy Kitson threw a tantrum one evening because the cold tap in her dressing room was dripping. Laurie Tichbourne caught a slight cold, which he treated as if it were an outbreak of cholera, and Nella Lewis ministered to him with hot lemon drinks and clean handkerchiefs. Rick Harmer hinted that his agent (that was his *acting* agent, of course, not his *literary* one) was having extremely interested enquiries about him for a major role in a major television series. Gay Milner insisted on lending everyone books about International Socialism, and Cherry Robson shrewdly started sleeping with a very rich local factory-owner. At meals after the show in The Happy Friend Chinese Restaurant and Takeaway, the Variety of Mr Pang's Ice Creams remained fixed at Vanilla.

Life, in other words, was normal.

And Charles Paris had nothing to do.

The ways that actors spend their time when they're working in the provinces are various. Some spend it acting. Particularly in repertory companies, many of the cast of the evening's show will pass much of their day rehearsing the next production. Though tighter Equity regulations have prevented the hours of work that used to be expected, this can still agreeably occupy most of the day.

But Charles Paris wasn't in the next production, the much-debated *Shove It*, and was so deprived not only of occupation but also the social life of rehearsal.

Some actors, though not actually rehearsing, can still spend the entire day preparing for their evening's performance. The deeply serious tune themselves like precision instruments, working through relaxation exercises, preparatory walks and concentration games. The deeply lazy, like Laurie Tichbourne, can quite easily pass a day doing absolutely nothing. He would rise around eleven to a large breakfast, cooked by a loving landlady (he, needless to say, always ended up with a 'treasure'), take a leisurely bath until lunch, eaten either at his digs or somewhere within strolling distance in the town, while away the afternoon perhaps with another sleep, then arrive at the theatre at seven o'clock complaining how tired he felt.

Charles Paris couldn't follow either of these courses. Even an actor marinated for a lifetime in Stanislavskian lore (which he certainly was not) would have had difficulty in 'thinking himself into' the role of the defunct Sir Reginald De Meaux. And the Laurie Tichbourne method didn't work either. Charles was one of those people for whom stasis meant depression; to sit around all day was simply to offer an open invitation to all his worst thoughts. And since what he could only regard as the 'loss' of Frances, those thoughts were even less welcome than usual.

Some actors marooned in the provinces are organized about their careers. They write lots of letters, to other theatres, managements, television producers, casting directors, anyone who might lead to another job. They ring their agents and other contacts, finding out what new shows are coming up. They work hard, and are occasionally rewarded.

Charles Paris had long since ceased to believe that his career would be affected by anything but the randomness of fate.

Some actors, who have the ability, use the time to write, trying out ideas, getting new shows together, trying to interest managements in their wares.

Charles Paris, who had the ability, seemed to have lost the desire to write.

Some actors take advantage of their environment. They join the National Trust, they spend their days visiting stately homes and other places of local interest.

Charles Paris never got round to doing that sort of thing. Some actors pursue their sideline. It's amazing how many extra talents actors have. Some are solicitors and do a little gentle conveyancing for their colleagues. Some are doctors and fit in the odd locum clinic. Some are collectors and use their time with profit scouring the antique shops or bookshops of the area.

Charles Paris had no sideline.

Of course, all actors go to the cinema in the afternoon.

Charles Paris did that.

But Rugland Spa only had two cinemas. And that left a lot of the week unfilled.

The *Rugland Spa Gazette & Observer* was in the newsagents on Thursday mornings, but Gordon Tremlett, who knew everyone and how to get everything in the town, came into his dressing room with a copy on the Wednesday evening.

It was just after seven o'clock. Charles Paris, now *very good* about being in for the 'half', sat there meekly, his Sir Reginald De Meaux gear complete but for the screw-on sword and a fresh splash of Kensington Gore.

'Well, love, we're all over the local rag!'

Charles wondered whether Gordon Tremlett, in his previous existence, had addressed those grovelling for overdrafts as 'love'. It seemed unlikely. No doubt such flamboyance was reserved for his wild evenings amongst the Rugland Spa Players.

'What do you mean?'

'The *Shove It* scandal, sweetie. Look, front page news.'

The headline read 'COUNCILLOR DENOUNCES "SMUTTY" PLAY'.

Charles shrugged. 'They say all publicity's good publicity.'

'Not sure in this case, love. Councillor Davenport's asking for an enquiry into the running of the Regent.'

'Oh.'

'He's not going to get it, of course. Herbie Inchbald slapped him down firmly at last night's council meeting. But I think it could all blow up into a rather nasty row. You seen the Mrs Feller Brigade outside the front?'

Charles nodded. As he passed the theatre that afternoon he'd noticed a cluster of aggrieved ladies' hats and banners exhorting the public to 'KEEP OUR THEATRE CLEAN', 'BAN PORNOGRAPHY' and allow 'NO OBSCENE SHOWS IN RUGLAND SPA'.

'But surely that's the sort of publicity the show needs. Nothing like a bit of a controversy to fill the seats.'

'Not here, dear.'

'People'll come along just to see what the fuss is about. Broaden their minds.'

'Oh no, love. People move to Rugland Spa specifically to have their minds narrowed. No, they'll stay away in droves.'

'Are you sure?'

'Positive. Seen it before. No, this is a pity for the theatre. There are a lot of people in this town who'd like to get rid of the Regent. A lot of people on the council, unfortunately. Councillor Davenport and his lot want it sold. It's a prime site – any developer who got hold of it'd knock the theatre down and make a mint.'

'But isn't the theatre a protected building?'

Gordon Tremlett shook his head wryly. 'Not old enough or architecturally interesting enough to be listed. It is protected in a way, but the council could reverse that whenever they wanted to.'

'Why does this Davenport bloke want to get rid of it?'

'Wants the money to build a Leisure Centre on the Leominster Road. His pet project. Always saying theatre's a waste of time; we should be investing in the health of the body rather than that of the mind.'

'Blimey.'

'Trouble is...' Gordon tapped the paper. 'Something like this doesn't do his cause any harm.' The former bank manager pondered for a moment. 'I wonder if all this has anything to do with what Donald was asking me...'

'What was that?'

'Oh, just wanted to pick my brains, share a little of my expertise.' Gordon looked up mischievously. 'You're not going to believe this, Charles, but I haven't always been an actor.'

Play along with him. 'No. Really, Gordon?'

'No.' With a complacent shake of his head. 'No. And I don't think you'd ever guess what I used to be...'

Oh God, here we go. The worst-kept secret in Rugland Spa. 'Why, what were you. Gordon?'

'Only a bank manager.'

'Good heavens.' And, in case that was insufficient amazement, Charles added, 'Well, well, what a turn-up.'

'Oh yes.' Gordon smiled like the sphinx unburdened of her riddle.

'But what was Donald asking you then?'

'Ah well, you see, love, during my wicked past...' Gordon chuckled at his wit, 'I developed a certain familiarity with figures, account books, what-have-you...'

'Not surprising.'

'No. Anyway, I gather Donald's found some inconsistency in the theatre's books, don't know what, but he asked if I wouldn't mind casting an eye over them when I've got a moment. I don't think he wants to bring the accountants in and make it official. It's probably nothing, but I was wondering whether this threat of an enquiry's made him a bit nervous.'

'Could be.'

'Yes.' Gordon Tremlett rubbed his hands with glee. 'Still, before I get on my slap and cossy to tread the boards...' (he always used far more theatrical slang than a real actor would) 'I will cheer myself up with a nice notice. Frank Walby's column – always on the Entertainments Page, always on page fourteen, always restorative to the poor thespian ego.'

He turned with relish to page fourteen, but the sudden change of his expression was enough to make Charles lean forward and read over the shoulder:

## DATED THRILLER FAILS TO THRILL

Every cliché of the whodunnit is present in the Regent's latest offering, THE MESSAGE IS MURDER by Leslie Blatt. Though the play had a modest success when it was first written in the fifties post-SLEUTH and DEATHTRAP, audiences require more sophistication in their thrills than this awkward little piece now has to offer. Throughout the evening disbelief is suspended so often that eventually one doesn't give a damn what happens next and only prays for a premature curtain to put the play out of its misery.

Nor are the show's chances improved by an untidy production by Antony Wensleigh. When the curtain rises on Hermione Halliwell's set, we suspect we are in for an evening of dated shabbiness, and nothing that happens subsequently dispels this impression.

The cast suffer the disadvantage of playing characters with no vestige of psychological credibility, but that doesn't excuse the display of hamming and fluffing to which we are treated. Kathy Kitson moves through her part like a shopwalker from Harrods and Laurie Tichbourne, as her son, is so wet you want to get up on stage and wring him out. Cherry Robson, as the maid Wilhelmina, sensibly makes no attempt to act and confines herself to looking pretty, while Gay Milner, an unlikely debutante, plays her part as if suffering from internal injury. Gordon Tremlett, impersonating a Colonel, gives a performance so unconvincing that it would not be tolerated by any amateur dramatic society in the country. The actor who emerges with most credit is Charles Paris, who is at least meant to behave like a dead body, and who has least opportunity to do anything wrong.

All in all, THE MESSAGE IS MURDER is a production to be forgotten as soon as possible, and one that raises disturbing questions about the Regent's methods of play selection and overall artistic standards.

'Good God!' Gordon Tremlett exhaled in a shocked whisper. 'He must have gone off his rocker.'

'What?' asked Charles, who was just working out that 'The actor who emerges with most credit is Charles Paris' was, if one forgot the rest of the sentence, a very quotable review.

'Well, I mean, Frank. He's had a brainstorm. He's gone, completely. He's never written like this about any other production.'

'Perhaps he's never thought any other production was as bad.'

'No, but I mean, some of the things he says here...I mean, Okay, it's a rubbishy old play – I was only saying so to Leslie Blatt the other day – but a critic should be able to look beyond the play. To say that I give a performance that wouldn't be tolerated in any amateur dramatic society in the country...I mean, those aren't the words of a sane man. Are they?'

'Well,' said Charles judiciously, 'it does seem a bit over the top.'

'Over the top? It's nothing short of lunatic. And so hurtful.' Gordon Tremlett slumped dramatically back in his chair. 'I don't think critics realize how fragile an artist's confidence is. We have to go out there and give of ourselves every night, build ourselves up, bolster ourselves. And then, to be confronted with something like this. It's very puncturing to the ego.'

Charles grimaced, recalling past punctures to his own ego. The bad reviews always stayed fixed, word for word, in his mind. Like the one from the *Aberdeen Evening Express*:

'With Charles Paris playing Dracula, dawn couldn't come soon enough for me.'

Or the *Yorkshire Post*'s comment:

'Charles Paris kept hitching up his Northern accent like a loose bra-strap.'

But perhaps the most wounding of all had been *Plays & Players* reaction to his performance in one of the great classical roles:

'Charles Paris' Henry V had me rooting for the French at Agincourt.

# ACT TWO

## *Chapter Six*

'NO, THERE'S NO doubt about it,' Professor Weintraub announced. 'Sir Reginald had been dead for at least eight hours when his body was discovered.'

(On the Wednesday night of the second week that was true. Charles Paris had been an exemplary cadaver and was now sitting quietly in his dressing room reading.)

'But I don't see how that could be true,' Felicity Kershaw objected. 'I heard him talking on the telephone in the study just before we went out to play tennis.'

'Yes, so did I,' her fiancé agreed, trying desperately not to sound wet, 'but we were fooled. That was just another part of the murderer's devilish plan. Look!'

Dramatically, he produced a spool of recording tape from his pocket. 'Father had just bought one of those new-fangled tape recorders, and someone had set it in motion. So when we heard his voice, he was already dead!'

'How horrible,' exclaimed Felicity Kershaw, starting to clutch at her stomach and then, not wishing to look as if she had an internal injury, stopping the gesture half-way.

'Oh yes, it is horrible,' intoned Miss Laycock-Manderley, feeling extremely grateful that the *Rugland Spa Gazette & Observer* had nor deemed her performance worthy of comment. 'There is evil in the air at Wrothley Grange. I fear Sir Reginald's death may not be the last disaster we have to face before the day is out. I have a strange tingling in my spine.'

'Now don't let's get things out of proportion,' argued Lady Hilda, who wore a black silk dress for Act Two. This had been a source of some disagreement during rehearsal. Kathy Kitson had insisted that Lady Hilda De Meaux was the sort of woman who would instantly change into black after her husband's death. Tony Wensleigh, thinking of his Wardrobe budget, had felt this was unlikely but, not for the first time in his life, had allowed himself to be swayed. However, when she had also announced that Lady Hilda was the sort of woman who would change into yet another silk dress (this time, she fancied, a pearl grey) for the dénouements of Act Three, he had said he really would have to put his foot down.

'Everything,' Lady Hilda continued, 'will be all right once the police arrive.' With an elegant flick of her arm she looked at her watch. 'I'm surprised they're not here yet. James, when you spoke to the station, did they say how long they would be?'

'About half an hour,' James De Meaux replied as drily as he could.

'Hmm. And that was two hours ago.'

'Ahah,' Professor Weintraub joked inappropriately. 'The good old English bobby travelling as usual on his bicycle, yes?'

'You're sure they said half an hour, James?'

'Oh yes, mater,' her son replied, because that was how Leslie Blatt thought the upper classes spoke. 'The woman who answered said half an hour at the longest.'

'Woman?'

'Yes.'

'And you rang the station in Winklesham?'

'Yes, mater.'

'But there aren't any women at that station. There's just Inspector Carruthers, Sergeant McIntosh and the two constables.'

'What on earth does that mean, mater?'

'Oh, there's something horrible going on,' Felicity Kershaw panted, again restraining herself from clutching at her vitals.

'Now let's keep calm. We'll ring the police again. Professor Weintraub, would you oblige?'

'Of course, milady.'

'Ask the operator for 253.'

'Yes, milady.' The Professor jiggled the buttons of the telephone. 'I am not seeming to be able to raise the operator. Ah no, somebody answers. Could I have, please, number 253? What? Who is this? Wilhelmina?'

Lady Hilda moved sharply across to him. 'Let me take it. Wilhelmina? What are you doing? Where are you? Oh. Well, will you please come here straight away?' She put the phone down.

'Wilhelmina?' emoted Felicity Kershaw, her hand going involuntarily to her stomach. 'You mean she planned it all? She murdered Sir Reginald?'

'No. She was in the study dusting when the telephone rang and she answered it.'

'But how on the earth...?' began Professor Weintraub.

'The telephone in the study is just an extension of this one. Someone has tampered with the machinery, so that when you ring from here, it can be answered from the study.'

'So I didn't speak to the police station at all?'

'No, James. You spoke to someone in this house.'

'Good heavens!'

'A woman. Did you recognize the voice?'

'Well, no. It was a very bad line. The voice was very muffled.'

'A handkerchief over the receiver,' Professor Weintraub announced. 'This is an old ploy amongst the criminal fraternity.'

James De Meaux looked menacing. 'How do you know that, Professor?'

'Well, I, er...'

But he was spared further confusion by the entry of Wilhelmina, who stood in the doorway, looking pretty. She had decided that this was probably her role in life after all. She was very tired, after a few late nights at clubs in Birmingham with her factory-owner. And since he, who was separated from his wife and didn't seem to know what to do with his money, had offered to take her on a trip to the West Indies, she couldn't wait for the end of the run. See how things sorted out. Maybe give up this acting lark.

'Yes, milady?'

'Wilhelmina, you just answered the phone in the study.'

'Yes, milady.'

'And spoke to us in here.'

'Yes, milady.'

'Has that ever happened before?'

'No, milady.'

'Are you sure?'

'Certain, milady.'

'Hmm. Now when James thought he was speaking to the police, in fact he was speaking to someone in this house. A woman.' (Leslie Blatt's constant repetitions showed he had no very high opinion of the retentive qualities of his audience's minds.) 'Who was with you in here when you telephoned James?'

'Nobody, mater. I was alone.' (This was true, as the audience could bear witness. Act Two had started with the relevant telephone call.)

'So it could have been anyone James, you had better get into the car and drive to Winklesham to fetch the police.'

'Yes, mater.'

'We have no other means of communication since the telephone is not working.'

At this moment (one of Leslie Blatt's personal favourites in the play) the telephone rang. The entire cast froze, looking at the instrument.

Wilhelmina was the first to move towards it, but was stopped by her mistress. 'No, I will answer it.' Lady Hilda raised the receiver. 'Hello, Wrothley Grange. Ah, Laurence. Where are you? Well, will you come to the Grange straight away. What? Where? The bridge? What do you mean – washed away? But –'

She looked at the receiver. 'We have been cut off.' She looked at the assembled company. 'That was Laurence. The butler,' she added, in case people had forgotten the earlier reference to him at the beginning of Act One. 'He was calling from Winklesham. The bridge over the River Wink has been washed away by the freak high tide.'

'Oh no!'

'But, mater, that means I can't drive to Winklesham to fetch the police.'

'No, James. And I didn't have time to inform Laurence of Sir Reginald's death before we were cut off.'

'No.'

'Oh! That means we're all trapped here!' Felicity Kershaw had by now lost any inhibitions about her natural acting style and clutched her stomach enthusiastically.

'Yes. Trapped with Sir Reginald's murderer. Who must be one of us.'

'Oh,' moaned Miss Laycock-Manderley. 'I knew there was evil in this house when I arrived. The deaths will not stop at one. The forces of evil demand their toll of blood.'

'Don't go on so,' reprimanded Lady Hilda (and most of the audience echoed the sentiment).

'No, we've got to be logical, think this through,' said James.

'Yes. The person we are looking for is a woman with a knowledge of the workings of telephones,' asserted Lady Hilda.

'Well, don't look at me. I'm an absolute rabbit at practical things. I can't even change a fuse.' Felicity Kershaw went off into a peal of high-pitched laughter, deliberately excessive to point up the essential vacuity of the property-owning class which she represented.

'But why are we just looking for one person?' asked James, atypically incisive. 'There might be a conspiracy. Suppose the woman who answered the telephone is in league with someone else, the one who actually tampered with the instruments. Maybe they planned the old man's murder between them.'

There was a pause for the cast (and audience) to assimilate this new idea, before James continued, turning his best profile to the auditorium, 'Professor, you brought a lot of recording equipment with you.'

'Yes, but this is because of my bird-watching. I make records of bird-song. I am very anxious to capture the singing of the cormorant. This is why I bring it.'

'But there are no cormorants round here. Not for miles,' James countered.

'Ah, well, sorry, a mistake. When I say cormorant, I did not mean, er...'

'I don't think you'd recognize a cormorant if one flew in your face. Or any other bird, come to that. I don't think you brought your recording equipment and cameras for bird-watching at all. I think you re more interested in the top-secret army research establishment in the pine forest.'

'No, I –'

'I think you're a spy, Professor Weintraub. And I think my father recognized you as such. You may not know it, but my father was Head of British Intelligence during the last war!'

Professor Weintraub looked around the assembled company with panic in his eyes. 'But I never knew this, I never knew it.'

'I think my father invited you here to expose you, to show you up for the dirty little spy that you are!'

'No, it is not true!'

The ensuing pause was ended by Miss Laycock-Manderley with an utterance which, surprisingly and for the first time in the play, was not reminiscent of Cassandra. 'If we're looking back to the last war,' she said with a dryness that James De Meaux envied, 'we might do worse than investigate Colonel Fripp's record.'

'What do you mean?'

'He was in the Signals. One of the top boffins in Communications.'

'Really?'

'Yes. Best known for his development of a new form of field telephone.'

'Good heavens!'

'Where is Colonel Fripp?' Felicity Kershaw asked suddenly.

'I don't know,' Lady Hilda replied with an elegant but redundant gesture of a silk-clad arm. 'I haven't seen him all afternoon.'

'Nor have I.'

'No, nor me.'

'Wilhelmina, have you seen Colonel Fripp this afternoon?'

'Not since tea, milady. He said he wanted to take a good long look at the Titians in the Long Gallery.'

'Oh. Well, would you see if he is still there, Wilhelmina?'

'Yes, milady.'

Wilhelmina moved across to the double doors on the opposite side of the set from the fireplace.

Up in the front row of the Circle, Leslie Blatt's hand gripped the thigh of the fifteen-year-old he had picked up in the Wimpy Bar. 'You'll enjoy this bit,' he hissed. 'Give you a real thrill.'

Wilhelmina swung both doors open. Framed in them was the dangling figure of Colonel Fripp.

'Oh no!' screamed Lady Hilda, and then, perhaps thinking the play was on radio, 'It's Colonel Fripp! He's hanged himself!'

At this point, to justify James De Meaux's next line, the body was meant to swing round with its back to the audience. But the body wasn't behaving at all in the way it had at rehearsal. It was twitching and struggling, but it didn't turn round.

James de Meaux said his line anyway. 'Not hanged *himself*, mater. Not with his hands tied behind his back!'

Colonel Fripp continued to twitch and struggle as the curtain fell on Act Two. There was nothing amateur or unconvincing about the performance he was giving that night. He was giving the performance of his life.

Or perhaps, as the noose tightened around his neck, it would be more appropriate to say *for* his life.

## Chapter Seven

'THE TROUBLE WAS the rope was too short.'

Nella Lewis seemed quite happy to go through the accident again for Charles although she had presumably had to give her version to the police and other curious members of the company. She wasn't making a big production of it, just telling helpfully because he asked. She really was a very nice girl, he reflected. And astonishingly pretty. Wasted on Laurie Tichbourne.

But before any lecherous intent could form, the thought of Frances, like a trapped nerve, stopped him. Now that she was presumably off his scene, the thought of her was far more inhibiting to him than it had been when there was a real tie to feel guilty about.

'But he wasn't just being supported by the rope, was he, Nella?'

'Oh, no. Haven't you ever been hanged, Charles?'

'No. I've been decapitated once or twice, and had unspeakable things done to me in *Edward II*, but never actually been hanged.'

'Well, it's like flying.'

'Oh, I've done that. On the old Kirby wire.'

'Yes. Well, for hanging you wear the same sort of harness, you know, round the torso and under the crutch, and the wire clips on to the shackle in the same way. And the rope, the noose, is run up the wire into the flies.'

'Right.'

'Obviously the important thing is to get the relative tension between the rope and the wire right. It's got to be the wire that takes the strain, but you can't have the rope too slack or it sags and any illusion you might be creating is destroyed.'

'But for poor old Gordon it was the rope that took the strain?'

'Yes, with the wire slack. I don't know how it happened. It was a terrible accident.'

'Yes.' If that was the right word. 'When did he get in position? Surely he didn't dangle there through the entire Act?'

'No. He'd get there about ten minutes before his appearance...I forget what the cue was exactly...but then either Rick or I would clip on the wire and arrange the noose for him.'

'But why didn't you notice there was something wrong then?'

'Ah, you see, he stood on a chair for that bit, so both the wire and the rope were slack. He only launched himself off on Kathy's line, "Wilhelmina, have you seen Colonel Fripp this afternoon?" That was Tony's idea – he reckoned it was more effective if the body was swinging when the audience saw it.'

'So Gordon was only being throttled for a few minutes?'

'Yes, that's what saved his life – the fact that we were able to get him down so quickly. Mind you, he was lucky he didn't break his neck when he left the chair. I suppose the wire must have taken a bit of his weight.'

'Yes. And then the rope just slowly tightened up.'

'Right.'

'How is he? Have you heard?'

'Still in Intensive Care, I gather. Still touch and go.'

'Hmm.' Two accidents now. A stabbing which caused no casualty, and a hanging which might have been accidental and which might yet prove fatal. Charles' mind struggled to detect a pattern to the sequence. And, with gloom worthy of Miss Laycock-Manderley, he wondered whether the sequence had ended or was going to get worse.

'And you've no idea how it happened?'

Nella shrugged. 'Rick fixed the rope up in the flies. I suppose he could have misjudged the tension, but it's unlike him. He's pretty careful about most things.'

'Yes.' Rick Harmer, on the other hand, was one of the potential suspects for the stabbing, in the scenario that saw Antony Wensleigh as the intended victim. But the A.S.M. had a motive against the Director; and apparently none against the thespian bank manager.

'The only idea I've had,' Nella offered hesitantly, 'came from something Laurie said...'

'Yes?'

'Well, you saw that review in the *Gazette*?'

'Yes.'

'It upset quite a few people.'

'Everyone, I should think. Except me.'

Nella smiled deliciously. 'Well, Laurie was saying how upset Gordon had been about it, and I just wondered whether he...shortened the rope himself.'

'Gordon? Surely he wouldn't over-react that much. I mean, I know it upset him, but he's not a suicidal type.'

'No, I didn't mean that. I meant that the review said he was unconvincing, and I wondered whether he said to himself, "Unconvincing, huh? Well, I'll at least make sure the hanging looks convincing."'

'And overdid it?'

'It's possible. It's the sort of daft, unprofessional thing he would do.'

Charles jutted out his lower lip. 'I suppose you could be right. Pretty violent, that review, wasn't it?'

'You can say that again.'

'And, I gather, not typical.'

'No. Total change of character. I think the booze must have got to him at last, rotted his brain away.'

Then she blushed, remembering an earlier meeting with Charles and not wanting him to think she was making comparisons.

He smiled to ease the tension. 'How did Laurie take it?'

She grimaced. 'Not very well. I'm afraid he's a bit childish that sort of thing. Threw a bit of a tantrum – said if that's what people thought of his performance, then he jolly well wasn't going to go on.'

'But did, nonetheless.'

'Yes, I managed to calm him down.'

'Massaged his ego a little?'

She smiled again, slightly guiltily this time.

'Things all right between you and Laurie?'

'Yes,' she asserted defensively. 'Well, I mean, yes. He's very sweet, but.., well, you know...'

'Yes. I know.'

'He really seems to want a mother rather than a girl-friend.'

'Yes. But you're quite gone on him?'

She nodded ruefully. 'And he seems to be pleased about that, but just sort of to take it for granted .

'Yes.'

'I'm afraid it's not at the moment a very *dynamic* relationship.'

'I don't think dynamics are Laurie's strong point.'

'No. Oh well, it's the same old story. A – i.e. me – loves B, B isn't as keen as A is, and meanwhile A is hassled by the unwanted attentions of C.'

But before the intriguing identity of C could be revealed, Rick Harmer came up. 'Charles, Donald wants a word. Could you nip up to the office?'

'Sure. Continue our chat tomorrow, Nella?'

'Yes. Ooh, no, I won't be here tomorrow. I've got to go to this All-Day Seminar thing in Worcester.'

'Don't I know it,' said Rick bitterly.

'What's this?'

Nella explained. 'It's something for an Adult Education Institute, I think. A sort of Symposium on the theatre. Tony's going along to talk, and he's insisting on taking along a member of the Stage Management to answer questions on that side of it. God knows why he's chosen me – I'm fairly new to the business.'

'He's chosen you,' said Rick, 'simply so that I'll be needed here and won't be able to have the day free for the recording of my radio pilot.'

'Oh. Do you really think so?'

'Yes, I do. Absolutely typical of him. Tony Wensleigh is a real bastard.'

Once again Charles found it difficult to reconcile this description with what he knew of the Artistic Director.

Donald Mason was once again on the phone when Charles arrived in the administrative office. And once again he appeared to be sorting our some cock-up of Tony Wensleigh's.

'Look, I'm sorry to go through it again, but I would just like to check I've got my facts right, because, you know, if there has been any funny business...Yes, thank you. Right. you received the order for the Henry VIII costume on November 10th? Yes, that would tally, because round then we were thinking of organizing a series of medieval banquets in the bar, as a fund-raising exercise. But then we dropped the idea, and the order should have been cancelled. Yes, I remember distinctly reminding the Artistic Director to cancel. Are you sure he didn't? Hmm. You see, the thing that makes it awkward from my point of view is that when the costume did arrive, he then wore it to a fancy dress party on New Year's Eve. Yes, and then it was despatched to you on January 2nd. No, no, I'm not blaming you in any way, I just want to get the facts right. You see, it could look – to an outsider – horribly as if he'd just ordered the costume for himself to wear to this party – and slapped the hire charge on to the theatre's account. So just in case anyone does start to make allegations like that, I have to know exactly what happened. Yes. I mean, I have to protect my Artistic Director. Right. Well, thank you very much indeed. You've been most helpful.'

He put the phone down and, with a disarming smile, said, 'Sorry, Charles. There's always something.'

'Don't worry. You, er, wanted to see me.' Once again Charles found himself feeling a bit Billy Bunterish.

'Yes.' Donald Mason rose from his chair and moved over to look out of the office's one small window. 'Our last interview was on a rather unhappy subject...'

'Yes.'

'Well, I think this one's going to be more cheerful. It's an ill wind and all that.'

What on earth was he talking about?

'As you know, Charles, we had a rather nasty accident last night. Poor old Gordon...Incidentally, I've just been on to the hospital and the prognosis, you'll be glad to hear, sounds a little more hopeful. But the fact is, Gordon's going to be out of action for some time, whatever happens.'

'Oh.' Was Charles about to be promoted from a stabbed corpse to a hanged corpse?

'Now Rick Harmer will be taking over from Gordon for the rest of the run of *The Message Is Murder*.'

No, he wasn't.

'Rick's a very talented boy and can easily age up for the part. But the thing is that Gordon was also playing a small part in *Shove It*...'

So that was it. Charles' great talents were about to be enlisted in the service of Royston Everett's mucky writing.

'As I say, it's only a small part, but Rick can't play it, because you can't do that with make-up.'

There was a slight pause before Charles asked, 'Er, do *what* with make-up?'

'Well, you can manage a face easily, but you can't make the whole of a young body look like an old body.'

'Ah. Do you mean this is a nude part?'

'Yes.'

All right, all right, thought Charles. Now don't tell me that it's all absolutely necessary to the plot and will be very tastefully done.

'You'll be one of the prostitutes' clients who are chased out when the police raid the flat.'

'Oh. Great.'

'There are a couple of lines. Nothing much. You just have to shout at the policemen.'

'Oh yes.' Charles could imagine the sort of thing he'd have to shout.

'I'd like you to do it, Charles – apart from anything else, to show there are no hard feelings about the other business. I have to tell you that Tony doesn't want you to have the part, because he thinks you're unreliable, but I'm prepared to overrule him on this occasion. That is, if you want to do it. It's another three weeks' work. What do you say? Will you do it – I mean, that is assuming that you're not going straight on to another job?'

No one who had been more familiar with Charles Paris' career would have asked the last question.

The letter had been directed on to the Regent Theatre by Charles' agent, Maurice Skellern. As soon as he recognized the writing, he felt a little welling of nauseous excitement in his throat. He didn't want to open it but at the same time knew he had to.

Dear Charles,

I had hoped to hear from you after my last letter, but, since I haven't, there seemed nothing for it but to write again. I've tried ringing Hereford Road a few times, but when I finally got through, one of the Swedes said you were working, though she didn't know where. I somehow couldn't bring myself to ring Maurice, so I've sent this letter c/o him.

I do want to talk to you, Charles, now more than ever. Nothing has really changed since I last wrote, least of all my state of utter confusion. And though I know that seeing you would only confuse me more, I also know that you are probably the only person I can talk to.

I gather that you spoke to Juliet and have had horrors since that anything she said may have misled you, though I'm not quite clear what she did say and what would constitute misleading information.

Charles, we must not lose touch, now more than ever. Please ring me, or write to me – contact me somehow. I so want to talk to you.

I hope whatever you're doing is going well, wherever you re doing it. And I hope you're more positively and consistently happy than I am.

Love, Frances

The letter threw him into a turmoil. Through his scrambled emotions he could identify individually anger, jealousy, pity, regret and even, infuriatingly, a little hope. Though hope for what he was not sure.

The one clear point that emerged was that he should phone Frances as soon as possible.

But, being Charles Paris, he put it off.

*Shove It* had been a *succès de scandale* of 1977. The production, much-praised at the Liverpool Playhouse, had transferred to the West End, where the critics, going through one of their self flagellating phases of gosh-we-must-stop-watching-all-these-light-comedies-and-thrillers-and-really-get-down-to-something-a-bit-searing-and-gritty, also praised it extravagantly. With three changes of cast, it ran for two and a half years, then did a national tour for another year, until finally the rights were available for provincial theatres to mount their own productions.

The play, a searingly accurate and unsentimental evocation of the tough area in which Royston Everett grew up, made him enough money to settle in the South of France, where he continued to make a great deal from writing screenplays of films that never got made, and settled down quietly to drink himself to death.

Nothing dates more quickly than yesterday's sensation, and by the time it reached the Regent Theatre, Rugland Spa, *Shove It* was more dated than the works of Thomas Shadwell and Colley Cibber. Its power to shock had been weakened by imitations on stage and television, the reliance of its original success on a series of charismatic performances was revealed, and all that remained was a rather shapeless piece, full of long ranting monologues, with a lot of apparently gratuitous bad language and nudity.

The performances that it was getting in Rugland Spa were not charismatic. Nor did they seem to be in tune with the mood of the play.

Certainly Kathy Kitson's wasn't. The first morning Charles arrived at rehearsal, she was already arguing with a very patient but pained-looking Tony Wensleigh.

'I'm sorry, Tony love, but I'm sure the madame of the brothel would wear a beige silk dress with blue flecks.'

'I honestly think that's unlikely, Kathy. The play is set in a very depressed area and she's meant to be very poor.'

'I know that, darling, but she's not the sort of woman who would let that sort of thing stop her from taking care of her appearance.'

'But she couldn't afford a silk dress.'

'Tony love, all the great courtesans of history have dressed magnificently, it's a well-known fact. I mean, Dubarry, Pompadour...'

'But she isn't Dubarry or Pompadour. She's a broken-down old whore, riddled with syphilis.'

Kathy Kitson extended her long neck. 'I don't think that sort of language is necessary, Tony.'

'It's nothing to what's in the play.'

'No. That's another thing I would like to have a long talk about.'

'Yes, okay, Kathy. Later. We'd better get on with rehearsal now.'

'I am quite ready to get on with rehearsal, Tony. I don't want to get side-tracked by all these discussions.'

'No. Right. Fine. Let's take it from where the two punters come in and you offer the girls to them.'

'Very well.'

The cast for the scene got into their positions. Charles, who was playing one of the punters, was shown where to stand. He didn't have many actual lines in the scene, just a few lewd grunts and obscene reactions as the prostitutes were pointed out to him and a brief résumé of their special skills given by their keeper. (This scene had been hailed by *Time Out* as 'a microcosm of English society, where the fat cats of plutocracy casually select which workers they intend to exploit.' Gay Milner, as one of the whores, was finding the part a lot easier to play politically than she did Felicity Kershaw.)

Tony Wensleigh clapped his hands, a gesture of authority which didn't suit him. 'Okay, Kathy, you begin with "If you're looking for a really good..." erm...etcetera...'

'Right you are, love.'

The whores posed, according to their middle-class views of how whores might pose. The punters tried to look like lecherous old men ( no great effort of character acting in at least one case). Kathy Kitson gave her eternally graceful impression of a shopwalker at Harrods.

'If you're looking for a really enjoyable evening,' she elocuted, 'perhaps one of these young ladies might prove a friendly companion for you. Sharon here has a great deal of charm –'

'Kathy, Kathy. Sorry, got to stop you.'

'I was just getting into my flow, Tony.'

'I know, I know. But those are not the lines in the script.'

'You can't expect me to be word-perfect at this stage in rehearsal.'

'That's not what I'm saying, Kathy. You are remarkably fluent for this stage in rehearsal. But what you are fluent in is not what Royston Everett wrote.'

'He wrote that she offers the girls – I'm offering the girls.' Kathy Kitson shrugged silk-clad shoulders.

'Yes, but he didn't write it in the words that you used.'

'I'm sure the audience will understand what I mean.'

'I'm sure they will. But that's not the point. The author's lines matter. I mean, how would you feel if Hamlet came on for his big soliloquy and said, "I can't decide whether to do myself in or not"?'

'This Everett person is hardly Shakespeare.'

'No, I agree. But we are doing his play, that's what we are paying him royalties for, that's what the audience will come to the theatre expecting to see, and so that is the text that we should be presenting.'

'I think what I am saying is much more tasteful.'

'I don't question that, Kathy. But Royston Everett is not trying to be tasteful. He is painting a picture of life as it really is, in the language which people really use.'

'Oh, I don't think life is really like this. This is all so impossibly sordid. I mean, Tony love, is your life like this? Do you move amongst prostitutes all the time? I mean, when did you last meet a prostitute here in Rugland Spa? Go on, tell me.'

'That is not –'

'Certainly, my life is nothing like this, I'm glad to say. My life's much more like a Noel Coward play than this sort of rubbish.'

'Kathy, all I'm saying is that we should perform the play as written. I'm not saying that your life is like the life depicted here, but then you can't expect to be playing yourself all the time. You have to play other characters as well – that's what acting's about.'

'Don't tell me what acting's about!'

'No, I'm sorry, I didn't mean that. I just mean that, okay, Royston Everett's language is not the sort of language you might use.'

'Certainly not.'

'No. It's bold, and it's frank, and it's designed to shock. But we mustn't be pussy-footed about it. We must just say the words, not be ashamed of them. When the script says, "If you're looking for a really good..." erm...then we mustn't shy away from it. We must say the word, we must say, "If you're looking for a really good..." erm...and so on...Okay, let's take it from the same place.'

They continued the rehearsal. Seeing the play acted did not raise the opinion Charles had formed from reading it. The cast seemed to be lost in a morass of vituperation, and Tony Wensleigh showed no signs of being able to lead them out of it. He looked puzzled and was vaguer than ever. Scenes got plotted and intonations corrected, but he had no overall vision of the play. *Shove It* needed a strong directorial hand to camouflage its deficiencies, and it wasn't getting it. The cast needed the inspiration that could only be given by directorial enthusiasm, real or faked (theatre directors have to rival prostitutes in faking enthusiasm). But Tony Wensleigh seemed distracted, preoccupied, anxious even.

He certainly showed no aptitude for directing that sort of play. He was workmanlike, the show would actually go on, but it was alien to the director's nature. He excelled at the subtleties of his craft, teasing performances out of small casts, and was lost amidst the strident brashness of Royston Everett's work.

Not for the first time, Charles wondered how the season's plays actually got selected. To choose one absolute stinker might be regarded as a misfortune: to choose two in a row looked like deliberate perversity.

That afternoon the cast was honoured by a visit from Herbie Inchbald. His entrance disrupted the rehearsal completely, though for the first time in the day some kind of flow had been established. With elaborate gestures and hushings he explained that he didn't want to disrupt anything, just slip into the back of the Drill Hall and watch a bit of the rehearsal. They were to ignore him and just continue as if he weren't there.

This was difficult. The presence of the Chairman of the Theatre Board – particularly his unexplained presence – was not easily ignored. But they did their best, and at least his being there inhibited Kathy Kitson's meandering from the text a little (though there were certain favourite words of Royston Everett which she refused to utter).

After about ten minutes, the scene which they were running came to an end, and Herbie Inchbald interrupted, 'Er, sorry, Tony, don't want to interrupt but if I could just say a couple of words...'

'Of course, Herbie.'

'Erm, okay. If you could all gather round, team...'

Ugh. Charles didn't like people who called the company 'team'. It seemed to him to fit in with people who called the theatre the 'thee-ettah'.

'Now, the reason I've come along today, team, is not anything that need worry you. Fact is, you probably don't need telling that this little show of yours is causing a bit of controversy in Rugland Spa. Its reputation has gone before it and, let's face it, it's got a few of the local biddies a bit upset.

'Now this doesn't worry me. The history of the thee-ettah has been the history of ruffling public sensibilities – that's the only way new ideas get an airing, and the thee-ettah is a very important medium for spreading new ideas.'

Gay Milner, slightly surprised at the source of this remark, still nodded agreement.

'No, it's my belief that, so long as what you're doing is artistically justified and is tastefully done, then it should be done. Our policy at the Regent – and particularly since Donald, our new General Manager, took over – has always been to provide varied fare. Okay, we do the standards, we do the panto, we do the Shakespeare, we do the Ayckbourn, we do a grand little thriller like *The Message Is Murder*. But we also have to be experimental – and that's why we're doing *Shove It*.

'You may wonder why I'm telling you all this. After all, you know it. But I wanted to come along in person and tell you that this little show has the full support of the Board – as well, of course, as that of the Artistic Director and General Manager. Don't worry about the opposition, don't worry about anything you read in the local paper. This is the sort of show the Regent ought to be doing.'

Charles' respect for Herbie Inchbald rose. His arrival at rehearsal had been a good psychological move, to revive a doubting cast by assurances of management support. But he couldn't remove a niggling doubt about the artistic judgement of someone who liked *Shove It*, who could describe *The Message Is Murder* as 'a grand little thriller' (and someone who pronounced theatre 'thee-ettah').

Herbie Inchbald had not yet finished his team-talk. 'You know, a few weeks back, I was talking to Michael Timson – you know, the M.P....'

They knew. The name had been all over the newspapers three months earlier when he had resigned on an issue of principle over defence spending.

'We're members of the same club in London...Blake's...'

The name was dropped very casually, but still had the desired effect of surprise. Blake's was one of the most exclusive clubs in the country. Obviously there was more to Herbie Inchbald than met the eye. He was, Charles had discovered, Managing Director of a local haulage company, fairly prosperous and socially acceptable in Rugland Spa, but not Charles' idea of a clubman. Still, the deceptiveness of appearances was a continuing source of amazement.

'And Michael and I got talking about his resignation, and, you know, he said something to me which I thought was very relevant to us here. He said, if you know you're right, do what you have to do, and all will turn out for the best.'

Usual politician's vacuous rhetoric, thought Charles with reflex cynicism.

'So let's all have the courage of our convictions, eh? The Regent Thee-ettah has weathered a few storms in its time, and I'm sure it'll weather this one. It's been closed down, it's been bankrupt, it's nearly been brought up for development I don't know how many times. But it's always survived and it always will, so long as we stick to our policy of choosing the best plays and putting them on according to the highest artistic standards of the British thee-ettah.'

Experience of many council meetings had taught Herbie Inchbald to bring a speech to a climax demanding applause (a device known in eighteenth-century theatre as a 'claptrap'), and he didn't fail this time. The company clapped dutifully.

'Thank you. And just remember, the best you can do for me, and the rest of the Board, and for Donald, and Tony is to do this show so well that our critics and the Massed Wet Blankets of Rugland Spa haven't got a leg to stand on. Make *Shove It* an artistic landmark in the history of the Regent Thee-ettah!'

Again, he got his applause.

And Charles felt the same unease that he had on his earlier encounter with Herbie Inchbald.

The Chairman of the Board's enthusiasm for the theatre was unquestionable and admirable. But did he actually know anything about it?

## Chapter Eight

REGENT THEATRE 'HANGING' – COUNCILLOR CONDEMNS
'NEGLIGENCE' – CALLS FOR ENQUIRY
by our Arts Correspondent, Frank Walby

The fortunes of Rugland Spa's beleaguered Regent Theatre suffered another setback last Wednesday with a near-fatal accident on stage to Gordon Tremlett, one of the theatre's regular actors (and former manager of Barclay's Bank in the High Street). A stage hanging in the Regent's current production, *The Message Is Murder* by Lesley Bratt turned out all too realistic for poor Gordon, who, in his own words, 'found the noose tightening round my neck'.

Speaking from his bed in the Chambers Kenton Hospital, where he is now recovering, the former Bank Manager is aware of how lucky an escape he had. 'I don't remember much about it, but I gather I spent two days in Intensive Care and it was touch and go for a while.' He paid tribute to the nursing skills of the doctors and nurses of the Chambers Kenton.

Gordon, who lives in Harfleur Avenue with his wife Anita and two children, Robert and Libby, and was a former star of the Rugland Spa Players before turning professional, says he won't let the accident deter him from continuing with his theatrical career. 'As soon as I'm fit, I'll be back. When the right part comes up. If you've really got the theatre in your blood, it takes more than a hanging to get you off the boards. Just for the time being I'm resting, but I'll be back,' he joked.

The incident, however, has a more serious side. Councillor Thomas Davenport, already severely critical of the running of the Regent Theatre, sees it as 'just another in a long line of disasters caused by mismanagement and negligence. Obviously the equipment had not been checked properly'. He complained that the theatre received a large grant from the Council 'which is just wasted money. Rugland Spa is not a wealthy town, and recent government spending cuts have put a serious strain on resources. Essential services like Meals on Wheels and pre-school playgroup facilities are having to be cut back, and there is a lamentable lack of sports facilities in the area. Maintaining the council's grant to the Regent is just pouring good money after bad. An enquiry should be held into the running of the theatre.'

(In recent years the council has matched the grant made to the Regent by the Arts Council. But the Arts Council too is being forced to cut back, and the continuation of their grant is by no means certain. If that was withdrawn, the

Council would be unlikely to find the full amount of the subsidy, and the theatre might be forced to close. This nearly happened five years ago, when the theatre was again threatened and nearly sold for development, but it was saved by a campaign of local people.)

Councillor Herbert Inchbald, answering Councillor Davenport's allegations, said Rugland Spa needed its theatre. As Chairman of the Theatre's Board, as well as a councillor, he felt a duty to provide this cultural amenity for the people of the area and not 'give way to the forces of philistinism'.

The theatre is also in the news at the moment, because of the controversy surrounding its next production, the outspoken West End success, *Shove It*, by Ryton Everitt, a play reputed to contain scenes of nudity and a great many four-letter words. Already opposition to the play is growing. Mrs Erica Feller, who is organizing the campaign against the production, says she is 'receiving up to ten phone calls of support a day'. She says the play, which she has not read, is 'disgusting and representative of all that is worst in this country at the moment'. Mrs Feller, who lives in Ronston Gardens with her husband Norman and has won prizes for flower arrangement led the successful campaign to stop the opening of a sex shop on Station Parade last year.

Councillor Inchbald said that the Regent Theatre has 'nothing to be ashamed of', but announced that there would be a special meeting of the Theatre Board on Friday 'to discuss ways of improving the Regent's public image, which has recently undergone a quite unnecessary battering'.

Grapes were not really Charles' style, but they were more his style than flowers or chocolates, so he took grapes to the Chambers Kenton Hospital on the Wednesday afternoon of the third week of *The Message Is Murder*. (Wednesday was matinée day, which meant no afternoon rehearsal for *Shove It*, so Charles changed straight out of his costume after his appearance as the defunct Sir Reginald De Meaux. He thought the matinée audience could cope without seeing him at the curtain call. Actually, he doubted whether they'd notice; the average age at the matinées was even older than usual in Rugland Spa – in other words, about a hundred and fifty.)

The nurse told him he shouldn't stay long and tire the patient, but Gordon Tremlett looked indefatigable. He looked very fit and rosy in his room in the private wing. (Retired bank managers can afford health insurance schemes in a way that very few actors can.) He was surrounded by enough cards for a royal baby, enough flowers for the Guernsey Carnival and enough grapes, Charles noticed as he added his meagre offering to the pile, to start producing his own Chateau Tremlett.

Gordon had recovered sufficiently from his shock to appreciate its dramatic possibilities and was more than ready to relive it for the benefit of any pair of willing ears. Most of the Rugland Spa Players had already been to pay their homage and listen to the action replay, so he was glad to see Charles as a new audience.

'It was my heart, you see, that's why I was so ill. The shock to the heart would you believe, it actually stopped three times.' He indicated the bandages round his neck dismissively. 'Nasty rope-burn round here, you know, but that wasn't what did the damage. No, it was the old ticker, love. Touch and go, for a time, it was.' He clearly enjoyed this phrase, because he repeated it. 'Touch and go, you know, love.'

'But you feel okay now?'

'Fit as the proverbial. Quacks say I'll have to take things a bit easy, but I'm sure once I get back on the green, Dr Theatre'll sort me out.'

Charles tried not to wince visibly at this barrage of theatrical slang. 'And any idea how it happened?'

'Who can say, love? One of those things. One of the A.S.M.s got the tensions wrong, I suppose. They're not very experienced, those two. Need a few years before they're real *theatre* people.'

'They always fixed it, did they?'

'Oh yes.'

'I mean, you never went up into the flies yourself to check the ropes?'

Gordon Tremlett looked at him aghast. 'Me, love? No! I have the most terrible head for heights – stand on a weighing machine and I get dizzy. No, no. Anyway, I can't be bothered with technical things when I'm on stage. Leave all that to the stage management. I'm always giving all my concentration to my performance.'

Yes, ensuring that it's so unconvincing it wouldn't be tolerated in any amateur dramatic society in the country, Charles thought. That reminded him of the review, and of Frank Walby. 'Have you seen this week's *Gazette*?'

This got a predictable actor's response. 'And how, love! Not a bad little spread, eh?'

Obviously sheer quantity of coverage had erased the memory of Frank Walby's qualitative strictures. Still, the journalist had obviously interviewed Gordon for the front page article. Might be worth probing a little.

'Frank Walby wrote it, I see.'

'Oh yes. Phoned through agog to talk to me, absolutely *agog*.'

'Did you mention his review?'

Gordon Tremlett's face took on a saintly expression. 'I think, Charles, something an actor has to learn...' He paused, and a note of reproof entered his voice, as if Charles had obscurely offended '...is magnanimity in the face of criticism. It is not for me to cast judgement on Frank's aberration, just to feel sorry for his circumstances.' In an elaborate whisper, he added, 'He *drinks*, you know.'

So that was it. The review had now been dismissed as a symptom of alcoholic dementia. The punctures in Gordon Tremlett's ego had been repaired and it had been reinflated.

Charles allowed a silence to ensue. He knew exactly what he wanted to say next, but he wanted to present it with that what-on-earth-can-I-think-of-to-say-next desperation common to all hospital visits.

'It never occurred to you, I suppose, Gordon, that the hanging was anything other than an accident?'

'Charles! What on earth do you mean?'

'Well, the rope had always been the right length before. Why should it suddenly be wrong?'

'What, you mean someone was trying to *get at* me?'

Charles shrugged. 'It's an idea.'

'Yes, it is. How *thrilling*.' Gordon seemed captivated by the suggestion, gleefully contemplating all of its dramatic possibilities. He no doubt had visions of inviting back all of the Rugland Spa Players to his bedside for sessions of intriguing speculation.

'You're suggesting, Charles, that someone might actually have *tampered* with the rope?'

'As I say, just an idea.' Charles made it sound as much as possible as if he was suggesting a game of I-Spy or some other device to while away the afternoon.

'Yes, well, I suppose anyone could have gone up into the flies and *tampered*. It was all right for the matinée on Wednesday, and there's never anyone in the theatre between the matinée and the evening show. Everyone rushes out to grab a drink or a bite to eat...'

'Right. So anyone who wanted to would have been pretty safe going up to the gallery and sabotaging the tackle.'

'Yes. Oh, Charles, how *exciting*!'

'Very unlikely to have been seen doing it.'

'You're right.'

'The question is – who?'

'Well, if they weren't seen, we've no way of knowing.'

Gordon had obviously never gone through the mental processes involved in detective investigation.

'No, start from the other end. If anyone had been *seen* tampering with the rope, it would probably have come out by now. Instead, let's try and think who might *want* to tamper with the rope.'

'Sorry, not with you, love.'

Good God, how had someone as thick as this managed to run a bank?

'I mean – who might want you out of the way?'

'Oh, I *see*.' The seriousness of the idea struck Gordon. 'Oh, I'd never thought of it like that.'

'No. Well, would you say you had any enemies in the company?'

'Oh, I don't think so. I mean, I'm just another actor, like the rest of you, you know, mucking in, sharing the knocks, the ups and downs of theatre life, the cameraderie of the company...'

Dear oh dear. Soon he was going to burst into 'Born In A Trunk', or produce a piano from under the bedclothes and say, 'Let's do the show right here!'

'Okay, if you haven't got any enemies, do you perhaps know something about someone that they might want suppressed?'

'Sorry?'

'People do have secrets. You might have stumbled on something they'd rather have kept quiet.'

'Oh, I'm with you. Well now, let me see.' He looked round with elaborate caution. 'I know that Laurie and Nella are having an affair.'

'Gordon, the whole company knows that.'

'Do they?'

'Yes. Anything else?'

'Well...' Again the Official Secrets routine. 'I have a strong suspicion that Kathy Kitson's hair is not naturally blond.'

Charles sighed. This was uphill work. 'That's hardly the sort of secret someone's going to commit murder to keep quiet.'

'No, I suppose not.'

'But there's no one else about whom you know anything discreditable?'

'I don't think so, no.' Charles rose. 'Well, except for Tony.'

'Tony?'

'Well, perhaps this is telling tales out of school...'

'You can't stop there.'

'No.' Excitement at the drama of the situation quickly overcame Gordon Tremlett's scruples. 'Well, I don't know if I'd mentioned this to you, love, and if I haven't, I think you may have difficulty in believing it – but before I came into the business I used to be a bank manager.'

'No, Gordon. Really?'

'Oh yes. Here in Rugland Spa. And Tony had his account at my branch and...well, be wasn't very good at managing his money.'

'What, anything criminal?'

'Oh no, love. Just incompetent. Always asking for overdrafts, you know, always hard up.'

'Aren't we all?' said Charles, to keep the conversation light.

Gordon looked puzzled. 'Are we?'

'Never mind. So Tony was always bad with money?'

'Terrible. With his own money, that is. He seemed to run the theatre all right, but his own affairs were in a terrible mess.'

'Did the theatre have its account at your bank too?'

'No.'

So in fact Gordon Tremlett didn't know how Antony Wensleigh ran the theatre's financial affairs. But he might have been about to find out. Donald Mason had asked him to look through the theatre's books to check some 'inconsistency'.

But Gordon Tremlett never got round to checking that 'inconsistency'. Before he could do it, he was nearly killed by an 'accidental' hanging.

# *Chapter Nine*

A DISTURBING NUMBER of variables fitted into the new scenario. Casting Antony Wensleigh in the role of villain explained a great deal which had hitherto been obscure. For a start, it made sense of the Artistic Director's anxious air of abstraction and his somnambulistic approach to the production of *Shove It*. If, as Charles was beginning to suspect, Tony had had his hand in the till of the Regent for some years, all the current demands for enquiries would naturally be very disturbing for him. And the threat of investigation by his former bank manager, who had no illusions about his financial affairs, might lead the Artistic Director to extreme measures.

Or maybe he had other reasons for wanting to silence Gordon Tremlett. Maybe there was something else that an investigation which questioned the actor might reveal. Charles wondered. The odd thing about Gordon Tremlett's status was how he had become a professional actor so late in life. His talent was not so exceptional for anyone to make an effort to secure his services, and yet he had got his full Equity card. The only way he could have done that was to be given one of the Regent Theatre's two provisional cards granted annually, and after great competition, to two Acting A.S.M.s, usually straight out of drama school. Why should Tony Wensleigh have awarded one of these prizes to Gordon? Previously Charles had just taken this as another example of the Artistic Director's bumbling bonhomie, based on his life-principle, 'I like everyone to be happy'. But his new suspicion put the incident in a more ominous light. Maybe Tony's magnanimity was in fact some sort of payment for services rendered. Had his bank manager showed especial liberality in the granting of overdrafts on the understanding that his way into the professional theatre would thus be eased?

If that were the case, it was not something that would do any credit to Tony Wensleigh if it came out in the course of an enquiry. And it provided a further reason for silencing the former bank manager.

Another variable which slotted in with unappealing logic when Tony was cast as the villain was the attack on Charles himself. Hitherto his recollections of the evening of the stabbing had been lost in a blur of alcohol, but now the new concentration of his mind brought its events into sharp focus.

He recalled, with great accuracy, the whispered conversation he had had with the Artistic Director backstage, persuading a sceptical Tony Wensleigh of his fitness to play Sir Reginald De Meaux. Charles remembered the excess of eloquence in which he had asked what threat was posed by 'one slightly drunken middle-aged actor'. It was not, he had said, as if he were about to expose the Artistic Director, denounce him to the Board, reveal a long history of fraud and peculation.

It had been random word-spinning, but to a man who actually had a long history of fraud and peculation, it must have sounded horribly pertinent and implied stores of knowledge of which Charles was innocent.

So Charles Paris, like Gordon Tremlett, had to be silenced. And only his drunken doze had made that silencing ineffective.

Charles shivered at the thought, because presumably he still posed a threat to the increasingly paranoid Artistic Director, and presumably there might be another attack.

He did not think that Tony Wensleigh was a deliberate criminal, just a weak man who had slipped into an escalation of crime. His first financial fiddling had probably arisen out of incompetence, and then increased until he could not manage without it. As its scale grew, so had his fear of exposure, which had led him to the two attempted murders. Like Watergate, the cover-up had been worse than the original crime.

But unfortunately, the new scenario remained conjectural. Charles had no hard evidence that Tony had been responsible for the two attacks. Nor did he even have evidence of any of the financial misdemeanours.

But he had a feeling that Donald Mason might be building up a dossier on those. In spite of his occasional assertions that he must support his colleague, the General Manager was clearly having to spend too much of his time dealing with Tony's administrative failures. The booking of the rehearsal room was just an example of negligence, but the incident of the hire of the Henry VIII costume was potentially more serious. If Tony really had hired it for a private function and slapped the charge on to the theatre's account, that might be symptomatic of a general tendency to regard the theatre's funds as his own private bank.

These petty malpractices might be overlooked in an Artistic Director of undoubted flair, but there now also seemed to be big question marks over Tony Wensleigh's artistic judgement. Choosing a play as totally inappropriate to Rugland Spa as *Shove It* was not an action likely to inspire confidence, and the way he was directing the piece was equally disturbing.

If Tony was into wholesale fiddling, Charles wondered for a moment why it hadn't come into the open earlier, but decided that Donald Mason's arrival a year before had stirred things. From all accounts, the previous General Managers of the Regent had been lazier, less forceful individuals, no doubt content to let the Artistic Director run his own company without too many questions as to how he was doing it.

Of course, Charles reflected, most of his suspicions against Tony arose from things he had heard from Donald Mason. But he felt inclined to believe them. His respect for the General Manager had risen considerably since their first meeting. Donald had shown such surprising humanity over his drunken lapse that Charles felt a debt of gratitude. Donald had also, in the face of opposition from Tony, offered Charles the new part in *Shove It*.

And he really did seem to care about the welfare of the Regent. Provincial theatres were very weak institutions and needed all the support they could get. It was a great bonus when someone of Donald Mason's undoubted administrative flair channelled his energies in their direction.

And if he had come to the theatre as General Manager to discover, presumably gradually, that the Artistic Director was not only lowering the artistic standards, but was also guilty of criminal malpractice, it must have put him in a very difficult position. The theatre was too exposed to survive a public scandal, and yet if its Artistic Director was a positive liability, some action would have to be taken.

And it would have to be taken before the Artistic Director took any further action himself. If Charles' conjecture was correct and Tony Wensleigh had deliberately tried to silence both him and Gordon Tremlett, then anyone else who knew anything to his discredit might also be under threat.

With Donald Mason as the most obvious next target.

Bad habits are quickly born, and on the Wednesday evening Charles decided that, his absence from the matinée curtain call having passed unremarked, nobody was very likely to notice whether or not he was there for the evening one. He therefore hastily shuffled off Sir Reginald De Meaux's mortal tweeds, and slipped out of the theatre towards the adjacent pub. He needed a quiet pint and a think.

There was a phone-box between the Stage Door and the pub door. He hesitated by it for a moment, contemplating ringing Frances, but then decided he'd do that with more confidence after a drink.

Armed with the requisite pint, he moved into the corner of the bar. It was fairly empty, that sagging time of the evening when the drink-after-work crowd have reluctantly returned to their loved ones and the drink-before-bed crowd have not yet arrived. Act Two of *The Message Is Murder* was still unwinding its tortuous convolutions, so there were no refugees from the Regent. The pub was given over to the dedicated drinkers, and Rugland Spa was far too nice an area for there to be many of those.

The ones who were there seemed to be on their own, so there was little conversation, except from the girl and boy behind the bar discussing cavity wall insulation. Of the customers only one old lady talked. She was probably on her own too, though that didn't prevent her from directing her monologue to a crumpled figure who sat at the same table, with his back to Charles.

'You see, I know you,' the old lady asserted, after a slurp of bottled Guinness. 'Soon as you come in here I recognized your face. You come in here often, don't you?'

'Oh yes, an habitué of all the pubs,' the slumped figure agreed. 'Here, the

George, the Railway Inn, the King's Arms, Hare and Hounds, you name it.'

'Thought so.' The old lady nodded her head complacently. 'Never forget a face, I don't, never. Got one of those photographic memories, I have.' She continued nodding, rather too long, in a way that left some doubt as to her mental fitness. 'Your name's George, isn't it?'

The slumped figure was unable to agree with this.

'Oh well...' The old lady didn't seem put out by her error. 'I knew a George once. Funny, he was. Used to wait outside the Convent and drop his trousers. Up the Angel, this was. You know Islington? Had a nice budgie, he did. Wanted me to take it when they took him to the Old People's. I said, no, I can't be doing with birds. All that cleaning out the cages, millet in your carpets...ooh, no. Not for me. Can you be doing with birds?'

'No.' The man had reached that stage of drunkenness when he would agree with anything. Perhaps he even regretted saying his name wasn't George. Anything for a quiet life.

'My daughter got a bird. Canary, hers is. Don't like that either. Not that I'd tell her. No, I'm grateful to her. She took me in when I had to move, didn't let me go to the Old People's. Not like George. So I wouldn't breathe a word against that bird, not in her presence. Might be hurtful.' She took a contemplative swig of Guinness. 'Still don't like it, though. Doesn't even talk. Can't see much point in having one that doesn't talk. I mean, there's no other point to them, is there? You'd think if you got one that didn't talk, you'd take it back. You would if it was a washing machine,' she concluded sagely and finished her Guinness. She held the glass up a long time, so that all the beige bubbles could drain down into her mouth.

Whether this was a deliberate hint, or whether he had just finished his own drink and felt full of alcoholic bonhomie, this prompted her companion to offer her another, which she simperingly accepted.

It was when he rose to get the drinks that Charles recognized the man as Frank Walby, theatre critic and arts correspondent of the *Rugland Spa Gazette & Observer*. He had the chipped plaster cherub look of Dylan Thomas. As Charles thought this, he realized that Walby's voice had the even lilt of Welsh in it. Local boy, probably. Rugland Spa was not that far from the Welsh border.

Charles drained his own pint and joined the critic at the bar, where the latter was trying to distract the staff from discussion of their heating bills.

'Frank Walby, isn't it?'

The arts correspondent agreed, without surprise, that it was. He had reached that stage of drunkenness when nothing seems incongruous, when the sudden appearance and conversation of strangers are part of a blurred natural sequence.

'I have to thank you for a very nice review in the Gazette.'

'Eh?'

'For the show at the Regent.'

'Oh.' Frank Walby hiccoughed a laugh. 'You can't mean the current production. No nice reviews there.'

'Yes, I do. My name's Charles Paris.'

'Oh.' The memory of the name had been eroded by alcohol.

'The dead body,' Charles prompted.

'Oh. Oh yes.' Walby laughed again. 'Rather back-handed compliment, though.'

'But quotable.'

'Yes. Must watch that. String together any two words that aren't downright abusive and some actor'll quote them.'

Their drinks orders came and Charles paid for them, which again seemed quite natural to the critic. Nor did he find it odd that Charles followed him over to his table.

'Here, I know you,' said the old lady.

'Oh, do you?' The words were out before Charles could stop them, a completely instinctive actor's reaction. What had she seen him in? Was she about to congratulate him on one of his rare television appearances?

'Your name's Lionel, isn't it?'

'No.'

Again she was not deterred by the put-down. 'Knew a Lionel once. Knew more than one, if the truth were out. One I knew best worked in the greengrocer. Had the impetigo...'

She might have continued reminiscing in this vein for hours, had not Frank Walby suddenly sighed and announced, 'I have immortal longings in me.'

Whether or not the old lady recognized Cleopatra's words, they had the effect of silencing her, and she addressed herself to the thick head of her new Guinness.

'I know what you mean,' said Charles.

'Sometimes,' Frank Walby mused, 'after a few drinks, the world seems very simple. Every ambition very easy, just hanging in front of me like a ripe fruit, ready for plucking.'

'Hmm,' Charles agreed, playing along.

'And then, when I haven't had a few drinks, the fruit is snatched away from my lips like Tantalus, and every ambition seems insuperable.' When he waxed poetic, he became more Welsh. 'But now,' he continued, with the elaborate logic of the drunk, 'when I have had a few drinks, I can't imagine the times when I haven't had a few drinks, and I feel I can reach out and pluck...' He relished the word and repeated it '...pluck anything I want out of the sky.'

'Ah, but a man's reach should exceed his grasp, or what's a heaven for?' Charles quoted.

'Good.' Walby nodded enthusiastically. 'Browning, good. You know, when I was young, I thought I was going to do everything. Thought it was all there, just waiting. Just waiting for the plucking.' Again he savoured the word. 'Fleet Street,' he went on, with an expansive gesture, the definitive novel, '...women – all waiting for me. Well, I did my bit on Fleet Street...eight months I did.

Not all it's cracked up to be. And of course there've been women...'

'What about them?'

He shook his head carefully, as though afraid too violent a movement might dislodge it. 'Not all they're cracked up to be either.'

'And the definitive novel?'

'That...still remains to be done. Will be, will be,' he hastened to assure Charles. 'But I'm not quite ready yet. Still...' He hiccoughed. 'Still gathering material.'

'And meanwhile filling the time and paying the bills by doing theatre reviews for the *Rugland Spa Gazette & Observer*.'

'Exactly.' Another cautious nod. 'Exactly.' He somehow contrived to put too many Ts at the end of the word. 'Just biding my time.'

'And changing your style, I gather.'

Charles hoped his probing was done with sufficient subtlety, but he needn't have worried. Frank Walby was drunk enough to be above suspicion.

'Changing my style, you're right. You see, until...until recently I didn't think the criticism mattered. I thought, don't stir it, keep everyone happy, they're all doing their best, give them the bene...' He took another assault on the word. '...benefit of the doubt. But you can't go on like that. You see, time passes and, before I make my mark with the novel, why shouldn't I make my mark as a critic. Don't worry about people's reactions, the critic has a sacred duty to uphold absolute standards of excellence, and any falling off from those standards should be casti...casti...' He took a few runs at this one before managing to say 'castigated'.

'But why the sudden change of mind?'

''Snot a sudden change of mind. I've thought that all along. I've seen some unbelievably terrible shows at the Regent, unbelievably terrible. Every time I was writing my copy, I was working out all these really vicious things to say.

'Then why didn't you write them down?'

'Ah, well, as I say, didn't want to offend people. That's part of it. But also, not just that, I know a lot about the Regent Theatre. I mean, I've covered its ups and downs ever since I've been on the paper – that's eleven years now...' The statistic seemed suddenly unfamiliar to him. 'God, is it? Eleven years? Yes, it is. Eleven years. Must move on soon. Other things to be done. Where was I?'

'You've followed the ups and downs of the theatre...'

'Right. And it's been on the verge of closure so many times. Well, I don't want that to happen. You see, I do actually believe in the Arts. I mean, when it says in the paper I'm arts correspondence – sorry, correspondent – it's not just the usual thing of someone being promoted from the gardening column or the sports pages. I do care about the Arts, and I don't want the Regent to close. And God knows there are enough people in the town who do want it shut down – councillors and all – so I thought if I gave really strong reviews, I'd just be adding fuel to their fire. Look, they could say, not only does it cost a dispro... disprop...disproportionate amount of money, it also puts on rubbishy productions – here, we've got press cuttings to prove it. I didn't want to give them that kind of ammunition. I mean, critics can be very powerful. Clive Barnes, you know, one of his notices could close a show on Broadway.'

'I know.'

'So I sort of held my fire, because I thought it would be best for the theatre if I was bland and ano.. . adenoid...' He gave up on 'anodyne'...'...bland.'

'And what changed your mind?'

'Well, when I discovered that that wasn't at all what the theatre wanted, that I was weakening their cause rather than helping it, that they were only going to be viable if they were judged by the professional standards of West End theatre, that harsh criticism would actually sharpen them up, raise the quality of their productions.'

'What, someone actually said that to you?'

'Yes. He said that the Regent needed to be taken seriously as a theatre, not some kind of protected species. So I should stop pulling my punches and start applying some objective standards to the shows. He also said that that way I would stand much more chance of making my mark as a critic. So,' Frank Walby concluded, 'I changed my style, and you've seen the result in my notice for *The Message Is Murder*. Much more trenchant, wouldn't you say?'

'Oh yes, certainly.' The very word. 'Who was it who suggested you make the change?'

'Donald Mason, the General Manager.'

Oh dear. One of Donald's ideas that hadn't come off. Charles felt sure it had been done from the highest motives, but he was equally sure it was a misjudgement. Notices like Frank Walby's last one could only help Councillor Davenport's anti-theatre lobby.

Perhaps the General Manager hadn't been aware of the pent-up stores of vituperation in the critic which his request would unleash.

As if conjured like the Devil by the mention of his name, Donald Mason appeared in the pub at this point. He seemed to be looking for someone and, when his eyes lit on Charles, appeared to have found his quarry.

'Sorry to interrupt you – oh, hello, Frank.'

'Evening, Donald.'

The old lady looked up from her Guinness and, stimulated by the new arrival, went into her routine. 'Here, I know you.'

'I don't think so. Charles, do you think we could have a word?'

'Yes, of course.'

'I do know you. From Islington days. Blenley Terrace, you come round to see me there.'

'In private, if you don't mind, Charles...'

'Of course. Would you excuse us, Frank?'

'Be my guest.' The critic made another lavish, but unfinished, gesture.

'Blenley Terrace it was, in 1972. Before I had to move out. I know your name, and all...'

The old lady was still maundering on as Charles and Donald left the bar. Frank Walby sat opposite her, smiling seraphically, as though listening to some virtuoso of the art of conversation.

To Charles' surprise, Donald didn't lead straight back to the theatre. Instead he indicated the stairs to the upper bar, which could not be seen from the one they had just left. 'I don't often come in here, but I could use a drink. Don't know about you.'

'Just had a couple, but I'll happily join you.'

Charles had had enough fluid content from the beer and moved on to a large Bell's whisky. Donald Mason ordered a sugar-free lager.

When they had sat down, he said, 'First, the official business. I'm afraid it's another reprimand.'

'Oh dear. What, for sneaking out before the curtain call?' Donald nodded ruefully. 'Sorry, it sounds very petty. but I'm afraid you do have to be on your best behaviour at the moment. As you've probably gathered, Tony didn't want you to stay and you're here on my say-so. And I've sort of vouched for your reliability.'

'I'm sorry. It's unprofessional. Won't happen again.'

'Normally it couldn't matter less. Most directors wouldn't insist on you being in the curtain call, anyway, with the part you have, but...I'm afraid Tony seems to be rather on his dignity these days.'

'Yes.'

'And I'm afraid he's out for anything he can get on me. So if you let us down, it's going to look as if it's my fault – or he'll certainly play up that side.'

'I won't let you down.'

'Sorry. As I say, just at the moment...Maybe the atmosphere will be a bit clearer after Friday.'

'What's happening then?'

'This Extraordinary Board Meeting you may have read about.'

'Ah yes. It's going to be a confrontation, is it?'

Donald shook his head sadly. 'I'm afraid it may turn out that way. Not that I want that, but when someone starts making untrue allegations about you, well, you have to defend yourself.'

'And even counter-attack.'

'I hope that doesn't become necessary, but if it does, there are a few interesting points I could raise about Tony's management.'

Charles could imagine what some of them were. He also felt, though he could not yet substantiate them, he could add some interesting allegations of his own, which might raise a few eyebrows amongst the Board members.

'So it's open warfare between the two of you now, is it?'

'I hope not, Charles, but it may come to that. The Board may have to choose between us.'

'If they do, I should think you'd be all right. Herbie Inchbald seems to think very highly of you.'

Donald grimaced modestly. 'Has to. He backed me for the job and, I gather, overcame quite a bit of opposition to see I got it.'

'And I'm sure he doesn't regret the decision. No, I'm afraid Tony's probably had things his own way for too long. Running the theatre for twelve years, obviously he's become a bit autocratic, doesn't like criticism, and seems rather to have lost his objective standards.'

'Yes. Well, I'm certainly trying to remedy all that.'

'By telling Frank Walby to write more savage reviews?' Charles asked with a smile.

The General Manager looked up sharply. 'He told you that?'

'Yes. I know what you meant, but I think that idea rather backfired.'

'Maybe. It's just the whole Regent set-up needs a few shocks to wake it out of its complacency. It has no cause to be complacent.'

'No.'

'The trouble is, Charles, Tony's so resistant to change, he fights everything every step of the way. Which is just so wasteful of time and energy. If we really worked together, I'm sure we could pick the theatre up out of this trough. As it is, we're just weakening it further. And if the divisions in the Regent's management become public…God knows, I do my best to present a united front, but it's not easy in the face of some of Tony's behaviour. I sometimes wonder if he's quite sane.'

'I think he may have lost touch with reality a bit.'

'Hmm. That's a charitable way of putting it. But whatever it is, it's not helping the theatre one bit. The Regent is so fragile at the moment, so vulnerable. Wouldn't take much to topple it. If we lose our Arts Council grant, I can't see the council coughing up the full subsidy. No, I reckon it would be dark within the month, sold and knocked down for development within the year.'

'Wouldn't somebody step in to save it?'

'Don't know who.' Donald Mason sighed. 'Still, don't let's anticipate disaster. I gather you didn't do your curtain call this afternoon either.'

'No. I'm sorry. I went to see Gordon.'

'Yes, that's what Nella said. How did he seem?'

'Revoltingly healthy.'

'Yes. Did he say anything interesting?'

'Like what?'

The General Manager looked at him shrewdly. 'I'd never thought of you as a great friend of Gordon's, Charles. Nor the kind of person to rush round fulsomely to any invalid with crates of grapes.'

Charles found himself blushing. 'What do you mean?'

'Your reputation has preceded you, Charles.'

'Hmm?'

'A certain interest in detective work, a little mild investigation, a what shall we say?...a nose for crime?'

'Ah.'

'I think that's why you went to see Gordon. I think you wondered to what extent his accident was accidental.'

Donald Mason was extremely shrewd. Charles paid him the compliment of telling him so.

'Thank you. And what conclusions did you form from talking to Gordon?'

Charles shrugged. 'Could have been an accident.'

'Yes?'

'On the other hand, the timing was odd...'

'In what way?'

'Because of what you had done that afternoon.'

Donald Mason flushed. 'What *I* had done that afternoon?'

'Yes. You'd asked Gordon to check through the theatre books for him.'

'Oh. That.'

'Yes. You'd asked him to check some "inconsistency".'

'Yes.'

'Was it some evidence of the books being fiddled?'

'I, er, don't think I should answer that.' The awkwardness of the reply was as positive an affirmation as if he had actually said 'Yes'.

'Fiddled by Tony?'

This time he would not even reply.

But his silence again spoke volumes.

And confirmed Charles' conjecture.

# *Chapter Ten*

CHARLES WOKE THE next morning feeling better than he had for some weeks. He also woke early, round seven o'clock, so he dressed quickly and left his digs before he could be subjected to more of Mimi's gloomy omniscience and another of her cremated breakfasts. He had woken up with a good intention and he wanted to realize it before it too got laid on the hardcore to hell.

He rang from a phone-box on the way to the station before eight. He knew she didn't get into the yellow Renault and drive to school till a quarter past.

Her voice, as she gave the number, sounded achingly familiar.

'Frances it's me.'

'Charles. Thank God you rang. I was beginning to worry that something had happened to you.'

'Nothing more unusual than a job.'

'Good. Where are you?'

'Rugland Spa.'

'My God. Knee-deep in retired Colonels and blue-rinsed widows.'

'You have it in one.'

'So no doubt the show you're doing for them is horribly genteel.'

'No. By no means. I am participating in a thriller so bad I won't even mention its name, but I am also rehearsing for a play you may have heard of, called *Shove It*.'

'Ah.'

'Know it?'

'By reputation. Doesn't sound Rugland Spa fodder.'

'It isn't. And let me tell you, this production features a significant first in British Theatre – a full-frontal Charles Paris.'

'Oh, my God. When do you open?'

'Tuesday. Today we have our first Dr... no, our first *Un*dress Rehearsal.'

He paused. The initial impetus, the initial excitement of talking to her, had slowed down, and he felt very aware of the false brightness of their conversation. He also felt a sudden access of all the old mixed emotions, with jealousy well to the fore.

'Are you alone?' he asked suddenly.

'Yes.' She sounded surprised. 'Why, shouldn't I be?'

'Well, I thought your...you know, this man...this David...'

Pretty inept. So much for the cool man-of-the-world sang-froid he had hoped to bring to the situation.

'No, of course he's not here. You've got the relationship all wrong.'

Absurdly, he felt a gush of hope at her words. Maybe, after all, they were just friends. Or maybe no longer even friends...

But her next words soon east him down again. 'We couldn't live together if we wanted to. David's married. Didn't I mention that?'

It was the familiarity with which she said the name that hurt.

'No. No. You didn't actually say...just that there were complications. So ...the affair is illicit?'

'Yes. I suppose so.' She giggled nervously. 'I need to see you, Charles.'

'Yes. I...' With an effort he held back from over-committing himself. 'It'd be good to see you too.'

'When are you through in Rugland Spa?'

'Not for a month.'

'Oh, I must see you before that. Now we've actually made contact. I do need to talk to you. There's so much I want to say.'

But she didn't get the chance to say it. At that point the pips went.

And Charles didn't have any more change.


The turn-out for the first Undress Rehearsal of *Shove It* seemed unusually high. Perhaps, Charles reflected, there were no more members of the stage crew there than there would be for any other Dress Rehearsal in an outside rehearsal room, but he did wonder about the motives of some of those present. Certainly he couldn't think of any reason why Leslie Blatt should be there other than prurient interest.

There was about the proceedings an air of unnatural casualness. People joked too loudly to show how relaxed they were. Actors and actresses studied their crosswords and knitting with much greater concentration than they could usually muster. The ones who weren't going to have to take their clothes off seemed guilty and quite as unrelaxed as the rest of the company. (There were actually very few who didn't have to strip. Royston Everett's dramatic method seemed to involve every member of the dramatis personae baring their all at some point. *Time Out* had hailed this as an important symbolic representation of the truism that men are born equal and free but are everywhere in the chains of class, convention and fascism'.)

Charles felt quite as nervous as anyone else. He reckoned it must be worse for the men than the women. Female modesty was a traditionally powerful force, but, on the other hand, they didn't have the one great worry that dominated his mind (and, he wouldn't mind betting, the minds of most of the other male actors in the company).

That worry was extremely basic, and it dated back a long time. It was a worry that had been present in changing-rooms at school, at Army medicals, and when wearing swimming trunks.

It was of course, What happens if I get an erection?

Though it was some years since Charles had worried about getting an erection at an inappropriate time (indeed, a more recent worry had been not getting one at an appropriate time), the anxiety had not diminished in intensity. The sense of shame involved was very primitive. (Presumably Adam's original recourse to the fig-leaf was born of some similar instinct.)

Charles tried to take his mind off psychosomatic stirrings in his underpants by concentrating on Tony Wensleigh. The revelations of the previous day made him see the Artistic Director in a completely different light, and his new disillusioned vision explained many inconsistencies of behaviour.

It explained, first and foremost, Tony's air of manic anxiety. The director was surely the veteran of too many productions to be that worried about the show (it wasn't as if *he* had to take *his* clothes off, after all). Even a play as disastrously chosen as *Shove It* was the sort of thing an experienced director of three-weekly rep ought to be able to take in his stride.

But, if one interpreted his anxiety as that of a man facing total exposure of many years of mishandling theatre funds, of a man prepared to kill to keep his secret quiet, everything became clearer.

The same applied to his general air of abstraction and lack of concentration on the job in hand. There was only one important date on Tony Wensleigh's horizon and that was the moment the following evening when he had to face the Theatre Board and try to prevent his own fall by shooting down his General Manager.

Tony Wensleigh was a desperate man, prepared to do anything to save his position in the Regent Theatre.

In spite of the strained atmosphere of this-is-all-perfectly-normal-nothing-unusual, some concessions had been made to the modesty of the performers. Two sets of screens had been set up either side of the acting area 'to represent the exits and entrances to the wings' (though tape markings on the floor had been thought sufficient at all previous rehearsals). The effect of this was to give a measure of surprise to each new entrance (as well as a measure of privacy to the shyer members of the cast).

Behind the screens Charles Paris, who had the advantage of making his first entrance with clothes on, chatted with heavy unconcern to a young actor, who had thrown off all his garments immediately on arrival in the rehearsal room.

'You done, er, this sort of thing before?'

'Oh yes, did a year in *O, Calcutta*.'

'Oh.' The new generation of actors had a totally different training from his own, Charles reflected.

'And of course a good few movies.'

'Ah. Yes. Of course.' The young man seemed amiable enough. Charles decided he dared to confide his great anxiety. 'Tell me, when you are doing that sort of work...'

'The movies, you mean?'

'Yes...do you ever have any trouble with...erections?'

'All the time, mate, all the time.'

'Really?'

'Oh yes. I've tried everything, nothing has any effect.'

'Oh dear.'

'Total disaster. Whatever I do, I can't keep it up.'

Ah, thought Charles, *that* sort of movie.

The opening scene of *Shove It* had been highly praised by the London critics. One of them, more pretentious and deluded than the rest, had found in it 'parodic echoes of Restoration drama, producing by linguistic inversion a comment on the conventions of theatrical artifice.' What he actually meant was that the scene had been lifted from *The Way of the World* and the language dirtied up in the approved Royston Everett manner.

The broken-down old whore and brothel-keeper, Sylv, like Congreve's Lady Wishfort, is, in the eighteenth-century phrase, 'at her toilet'. The maid, Foible, is represented in the modern version by the retarded teenage prostitute, Tracey. But, whereas the audience only sees selected sections of Lady Wishfort's preparations to face the world, Sylv enters stark naked and goes through the whole process of dressing and painting.

Her first line is the repetition, five times, of a well-known four-letter word, which one Liverpool critic, intoxicated by the righteousness of the play's social comment, actually had the nerve to compare to King Lear's 'Never, never, never, never, never'.

In the Rugland Spa production of *Shove It*, the part of Sylv was being played by Kathy Kitson.

There was more than the usual anticipation at an outside Dress Rehearsal as the A.S.M.s called for quiet and the Act One beginners crowded behind the screens. Tony Wensleigh, his large eyes glistening with anxiety, announced, 'Okay, let's take it from the top. As straight through as we can make it. We'll only stop if there's some really major disaster.'

There was a silence. The acting space between the screens was empty.

Then Kathy Kitson entered.

She was dressed in a beige, silk ruffled negligée.

'Oh dear,' she said, in her usual beautifully modulated but totally characterless voice. 'Oh dear. Oh dear. Oh dear. Oh dear.'

'Sorry. I've got to stop you there.'

Kathy Kitson turned innocently to the Artistic Director 'You said you'd only stop for major disasters.'

'Kathy, this *is* a major disaster. Look, you know you're meant to be making this entrance completely naked...'

'Yes.' She nodded confidently, as if she had given a complete answer to his question.

'Well, Kathy, I mean I hesitate to state the obvious, but I think it must be clear to everyone here that you are not naked.'

'Oh, is *that* it?' She spoke chidingly, as if he had picked her up on some minuscule detail of performance.

'Yes, that is it. Look, I'm sorry, Kathy, but we're beyond the moment for coyness. When you read the script and agreed to play the part, it was made quite clear to you that you would have to take your clothes off. I remember, we had long discussions with your agent about that very matter and got his full assurance of your agreement.'

Kathy Kitson stretched her neck loftily. 'Tony dear, when you book an experienced actress, you don't only book the actress, you also book the experience and the judgement that that experience brings. And my judgement is that this scene is more effective with me *acting* naked than actually *being* naked.'

'*Acting* naked?' the director repeated weakly.

'Yes, darling. I knew you'd agree.' Kathy Kitson moved back towards the screens with an air of triumph. 'Would you like me to make the entrance again?' she asked with sweet humility.

'Kathy...' Tony Wensleigh spoke with great weariness. 'That's not all.'

'Something else, love?'

'The line you spoke was not the line that Royston Everett wrote.'

The actress conceded that this was indeed the case. 'But my line does get over the same feeling as his. And so much more tastefully, don't you think?'

The rehearsal did proceed, after a fashion, though Kathy Kitson resolutely continued to wear her negligée. At the moment she was meant to put on her dress, she removed the garment to reveal a delightful silken petticoat.

She also resolutely continued to expurgate Royston Everett's lines.

And Tony Wensleigh, sunk in an apathetic gloom whose cause Charles felt confident he now knew, made no further attempt to stop her.

The rest of the cast who had to strip did so without demur. As garment after garment slipped off, revealing no greater excitement than the odd appendix scar and some surprising evidence of dyed hair, both female and male, Charles felt his main anxiety recede. Human flesh is not aphrodisiac under all circumstances, and in the goose-pimply chill of the Drill Hall, Rugland Spa, it had the opposite effect. Charles found his mind dwelling on butchers' shops rather than sex, and when his own turn came to reveal all, he hardly thought about what he was doing.

The only person who did seem to find the flesh on display exciting was the one person who shouldn't have been there, Leslie Blatt. Given the evidence he had already shown of a Peeping Tom mentality, it was no great surprise, but Charles did find it mildly revolting. The playwright was of a generation to whom permissiveness, if it came at all, had come late, and his reactions were those of a twelve-year-old sniggering over a dirty picture.

Charles felt glad for Nella Lewis's sake that she wasn't in *Shove It*, because she was so obviously the centre of the old man's smutty desires. Laurie Tichbourne wasn't in the play either, so he was not around to protect her from unwanted attentions. On the other hand, Charles reflected, he couldn't actually see Laurie doing anything so positive, even if he had been there.

Nella was prompting, because at this stage of rehearsal the lines were still a little shaky, arid, since no one could ever quite predict what cue they were going to get from Kathy Kitson, there were frequent breakdowns in the dialogue. The A.S.M. sat demurely on a chair behind one of the screens, her eyes fixed on the page, perhaps just in punctilious discharge of her duties or maybe out of modesty in the face of all that naked flesh.

Leslie Blatt hung around behind the same screen, alternately ogling other female members of the cast and passing comments to Nella. As Charles made his naked exit after the police raid on the brothel, he heard the old man breathe in the A.S.M.'s ear, 'Pretty strong meat, this. Couldn't have written this sort of stuff in my day. Didn't know what I was missing, eh?' He sniggered adolescently. 'Still, healthier times now. Healthier attitudes people've got. Very healthy, very nice to see all these naked bodies around, eh?' Then he leant forward, pressing himself very close against the back of Nella's chair. 'Though, of course, there are some one would rather see than others.'

The girl's eyes did not leave the page, nor did any part of her body move except for her right arm. But that moved decisively, and the sharp point of its elbow was unerringly accurate.

'Mmmf' squeaked Leslie Blatt.

And 'Good girl,' thought Charles Paris, as the old man moved away from the chair, doubled up with pain.

The police raid ended Act One of *Shove It*. It was a kind of climax and, given Royston Everett's dramatic method, this meant that more people had their clothes off at that point than at any other in the course of the play (except for the end of Act Two). The last words before the interval were spoken by Sylv and were an exact repetition of the five with which she opened the play (a device which had prompted one of the sillier critics to speak of 'an almost classical demonstration of cyclical unity').

The naked gathered behind the screens as Kathy Kitson moved to centre stage (a habit she had) to deliver herself of the same – or who could say, perhaps some new – euphemism. But what she would have said at that rehearsal was never revealed.

Because at that moment came the Invasion of the Hats.

The doors of the Drill Hall burst open and, led by the redoubtable hat of Mrs Feller, in marched the Massed Hats of Opposition to *Shove It*.

There were about a dozen of them. Most carried banners. To those with which they had picketed the theatre had been added such choice slogans as 'DON'T POISON THE MINDS OF OUR CHILDREN', 'NO ROMANS IN BRITAIN HERE', 'FILTH CORRUPTS' and, rather surprisingly,

'YOU KNOW WHERE YOU CAN SHOVE IT!'

In the wake of the hats, shamefaced and wishing he was anywhere else in the world, was dragged a very young policeman.

The aim of the demonstration was disruption and the first action of the hats, loudly shouting out the slogans on their banners, was to knock down the two screens. The sheer size of the nudist colonies these revealed struck them dumb.

In the ensuing silence Tony Wensleigh's voice could be heard weakly asking what on earth they thought they were doing.

'There!' Mrs Feller pointed an accusatory finger, as far as Charles could see, directly at him, and turned to the young policeman saying, 'If that isn't an obscene display, I'd like to know what is.'

'Well, erm…' The wretched young man blushed beetroot. 'In fact, the law on obscenity is not always clear.'

'But this is clearly obscene,' insisted Mrs Feller.

'Well, it might be, but, even if it were, I'm not quite sure what I could do about it.'

'Not sure? I'll tell you exactly what you could do – and exactly what you should do – arrest the lot of them!'

The young policeman looked even unhappier. The prospect of rounding up a dozen naked men and women and marching them through the streets of Rugland Spa to the police station was not one that appealed to him.

He tried to look authoritative by getting out a notebook and pencil. 'Right,' he began tentatively. 'Who's in charge here?'

'I am,' Tony Wensleigh replied.

But not for long, thought Charles. This latest incident was just what the Artistic Director didn't need. Charles wouldn't have offered much for Tony Wensleigh's chances at the Extraordinary Board Meeting the following evening.

## Chapter Eleven

MRS FELLER DID not get any arrests, but she achieved the lesser objective of totally sabotaging the Undress Rehearsal. By the time the Hats had been cleared from the Drill Hall, the cast had all apologetically put their clothes back on again and it was too late to start on Act Two of Royston Everett's little masterpiece. Even if the cast of the evening's show had forgone the break due to them between rehearsal and performance, there wouldn't have been time. So a somewhat sheepish little group traipsed back to the Regent Theatre.

Where at least one of them was met with a further set-back. Charles, now feeling that he should watch the Artistic Director's every move, had walked back with him from the rehearsal room but there had been little conversation. Tony Wensleigh was sunk in a gloom of his own.

But they were still walking together when they entered the foyer of the theatre, and so Charles overheard the words of Donald Mason, who rushed up anxiously to his colleague as if he had been awaiting his return for some time.

'Tony,' the General Manager whispered as Charles moved away, 'just had a call from Nigel Hudson.'

'Nigel Hudson?'

'My contact at the Arts Council.'

'Oh yes.'

'Well, it wasn't so much a call as a tip-off. Apparently our grant prospects are dicier than we thought.'

'Oh.'

'They're going to make their recommendations within the next fortnight.'

'Oh yes?'

'And they're sending the assessment team down to the first night of *Shove It* to, as Nigel charmingly put it, "give us a final chance".'

Which, Charles reflected as he left the foyer. was considering the current state of the production, tantamount to a straight refusal of the grant.

But the new blow aroused very little reaction in the traumatized Artistic Director. All it got was another dulled 'Oh yes?'

Charles was surprised to find there was a telegram from him backstage. There are perhaps actors whose lives are full of ecstatic messages from fans and urgent news from agents about film offers, but he wasn't one of them.

His first reaction was that something awful had happened to someone in the family. Juliet was ill. One of the grandchildren had been in a car accident.

It was family. But it wasn't bad news. Or, he decided quickly before his mind was swamped with mixed emotions, it probably wasn't bad news.

'COMING DOWN TO RUGLAND SPA FOR LUNCH ON SUNDAY. RING ME IF YOU CAN'T MAKE IT. LOVE. FRANCES.'

The dear departed Sir Reginald De Meaux was now on his best behaviour. He had given his word to Donald Mason and, not wishing to add to the dissension between General Manager and Artistic Director, he therefore did not even contemplate a visit to the pub after he had discharged his artistic duties in the Thursday night performance of *The Message Is Murder*. He would wait around for the curtain call, following Tony Wensleigh's desires.

Other nights he would have been content to sit quietly with a book (he was re-reading Samuel Butler's *Erewhon* and enjoying the experience), but on this occasion he felt twitchy and couldn't concentrate. His dressing room chair felt uncomfortable, and Leslie Blatt's banal dialogue, half-heard over the loudspeaker, was a constant distraction.

Partly, he knew, it was the telegram. The prospect of seeing Frances filled him with reactions he didn't want to itemize.

But there was also a general air of tension in the theatre. The afternoon's débacle would normally have been laughed off by the company, but it merely added to the anxiety over *Shove It* The show was due to open the following Wednesday and everyone was aware that it was well behind schedule. They were also becoming aware, given no assurances to the contrary from their director, that it was not a very good play.

The state of the Regent's internal politics was also starting to have its effect on the company. The conflict between General Manager and Artistic Director could no longer be disguised. Nor could the importance, for the future of the theatre, of the following evening's Extraordinary Meeting of the Board. All this added pressure to the normal anxieties of a week before a new production opens.

For Charles, who reckoned he had deeper insight into the real causes of the divisions in the theatre, the stress was greater. He could recognize the increasing strains on Tony Wensleigh, feared that they might resolve themselves into violence, and yet felt impotent to stop the escalating sequence of crime.

If only he had some proof of Tony's involvement in the earlier attacks...

He decided to go up into the gallery and watch the Act Two hanging of Colonel Fripp (now being played with rather more conviction, because, in spite of his years, he had more talent than Gordon Tremlett, by Rick Harmer). Seeing the effect repeated might give Charles some clue as to exactly how the accident had been staged.

The top floor of the Regent Theatre was quite complex. The central area was the decorated ceiling of the auditorium with the roof directly above it. Above the stage was the flying space with a gallery on either side. In the front of the building, above the bar, was the space into which the administrative office was crammed.

But along the sides, joining the front of the theatre to the back, were two broad passages. The primary function of these was to give access to the catwalk round the auditorium from which much of the lighting was fixed, but because storage space is always at a premium in a repertory theatre, they were also used for other purposes. One side, on long mobile rails, was kept the company's stock of all-purpose costumes (the sort of peasant blouses and leather jerkins which would see service in anything from medieval mystery plays, through pantomime, to Robert Bolt). The other side was used as a prop store, where Roman helmets nestled side by side with papier-maché marrows, rubber skulls dangled by strings of plastic onions, glass jewellery hung from deer's antlers, and tennis rackets poked from witches' cauldrons.

Both of the stores had doors at either end, giving access to the flying gallery and the administrative office area.

Charles had climbed up the wall-ladder to the gallery and was inspecting the counter-weighting of the wire from which Rick Harmer was about to be suspended when he heard a noise from the props store.

The door was closed. Charles had seen Nella, Rick and the other members of the Stage Management down at floor level. They were the only people who might have legitimate cause to go to the prop store during a performance. Alert to the danger of another act of sabotage, Charles decided that he should investigate.

He opened the door with extreme caution, but the light it admitted put the intruder on his guard. From the far side of the gloom a torch-beam swung round into Charles' face, blinding him.

'Charles.' The voice, which he recognized, sounded relieved. Then Charles thought he heard a click, like the throwing of an electrical switch.

There was sufficient light from the door for him to see a light-switch on the wall nearby. He flicked it. Two naked hanging bulbs illuminated the scene. He stepped inside and closed the door.

Tony Wensleigh was momentarily thrown by the sudden light and froze. He was crouched in the far corner of the store by a fibreglass sundial and a pile of breastplates made of stiffened felt. In his hand he held a World War I army revolver.

After the shock he moved hastily, shuffling the breastplates back against the wall, tucking a dangling string behind a grandfather clock before he turned back to Charles with apparent insouciance.

'What on earth are you doing here?'

'Just heard a noise and wondered who it was.'

'Oh.'

The monosyllable seemed to require further explanation.

'I was just going for a walk round the gallery, you know killing time.'

'Yes, of course. You do have a long wait between your appearance and the curtain call.'

'Yes,' Charles agreed, with some edge.

'Why do you do it?'

'What?'

'Why do you wait? Why not just get changed straight away? I'm sure no one notices whether you're there or not at the curtain call.'

Charles looked at the Artistic Director in amazement. 'I do it because you specifically asked me to.'

'Oh, did I?' Tony looked confused, suddenly like an old man. 'I'm sorry. I keep mixing things up. Do things and can't remember I've done them. Don't do things and think I have done them. Sorry.' He rubbed his hand across his brow, as though his mental state were something external, that could be wiped away.

'You've been under a lot of pressure recently, Tony,' said Charles gently.

The Artistic Director gave a weary smile. 'That is a wonderful understatement. A lot of pressure, yes. I wonder how much pressure it takes before a man cracks. How many straws can a camel take cheerfully, and how does he recognize the one that's going to do the damage? Does it carry a Government Health Warning?'

He let out a bark of nervous laughter. Then silence came between them. With surprising clarity further banalities by Leslie Blatt filtered up from the stage.

Charles kept his therapist's tone of voice. 'Tony, you don't have to crack up completely. You can save yourself, you can talk, tell the truth.'

'Yes, I firmly intend to. Get the truth out into the open, then the pressure'll go away.'

'Exactly. And you'll feel a lot better.'

'Yes.' The Artistic Director seemed calmer. 'Yes, I'll get people to listen to my side. Then they'll realize I'm not mad.'

'Of course they will,' Charles soothed.

'And the nightmare'll soon be over.'

'Yes. You can put an end to it whenever you want to. It's up to you.'

'You're right, Charles.' The Artistic Director looked directly into his eyes. 'It's all a lot clearer now, what I should do. I've been very confused the last few weeks, but now its coming clear.'

'Good.'

The revolver was still in Tony's hand. Charles thought the atmosphere had relaxed sufficiently for him to mention it.

'Where did that come from, Tony?'

The Artistic Director looked down, as though noticing the weapon for the first time. 'Oh, that. I just found it up here. Forgotten we'd got it. Came from one of my first productions at the Regent, *Journey's End*. In the early days we didn't have any money. We could just afford the cast, but nothing left for costumes and props...So we put out an appeal in the *Gazette* – any one got any First World War uniforms and stuff they'd lend us. Quite a good response. This came from an old girl who'd had two brothers in the war. They'd both been wounded, and she'd nursed them both until they died. She'd kept everything...all their uniforms, everything...and she said we could borrow them because of the play...because *Journey's End* was against war, and she hated war. I don't know why we've still got this. We should have given it back...I can't remember.'

Once again the clouds of confusion were gathering. He pulled himself together with an effort. 'The old lady gave us all the ammunition, too. She'd kept that.' He gave a little laugh. 'We shouldn't really have used a gun like this on stage. Not one that works. Should have had a spiked one, but...' He shrugged. '...I'm sure we were in a panic as usual, and the important thing was to get the production on. I think that's always been the important thing – to get the production on – and it's never left much time for anything else. Plays are easier, too – I find plays easier than everything else. Other things just get so...complicated...'

This comment seemed to encompass his whole life. He drooped, exhausted.

'Tony,' said Charles very quietly, 'why don't you give me the gun?'

There was an instantaneous change as the man's body snapped alert. 'Oh no. I may need it.'

'What do you mean?'

'There are people out to get me. People who aren't afraid to use violence.'

His words sounded like the definitive statement of paranoia.

'But, Tony, you can't go round shooting people.'

'Only in self-defence. I hope it won't come to that. I'm sure it won't. But if someone attacks you, you have to defend yourself. Those who offer no resistance get trampled on, and I've been trampled on for long enough.'

'Tony –'

'No, Charles. I know what needs to be done. It's all very clear to me now. I know what needs doing, and at last – thank God – I'm ready to do it.'

'What do you mean?'

'I mean that all the cheating that's been going on, all the things that have been wrong with this theatre, are about to be sorted out.' He sighed, anticipating the relaxation this moment would bring. 'Soon it'll all be over. One confrontation...if I have the strength to do it...and it'll all be over.'

This was beginning to sound uncomfortably like a statement of intent to murder. Charles moved forward. 'Tony, I think you'd better give me that gun.'

'No. I'm sorry. I need it. To protect myself.'

Charles stretched out a hand. 'Tony...'

The noise of the gunshot in the enclosed space was thunderous. Charles heard the lightbulb above him shatter and felt the rain of glass on his shoulders.

He looked for a second at Tony. The man's face seemed to register surprise as he looked at the gun, almost as if the firing had been accidental.

But Charles didn't feel inclined to explore that possibility. The barrel still pointed at him, and he was no hero. He turned and rushed out of the door, slamming it behind him.

He had reached the bottom of the wall-ladder and was at stage level before he realized that there were no sounds of pursuit. He froze for a full minute, then gingerly climbed back up the ladder and on to the cast-iron floor of the gallery. He inched his way towards the prop room door, his ears straining for any unexpected sound.

All he could hear came from down below. 'The deaths will not stop at one,' Miss Laycock-Manderley was saying. 'The forces of evil demand their toll of blood.'

He reached the door and, leaning against the adjacent wall in best television detective style, reached for the handle. He gave it a sharp turn and a push.

The door did not shift.

He tried a more forceful shove.

Nothing. The door had been locked from the inside.

He put his ear to it. No sound.

He banged on the door with increasing force. But there was no response.

Then he remembered the other exit from the prop-store, the exit that led to the front of the theatre.

That was the way Tony Wensleigh must have gone, crazed by paranoia, with the gun in his hand.

Straight into the administrative office.

Where he was likely to find the man he saw as his greatest enemy – the Regent Theatre's General Manager – Donald Mason

ACT THREE

## *Chapter Twelve*

'WHAT MAKES IT all so gruesome,' announced James De Meaux, 'is the fact that it must all have been planned. Someone worked it all out, every ghastly move.'

He stifled a yawn. He really was feeling very tired. Of course, he was playing a major role, and it was the third week, but that shouldn't make him feel so absolutely *drained*. He knew what it was, of course – Nella. Lovely girl, but so inconvenient that she was at *Shove It* rehearsals all day. He could have coped with her very nicely in the afternoons, but all this late night emotion was very wearing. Sex was very nice, he reflected, but not when it interfered with sleep. Be quite a relief really, to get back to his nice little flat in Pimlico. Have a few days' sleep.

'Yes, but who?' asked Felicity Kershaw. 'We're still no nearer to working out who did it.'

She was also tired, but happier about it. The guy who'd directed *Scrag End of Neck* at the Bus Depot had turned up to the night before's performance and said she acted like 'a real cow', which she had taken as a compliment. He had then let her buy him a meal (including Vanilla Ice Cream) at Mr Pang's, while he expatiated on the rights of women. He had gone back to her digs, made love to her relentlessly all night and left after breakfast, having borrowed fifty pounds. She felt fulfilled as a woman.

'Well, Colonel Fripp was certainly involved. He must have tampered with the telephone. Why else should he bring that great array of screwdrivers in his luggage?'

'But he didn't hang himself. That was the work of his accomplice.'

'The mysterious woman.'

'Whoever she may be.' Felicity Kershaw let out another of her laughs, confident that she was showing exactly what sort of bourgeois cow would be first against the wall, 'come the revolution'.

James De Meaux looked thoughtful. An infatuated First Fairy had once told him he was very sexy when he looked thoughtful, so he did it whenever possible.

'We've heard from Professor Weintraub's examination of the body that Colonel Fripp probably died between four and five in the afternoon. It might be worth checking what everyone was doing round that time.'

'Well, if you want to start with me, darling, my movements were quite simple. I remember exactly. I went for a walk with Miss Laycock-Manderley.'

'In the rain?'

'Yes. It was pouring.'

'Precisely. Pouring. Which makes one thing rather odd.'

'What's that?'

'I refer to the fact –' James De Meaux rounded on his fiancée ' – that, when you returned from that walk, your overcoat was dripping wet, while Miss Laycock-Manderley's was not even damp.'

'Ah.' Felicity Kershaw was meant to look trapped, and expressed this by clutching her stomach.

'Do you have any explanation of that for me, Felicity?'

'Well...'

'Or let me put it another way – what evil hold has Miss Laycock-Manderley over you that would make you lie to provide her with an alibi?'

Then followed one of Leslie Blatt's favourite dramatic devices, which was used liberally throughout his work. Just at the point when a character had asked a relevant question, one that threatened to unravel the plot a little, another character would enter and prevent the answer being spoken.

In this case, the interruption came from Lady Hilda De Meaux. She swept on in her Act Three pearl grey silk dress (Tony had put his foot down, but she had overruled him) and recited, 'I thought we could all do with a drink, so I've asked Wilhelmina to bring them in here.'

As she said this, she decided definitely that Sylv would wear a midnight-blue silk dress for Act Two of *Shove It*. That's what the character would do. She was, after all, going to appear in public, in the court, and Sylv was the sort of person to really care about her appearance under such circumstances. If she wore that thing Wardrobe had provided, she would look less smart than the two policewomen who flanked her in the dock. That wouldn't do. No, midnight-blue definitely. She would speak to Tony.

'What a good idea, Lady Hilda,' said Felicity Kershaw, glad of the change of subject. 'It's not my usual drink, but I could do with a large whisky after all this.'

'I think I might join you in *one*,' agreed James De Meaux. He'd tried putting the emphasis on every separate word of that line, and none of them sounded right. Tonight's experiment, hitting the 'one', seemed no more successful than the others.

Wilhelmina appeared in the doorway with a silver salver bearing the impedimenta of whisky and sherry decanters, soda syphon and cut-glass tumblers. 'Where would you like me to put these, milady?' she asked.

Her mind supplied an obscene suggestion to answer the question. She was now even more tired, the midnight excursions with her factory-owner having continued through the run of the play. She was also disgruntled that he had made no further reference to the West Indies, and wondered whether he had been spinning her a line all the time. On top of that, her period was a couple of days late, which was all she needed.

'Oh, over by the fireplace, thank you, Wilhelmina. And would you like to call Professor Weintraub and Miss Laycock-Manderley?'

'No need in my case. I am here already,' said the Professor leaping friskily through the French windows.

Three more performances, he was thinking. Get this one finished and then there are only three more. Then, first thing on Sunday morning, shake the dust of Rugland Spa off my feet and get back to Jerome and the chihuahuas.

'I wonder,' mused James De Meaux thoughtfully, because Leslie Blatt had to fill in the hiatus till Miss Laycock-Manderley's entrance with something, 'if there's any way we could make contact with the police. Do you think they'd see, mater, if I did semaphore from the tower?'

'With the weather like this?' asked Lady Hilda rhetorically. The man in charge of Sound tweaked up his volume control and it rained heavily. 'They'd never see you, James. When the wind's coming up from the sea, the Grange is virtually invisible from Winklesham.'

'Oh just an idea.'

Wilhelmina returned. 'Miss Laycock-Manderley will not be a moment, milady. She is just powdering her nose.'

If I actually am pregnant, she was thinking, I could tell him it's his (which it quite possibly could be) and maybe he'd marry me. Hmm, on the other hand, he has already got a grown-up family. And he doesn't really give the impression that children are any longer what he wants from a woman. Have to ask him directly tonight about the West Indies, at least find out where I stand.

'Thank you, Wilhelmina. Would you care to serve the drinks?'

'Yes, milady.'

'[AD LIB SERVING DRINKS DURING THE ENSUING DIALOGUE]' it said in the script, which is always a risky thing (and often a lazy thing) for a playwright to write, because actors vary so much in their improvisational skills. Some are struck dumb as soon as they have to leave the printed text, while others seize the opportunity to weave elaborate fantasies, build in complicated sub-plots which bear no relation to the main action. Without a strong directorial hand, chaos can ensue.

But Antony Wensleigh's had never been a strong directorial hand. And Felicity Kershaw saw the stage direction as an opportunity to aggrandize her part and to make more of a political statement. On this particular night, fired by the militancy of the director who had spent the night with her, she embroidered more than usual.

'Oh, a sherry for me. Just a teensy-weensy sherry. I do hope it's South African. I really do so approve of South Africa – at least it's an ordered society. Like it used to be here. Till all these trades unions started to take over with all their unhealthy leftist talk...'

She thought that was probably sufficient to make her ironic point and cause discomfort amongst any plutocrats in the audience who would realize that they were being pilloried, so she returned to the line they had rehearsed. 'Yes, just a small sherry, please.'

The trouble with that sort of ad libbing is that the 'ensuing dialogue', the dialogue which is meant to be heard, is lost completely. But since this main dialogue conformed to Leslie Blatt's usual standards, it didn't matter that much.

When they were all supplied with drinks, Lady Hilda raised her sherry glass and said, 'What is the toast to be?'

This was the cue for the spectral entrance of Miss Laycock-Manderley, with the line, 'How about absent friends?'

But Miss Laycock-Manderley did not appear. There was an ugly pause.

'Um, how about "Cheers"?' offered Felicity Kershaw, trying to save the situation.

'Or "Prost!"?' suggested Professor Weintraub, rather overdoing the character bit.

'"Your good health" maybe?' was Lady Hilda's suggestion.

James De Meaux realized it was one of those awful moments when he ought to *do* something. Everyone else had had a go; he had to come up with something. 'What about "Bottoms Up", mater? "Down the hatch"...? "Here's mud in your eye"...? Um...'

He was saved from further meanderings through *The Book of Your Favourite Toasts* by the belated appearance of Miss Laycock-Manderley. She was meant to look spectral at this point, but it was a shock to all the cast just how spectral she looked. She was in a state of shock, wide-eyed and trembling.

'How about...' she quavered, '...absent friends?'

'I find that in rather bad taste, Miss Laycock-Manderley, rebuked Lady Hilda, homing in again on Leslie Blatt's text.

'Simply honouring the dead, Lady Hilda.' Miss Laycock-Manderley's teeth were chattering now, as she continued, 'And those about to die.'

Lady Hilda looked at her curiously. 'Would you care for a drink, Miss Laycock-Manderley?'

'Yes, please. A small sherry would be most welcome.'

Looks more like she needs a massive brandy, thought Wilhelmina, as she poured out the apple juice.

'Or, no – I think I'll have a whisky.'

Wilhelmina changed decanters and started to pour the cold tea.

'What did you mean, Miss Laycock-Manderley, when you spoke of "those about to die"?'

'Ha, Lady Hilda. Do you really believe we have seen the last death of this weekend at Wrothley Grange?' As she spoke, she swayed, threatening to fall.

Wilhelmina took the cold tea across to her. '*Are you all right?*' the maid hissed.

'*Terrible news. Just heard backstage,*' was all that could be hissed back before Lady Hilda had finished saying, 'I think you're being overdramatic, Miss Laycock-Manderley.'

'I wish you were right, Lady Hilda. Excuse me...' She fumbled in her handbag. 'I have a slight headache and will just take one of my pills.'

'You can't be serious about more deaths.' Felicity Kershaw clutched at her vitals as she spoke.

'Oh yes.' Elaborately Miss Laycock-Manderley put a pill in her mouth and tried to wash it down with cold tea. Her hand was shaking so much the liquid slopped all over her dress.

'*What on earth's up with her?*' James De Meaux whispered to his mother.

'*The bottle, I would imagine*,' Lady Hilda replied through closed teeth, before continuing, 'No, I think the sequence of deaths has ended. What is more, I think that James and I know who is responsible for them. Perhaps you would like to tell us, Miss Laycock-Manderley, what you were really doing while you were meant to be taking a walk with Miss Kershaw?'

'What?' Miss Laycock-Manderley's hand flew to her throat. Given the state she was in, it was hard to tell whether this was acting or not.

'And also,' James De Meaux chipped in, 'what you were actually doing at the time of my father's death last night when you were supposed to be playing patience in the library?'

'I don't know what you are talking about.' She started to sway and totter. She was meant to sway and totter at this point in the play, but the rest of the cast, who had never seen her sway and totter before in quite the same way. watched, mesmerized.

'Are you all right, Miss Laycock-Manderley?'

'No, I...er...' With another clutch at her throat, she slumped down on to a convenient sofa.

Wilhelmina knelt beside her and loosened her collar. '*For Christ's sake, what's happened?*'

'*It's awful. I just heard...*'

'*WHAT?*' Wilhelmina hissed in frustration, as she felt the slumped figure's pulse.

'Is she all right, Wilhelmina?'

The maid rose. 'She's dead, milady.'

'Good God!' James De Meaux crossed over to them. 'Are you sure?'

'Certain.'

James De Meaux picked up the bottle from which Miss Laycock-Manderley had taken the pill and sniffed it.

Wilhelmina, to the surprise of the rest of the cast, because she had never done it before, again knelt down by the latest victim of the Wrothley Grange murderer. '*Tell me what's happened!*'

'Cyanide,' James De Meaux announced with the air of a connoisseur of fine wines.

Miss Laycock-Manderley's lips didn't move as she murmured the news. '*Tony Wensleigh's shot himself!*'

'Good God,' said James De Meaux.

And Leslie Blatt's dialogue showed more sense of dramatic timing than usual as he went on. 'It was suicide!'

## Chapter Thirteen

'WHY DID YOU find the body, Mr Paris?'

'Why?' The detective gave him a long-suffering look. 'Oh, I'm sorry, I see what you mean. You mean why did I go up to the administrative office in the middle of a performance?'

'Precisely.'

'I went because I was worried about what Tony was going to do.'

'You suspected that he might be about to kill himself?'

'No. I suspected that he might be about to kill someone else.'

The detective sighed. There is no natural affinity between policemen and actors. With an expression of long-suffering, he asked, 'Who did you think he was about to kill?'

'Perhaps I'd better explain from the beginning.'

'That might help.'

Briefly Charles outlined his encounter with the Artistic Director in the props store, concluding, 'Because he was waving the gun around and talking about ending the pressure and sorting things out, I thought he meant he was going to commit murder...but I see now that most of what he said could have referred to suicide.'

'Yes. You hadn't had a quarrel in the props store?'

Charles looked bewildered. 'No. What made you ask that?'

The detective became fascinated by the end of his pencil. 'Oh, I don't know. I just thought you might have been friends and...you know...had an argument and he might have...'

Oh, I see. The old all-actors-are-gay syndrome. The detective was trying to find a lovers' tiff as an explanation for the suicide.

'No. If you're looking for a motive, I'm afraid you don't have to be as devious as that. Tony Wensleigh was under a lot of pressure in his job. There was a Board Meeting planned for tomorrow evening, when it seemed likely that certain questions were going to be raised about his running of the theatre.'

The detective looked interested for the first time. This sounded like something he could understand. 'What, you mean he'd got his hand in the till, he was ripping the theatre off?'

Though this coincided closely with Charles' conjecture, he had no proof and reckoned the dead deserved some loyalty. 'I don't know.'

'But this meeting was going to put him on the spot?'

'Certainly. It was the culmination of a long, unhappy period of conflict.'

'Conflict with who?'

'With the theatre's General Manager, Donald Mason. They had rather different methods of running the Regent and I think these were going to be discussed at tomorrow's meeting.'

'And you reckon this Mason had caught Wensleigh on the fiddle?'

'I don't know. You'd have to ask Donald.'

'Yes, I'll do that. But, anyway, this meeting tomorrow looked like being a showdown?'

'Yes.'

'So, if Wensleigh knew he was going to lose, that'd give him the perfect motive for suicide.' The detective sounded pleased to have got that sorted out so quickly.

'It might do,' said Charles cautiously.

'And when you said you thought he was intending to murder someone, you were thinking of this Donald Mason?'

'Yes. But I misunderstood him rather seriously.'

'Hmm. Could we just go through your movements again, after your conversation in the props store?'

'Okay. Well, after he fired the gun at me –'

'Do you think he did actually intend to hit you?'

'No, I don't. I did at the time, which was why I ran out, but, in retrospect, I don't think he even intended to fire it. He looked very surprised when the gun went off.'

'Right. But you ran, anyway...'

'Yes. I got right down as far as the stage. Then, since he obviously wasn't following me, I went back up again.'

'Why?'

'To talk with him further. To reason with him. He was obviously in a very emotional state. I thought I might be able to help him.'

'Hmm.'

'But when I got up there, I found the props store door locked, so I assumed that he had gone forward to the administrative office.'

'Where he shot himself.'

'Yes.'

'But you thought he was going forward to commit a murder.'

'Yes. I was wrong. It was just that Donald Mason was quite likely to be in the office.'

'But he wasn't.'

'I gather not. I met him backstage later: He'd been there most of the evening.'

'I see. So let's just get the time-scale sorted out. After you'd found the props store locked, what did you do?'

'I went back down the ladder and then, after a bit, I went round the outside of the theatre, in through the front doors and up the stairs to the administrative office.'

'"After a bit", Mr Paris?'

'Yes, well, I wasn't quite sure what to do next. I went to my dressing room for a moment. I...dithered.'

'You thought a murder was about to take place and you dithered?'

'Yes.'

The detective did not add any verbal comment to this; it seemed unnecessary.

'So how long would you say elapsed between your last seeing Wensleigh in the props store and finding his body?'

'Ten, fifteen minutes. I know when I went out of the Stage Door to go round the front, they were just getting to the end of Act Two, just about to do the hanging. And I remember a line I heard while I was up in the gallery, so we could work it out exactly from the running time of the play.'

'Probably won't be necessary, but it might be useful. So let's move on to when you got to the administrative office. Was everything exactly as when we arrived?'

'Yes. It was clear what had happened. There was so much blood, I could see be was dead, so I didn't touch him. I didn't touch anything.'

'Not even the telephone?'

'No. I phoned for the police from backstage. I thought I should tell someone official before I contacted you, so I went back backstage and found Donald. In fact, Councillor Inchbald was also there, so I was able to tell him.'

'Right. Could you just describe Wensleigh's posture when you found him?'

'He was sitting in his chair, slumped forward over the desk. The top drawer of the desk was slightly open. There was blood everywhere. The gun was in his right hand – or rather half-out of his right hand, lying on the desk.'

'That sounds about right. And you didn't read the note?'

'I didn't see a note, let alone read it.'

'Ah.' The detective took out of his file a polythene bag containing a white Regent Theatre envelope. 'It was in the drawer.'

'I see. What did it say?'

'I'm afraid I don't think I should really tell you that, Mr Paris. There is a certain privacy about these things. If you were his widow, of course you should see it, but...'

'Okay, don't worry.' Charles looked at the detective. 'It was a suicide note, I take it?'

'I think there's little doubt about that, Mr Paris. Self-recrimination, apologies for his life...Always a great relief when they do leave a note – makes our job easier.' The detective rose. 'You've been most helpful, thank you. I've got to talk to other people, obviously, and I may need to ask you a few supplementary questions.'

'Fine.'

'And you'll almost definitely be required for the inquest.'

'Yes. Any idea when that's likely to be?'

'Next few days. Can't say exactly.'

'Okay.'

The detective rubbed his hands. 'No, this is really a very satisfactory case, as suicides go. Clear statement of intent from the victim – though in fact you misunderstood it. Clear motive, in that he was building up to a crunch meeting which threatened his career And, just to put the cherry on the cake, a nice note, as well. All in all, nice, straightforward little suicide.'

Frank Walby made it to Fleet Street again on the Friday morning. Just.

He had been seized by the hold-the-front-page glamour of the suicide at the Regent Theatre, talked to anyone who would talk to him there, used his contacts in the local police and, with a bottle of whisky by his typewriter just like in the movies, hammered out a dramatic couple of columns for the national press.

He had then rung it through to an old Fleet Street contact, now a night editor, and finished the bottle of whisky in celebration of his scoop.

The next morning the story appeared, subbed down to two lines, without Frank Walby's by-line. It was dropped completely from later editions.

No one really expected there to be a rehearsal for *Shove It* on the Friday morning, so most of the cast went to the theatre to see if there was any notice on the Green Room board to tell them what to do.

There was. Donald Mason was too efficient to allow his company to go wandering around like lost sheep, whatever the disruption. A meeting would be held on stage at eleven o'clock to outline future plans. The company sat around until then making coffee and comparing previous theatrical disasters. Laurie Tichbourne told how he had once played Rosencrantz with a cracked bone in his toe, 'undiagnosed for *a whole week*'.

Charles wandered round restlessly backstage. He had slept badly and was still in a state of mild shock after discovering Tony's body. Mimi's so-called kedgeree hadn't helped. He also felt a pang of useless guilt. If only he'd understood what Tony had been saying, he might have been able to do something to prevent the suicide. If only...sometimes he reckoned that's what he should have engraved on his tombstone.

He met Donald Mason, who was just finishing a conversation on the backstage pay-phone. The General Manager grimaced as he put the receiver down. 'Just ringing round the Board members to tell them the meeting's off. Not an ideal place to work from.'

'Police still checking out your office?'

'Yes. Say I may be able to get back in late this afternoon. It's a bloody nuisance, though. All the files I need are up there.'

'Yes.'

'I should be ringing round to try and find a new director to come in and salvage *Shove It*.'

'Yes, of course. I hadn't thought of that.'

'I mean, I don't think we'll manage to open on Wednesday, but if we could just postpone for a couple of days...The one thing we mustn't do is have the theatre dark. That'd be playing right into the hands of the anti-theatre lobby. Have to be seen to be doing something, or the Regent's finished.'

'You're right. Did you have a long session with the police?'

'Not that long. They seemed to think everything was pretty cut and dried. It's an absolute disaster, though. It never occurred to me that Tony'd do something like that. And I feel terrible for hounding him so much. I was just trying to make him a bit more efficient, get the theatre back on to an even keel...Now I almost feel as if I've driven him to it.'

'I feel I should have been able to stop him too.'

'Yes.' The General Manager sighed. 'Poor old Tony. He was inefficient – and possibly even worse – but he really did care about the Regent. As much as I do. I suppose the best I can do for his memory is to ensure that the theatre survives – and make it as successful as it's in my power to make it.'

Herbie Inchbald addressed the eleven o'clock meeting. The little man with the mane of hair took his responsibilities as Chairman of the Regent Board seriously, and obviously enjoyed giving his team-talks, even under such clouded circumstances.

'I think you'll all have heard by now what happened last night. I was one of the first to hear the news backstage, and if you're feeling the same sort of shock as I'm still feeling, I know you must be pretty shaken.

'I'm sure I speak for all of us when I say how upset I am about Tony's death. We all appreciated him as a director and friend, and I only wish that we had recognized the symptoms of the breakdown which was coming and which led him to...do what he did. But Tony was a reticent chap, didn't talk a lot about his feelings.

'But we can't look to the past. The time will come for a memorial service for Tony, when we can all voice our appreciation of him, but at the moment our first priority is to get on with the work of the theatre.

'You probably know by now – and I'm not pretending otherwise – that the Regent has been going through a fairly rough time recently, and this new disaster couldn't have come at a worse moment. This town's full of people who don't give a damn about the Arts, and, if we have to close the theatre down, they'll do their level best to see that it doesn't reopen.

'So we must keep going. *Shove It* will open, don't worry. May take us a day or two to find a new director, but it will open – you take my word.

'So I must ask you all to be patient and co-operative, and we'll let you know as soon as there's anything to let you know. Meanwhile, there's a performance tonight and two more tomorrow of *The Message Is Murder*. And the best tribute you can all give to the memory of Tony Wensleigh is to make sure that all three performances of his last production are real little crackers!'

The Councillor's experience again told, and he secured his required round of applause.

There was no question about the commitment of the General Manager and the Chairman of the Board. Charles wondered whether, after all, Tony's death might not prove a blessing to the Regent Theatre. His financial irregularities would probably now never be investigated, and his departure had cleared the air. The new Artistic Director, when he was appointed, would start with a clean slate and, given the back-up of Donald's efficiency and, presumably, better judgement than Tony had demonstrated, might well be able to lead the theatre into a new era of success.

Assuming, of course, that the Regent could survive the hazardous period of interregnum.

He had given his all (insofar as a dead body is capable of giving its all) in the Friday night performance and was unscrewing the sword from his chest, when there was a tap on the dressing room door and Nella entered.

'Charles, there's a lady at the Stage Door who would like to speak to you.'

'Oh?'

'She looks upset. Could you come down?'

'Do you know who it is?'

'I'm not sure, but I think it's Tony's widow.'

She did look upset, but seemed to be in control. She introduced herself as Martha Wensleigh, and agreed to his suggestion that they should go over to the pub and have a drink. Even on Friday night, he assured her, it would be pretty empty at this time.

As they crossed the bar, the old lady with the Guinness, who seemed as much a fixture as the dart-board, claimed to recognize them both, but Charles ushered the new widow past to a sheltered corner. He had a large Bell's and she agreed to his suggestion of a large brandy.

'I'm very sorry,' he began conventionally.

'Thank you. I haven't really started to feel yet.'

'No. It'll take time. He was a fine man.' The clichés jolted out uneasily. He wondered how much Martha knew of what had brought her husband to his death. It struck him that in the three weeks he had been in Rugland Spa, he had never heard Tony's wife even mentioned. She hadn't been at the first night party, and the fact that Nella had been uncertain in identifying her suggested that she was not often at the theatre. This was unusual; in most of the provincial theatres he had worked where the Artistic Director had a wife, Charles had been aware of her presence. (In one particular company he couldn't avoid it, because she played all the female leads.) Maybe the Wensleighs' marriage was breaking up.

Martha scotched that idea straight away. 'Tony and I were very close.'

'Ah.'

'He wasn't very outgoing to people he didn't know, but he talked to me. Whenever he got the time, he talked.'

'Yes.' The conversation wasn't really flowing. 'He can't have had much time. The Regent was a very demanding job.'

She nodded. 'Sometimes it seemed he only came home to sleep. Sometimes not even that. All-night lighting, that sort of thing.'

'Of course.' Charles wondered if she had disliked the theatre, kept away from it deliberately as some mark of disapproval.

Again she answered his unspoken question. 'Tony liked to keep his work and his home life separate. He gave a lot of himself during the days; and then at home I like to think he could relax, recharge his batteries.'

'Yes.'

'When we first started living together, I thought he wanted me as part of his work. I used to do Wardrobe. But then it was clear he valued me more as someone outside it all, someone who could be objective, who wasn't involved in all the ups and downs of productions and politics.'

Charles nodded. He knew a lot of people in the business who kept their marriages and sanity intact that way. Choose a partner outside the theatre and you've got someone with whom you can laugh about the obsessive dramas and crises of rehearsal and performance. If you ever see them...That had been the problem with Frances all those years before. He was never there, always off in the alien single beds of the nation's Mimis. Acting and marriage had different imperatives, which were hard to reconcile.

Martha Wensleigh broke into his maudlin reverie with an abrupt change of subject. 'I thought of you because of something I heard from a man called Spike.'

'Spike?'

'His real name was Gareth Warden. He stage-managed at the Regent a few years back.'

'Oh, I remember him.' It came back. Spike had worked on the pre-London tour of the musical, *Lumpkin!*, a show whose progress had been bedevilled by a series of unexplained crimes.

'Spike talked about you one night when he was a bit drunk. Said you were not above a bit of detective investigation.'

'What a nice way of putting it.'

'I want you to undertake an investigation for me.'

'Into Tony's death?'

'Yes.'

Charles looked at the widow with pity. 'I think I'm unlikely to unearth a satisfying murderer. There seems to be little doubt that he did kill himself.'

'I know that. I don't want you to unearth a murderer. I just want to know what drove him to...do what he did.'

Strange, that she should use exactly the same euphemism as Herbie Inchbald. Or perhaps not strange. Anything rather than define the unpalatable truth too closely.

'Tony had been under a lot of pressure for a long time,' said Charles gently. 'I think he was very confused.'

'You don't have to tell me that, Charles. I lived with him.'

'Yes. Of course. What I'm saying is, I think that confusion impaired his judgement. He had done a series of strange things recently. I'm afraid taking his own life may have been the culmination of those. What's the phrase – "while the balance of his mind was disturbed"?'

'Yes, but what disturbed it?'

Charles shrugged. 'As I say, a series of things. The Regent's been under threat for a long time, you know that – that was one continuing pressure. Then...' Charles fought shy of mentioning the financial fiddles and the attempted murders. 'There were other things,' he ended lamely.

'But he used to be able to cope with pressure.'

'One day it just gets too much. He had been getting worse – forgetting he had done things, not doing things he thought he'd done.'

'He talked about that. It worried him a lot. There were letters he swore he had written, and then it turned out he hadn't...very strange...'

'He was always at rehearsal,' Charles explained soothingly. 'Administration was never one of his strengths.'

'I know that. But what I do want to find out is what the final pressure was. What made him...do it?'

'Didn't he talk to you about it?'

'Only in general terms. He said he didn't want to go into details until he'd sorted everything out. And I thought he had. He rang me the evening he died.'

'Did he?' Charles was instantly alert. Have you told the police?'

'Oh yes,' she replied wearily.

'What time did he ring?'

'About eight.'

Before Charles had met him in the prop store. 'And what did he say?'

'He said he'd finally sorted it out. He said it had all been very confusing, but he was getting there. Soon he'd have it all taped and the pressure would be off.'

Charles grimaced ruefully. 'That's pretty much what he said to me later on. It's ambiguous, to say the least.'

'Yes. The police...'

'I can imagine. Took it as further evidence that he intended to do away with himself.'

'Yes.' Martha Wensleigh looked discouraged and, for the first time, as if she was about to break down.

'He didn't say anything else, anything more specific?'

'He said something rather strange. I can't remember the exact words, but, more or less, he said, "At least I'm not paranoid. A paranoid *thinks* he's being persecuted, but now I *know* I've been being persecuted".'

'I'm afraid that's exactly what a paranoid would say.'

He hadn't said it gently enough. Martha Wensleigh flared up. 'Oh, for God's sake! Can't you say anything more helpful than that?

'I'm sorry.'

She looked at him. Her eyes had the same dark vulnerability as her husband's. Grey-haired lady in her fifties, not particularly attractive. And now a widow. What did the rest of her life hold for her?

She swallowed down a sob as she spoke carefully. 'I'm sorry too. It's just that Tony was convinced someone was out to get him, that someone at the Regent was trying to ruin his career. He said it more than once. He didn't say who, and he didn't say how – just that someone was out to destroy him and the theatre.'

'I'm sorry to have to say it, Martha, but that again sounds very like paranoia.'

'Yes, I agree. It could. But I sort of got the impression that Tony was building up some sort of case against his...enemy. When he rang last night, I thought he meant his case was complete.'

Charles looked sufficiently dubious for her to lose her temper again. 'Oh, you're just like everyone else! You don't want to help and –'

'I do. It's just...'

'Forgive me.' Once again she made a supreme effort to control herself. 'As I said, I'm not feeling properly yet. Not feeling the things I will feel. Soon I'm going to break down and weep for a year. But at the moment all that's coming out is anger, anger and the need to do something. I can't bring Tony back, but at least I can find out who persecuted him so much that he killed himself. Or if I can't...' She softened, and for the first time Charles was aware of her as a woman, as someone with a sexual identity, 'perhaps you can.'

The appeal was strong, and he would have liked to agree to what she asked. But he felt certain that she was going to be disappointed in her quest, and thought it better that that disappointment came sooner rather than later.

'Martha, from what I can gather, Tony had been cracking up for some long time. His artistic judgement seemed to have gone.'

'What do you mean?'

'Well, I don't know when the season's programme is decided...'

'Oh, about eight months back. Has to be finalized round June.'

'Then I reckon he had started to crack back in June. Do you really think that choosing *The Message Is Murder*, followed by *Shove It*, is the action of someone whose artistic judgement is intact?'

Martha Wensleigh stared at him, surprise so dominating her face that it drove out the pain and distress. 'But he didn't want to do those plays.'

'What?'

'Tony thought they were both awful. Directing them made him utterly miserable.'

'Then why on earth did he choose them?'

'He didn't. That's done by the Play Selection Committee.'

'Isn't he even on the committee?'

'Oh yes, but he could be overruled by the others.'

'Who are the others?'

'The Chairman of the Theatre Board, the General Manager, and there's always a Creative Consultant. This year it was Leslie Blatt.'

## *Chapter Fourteen*

CHARLES HAD TO parry offers of tea, coffee, cocoa and rock cakes from Mimi before he could get to bed and look at the file that Martha Wensleigh had given him.

It was her revelation about Tony's dislike of the plays that had persuaded him to go further. So much of his thinking about the collapse of the Artistic Director's judgement had been based on the two choices, that he now felt the whole case needed re-examination. Also, the knowledge that Wensleigh's opinion of *The Message Is Murder* and *Shove It* coincided with his own made him feel closer to the dead man than he ever had during their acquaintance.

So he had agreed that he would investigate, but with no very lively hope of success. It was the nakedness in Martha Wensleigh's eyes that had swayed him, though deep down he suspected he would find out nothing that was not already obvious.

The file she had brought with her was all that Tony had kept at home. Any hope that it would prove to be some kind of dossier, evidence in the 'case' his wife had suspected he was building up against his 'enemy', was soon dashed.

The file was a further demonstration of Tony Wensleigh's disorganized mind, of his lack of administrative ability. It was just bits and pieces, carbons of letters and photocopies of documents jumbled up with photos of actors, programme proofs, rehearsal notes scribbled in his cramped handwriting, props lists, snippings of Frank Walby reviews, Board Meeting agendas, designers' sketches for sets, phone numbers on backs of envelopes, restaurant bills and other less decipherable scraps.

There was no system in the collection; it was as if the Artistic Director had every now and then emptied out his jacket pockets and shoved whatever he found into the file.

Just sorting through the mass of paper would be a long job. Charles was glad he had taken the precaution of buying a half-bottle of Bell's from the pub. He took a long swig and, propping himself up on Mimi's brushed nylon pillows, started to wade through.

After about an hour, he had winnowed out four single sheets and one stapled bunch of papers which he thought might have some bearing on the case, or which, failing that, might at least provide some background to recent events at the Regent Theatre.

The first confirmed what his widow had said about Tony Wensleigh's view of the plays in the current season. It was a duplicated sheet, headed 'Play Selection Committee – Proposals', containing a list of play titles. Presumably, since there were only seventeen in all, these represented some sort of short list. Five shows in the season, no argument about the pantomime (which had been *Puss In Boots* that year) and, it seemed, one nomination from each committee member for each of the other four slots.

It was clear, from his underlinings and comments, which had been the Artistic Director's own suggestions. *Much Ado About Nothing, Sleuth, Kiss Me Kate* and Ayckbourn's *Ten Times Table*. Not wildly original, perhaps, but a fairly well-balanced programme of Rugland Spa fodder.

What was striking about the committee's voting was that in every case the Artistic Director's proposal had been voted out, and in each case replaced with something inferior. Even *Much Ado*...had given way to *All's Well That Ends Well*, a much more difficult and less readily accessible play.

Whether the committee's voting reflected lack of artistic judgement or something more sinister it was hard to be certain. The first was quite possible, Charles reflected. He already had serious doubts about Herbie Inchbald's knowledge of the theatre; *The Message Is Murder* did not inspire much confidence in Leslie Blatt as an arbiter of taste; and, he suddenly realized, though he had heard Donald Mason talking about a lot of administrative matters, he had never heard an artistic judgement from the General Manager.

On the other hand, the unanimity of voting against Tony Wensleigh suggested that his suspicion of organized opposition was not completely fanciful.

The Artistic Director's view of one of the plays ultimately selected was left in no doubt by a carbon of a letter dated a few days before the Play Selection Committee Meeting.

Dear Leslie [it ran], thank you very much indeed for letting me see the script of *The Message Is Murder*, which I return herewith.

I am afraid your submitting it puts me in a difficult position, because, having known you so long, I would like to be able to write back with enthusiasm, but I'm afraid I can't. I am sure that, as you say, the play was well received when first produced in the fifties, though I feel the fact that its run ended on its pre-London tour may suggest that it lacked a certain West End gloss.

Anyway, that need not matter. Frequently a revival can completely change a play's fortunes. But I'm afraid I cannot see that happening in this case. To be brutally frank, the play has dated badly and now seems painfully contrived. The characters have no inner life or psychological continuity, and, speaking as a director, I can foresee massive problems in giving the play any credibility at all.

I am sorry to have to write like this, but I feel that it is better to be frank at this point than by politeness to get caught in a project which should not have started.

Please rest assured that I have often had occasion to respect your judgement in the past, and am sure that I will be grateful for your advice in the future. I am only sorry that I cannot agree with you about the suitability of *The Message Is Murder* for production at the Regent in the 1980s.

Yours sincerely,

Tony.

The letter interested Charles a lot, not only because it confirmed Tony Wensleigh's dislike of the play, but also because it revealed a core of good sense and professional skill which he had not seen during his brief acquaintance with the director. Tony Wensleigh might have cracked up in the intervening months, but he hadn't cracked when he wrote that letter.

The next document of interest was a letter from Herbie Inchbald, dated some three years previously. It spelled out precisely the threat to the site of the Regent Theatre.

Dear Tony,

As you know there has been a great deal of toing and froing on the Council recently over the future of the Regent and, both as a Councillor and as Chairman of the Theatre Board, I think it's up to me to keep you informed of developments.

As you don't need telling, the theatre holds a prime position in the Maugham Cross area, the whole of which is badly run down and will at some point require redevelopment. I don't question that that will have to happen in time, but what I and my supporters on the Council are trying to ensure is that any development plans guarantee the survival of the Regent in its current form. As you have probably gathered, not everyone on the Council agrees with me. Like everything else, it has become a political matter, and we're spending an awful lot of Council time debating the merits of theatre v. Leisure Centre and God knows what else.

The issue has become more pressing, because we have now had a definite offer on the whole Maugham Cross area from Schlenter Estates. It is an attractive offer and the majority of the Council favour accepting it and appointing Schlenter Estates as developer. They seem to be well backed and have presented us with convincing plans, demonstrating how they will raise development money from a pension fund, etc. They seem to know what they're on about.

And Rugland Spa could use the money. Apart from a guaranteed minimum income from the project, we would also receive a healthy percentage of the gross rents for the completed development, just the sort of financial boost we need in these straitened times. And, of course, we would control the way the development is done, to keep it in tone with the rest of the town centre.

But Schlenter do want the Regent site as part of their development and I think they'd be prepared to do anything to get it. I've already had the soft soap treatment from them, invitations to look round one of their completed projects near Birmingham. I went along, out of curiosity. Most of the day was spent being whisked between expensive restaurants in Rolls-Royces, being fed to the gills with excellent food and champagne (and with a fairly unambiguous offer of a girl at the end of the day if I fancied it). Well, of course, they'd backed the wrong horse with me. I can recognize a bribe a mile off, and am fortunately sufficiently comfortable not even to be tempted. But it does show how important the development is to them, and what they'd be prepared to do to get that site.

As I say, a lot of the Council would let them have it without a backward thought, so we're going to have to fight hard to save it.

I'm sure we'll succeed. As we discussed, I've written to Lord Kitestone asking him to be our patron. His name on our notepaper will give us a lot of respectability. And then we must organize public opinion. I'm sure we can guarantee a good outcry when the proposal to demolish the theatre becomes public, and I'm sure we'll be able to stop it. Either the development will go ahead, leaving the Regent untouched, or else the whole project will be shelved.

But, even if the second happens, this has been a grim warning and it's the kind of thing that's bound to come up again. It's down to us to ensure that we maintain such a high standard of theatre at the Regent that no one even dares to suggest closing us.

Anyway, thought you ought to know the state of play. Rest assured of the continuing support of myself and anyone else on the Council who I can speak for (and pray that there won't be a disaster at the elections!).

Yours sincerely,

Herbie.

The letter confirmed – if it needed confirming – Councillor Inchbald's whole-hearted backing for the Regent, but it also defined the reality of the threat to the theatre's future. And its total reliance on Council support.

That had been three years before. The Regent was still standing, and the area in which it stood, Charles had noticed, was, by Rugland Spa's genteel standards, pretty shabby. So presumably the deal with Schlenter Estates had not gone through. But the more run-down the Maugham Cross area became, and the lower the artistic standards of the Regent fell, the greater became the likelihood of another similar offer. An offer which, after recent disasters, the pro-theatre lobby might find difficult to fight off.

Charles then turned his attention to the stapled sheaf of papers, which turned out to be photocopies of Donald Mason's c.v. and references when he applied for the post of General Manager at the Regent Theatre just over a year before.

These made fascinating reading. Charles realized that he knew almost nothing about Donald's past. Whereas much of actors' conversations is spent in asking each other where they've worked and who with, such questions are rarely addressed to General Managers. Indeed, in many theatres, the cast are hardly aware of the General Manager's presence.

Donald Mason had started out in 1970, it appeared, as an estate agent, which, he wrote, 'taught me the basic skills of administration without in any way stimulating my mind, which was becoming increasingly set on the idea of working in the theatre'. Difficulty in finding an opening in this country had led him to try his luck in Australia, where, starting humbly as an Assistant Front of House Manager, he had risen through various companies, until he reached the status of General Administrator at the Kelly Theatre in Sydney. Wishing to try his luck again in his native country, he had returned to England six months previously and found, like many before him, that experience abroad did not count for as much as it should. But, determined to build up his career again, he had been prepared to go a few rungs back down the ladder, and accepted a job as Assistant Front of House Manager at the Pavilion Theatre, Darlington. It was from there that he was applying for the Rugland Spa job.

That career history was adequate for the job; what made it exceptional was the quality of the references that accompanied the application. Charles knew that in the theatre a good reference was sometimes a way of getting rid of a member of the administrative staff who didn't fit in, but that could not explain such unanimity of praise as Donald Mason had received from his Australian employers. Charles didn't know the antipodean theatrical scene, so the names didn't mean anything to him, but there was no doubting the enthusiasm of Ralph Johnson of the Theatre Royal, Adelaide, Rich Coleman of the Dominion, Perth, Greg Avon of the Hippodrome, Melbourne, and Jim Vasilis of the Kelly Theatre in Sydney. They all praised Donald Mason's administrative skill, tact and general flair for the theatre; and they all very much regretted losing him. The letters made impressive reading. Rugland Spa had been lucky to catch Mason at a low point in his career, because he was clearly destined for higher things.

The final piece of paper from Antony Wensleigh's file was further confirmation not only of Donald's suitability for his job, but also for the Artistic Director's endorsement of the appointment. The duplicated sheet was headed 'General Manager Applicants' and dated nearly a year before. There was a list of five names with times half an hour apart, presumably for their final interviews. There were comments beside all the names in Tony's tiny writing, but against Donald Mason's were four asterisks, an exclamation mark and the remark, 'This one by a mile!'

So, though conflict seemed to have developed between the Artistic Director and the General Manager, there was no question of Tony having had Donald foisted on him. He had supported the new appointment unreservedly.

If his feelings of persecution were more than fantasy, then the contents of the Artistic Director's file gave no clue as to the identity of his persecutor.

There was only the business of play selection, which could perhaps show organized opposition to Tony, and that seemed more likely to be just the workings of innocent philistinism.

A natural instinct for tidiness made Charles drain the half-bottle of Bell's. Then he switched out the light and tried to snuggle into the brushed nylon sheets (though snuggling and brushed nylon sheets don't really go together). The stuff in the file had been interesting, he reflected, but it hadn't really got him any further in what probably wasn't even a case.


'There was a phone message for you this morning,' Mimi announced, as Charles tried not to meet his kipper in the eye. What a hell, he thought, for a fish. Being caught is bad enough. Being kippered adds to the agony. But then to have to suffer the final indignity of being cooked by Mimi...it made hanging, drawing and quartering seem humane.

'Who from?'

Disbelief flooded Mimi's face, before drenching her words. 'She said she was your wife.'

'Why on earth didn't you wake me?'

'Oh, didn't want to disturb you. I said you were sleeping it off.'

So that was going to be the regular line, whoever rang while he was asleep. Thank you very much, Mimi just wait and see what I write in your Visitors' Book. I will. I really will.

'Am I to ring her back?'

'No. She said she'd leave a message.' Mimi stopped, as if that were all she had to communicate, and started further adulterating her tea with tepid water.

'What was the message?'

'Oh. You want to know?'

'Yes.'

'Well, you can never be sure. Some of my gentlemen don't want to hear from their wives, tell Mimi not even to admit they're here if their wives ring.' She looked at Charles balefully. 'You behind on the maintenance?'

'No, I am not. We are not divorced.'

'Oh. Happily together, eh?'

Charles restrained himself. 'What was the message?'

'She said she couldn't make lunch tomorrow.'

The slap of pain made him realize how much he had been looking forward to seeing Frances. Whatever the situation was, however awkward the meeting, he wanted to see her.

'Oh, well...' he said miserably.

'But...' Mimi took her time, 'she said could you make it dinner instead? An early dinner. She's booked for seven-thirty Sunday. If you can't, ring her between six and seven tonight.'

Charles felt such a flood of boyish joy at his hope restored that he forgot Mimi's awfulness. 'Terrific,' he said, rising from the table.

'Now you're not going to leave that lovely kipper, are you?' demanded Mimi.

Charles felt guilty about Martha Wensleigh, guilty about the anguished appeal he had seen in her eyes. He felt he should have something for her, but knew he had nothing to give.

Still, one new idea had come with the morning. It was tiny and undeveloped, but pursuing it would at least give him the illusion of doing something on the widow's behalf.

The thought he had had arose from something in Herbie Inchbald's letter about the proposals to redevelop the Maugham Cross area. The Councillor had made it clear that Schlenter Estates wanted the site very much, and had even tried tentatively to bribe him as a way of getting it. Was it just possible that they had also found a way of putting pressure on Tony Wensleigh, hoping through him to weaken the theatre's status in the town and make their course easier?

It was fanciful, but no more fanciful than a great many of the blind alleys Charles had run up in the course of his detective career.

The trouble was, he knew nothing about the workings of property companies. However, he did have a friend who might be able to help him.

He phoned from a public call-box, wary of Mimi's telescopic ears.

Kate Venables answered. 'Charles, what a pleasure to hear from you. Not to say a surprise. Look, I must dash – taking one of the kids out for her riding lesson. I think Gerald's still here – he's just on his way out to play golf. Just a sec. Lovely to hear you.' The receiver was put down and Charles heard receding cries of 'Gerald!'

Charles could visualize the house in West Dulwich, a beautifully appointed example of 1970s Georgian. Money had been lavished on it like plant food on a Chelsea Flower Show exhibit. Everything was of the best and of the most expensive. Riding lessons for the children, golf for Gerald, facials for Kate – everything perfect, everything money could buy. Occasionally, in reflective moods, Charles tried to imagine just how much money Gerald Venables made but usually gave up early on in disbelief There was the basic profit from the highly successful firm of show business solicitors, but that was now only part of a huge investment income. Gerald was one of the few consistently successful 'angels' who actually made a profit from putting money into shows; but he also had stakes in television companies, commercial radio stations and God knew what other lucrative projects.

The two had met at Oxford and, in spite of the fact that Charles' annual income probably represented a month's pocket money for Gerald, had remained friends. Part of the reason for this was Gerald's fascination with detection and childlike eagerness to get involved in any investigation that Charles initiated.

That this eagerness remained undiminished was confirmed by his first words when he reached the phone. 'Charles, are you on a case?'

'Not sure. I might be.'

'You must be. I don't hear from you from one year's end to the next, and when I do, it's always a case. Spill the beans.'

'I'm at Rugland Spa.'

'Ah, taking an early retirement?'

'No. Thing is, the Artistic Director of the local theatre has just committed suicide.'

'But Charles Paris is convinced it was really murder?'

'No, I'm sorry. Nothing so dramatic. Seems no doubt he actually did away with himself. I just want to know why.'

'Ah. And you think I can tell you? You overestimate my powers, I'm afraid. I'm not psychic.'

'I just want you to find out some information for me.'

'Showbiz?'

'No. It's a bit outside your normal field, but I thought you might be able to root something out. It's about a property company.'

Gerald didn't immediately reject the idea that he might know something. As Charles had suspected, the solicitor's investments were well diversified.

'Which property company?'

'Schlenter Estates.'

Gerald made a little whistle through his teeth. 'The original wide-boys.'

'You mean they're crooks?'

The solicitor tutted. 'You really must learn to moderate your language, Charles. There are laws of slander in this country. Anyway, a crook is someone who has been found guilty of a crime. Schlenter Estates have never been found guilty of anything.'

'But...?'

'But nothing. They are now a highly respected company with international interests. They're even more respectable since they were taken over by Fowler Rose Stillman.'

'They're big, aren't they? Even I've heard of them.'

'Oh yes. Fowler Rose Stillman are very big. And highly respectable.'

'Then why did you refer to Schlenter as wide-boys?'

'I was being indiscreet.'

'Go on, Gerald, don't be coy.'

'Well, it's going back a few years. During the property boom. Round 1970. Then there were a few uncharitable rumours going around about Schlenter. No property companies had a very good reputation round then.'

'Anything specific?'

'On Schlenter? Can't say off the top of my head. I could check round on the office on Monday, ask a few people, if you like.'

'I'd be very grateful.'

'What do you want exactly?'

'Don't know, really.'

'That's helpful.'

'Well, sort of anything about them. Who really owns them, what they do...any dirt, certainly.'

'Just that. Uhuh,' said Gerald with heavy irony. 'I'll see what I can do. Where can I contact you?'

Charles had to give Mimi's number. It wasn't private, but at least it wasn't actually in the Regent.

'I'll have to ring either before eleven or else considerably later,' said Gerald. 'I've just remembered I've got a client coming in at eleven. He's joining the National as an Assistant Director and we're going through his contract. That'll mop up lunch – mop up most of the day, actually.'

'I'll stay in till eleven.'

'Fine. Actually you might know him.'

'Your client?'

'Yes. It's Bill Walsingham – have you worked with him?'

'You bet. Bloody marvellous director.'

'Yes.'

'Oh, well, give him my love.'

'Will do.'

'And now I won't keep you from your golf any longer. Hope to hear from you on Monday.'

'Do my best. Oh, incidentally, Charles, isn't it good news about Frances?'

The change of subject was too sudden for Charles. 'What about her?'

'Well, I mean this new bloke.'

'Ah.'

'David. Seems an awfully good thing.'

'You've met him?'

'Yes. Absolute charmer.' Charles didn't say anything. 'No, I'm so pleased for both of you really. I mean, it's been obvious for years that you and Frances wasn't going to work out. Kate and I had hoped it would when you first split up, but...And Frances has needed someone. So now you must feel a lot freer.'

'Freer?' Charles echoed.

'Yes, for all those little actresses, eh? No doubt you've got another little cracker on the scene at the moment.'

'No doubt,' Charles agreed, feeling emptier than he could ever remember.

# Chapter Fifteen

*The Message Is Murder* was given its two final performances on the Saturday, and then returned to its vault, surely never to rise again.

Both the matinée and the evening show were subdued, which was hardly surprising, considering the circumstances. The Methuselahs of Rugland Spa clapped politely at the matinée, and a fuller, fractionally younger audience gave exactly the same reaction to the evening show. Charles unbuckled the Waspee belt of his duelling sword for the last time, and vowed to do something unprecedented. He would turn down work. He would tell his agent on the Monday – if anyone else comes offering a part as a dead body, Charles Paris is unavailable.

The end of the show left everyone in limbo. A director had still not been appointed to rescue *Shove It*, so that production's future remained uncertain, and some members of the company were not sure whether they should be doing a full goodbye routine or if they'd all meet up again for rehearsals the following week.

A subdued little party went for a subdued little celebration at The Happy Friend Chinese Restaurant and Takeaway. Mr Pang welcomed them with his usual impassive smile.

There was little conviviality around the table. Laurie Tichbourne sat beside Nella, looking at her soulfully. A stranger might have seen this as evidence of a love too deep for words, but Charles recognized the plight of someone who just couldn't think of anything to say.

Cherry Robson was there with her factory-owner, though they were in the middle of some complicated row or negotiation. Half-way through the meal, he stormed out and, after two minutes of truculent deliberation, Cherry followed. She wasn't going to let all that money get away so easily.

Leslie Blatt, no doubt to the relief of the females present, was not there.

Rick Harmer and Gay Milner sat either side of Charles, apparently talking to him, but in fact engaged in long individual monologues. Rick was going on about how successful he was going to be, how almost certain he was to get this major television role, apart from getting this television sit com series to write, and how he wasn't really sure whether his agent had big enough ideas for him. What did Charles think?

Gay Milner was talking about sexual relationships and their relevance to their political context. Most of what she said was direct quotation from the director of *Scrag End of Neck* at the Bus Depot, who appeared to have found a new rationale for that oldest of masculine pursuits – how to get sex without responsibility. It was very important that sexual relationships remained egalitarian, Gay quoted. There was, after all, capitalism in sex as well as other forms of property-owning. It was important that relationships should not be limited by the use of glib emotive buzz-words like 'love'. What did Charles think?

Since he had no thoughts at all on what either of them was talking about, he said nothing, but that did not deter them from continuing to circle round their subjects right through the meal.

At the end Mr Pang was once again asked what Ice Creams (Various) he had, and once again he said Vanilla.

The Sunday was a twitchy day for Charles. He would have liked to wake very late, but Mimi decided to hoover the landing outside his bedroom at eight o'clock. She seemed to have some in-built monitor which made her hyper-sensitive to her gentlemen's desires; she must have done, otherwise she couldn't so consistently have ensured that they were frustrated.

When she finished hoovering, Charles turned over, still with a good chance of going back to sleep. He achieved this, but after five minutes was woken by a knock on the door and ordered down for what Mimi had the nerve to call an omelette.

He got out as soon as possible and was faced with the prospect of a day to kill in Rugland Spa, a day when the pubs didn't open till twelve or the cinemas till three. At least, thanks to *Shove It* rehearsals, he hadn't seen either of the films that had started on the Thursday. But did he really want to go to *Bambi*? Or *She Lost Her Swedish Knickers*, come to that? (He wondered idly whether Mrs Feller spent her spare time picketing the cinema or whether she'd given it up as a bad job.)

The day stretched ahead, one of those awful sagging Sundays in rep. In the old days, he remembered, they had been rare. Sundays had meant tech runs and Dress Rehearsals for a Monday opening. But Equity had tightened up the regulations, now there were overtime rates for Sunday working and as a result few theatres did it. Shows opened now on Wednesday, and usually ran two-and-a-half weeks. The old manic days of weekly rep were gone.

He trudged round the streets of Rugland Spa. Anything of interest the town had to offer (and there wasn't much) he had already seen. He felt mournful and self-pitying.

And he knew that part of the reason was the evening that lay ahead. His mind vacillated between desperately wanting to see her and blind panic. At times he contemplated not turning up at all at the hotel. It might be simpler that way.

The day passed somehow (*Bambi* was actually much better than he'd remembered it), but he still found himself at the Rugland Spa Hotel half an hour too early. But by then his feet were so tired, he couldn't face another aimless circuit of the town. Anyway, at seven o'clock he would be able to get a drink and he felt he was going to need a couple of stiff Bell's to set him up for the evening.

The Rugland Spa Hotel had been built in the days when the spa meant something, when people actually ventured out to Herefordshire to take the waters, when the town was, if not a wildly fashionable resort, at least an active one.

But health fads change and the people who in the nineteenth century might have taken courses of baths were, in the 1980s, jogging, cramming themselves with vegetable fibre or listening in the privacy of their own homes to their biorhythms. And anyone so cranky as actually to want to take the waters would have been frustrated. The baths complex had fallen into disrepair, been declared unsafe in the 1950s, and ten years later been demolished and supplanted by a supermarket.

But the hotel had remained. The site, on the way out of the town towards Ludlow, had been chosen for its proximity to the baths, but a supermarket didn't attract guests in the same way. The hotel was no longer independently run, but had been taken over by one of the smaller chains, who were having a hard job to keep it going. It was built on too grand a scale. A few elderly people liked to stay there, occasional families were lured out from the cities by offers of 'Bargain Breaks', some resolute foreigners 'doing Britain' might end up there, but there was no continuity of trade. Businessmen and travellers in the area seemed to prefer the anonymous uniformity of the new motel the other side of town, with its colour television, in-house video and 'conference facilities'.

The hotel's exterior reflected its declining popularity. Its former splendour carried an almost shamefaced air. The name stuck boldly on the fascia in large metal letters, had tarnished and the 'L' dangled diagonally. Creeper threatened to swallow up whole wings and the paintwork on the finely-shaped windows was cracked and stained.

It was, thought Charles, as he entered the apologetic portico, another site suitable for development.

He had checked in the car-park for Frances' yellow Renault, but there was no sign of it, so he went straight through to what was called 'The Kitestone Bar'.

At seven o'clock on a Sunday it was almost uninhabited. Any trade they did get on Sundays tended to be lunchtimes; there were still local farmers and wealthy sons of retired parents who believed in bringing family parties out for 'Roast beef, Yorkshire pudding, the full works'. But the evening trade was very slack.

There was only one other customer, sitting in a bay window, so Charles had no difficulty in engaging the attention of the adolescent barman. That young man, looking, in a red braided jacket too big for him, like a pen in an envelope, had a bit of difficulty in locating the Bell's whisky, but compensated for this by pouring out a huge measure and charging for a single.

The evening was pleasant, so Charles wandered over to the window. As he sat down, he realized that he recognized the bar's other customer.

'Excuse me,' he said. moving across to her, 'but its Mrs Inchbald, isn't it?'

The pudgy face looked up at him. 'Oh...er...We met at the theatre, didn't we?'

'Charles Paris.'

'Of course.'

'Do you mind if I join you? I'm waiting for my wife,' he added quickly, lest she should think his intentions anything but honourable. No doubt even so fat a lady as Velma Inchbald regarded herself as a potential target for a predatory male.

'Oh, do, please.' The slight exaggeration in her speech, and the wide gesture which accompanied it suggested that the pink gin in front of her was not the first she had had that day.

'Herbie,' she explained, 'is up in London.'

'Ah.'

'A weekend conference, related to his business,' she said importantly.

'Road haulage?'

She looked a little put out to have her husband's business so precisely defined, but conceded that this was so. And she quickly regained any social ground that might have been lost by saying, 'Of course, it's so simple now when Herbie goes up to town, because he stays at his club. All the other delegates are stuck in these awful hotels, but he spends the night in comfort at Blake's.'

'Very nice indeed.'

'Oh yes. He meets such interesting people there, you know.'

'I'm sure.'

'The sort of people who he mixes with naturally. The sort of people he should have been mixing with all his life, but, you know, the demands of the business have kept his social circle...parochial until now.'

'And he'll be back tomorrow, will he?'

'Very late this evening.'

They were silent. Charles looked out of the window. The view was magnificent, rolling hills shading away towards the distant mountains of Wales. The only building in sight was a huge square mansion about two miles away, set on a hill-top, dominating the entire landscape.

Velma Inchbald must have followed his gaze, because she identified the mansion. 'Onscombe House. But you probably knew that.'

'No, I didn't, actually.'

'Willie Kitestone's place.'

'Oh.' He sensed that Velma wanted him to ask further about this familiarity. 'You mean Lord Kitestone?' he asked, with a sufficiency of awe in his tone.

A smile irradiated her fat features. He had said the right thing. 'Yes. Willie and Herbie are *such* good friends. You know, it's what I said about Herbie mixing with more interesting people. I mean, he hasn't got all the education and that, he's made his own way, but Herbie really is a member of Nature's aristocracy. He and Willie have such respect for each other. It was Willie who put him up for Blake's, you know.'

So that was one little mystery explained. 'Lord Kitestone's the Patron of the theatre, isn't he?' asked Charles.

'Yes. That was one of Herbie's brainwaves. The Regent was being threatened at the time and Herbie thought, let's get the biggest name in the area on our side, so he wrote to Willie. That's really how they got to know each other.'

'Ah.'

'And they got on like a house on fire from the start. Oh, we're quite often invited up to Onscombe, you know.'

Charles made suitably impressed noises.

'Such a generous man, Willie. I mean, I don't think he's that well off...Well, obviously he is by our standards, but not for someone keeping up an establishment like that. No, I'm sure there were rumours some years back that he was going to have to sell Onscombe. But you'd never know it. He is such a generous entertainer. Do you know, he let us borrow his villa in Corsica last summer...?'

'Really?' Had that been some sort of bribe, Charles wondered, though he couldn't for the life of him imagine why Lord Kitestone should want to bribe Herbie Inchbald. Some question of planning permission, perhaps?

But such speculation was dashed by Velma's next words. 'Of course. Herbie insisted we pay him rent. Never take anything for nothing, Herbie wouldn't. Sometimes I think he's *over*-scrupulous about that sort of thing. But he always says to me, "No, Velma, someone in my position can't be too careful. Local Councillors are constantly under public scrutiny, and even a simple little goodwill gesture can be easily misinterpreted. No, Velma, I never accept something for nothing."'

Years of living with him had enabled her so to take on her husband's intonations that it sounded as if Herbie himself was speaking.

Charles said, 'Good principle' or some other vague cliché.

And then he noticed Frances standing in the doorway of the bar. 'Oh, er, Mrs Inchbald, would you excuse me? My wife's arrived.'

Velma shifted her bulk in the chair as if to suggest that Frances might come across and join them, but Charles, unworried by his rudeness, said, 'No, I'm sorry, but I need to see her on her own.'

'Oh, I'm sure I wasn't wanting to...'

'I haven't seen her for a long time,' said Charles, as he walked across the room.

Somehow they both wanted to be outside, so before they had a drink, they took a turn round the hotel garden. This showed the same neglect as the rest of the premises. The straight lines of its formal design were shaggy with weeds. The gravel of the paths rose up in uneven hillocks. The white painted trellis of an arbour had collapsed in a tangle of lathes. Dandelions and plantain broke up the surface of the croquet lawn.

It was getting dark. They walked hand in hand. He could feel on her thumb the familiar scar a kitchen-knife had made once when they were together.

'I'm sorry I had to change the arrangement,' Frances said rather formally. 'About lunch. I thought I'd be free all day, but .something came up.'

'David?' Charles was determined not to avoid the name.

She nodded. 'I thought he'd be tied up with his family all day, but then his wife got invited out to lunch and he was free and he expected me to be free, and I couldn't tell him where I was going and...God, it's so complicated.'

'He doesn't know you're here now?'

She shook her head. 'But I had to see you. Now it means I've got a three-hour drive back in the small hours. Never mind.' She stopped and looked at him. 'I am just so confused, Charles. I've never been in this situation before.'

'You mean, having an affair with someone married?'

'Well, no, I haven't done that, I agree. I had no idea how complicated it was...all the times you can phone, times you can't phone, meeting in places you won't meet anyone you know...I don't know how people manage.'

'They do. Always have.'

She caught the additional meaning in his words and grinned at him ruefully. 'Of course. You know all about it, Charles.'

'Not all. A little. Maybe I should give you a few tips.'

Frances laughed out loud. They put their arms around each other and kissed.

'It's not just that that's complicated,' Frances giggled. 'He also seems to be jealous of you.'

'I suppose that's flattering.'

'Maybe. But it means I daren't even talk about you. And then I start feeling guilty towards you – though God knows I have no need to. And then...God, I don't know...' She gestured at herself pitifully. 'And see the result – one totally mixed-up mess.'

They looked into each other's eyes in the growing dusk. Each saw pain, and confusion, and resignation, and a spark of humour.

'Frances,' Charles asked gently, 'is he the real thing?'

'David?'

'Yes.'

She looked away. 'I don't know. Just don't know. When it started, it was just so...unexpected. I was carried along. Yes, it was wonderful, but sort of unreal. Then I started to feel confused. Now...I don't know. So much of the relationship is intrigue, the times we spend together are so rushed...we don't seem to be together for long enough to judge whether it's actually working or not.'

'A lot of affairs survive for a very long time on that sort of excitement.'

'Maybe. I'm not sure that my nerves are up to it.'

It was odd talking to Frances about her having an affair. He felt very close to her. The fact that there was another man she slept with did not seem relevant. It was something that he could appreciate intellectually, but not imaginatively. It did not make any difference to the warmth there was between them.

'Perhaps,' he suggested sagely, 'you should employ me as a consultant on how to conduct an illicit affair...'

'Why, Charles? What's your success-rate like?'

'Abysmal,' he confessed.

And Frances laughed again, a clear relaxed laugh.

As the meal progressed, they both knew what was going to happen, but it was over coffee and Armagnac that Charles actually put it into words.

'I want you, Frances.'

'I know. I want you too, Charles.'

'I wouldn't recommend my digs. They are guarded by something that Hercules ought to have mopped up as one of his labours.'

'Ah. So...?'

'They don't appear to be overbooked here. I'll go and see.' Charles rose from the table. 'What name shall I say – Mr and Mrs Smith?'

'You may joke, Charles, but I feel as if I'm doing something utterly criminal.'

'Why? We are married.'

'I know,' said Frances. And it was not said in a tone of unqualified approval.

It was good. They needed each other, they knew each other, they wanted each other, and it was good.

Nothing was solved. Nothing was sorted out. Nothing was said about anything relevant, no plans, no intentions for the future, no discussion of what would happen to Frances and David, no demands that Charles would give up other women, nothing.

Nothing but their pleasure in being together at that moment.

Frances had to leave at five to make it back to town for a day's head-mistressing. A night-porter (the adolescent from the bar the night before) was roused to let her out.

It was cold out on the gravel of the car park. Both felt tired and a little shocked by what had happened.

They stood by the yellow Renault. Frances' face looked drained as Charles kissed her, this time without passion.

'We'll see each other again,' he murmured, as usual supplying no place, no date.

'Yes.'

She sighed deeply and got into the car. She wound down the window and said to him without resentment, just as a statement of fact, 'Thank you, Charles Paris. I think you've just ruined my life again.'

And she drove back to London.

# *Chapter Sixteen*

'OF COURSE,' GRUMBLED Mimi, 'I've had gentlemen stay out all night before. Some been drunk, some been philandering. I know all about it. They tell Mimi.'

She paused, waiting perhaps for Charles to pour out his confession. If so, she waited in vain.

'Because they know Mimi doesn't pass judgement. I accept human beings for what they are, warts and all. A lot of my gentlemen've brought back women here, knowing they're safe, knowing Mimi'll understand.'

It was half-past ten and Charles had just got back. He had returned to bed at the Rugland Spa Hotel and woken again at nine, feeling more peaceful than for some weeks.

Under Mimi's relentless barrage, he would normally have gone straight out again. But he had given Gerald the number there and had a slight hope of hearing from the solicitor before eleven.

'I suppose you'll be wanting breakfast now.' Mimi gathered her green candlewick about her, preparatory to rising. 'Most of my gentlemen want a really big breakfast after the sort of night you've just had.'

'No, thank you.'

'Oh, they do. I remember when one of my gentlemen was having an affair with the hairdresser in Raleigh Street…Big secret it was, but he told Mimi, because he knew I'd be discreet. Anyway, he'd be out all night and come in so hungry you'd –'

'No, really, thanks. I had a very good breakfast at the Rugland Spa Hotel.'

'Rugland Spa Hotel,' Mimi repeated, and Charles cursed himself for giving her even the smallest solid fact. He knew it would be filed away and provide anecdote-fodder to which some other poor gentleman would be subjected.

'I've heard the Rugland Spa Hotel breakfasts are very stingy.'

'No, it was fine.'

'Because it's a matter of moments for me to rustle up some scrambled eggs for you.'

'No. Really.'

'I mean, there's nothing like home cooking.' She made it sound like an accusation.

'No.'

She subsided back into her folds of candlewick, and looked at Charles with ill-disguised disapproval. 'I'm surprised you haven't gone off to rehearsal yet.'

'Not called till later.' He didn't want to go into all the circumstances which had caused *Shove It*'s rehearsal schedule to be suspended. Though Mimi probably knew anyway. 'And also I'm vaguely expecting a phone call.'

'Oh.' Mimi digested this information for a moment, and then said casually, 'Someone did ring for you just before you come in.'

'Why on earth didn't you tell me?'

'I told him you was out on the razzle,' she continued, ignoring his question.

'Who was it?'

'Somebody Venables.'

Mimi said no, she didn't mind him using her phone, but it was clear that her sitting there eavesdropping was part of the deal. Still, if Gerald had an appointment at eleven, there wasn't time to go anywhere else.

'Oh, morning, Charles,' said the solicitor when he got through. 'Gather you've been being a naughty boy again.'

'Ha. Ha.'

'Another nice little actress? Don't worry, I won't tell Frances – though I suppose we don't have to worry about that any more.'

Charles did not wish to pursue the ironies of that particular line of conversation and asked brusquely, 'Did you get anything on Schlenter?'

'A bit. Nothing very criminal. Just basic background.'

'I'd be glad to hear it. There might be something.'

'Okay then. Here's a quick history: Schlenter and Schlenter – two brothers, I think – started as ordinary estate agents in the sixties, North London… Highbury, Islington, that area. Did very well in the property boom of the late sixties, early seventies. Just residential then – you know, that was an area where a lot of the old terraces were being gentrified – old tenants died off, plenty of grants available to tart up the properties – there was a killing to be made and Schlenter and Schlenter were right in the middle of it. If you're looking for anything criminal, that's the time you should be concentrating on.'

'What do you mean?'

'It was the hey-day of the "winkler". A lot of the property companies had them, to winkle out sitting tenants in premises they had bought.'

'How did it work?'

'Variety of ways. Little old lady sitting in her little flat, feeling secure – smooth young man from estate agent comes round with cheque-book, offers her something to get out. Not much, but probably more money than most of the little old ladies had ever seen, so a few accepted. Those who didn't remained sitting in their little flats, feeling a little less secure. Next time maybe the smooth young man has a big growling Alsatian with him when he comes round. Or builders arrive saying the garden wall's not safe, needs replacing. They knock it down, cover the debris with a tatty tarpaulin and disappear for a few months. Or pipes get broken, or essential repairs don't get done.

Usually the little old ladies reach some sort of breaking point and get out.'

'Leaving a property with vacant possession?'

'Exactly. Worth a great deal more money.'

'And the Schlenters were right into all that?'

Gerald Venables' professional caution stepped in. 'No, I didn't say that. All I said was that a lot of that sort of thing went on in the area where Schlenter and Schlenter had their operation.'

'Okay.'

'And it's not the sort of allegation to flash around carelessly. They are now extremely respectable and quick on the draw with writs.'

'I will be very circumspect. How did they become so respectable?'

'That started round 1970. They were coining it from the residential property and starting to buy up other local estate agents...Ringling and Sons, Spielberg, Pugh and Fosco, Dutters...and a few more. Then they incorporated the lot into Schlenter Estates and started to diversify into bigger projects...you know, hotels, town centre developments, that sort of scale.'

'Any evidence of corruption?'

'Oh, I'm sure all the usual things went on. A few local councillors suddenly might appear with new cars, the odd inconvenient building might burn down, small stores might find they were having difficulty getting their deliveries through...But all very discreet, nothing you could ever make stick. Just normal business practice, if you like.'

'Where were their town centre developments?'

'All over. Good few in Wales, traditionally the centre of local council corruption. But they weren't just operating in England. Expanding abroad during those boom years...Africa, Australia, Hong Kong, even further afield. God,' said Gerald with wistful respect, 'they must have made a lot of money.'

'Then what happened?'

'Well, the property boom really peaked in '72. Then whatever you did made money. But the crash came, inevitably. '74, '75 were probably the worst. A lot of people got their fingers burned. A lot of property companies went out of business. Schlenter Estates were particularly vulnerable. They'd expanded so quickly, they'd got all these developments stretched all over the world, and suddenly there wasn't any money to be made in property.'

'But they didn't fold. They're still around.'

'Yes. But they very nearly went under. Round 1975 I think both of the original Schlenters died, and it looked like the end. But then they got taken over.'

'By Fowler Rose Stillman?'

'Ye-es, but not directly. They were actually absorbed by Clarton Investments, which is a subsidiary of FRS.'

'Oh, I see. But Fowler Rose Stillman is the top of the pyramid?'

'By no means. Everything, it seems, is owned by someone else. The average member of the public would have a fit if it was actually spelled out to them how few companies own almost everything in this country. No, Fowler Rose

Stillman was taken over a couple of years back by Polycopius...'

'The hotel chain?'

'Hotels, television, record companies, films, you name it. Anyway, Polycopius merged eighteen months ago with Carker Glyde Securities.'

'So Schlenter Estates are actually owned by Carker Glyde?'

'Yes. Or were at the end of trading on Friday. And you can't get more respectable than that. Long established in the City, high international reputation, half the House of Lords on their Board...'

'Really? Like who?'

'What, you want their names?' asked Gerald in bewilderment.

'If you've got them.'

'Just a sec. I've got their annual report somewhere. Ah, here we are. And you want me to read out the list of directors?'

'Please.'

Charles could visualize his friend shrugging as he began to read. But the actor felt insanely confident, and when the name came up, he asked Gerald to stop and repeat it.

'Lord Kitestone.'

'Thank you. And you say the take-over was eighteen months ago?'

'Give or take a month.'

'Thank you very much.'

'Charles, what are you on about?' But before he could be answered, Gerald was interrupted, apparently by someone entering his office. 'What, Polly? Oh yes. Great. Send him in. Listen, Charles, Bill Walsingham's arrived, so I'm going to have to find out the rest later.'

'That's fine. I've got what I wanted. I'll –'

'Bill, how are you? Great to see you! How was Australia? Just a sec. Talk later, Charles. Okay?'

'Fine. 'Bye, Gerald. And thank you.'


Inchbald Haulage Co. was a little way out of Rugland Spa on the London Road. The main gates opened on to a large yard, in which three yellow articulated lorries boasted their owner's name in red letters. The office was a low cedar-clad one-storey building with a lot of windows. The secretary's room was animated with displays of plastic flowers. Everything was neat and tidy, reflecting a well-run and probably profitable business, but it was not the setting in which one expected to find a member of Blake's Club.

'My name's Charles Paris. To see Mr Inchbald. I rang earlier.'

'Yes, of course. Mr Inchbald, Mr Paris has arrived,' she breathed into the intercom.

'Send him in!'

Herbie Inchbald's office was as neat and prosperous as the rest of the outfit. Its furniture was low and Scandinavian. On the walls fluorescent paintings on black velvet and framed cars made of clock-parts once again made Charles wonder about the Councillor's artistic standards.

'Come in, Mr Paris. Sit down. Would you care for a coffee?'

'No, thank you.' Charles thought the confrontation might become ugly, and didn't want to start it on too cosy a level.

'When you rang, you said it was something about Tony Wensleigh's death.'

'Yes.'

'Terrible tragedy, that.'

'It was. But it's just one in a sequence of things that have been going wrong at the Regent.'

'What, you mean Gordon Tremlett's accident? Oh, I wouldn't call that a sequence.'

'Not just that. I mean, the way the artistic standards had been slipping.'

'Did you really think they were?' The little man ran his fingers through his mane of hair as he reflected on this idea. 'Well, maybe Tony was getting a bit past it. Perhaps, though it's an awful way for it to happen, having to bring in a new man may be the saving of the the-ettah.'

'I wonder whether the theatre *can* still be saved.'

Herbie Inchbald looked very affronted. 'What on earth do you mean?'

Charles stared straight at him. 'It's my belief that someone very closely connected with the theatre has actually been trying to sabotage it, to ensure that it's in such a bad state when the Maugham Cross development is next discussed that nobody will be able to argue persuasively enough to save it.'

'That's a rather extreme allegation, Mr Paris.'

Charles shrugged. 'Maybe, but I think it is the case. I think Tony knew too, and I think it was fighting against the pressure of that sabotage that drove him to suicide.'

'But who would possibly want the theatre to close?'

'Schlenter Estates would, for a start.'

'Yes, obviously, but –'

'I wouldn't think it would be long before they come in with another offer for the whole Maugham Cross site.'

Herbie Inchbald coloured. 'Well, er...'

'You mean they already have?'

He nodded. 'Just heard this morning. Bigger offer, quite a bit bigger.' He looked miserable.

'Quick off the mark. They're shrewd operators. And what kind of luck do you think you'll have this time persuading the Council that the Regent is a hyper-efficient bastion of culture that must be preserved at all costs? What have we had in the last three weeks – disastrous production of a disastrous play, public demonstration about the next production, one near-fatal accident and the suicide of the Artistic Director under something of a cloud over his handling of the theatre's funds? What do you reckon your chances are this time, Mr Inchbald?'

The head sagged forward. 'Low,' came the reply. 'Very low.'

'Okay, it could just he a sequence of bad luck. I think there's more to it. I think it's been organized.'

'But who by?' The Councillor now looked shifty, cornered.

'Ultimately by Schlenter Estates, but I think a few other people have been used on the way. People who are not above bribery.'

The Councillor bridled. 'If that remark's aimed to me, I'd advise you to withdraw it. I have never accepted a bribe in my life. Schlenter tried it on with me, I don't deny it. They made some very attractive offers to me – cars, holiday homes, you name it. But I am proud to say I turned down every one of them. I'm not the kind of man to be bought that way.'

'No. I agree. Not that way.'

'I resent your tone, Mr Paris.'

'You wouldn't be bought by a direct offer of a gift, nor by any material inducement. No, somebody who wanted to buy you would have to appeal to your snobbery.'

Herbie Inchbald rose from his seat to his full height, which wasn't very high. 'Get out of my office!'

'Not yet. I want to ask you about your friendship with Lord Kitestone.'

'What of it?'

'You've seen a lot of him in the last few years.'

'So what? Who the hell do you think you are – asking me about my friendships? Lord Kitestone has been a friend since I asked him to be Patron of the Regent. We hit it off very well together, as it happens.'

'And you were great friends right from the start, right from when you asked him to be Patron?'

'Well, no, we took a bit of time to get to know each other. And he was very tied up at the time, problems with the estate and that, thought he was going to have to sell up, in fact. But in the last year or so, we've seen a lot more of each other, built up a great deal of mutual respect...'

'In the last eighteen months?'

'Yes.'

'So much so that he's allowed you to use his holiday home in Corsica.'

This again caught the Councillor on the raw. 'Don't try it, Mr Paris. I paid him the rent for the villa, and I can prove it.'

'I know. Are you aware who owns Schlenter Estates, Mr Inchbald?'

'I assumed they were independent. Well, perhaps they're part of some conglomerate...I don't know.' It was hard to tell whether this hesitant answer was the truth, or whether the Councillor was bluffing.

'Let me outline a little story for you, Mr Inchbald. Fiction, of course, but maybe you'll find something relevant in it. Let's say we have a peer of the realm with a large estate to maintain and he's feeling the pinch...His income just isn't big enough to cope with it all. True, he's got a few directorships which bring in a bit of loot for no effort, but it's not sufficient money. And then let's say one of the companies of which he's director takes over, through a fairly lengthy chain of ownership, a property company. Normally, it wouldn't interest him much, but in this case he does become involved. Someone in the property company comes to him with a proposal...a new mortgage, a loan maybe, something anyway that will let him off the hook financially...'

'Sounds good, says the noble lord, adding cautiously, is there anything I have to do in return? Yes, the property company replies soothingly, but it's something very small. All we want you to do is to get chummy with a local councillor in your area and –'

'I've heard enough of this!' snapped Herbie Inchbald. 'It's slander and I will see to it that –'

'As I said,' Charles overrode him, 'it's only a story. To make it even begin to be slanderous, you'd have to fill in some of the names. Call the peer of the realm Lord Kitestone, for example...Call the company of which he's a director Carker Glyde Securities...Call the property company they took over eighteen months ago Schlenter Estates...Call the Councillor –'

'Stop.' Herbie Inchbald's face was ashen. 'Is he really a director of the company that owns Schlenter?'

'Yes. You can check it. What's that very useful book called – "Who Owns Who"?'

'Oh, my God.' This time the Councillor did not appear to be acting. His shock at the revelation was quite genuine.

'So, to complete my little story, all I need to know is what the noble lord was delegated to get from the Councillor. What was the little favour? I think I know what the Councillor got in return.'

Inchbald picked himself up and returned aggressively to the fray. 'You're on a hiding to nothing, Paris. I've never accepted a bribe from anyone, and certainly not from Lord Kitestone. You can check my bank accounts, search my house if you like. You won't find anything.'

'I'm not talking about anything as crude as money. As I said, it had to be something that appealed to your snobbery, something that the noble lord could give at no cost to himself, but something that you could not get from any other source.'

'I don't follow you.'

'No? I am right, am I not, in saying that Lord Kitestone put you up for Blake's Club?'

'Yes, but...' The Councillor looked very angry again. 'That was just a friendly gesture on his part, because we got on so well. Good God, can't friends do each other favours nowadays without everyone getting suspicious?'

'Of course they can. And what favour did you do him in return?'

'Nothing. Well, I mean, hardly anything. He just gave me some advice and I took it. Wasn't even a favour to him, as it happened. Favour to someone else, another example of Willie's generosity. Turned out to be a favour to me too, as things worked out.'

'But, nonetheless, he didn't put you up for the club until you'd agreed to accept his advice?'

'God, you make it sound so cold-blooded. It was just two friends helping each other out, that's all.'

'You scratch my back...'

'Exactly...'

'Okay, I know how Lord Kitestone scratched your back. How did you scratch his?'

'It was nothing. It was just...'

And Herbie Inchbald told him.

As he finished, he smiled weakly and said, 'And if you can find any corruption in that, good luck to you. It's been a positive benefit to the theatre, and without Lord Kitestone it wouldn't have happened. I think you're barking up the wrong tree with all your talk of sabotage, Mr Paris. You certainly are if you're trying to point the finger at me.' Herbie Inchbald sat down and tried to regain some composure behind his desk. 'I am a devoted supporter of the Regent Theatre. And so is Willie Kitestone.'

Charles gave the Councillor the benefit of the doubt and believed his first assertion.

But not the second.

## *Chapter Seventeen*

CHARLES' MIND WAS now working well. He hadn't slept much the night before, but the tiredness heightened his efficiency rather than diminished it. He was on a high, feeling good, and his mind responded, making sudden new connections in the case.

After his interview with Herbie Inchbald he returned to Mimi's and, ignoring her curiosity as to what he was doing there at that time of day, went straight up to his bedroom. There he got out the file Martha Wensleigh had given him and took another look at its contents.

The brainwave came quickly. He looked at his watch. Quarter to one. Might just make it. Clutching some of the papers in his hand, he ran downstairs to the telephone and, oblivious of Mimi's eavesdropping, dialled.

'Gerald.'

'Charles? Look, this is rather inconvenient. I said –'

'I know. You're just about to go out for a long, good lunch. Where?'

'Langan's, as it happens.'

'Of course. Well, you can spare me two minutes. Listen, is Bill still with you?'

'Right beside me.'

'Put him on. I want a word.'

'Very well, but...'

'Hello?'

'Bill, hi. This is Charles Paris.'

'Oh. Good to hear you. What can I –'

'I want to pick your brains.'

'You're welcome to anything you can find there.'

'Right. You've just come back from Australia, where you've been directing...'

'For the last five years, yeah.'

'So you know the theatrical scene out there pretty well?'

'Such as it is. Yes, I guess I do.'

'Right.' Charles consulted the sheets in his hand. 'Do you know the Theatre Royal, Adelaide?'

'Sure. Nice old building.'

'And the Artistic Director, Ralph Johnson.'

'Ralph who?'

'Johnson.'

'Never heard of him.'

'This'd be back in...'

'Before my time. I'd have thought I'd have heard the name, though.'

'Okay. Try another. The Dominion, Perth?'

'Know it well.'

'Artistic Director, Rich Coleman?'

'Never heard of him. Jed Spencer had the job all the time I was out there.'

'What about the Hippodrome, Melbourne?'

'Know that too.'

'And the Artistic Director there in '79 was...?'

'Bruce Wade.'

'Not Greg Avon?'

'Never heard the name. What is this – a *Mastermind* special subject on the theatres of Australia?'

'No. I will explain. I haven't got time at the moment. There's only one more. Do you know the Kelly Theatre in Sydney?'

'Should do.'

'And you're going to tell me the Artistic Director there last year was not Jim Vasilis.'

'That one, Charles, I can confirm without a shadow of a doubt. For the last five years *I* have been Artistic Director of the Kelly Theatre in Sydney. That's the job I've just finished.'

Charles sighed with relief. 'Thank you very much, Bill.'

'No problem. I wish I knew what the hell it was about.'

'One day, Bill, over a very long and very drunken lunch, I will tell you.'

'I look forward to that, Charles.'

'Could you put me back to Gerald, just for a sec?'

'Okay.'

'Gerald, listen, have you got a copy of *The British Theatre Directory* there?' The solicitor grunted assent. 'Could you look up the Pavilion Theatre, Darlington for me?'

'Okay just a sec. I wish you'd explain, Charles.'

'If I did it might make you late for your lunch.'

'Oh, that's true. Some other time then. Right...the Pavilion, you said. It's owned by...ah, the site was bought up quite recently.'

'By whom, Gerald?'

'Schlenter Estates. Is that significant?'

'Yes, Gerald. It is.'

So all the references were quite meaningless. The Australian ones were forged, and the Darlington one presumably dictated by Schlenter Estates. No, more likely it was genuine. After all, that one could be checked easily, and Donald Mason must have spent some time finding out about theatre administration. Six months as Assistant Front of House Manager at Darlington would have given enough background to someone with a genuine flair for organization. And Schlenter had presumably arranged for him to take the job.

They had also assumed, correctly, that the average provincial rep theatre would know nothing about the Australian scene, and be too mean to ring up the other side of the world to check the references.

Charles now knew what Donald Mason's career hadn't been and, his memory working well, thought he might be able to find out what it *had* been.

The old lady was in her usual niche in the pub behind the theatre and accepted another bottle of Guinness gratefully.

'I *do* know you,' she said. 'Seen you before, you know.'

'In here. Just the once.'

'That's right,' she said, raising his hopes that she would prove to be a reliable witness. 'Your name's Lionel,' she continued, dashing them.

'Charles.'

'That's right, Charles.' She nodded her head, which seemed loose on her shoulders. 'Charles, I knew another Charles once. Had this nasty habit in the park. He used to –'

Charles didn't want to get too involved in irrelevant reminiscence, so he nudged the conversation on by asking, 'Was this in Islington?'

'Round the Angel, yes.'

'Where you used to live?'

'That's right, yes. Don't live there no more. Had this nice little flat. Now I live with my daughter. She wouldn't let me go to the Old People's, not my daughter. She's got this bird, my daughter has. Canary, it is. I don't care for canaries…'

Once again Charles had to stop the conversation from straying too far off course.

'Your flat was in Blenley Terrace, wasn't it?' he asked, memory working overtime.

'Blenley Terrace, that's right.' Again she started the unnerving nodding. 'Nice place it was, round there. Nice people, like a village. Not now. All been tarted up now.'

'Yes. Listen, I want you to try and remember something.'

'You come to the right person.' She stopped nodding and fixed her faded eyes on him seriously. 'I got one of them photographic memories. Never forget a face. Nor a name, Lionel.'

'Charles.'

'That's right. Charles.'

'Listen, when I last came in here, week or so ago, someone else came in, someone you said you recognized from Islington.'

She looked at him blankly. Her mouth sagged. Charles feared he had hoped for too much. Her mind had really gone.

'Man about thirty. Tall, pin-striped suit. Blond hair.' Something in this description struck a chord in her memory, because her expression changed suddenly. 'Oh, I remember *him*,' she spat out venomously. 'He was why I left my flat.'

'What do you mean?'

'He said he come from the estate agents. Offered me money to move out. But I didn't want to. I liked it there. All my friends there. Didn't care how much money, I told him, I didn't want to move. He kept coming back and I kept saying no. Then he started coming strange times, very late at night, six in the morning. But I still said no.

'Then I didn't see him no more, but...things started happening.'

'What sort of things?' Charles asked softly.

'Be knocking on my door in the middle of the night. Then someone bunged a brick through my window. Plumbing started going funny. Bath overflowed and soaked the people downstairs. I never left it on, I know, but they got in the social worker. And then there was the gas.'

'Gas?'

'Yes. Gas was left on on all my rings. Nearly a big explosion. They said I wasn't safe living on my own. But I ask you, would I leave all of them on? Anyone could leave one on by mistake, but not all of them.' She sniffed. 'Anyway, the social worker got on to my daughter and she come, and the social worker said I couldn't manage alone, and I'd have to go to the Old People's. And my daughter, bless her, says no, and brought me up here.'

'So you never went back to the flat?'

'No.'

'And you think the man you saw in here was behind it?'

'Bloody sure. I remember, the estate agents was called Spielberg, Pugh and Fosco. And his name was Mr Mason.'

Charles bought the old lady another Guinness. She had earned it.

As he stood at the bar, he pieced it together. So Donald Mason had started out as a 'winkler' for one of the estate agents the Schlenters took over. Then he probably had gone to Australia as the property company expanded in the early 1970s. Back to England, brief spell in Darlington to learn the new business, then, with Lord Kitestone leaning discreetly on Herbie Inchbald, he got the Rugland Spa job. Winkling again.

Just the same, but on a larger scale. Instead of getting rid of one old lady to clear a house, his job was to get rid of a theatre to clear a town centre site for development.

He was going to have to go and talk to Donald Mason.

He ordered himself a large Bell's as a bracer.

## *Chapter Eighteen*

LESLIE BLATT WAS coming out of the administrative office as Charles reached the top of the stairs. The elderly playwright looked extremely pleased with himself.

'Hello, Charles,' be said, rubbing his hands together. 'We're going to be working together.'

'What do you mean?'

'Donald's just asked me and I've said yes. It's a few years since I've done it, but I'm sure I'll manage. It's a real challenge.'

'What are you talking about?'

'*Shove It*. Donald's just asked me to take over as director.'

'What!'

'Well, don't sound like that. I used to direct, you know. Still got a lot of ideas, and I've been following most of the rehearsals. I'd really like to get my hands on a play like this.'

Not just on the play, either. Charles visualized the chaos that would be caused among the naked actresses by Leslie Blatt's wandering hands as he 'directed' them.

'Well, aren't you going to congratulate me, Charles?'

'What? Oh yes. Congratulations.'

'We're hoping to get ready for an opening on Friday. Only two days late.'

'I see.'

'Rehearsal ten sharp tomorrow morning. See you then.' The old goat pranced downstairs, chuckling to himself.

Charles knocked on the office door, and was bidden to enter.

Donald Mason sat behind his desk, every bit the smart executive in another pin-striped suit. Too smart, really, for the theatre. Charles felt he should have smelt a rat earlier. But no, he – presumably like everyone else – had been just relieved to see someone who appeared to be efficient in the role of General Manager.

'Charles. What can I do for you?'

'I just met Leslie. Gather he's going to take over directing *Shove It*.'

'That's right. Seems ideal. Difficult to get in someone from outside at this stage, and at least he's been following the production.'

'He'd follow anything where he knew women were going to take their clothes off.'

Donald Mason looked up sharply, surprised by Charles' change of tone. 'Have you been drinking?'

The actor shook his head. 'Not enough to affect my judgement.'

'Oh. Well, Leslie is going to be directing. I've made the decision.'

'Yes. I'm sure you have. Yet another in a skilfully composed sequence of wrong decisions.'

The General Manager was stung by this. 'What are you talking about?'

'I think it was almost a compliment, Donald. You've managed the whole thing very well. Constantly talking about the importance of right decisions and ensuring that the wrong ones are made. Constantly stressing the need for company loyalty and spreading divisive rumours behind people's backs. Constantly saying how much you want the Regent to survive and all the time undermining it.'

'Are you going to explain what you're on about, or do I have to listen to more of this abusive rhetoric?'

'I'll explain.' Charles took a deep breath. 'I've blown your cover, Donald.'

'What does that mean?'

'I know that all the references you produced to get this job were forgeries. I know that you never worked in the theatre in Australia. I know that you started working for an estate agency called Spielberg, Pugh and Fosco and I reckon that you're still in the pay of Schlenter Estates!'

There was a silence. Charles tensed. He didn't know what to expect after his outburst, but was ready for some form of physical assault.

To his amazement, he heard Donald Mason laughing. 'Very good, Charles, very good. I heard you had a bit of a reputation as a detective, and I'm most impressed by this demonstration of your skill.'

With the wind momentarily taken out of his sails, Charles blustered. 'Do you deny that you were put into this job to bring the theatre to its knees?'

'No, I don't.'

'Pretty easy, too, wasn't it? You could run circles round Tony Wensleigh. So vague he was, so abstracted, so trusting…Always out at a rehearsal, so that you could do what you liked here. Spread rumours about his inefficiency, libel him – always with an expression of deep regret that you had to do it.

'The sabotage went deep. The choice of plays…you contrived that very well. You knew Herbie was totally ignorant about art, and you knew Leslie would agree with anything so long as his dire little thriller was included. So you lumbered Tony with this awful programme, and then had the nerve to tell everyone that he had chosen them, and that his judgement was going.'

Donald Mason shrugged. 'Yes,' he said with an air of indifference.

'You're not making any attempt to deny it.'

'Why should I? It's all true.'

'But…' Charles found himself blustering again. It was like trying to get satisfaction out of punching a sponge. 'I mean, the way you played us all along, making us believe you were the long-suffering one, constantly clearing up after Tony. Little calculated touches of humanity – like when you didn't sack me, like when you offered me the part in *Shove It*..'

Donald smiled with something approaching insolence. 'Yes. Of course that was not just magnanimity.'

'What do you mean?'

'I thought keeping a piss-artist like you around in the company was another good method of disruption.'

'Good God.' Charles was almost lost for words. He found himself getting angry. This was not at all how he had intended the interview to turn out. 'So that's why you went against Tony's advice and kept me on.'

'Oh I didn't go against Tony's advice. He wanted to give you a second chance.'

'But you said...'

'Yes. And you believed me. I've often been told that one of my great strengths is my plausibility.'

'But...but how can you be so bloody cool about it all?'

'Why shouldn't I be cool? I was put into this job to see that the theatre closed within a year, and I reckon I've pretty well achieved that.'

'But what's going to happen when I expose you?'

'Expose what? Have you proof of any crime that I've committed?'

'Well...That accident to Gordon Tremlett – I bet you were behind that.'

'Proof I said, Charles, proof. Even if I did fix it – and I'm not saying I did, in case you have some tape recorder hidden away – how could you prove it?'

'Well...' Charles felt momentarily lost. 'What about Tony? You hounded him so much, confused him, accused him...you drove him to kill himself.'

The General Manager smiled again, infuriatingly. 'That I think you'd find even more difficult to prove, Charles.'

The actor gaped.

'You see, it's so easy to fool people. They set themselves up. They want to be conned. I mean, someone like Tony was just a sitting target. So trusting, as you said. So incapable of fighting back, assuming he could ever identify his enemy. Ultimately so stupid.'

'But there have been crimes committed!' Charles insisted, rising involuntarily from his chair with fists clenched.

Donald gave him a cool appraisal. 'If you were to hit me, that would be a crime. And I would see that you were charged with it.'

Charles subsided, trying to calm himself. Slow down, slow down, stick to the one crime he could prove. 'What about those forged references? Those are real enough. They're proof against you.'

'Okay.' The General Manager still refused to be ruffled. 'So what would that be – a charge of False Pretences, maybe? Might get a few months for that I suppose.

'Yes,' said Charles, with a hardly adequate feeling of minor triumph.

'If, of course, you could find anyone to charge me...'

'What?'

'Listen. As you have so cleverly worked out, I was infiltrated here to put this theatre out of business. I think I've done pretty well. With this new offer coming in from Schlenter, with *Shove It* causing public demonstrations, with the Artistic Director committing suicide under a cloud, the whole set-up looks pretty shaky. Not a great deal of faith around Rugland Spa in the Regent's management. Do you think that that faith would be increased by the revelation that that very management appointed as their General Manager someone with forged references?'

Slowly Charles let this sink in, and felt the full crushing power of its logic. The one charge that could be proven against Donald Mason would never be brought.

# Chapter Nineteen

THE FRUSTRATION WAS total. It was even more frustrating than when he couldn't make sense of the case. Now he could, now he had arrived at the truth, only to find that truth brought no resolution. It was like chatting up an apparently avid girl all evening only to have her favours abruptly denied.

Charles fumed, because he knew Donald was right. He had been planted to bring down the theatre and the revelation of the subterfuge would only hasten its collapse. If there were someone strong around to handle the exposure it might work, but there wasn't. Tony had found the pressure too much and was no longer available. And Councillor Inchbald wasn't going to publicize the way he had been manipulated by his 'friend', Lord Kitestone.

If only there were something else, some actual crime that could be proved against Donald Mason. He had as good as admitted to engineering Gordon Tremlett's accident, but in the full confidence that no proof could ever be produced. Maybe he had also been responsible for the stabbing Charles had so narrowly escaped. It didn't seem in character, too rash an action for someone who planned so cold-bloodedly, but it was possible Donald had arranged it as another random act of sabotage, another incident to get the anti-theatre councillors baying for enquiries.

But, even if that had been the case, evidence of Donald's implication remained as elusive for the stabbing as for the hanging.

Charles' fury was increased by the General Manager's arrogant confidence. He had taken the job knowing that it would end in collapse and presumably had some fatly-paid post lined up with Schlenter Estates for when he finally left it. And he had done what was required very efficiently, without a moment's hesitation on moral grounds. Driving Tony Wensleigh to suicide was clearly a feat he regarded as a major professional coup, not an action affecting the life of a fellow human being.

Tony, Donald had said, had been stupid. Stupid for showing normal human qualities like trust, stupid for giving people the benefit of the doubt, stupid for letting the pressure get to him.

No doubt Donald would apply the same adjective to Charles. Everyone in the world was stupid to Donald, because he knew he could run circles round any of them. A person with no moral sense at all is capable of much greater efficiency than those trammelled by doubt and benevolence.

And Charles could see no way of unsettling Donald Mason's evil complacency.

He stumped round the now-hateful streets of Rugland Spa, waiting for the pubs to open.

On the dot of five-thirty he went into the one behind the theatre. He had vague thoughts of seeing the old lady again, asking her more about the young winkler who had made her life a misery. He didn't know what he hoped to find out. It was all so long ago. To prove criminality at such a distance and after so long would be virtually impossible.

Anyway, the old lady hadn't appeared, so the idea was academic. Charles settled down to an evening of heavy drinking which might, in time, induce oblivion. He didn't drink beer; he went straight on to the Bell's.

So the wheel of his Rugland Spa drinking had come full circle. It had started badly, even to the extent of his being hopelessly drunk on stage; then he had reformed; and here he was deliberately going back to the bad ways.

Then came the unwelcome thought of what had started him drinking the first time. Frances. Frances and her announcement of her new lover. He was still shocked by how much that had affected him.

But the previous night he had seen her, had spent with her. The confrontations of the day had pushed that to the back of his mind. But it had been good. They had so much together. He couldn't just let her slip out of his life.

In his increasingly maudlin state he made various resolutions. He must get Frances back. David he dismissed as an irrelevancy. Surely, if he really asked her to, Frances would come back to him, permanently. Of course, he'd have to reform, he knew that. Moderate the drinking, though that wasn't what really annoyed Frances; she had always been pretty tolerant about that. No, it was other women. She really didn't like him being unfaithful. And he had always found it hard to resist the appeal of a young actress. That had been the root of the trouble, that and the long separations caused by his work.

But he was fifty-five now and his prospects with young actresses waned further with each passing day. No more, he decided virtuously. Concentrate on Frances. Concentrate on getting Frances back. She was the only woman who really mattered to him, she was the only one who could cope with his low moods. He needed her.

'Charles Paris, isn't it?'

A Welsh voice broke into his earnest resolutions.

'Yes.' He looked up into Frank Walby's bibulous baby face 'Hello. Can I get you a drink?'

He spoke with enthusiasm. Having taken the decision to get drunk, he knew it would be more pleasant to have a companion in his excesses, and also knew that Frank Walby was probably the most suitable candidate for that role in all of Rugland Spa.

The journalist accepted the offer with equal enthusiasm, specifying 'a pint of Old and Filthy – they'll know what you mean'.

Charles got himself another large Bell's and the two sat down and toasted each other.

Frank Walby emitted a long, lugubrious sigh. 'Who was it who described his life as a long disease?'

'Alexander Pope, I think.'

The journalist nodded. 'Sounds right. And somebody else said it was incurable.'

'That, I happen to know, was Abraham Cowley.'

Frank Walby mimed clapping. 'Oh, go to the top of the class, that boy. Very good.'

'I seem to have a knack of remembering depressing quotations.'

'Oh, you should do a book of them I can see it – *The Oxford Book of Depressing Quotations*, edited by Charles Paris. "Ideal bedside reading for all would-be suicides." Sell like hot cakes, that would.'

Charles grinned. Maybe the evening wouldn't turn out so badly after all.

'You've heard you'll have to wait a bit to review *Shove It*?'

'Yes. Friday, isn't it?'

'Uhuh. Should be. Are you going to do another of your swingeing notices?'

'I'm not sure. I don't know that the last one really did the theatre much good. And, God knows, it needs all the help it can get at the moment.'

'Yes.' With his new knowledge of Donald Mason, Charles now realized that the appeal for Walby to judge the Regent's productions more rigidly was just another cynical device to weaken the theatre further. 'No, I think you should go back to your old cosy style.'

'You may be right. Will I like *Shove It*?'

'Well, don't let me prejudice you in any way, but I think you'll hate every minute of it.'

'Oh dear.' Walby groaned. 'I can imagine exactly what I'll write The bold decision to stage that controversial play, *Shove It*, was fully justified at the Regent Theatre last night. A splendid cast did more than justice to...' Pap, pap, pap.'

'But generous to an ailing institution.'

'Yes. And at least it won't get me any threatening letters.'

'Why? Did the last one?'

'Oh yes. Didn't I show you this?' He pulled a crumpled letter out of an equally crumpled jacket and handed it over.

Charles skimmed the contents. '...filthy abuse of my work...showing your total ignorance of the theatre...not the sort of thing I take lightly...would advise you to be careful walking round after dark...not the first time I've had to defend myself from bastards who attack my work...' He looked up. 'It's not signed.'

'No, but it's obvious who it comes from, isn't it?'

'Leslie Blatt?'

'Yes.' Walby chuckled. 'Out to murder me – and presumably anyone else who disparages his magnum opus.'

Charles stared. His mind was racing. 'He hasn't made any attack on you?'

'No,' Walby replied with a grin. 'I wait in fear and trembling.'

'Maybe you should,' said Charles slowly.

He pieced it together. Perhaps there were two parallel but unconnected sequences of crimes. The crimes against the theatre, perpetrated by Schlenter Estates' cuckoo in the nest. And crimes against individuals, perpetrated by a crazed failed writer.

First, the stabbing...Leslie Blatt had thought 'young Mr Smartypants' was in the cupboard. And Rick Harmer had constantly derided the quality of *The Message Is Murder*.

Then the hanging...Gordon Tremlett, in his unthinking way, had spoken to the author of his 'rubbishy old play'.

And Antony Wensleigh, in his letter to Leslie Blatt, had said what he thought of it in no uncertain terms. And Antony Wensleigh had died.

For the first time, Charles wondered whether it really had been suicide.

Frank Walby was looking at him, rather puzzled by his silence.

'Frank, total change of subject – Tony's death...'

'Yes. What about it?'

'You covered it for the press, didn't you?'

'Yes. Even made the nationals – just.'

'You think it was for real, don't you?'

'What do you mean?'

'That it really was suicide?'

'Oh, you want it to be a murder, do you?' The journalist chuckled. 'High drama that would be, wouldn't it? No, I'm sorry, Charles. It was obviously intentional. He left this note. The police showed it to me.'

'Who was it addressed to?'

'Nothing written on the envelope. Just an ordinary Regent Theatre one.'

'Can you remember the exact wording?'

'Don't know, but I wrote it down.'

The crumpled jacket yielded an equally crumpled shorthand notebook. Frank found the place and handed the book over.

The words Charles read he had seen before.

'SORRY ABOUT THE TOTAL COCK-UP OF EVERYTHING. NO EXCUSES. YOURS ABJECTLY, TONY.'

Charles rushed into the theatre. His mind had done a complete U-turn, but was picking up speed in its new direction.

He was no longer thinking of Tony's apparent suicide as the work of Leslie Blatt. His suspicion had returned firmly to Donald Mason.

The coincidence was too great. Tony wouldn't have couched his suicide note in exactly the same words as his apology of the rehearsal room booking mix-up, though to someone who had not seen the letter in its original context, it could well read that way. Donald Mason had recognized that ambivalence and its potential future value when he had pocketed the note. And forgotten that Charles Paris had witnessed his action.

Nella Lewis was in the Green Room, sorting through some *Shove It* props. She looked mournful, bereft of Laurie Tichbourne and knowing that she was pretty unlikely ever to see him again. But Charles had no time for chat and sympathy. He just waved and went on stage to the ladder to the gallery.

He tried to remember exactly what Tony Wensleigh had said on the evening he died. He had been manic, nearly hysterical, but certain points had emerged both in his conversation with Charles and in his phone-call to his wife.

One was that he reckoned he definitely had an enemy within the Regent Theatre set-up. Charles could now confidently identify that person as Donald Mason.

The second point was that, after a long period of confusion, Tony implied that he had at last made some breakthrough, perhaps found actual proof of his enemy's malpractices.

Third, he intended to confront his enemy. And, perhaps already suspicious of his opponent's ruthlessness after the accident to Gordon Tremlett, he wanted to have the gun with him when he made the confrontation.

Charles had rushed out of the prop store when Tony fired at him (a firing he now felt sure had been unintentional). Tony hadn't followed him, but had locked the back door and gone out at the front into the administrative office. Before the details of the suicide came out, Charles had assumed that the Artistic Director had gone to confront his General Manager.

Suppose, after all, that was what had happened. Tony had bearded Donald in his office and presented him with the evidence of his misdoings. An argument had developed, in the course of which Donald had got hold of the gun and shot his accuser. He then arranged the scene to look like suicide, put the note he had kept in the drawer, and went backstage.

He would have had plenty of time to do this before Charles arrived. And, while the actor had gone the long way, round the outside of the theatre, Donald could have cut through either the props store or the Wardrobe store. (In fact, Charles reasoned, if he had taken the latter course, he could almost guarantee not to be seen. It would have been towards the end of Act Two, when almost all of the stage staff were busy arranging the hanging of Colonel Fripp, and all of the rest of the cast were on stage.) Donald could then sit in the Green Room with a paper, which was how Charles found him when he broke the news of Tony's death, and give the impression he had been there for hours.

But what was the evidence that Tony had produced which so threatened Donald? Perhaps he had found out the Schlenter connection and intended to reveal it at the Extraordinary Board Meeting of the following evening. Though Donald was unworried by exposure after Tony was dead, an attack from the living Artistic Director might ruin his plans and build up sympathy for the Regent's plight.

Whatever it was, Charles felt convinced that the key to the secret lay in the props store.

He opened the door and switched on the light. The nearer bulb, which Tony Wensleigh's bullet had shattered, had not been replaced, but the far side of the room, which was the part Charles was interested in, was clearly illuminated. He moved across through the bizarre juxtaposition of halberds and croquet mallets, fridges and thrones, wooden lamp-posts and polystyrene boulders.

He remembered Tony Wensleigh shuffling together a pile of breastplates when Charles had disturbed him. Had he been hiding something?

Charles started cautiously sifting through the armour. The breastplates were just the top of the pile. Beneath was an assortment of small props – cigar boxes, biscuit tins, ice buckets, jewel cases.

It didn't take him long to find what he was looking for.

They were inside a treasure chest. It was crudely painted, like something out of a pirate cartoon, and presumably only got an airing when the right pantomime came up. A fairly safe hiding-place, unlikely to be investigated from one year's end to the next.

They were papers, most of them with Antony Wensleigh's signature. Some meant nothing, but one or two Charles could identify.

There was a letter to the costume hire company, cancelling the order for a Henry VIII ensemble.

There was a letter to the caretaker of the Drill Hall, confirming that the Regent Theatre wished to continue their booking.

There were cheques to settle accounts with wigmakers and scenery builders, cheques that never arrived, prompted reminders and lowered the theatre's public credibility.

There were charming letters to actors, which they never received and so added the Regent to the list of unhelpful theatres that didn't give a damn.

There was the whole history of the tarnishing of the public image of Antony Wensleigh and the theatre he so loved.

It must have been so simple. The prop store was directly next to the administrative office. Tony Wensleigh would rush in early, before rehearsal, or late, after rehearsal, and scribble off a few letters. Donald Mason, in the office all day, would have leisure to select which letters could be mislaid to best effect and slip them into his secret cache whenever he wanted to. Then he had only to play on the Artistic Director's natural abstraction and vagueness to convince him of his omissions, meanwhile maintaining a whispering campaign about his colleague's inefficiency and perhaps worse.

But Tony had discovered what was going on and intended to reveal all to the Board at their Extraordinary Meeting.

First, though, he had confronted his enemy.

Charles decided to do the same. The discovery of the papers made him so angry that, whatever the risk, he had to satisfy the anger by another confrontation with Donald Mason.

He braced himself behind the front door of the props store.

Then he swung it open.

As he suspected, it opened straight into the administrative office.

But there was nobody there to confront. The room was empty.


Back in the props store, he looked again at the papers and realized their worthlessness. They confirmed Donald Mason's position as saboteur at the Regent, but he had already confessed to that. And that was the crime he would never be charged with.

With regard to murder, Charles still had nothing. Nothing but a strong conviction.

The note was not enough. He had been alone when he witnessed Donald pocketing it. Maybe forensic tests could prove it had been written a few weeks earlier than it was supposed to have been, but Charles didn't reckon much on his chances of persuading the police to get to the point of forensic tests.

No, he was stymied again. Lots of suspicion – no proof.

He felt furious. He looked at his watch. Still not half-past six. Frank Walby would probably still be in the pub. Back to Plan A for the evening. Get hideously smashed.

He stood there for one last moment in the props store.

Vividly his mind played back his last encounter with Tony Wensleigh.

The man had straightened the pile of breastplates and...something else. A string or something. He had tucked a string behind the grandfather clock.

Charles moved towards it. He couldn't see anything.

He shifted the clock round and light spilled into the spaces behind.

It wasn't a string. It was a wire.

A thin grey wire.

One end led down to a ventilation brick in the wall to the administrative office.

The other led up into the back of the grandfather clock where the movement had once been, but where now nestled a portable cassette recorder.

The 'Play' button and the 'Record' button were both pressed down. But when Charles cancelled them and tried to rewind, nothing happened. The batteries had been allowed to run down. No one had ever switched it off.

The man who switched it on had not lived to switch it off.

Metaphors, Charles reflected wryly, do also have literal meanings, as he recalled Martha Wensleigh's report of her husband's words on the evening of his death:

'He said he'd finally sorted it out. He said it had all been very confusing, but he was getting there. Soon he'd have it all taped and the pressure would be off.'


Nella was still in the Green Room.

'Is there a cassette recorder anywhere in the building?' Charles asked, panting after his rush down the ladder.

She looked surprised. 'Yes, there's one we sometimes use for playing in sound effects at outside rehearsals.'

'Can I use it?'

The Green Room, he decided, was too public; the wrong person might walk in; so he took the recorder to the Number One dressing room, which had a door which locked.

'You come and listen, Nella. I want a witness.'

'What is all this?'

But she was intrigued and followed him into the dressing room. He locked the door and put the cassette in the player. He switched on.

After the leader of the tape ran through, there was the sound of distant voices. "Do you recognize it? asked Charles.

The pretty A.S.M. shook her head and craned forward to listen more acutely.

'You should recognize it. You've heard it enough times. It's the second Act of *The Message Is Murder*.'

'Oh yes.'

'As heard from the props store above the stage. Which is excellent, because it gives a time reference.'

'But why is –'

'Ssh!'

Much closer than the voices, there was the sound of a door opening.

*'Tony! What have you been doing in there?'*

The voice was unmistakably that of Donald Mason.

*'I've just been looking at some very interesting papers.'*

*'Oh. Interesting to whom?'*

*'Interesting to the Board, certainly. As they will find out when they see them tomorrow evening."*

*'You still haven't said what you are referring to.'*

*'I'm referring to all the letters of mine you've filched, as part of your campaign to get me out of this job."*

*'Ah.'* The monosyllable was uttered with the same infuriating coolness that Charles had suffered that afternoon.

*'I don't know why you want to do it. I don't know whether it's me you're trying to destroy or the theatre, but I tell you, Donald, you won't succeed. Oh, you nearly got me. I nearly cracked. You did it very well, confusing me, making me unsure what I had done, what I hadn't done, getting me so that I didn't trust my own judgement. Yes, you nearly succeeded. But now the tables are turned. I am going to shoot you down in flames, Donald Mason. You'll never get another job in any theatre in the country after I've finished showing you up.'*

There was a short laugh from Mason. *'I'll survive that. I don't want another job in any theatre in the country. All right, you go to the Board, Tony. Tell your tales out of school by all means. What do you think'll happen?'*

*'You'll get the sack."*

'*Possibly. And what will happen to the Regent? Just another example of shaky management, internal bickering. So I took a few letters – I don't call that a major crime.'*

'*And what do you call attempted murder?*'

'*I don't know what you're talking about.*' The bantering tone was abruptly gone from Mason's voice.

'*I was checking something in the Wardrobe store the Wednesday before last. Between the matinée and the evening show. I saw you adjusting the rope for Gordon's hanging.*'

There was a grunt from the General Manager, as if he had been winded and the Artistic Director went on. '*It never occurred to me  what you were doing, or I would have gone and undone it. When Gordon was  injured I still couldn't believe it. But now, Donald, I'm beginning to realize just how cold-blooded you are.*'

'*You don't plan to tell the Board about the hanging, surely?*'

'*Oh yes, I do. Though I think I might tell the Police first.*'

There was a sudden sound of movement, then a scuffle, then Tony's voice, very tense, saying, '*Keep back.*'

'*Oh, a gun. How convenient.*' The tone of grim banter was back. '*If it had to come to this, I had planned to use a syringe. But a gun with your finger-prints on it – even better.*'

'*Keep away, Donald! I'm not afraid to use this.*'

'*Oh, but you are, Tony. Just let me get my gloves on and –*'

'*I will use it!*'

'*No. You haven't got it in you, Tony. It's not in your nature. You're just like everyone else – too full of the milk of human kindness to be properly efficient. Unlike ME!*'

The last word was the cue for another assault. There was a tussle, then silence. When Tony's voice was heard again, it sounded very frail.

'*No, Donald. You mustn't. You can't.*'

'*Sorry. You've left me no alternative.*'

The bang was hideously loud, but unfortunately it was not loud enough to cover the liquid gurgle from Antony Wensleigh, nor the thump of what remained of his head hitting the desk.

Charles Paris looked up at Nella. Her eyes were full of tears.


This was no time for another amateur confrontation. This time he had strong enough evidence to take to the police.

Their initial scepticism vanished when they heard the tape. They accompanied Charles to the Regent Theatre and looked with interest as he showed them the cassette recorded and the cache of papers.

Later that evening, Donald Mason, rising property developer and the most efficient General Manager the Regent had ever had, was arrested at his flat and charged with the murder of Antony Wensleigh.

## Chapter Twenty

'...BUT EVERYTHING was passed on and subtly distorted by Donald,' said Nella, slightly breathlessly. She looked sensational, her colour heightened by the wine and excitement. 'I mean, do you remember Symposium thing I had to go to with Tony...you know, the thing that meant Rick couldn't go to his radio recording...well, we all assumed that was just Tony being awkward, but it wasn't. Tony told me when we were there. Donald had accepted on his behalf and Donald had nominated me to go with him.'

'Poor old Tony. He just wouldn't stand up for himself. It took him a long time to accept that anyone would be capable of that kind of deceit.'

'I know. Did you talk to his wife – widow, I mean?'

'Yes, I rang her before I came here.'

'How did she sound?'

'Pretty terrible. But she was pleased when I told her. I mean, nothing's going to bring Tony back, but at least his name had been cleared from any suspicion.'

'Yes.'

There was a peaceful lull in their conversation. They were now the only customers in the Happy Friend Chinese Restaurant and Takeaway. Those people in Rugland Spa daring enough to eat Chinese food were certainly not daring enough to do so after eleven o'clock in the evening.

Charles sighed. 'Thank God we got him. I thought he'd get away with it all. And what he was doing was so easy. The old "Divide and rule" principle. And there can't be many places where it's easier to foster division than a provincial rep.'

Nella smiled. She really was very pretty.

Charles tried not to look at her too lustfully as he continued, 'So he carefully built up a general atmosphere of distrust, then staged the odd accident to keep the situation on the boil. Like poor old Gordon's hanging – bound to lead to more demands for an enquiry. And all the time he was just trying to put the theatre out of business. The sad thing is...' He took a rueful sip of wine. 'he's probably succeeded.'

'You think the Regent'll close?'

'I can't see it avoiding it this time.'

'But surely Schlenter Estates won't get the development?'

'Don't see why not.'

'But once their connection with Donald is shown...I mean, he'll be a convicted murderer and...'

'I'll lay any money you care to mention that the connection could never be proved. People in a company like Schlenter are very canny – and particularly when they've got Carker Glyde behind them. No, if there ever were an investigation, it would be proved that Donald Mason was acting off his own bat.'

'They'd just drop him like that?'

'You bet. They'd show the same qualities of loyalty as he did.'

Nella looked pensive. She was young, perhaps she still nursed some illusions about how the commercial world worked.

'Do you fancy a sweet, Nella?'

'Wonder what he's got.'

'Mr Pang!'

'Yes, sir.'

'What have you got in the way of Ice Creams (Various)?'

'Today, sir,' Mr Pang announced with a huge conspiratorial grin, 'we have Vanilla.'

Through their laughter Charles and Nella agreed that they'd both have one. As the giggles subsided, Charles said thoughtfully, 'One thing I still haven't worked out.'

'What's that?'

'Going back to the second night of *The Message Is Murder*...the night when I got so disgracefully pissed...'

'I remember.'

'Well, somebody tried to stab me through the flat at the back of the cupboard and I never -' He looked at Nella. She was blushing deeply. 'You?'

She nodded. 'I've felt awful about it ever since.'

'Well...What had I done?'

'It wasn't aimed at you, you fool.'

'Then who did you think was in there?'

'No, I knew you were in there. Listen, if you remember, I was on the book that night, actually stage-managing the show, which meant I had to sit at the desk and couldn't move about much. And someone took advantage of that.'

'Leslie Blatt?'

'Got it in one. He kept sneaking up behind me and making the most disgusting suggestions. And then touching me up and...ugh. Eventually I got so furious, I just jumped up and chased him with the sword. I really wanted to kill him. I lunged at him.'

'And he moved out of the way?'

She nodded shamefacedly. 'Yes. I felt terrible when I realized what I'd done. I thought I'd killed you for sure.'

Charles grinned. 'Well, you didn't.'

'No. Thank God.'

'Must be pretty ghastly,' he said casually, 'for a young girl, being touched up by older men.'

She turned her astonishingly beautiful face to him and gave a little shy grin. 'Depends on the older man.'

Charles Paris looked at her hand lying on the table. Nice hand – small, but strong. No rings, nails a bit grubby from making props all day.

His hand moved forward and hovered over hers...

Charles' prognostication for the future of the theatre proved too pessimistic. The new offer from Schlenter Estates had its predictable effect in the Council Chamber, and it seemed that the Regent would finally be demolished as part of the Maugham Cross redevelopment scheme.

But local support came from an unlikely source. Mrs Feller, seeing there was a cause to champion, marshalled her Hats and, after a well-orchestrated sequence of banner-waving demonstrations and letters in the *Rugland Spa Gazette & Observer* (backed up by fighting leaders from Frank Walby), the Council decision was rescinded. Councillor Davenport was furious, and Councillor Inchbald was delighted.

The Arts Council, too, decided to give the theatre another chance. Given the fact that there would be a new Artistic Director and General Manager, the Regent got its grant. And the Council agreed to match it.

Herbie Inchbald remained as Chairman of the The-ettah Board. But Lord Kitestone also remained as the Regent's patron; and the Maugham Cross area got increasingly run down; one day it would have to be developed. So the theatre's ultimate future remained uncertain.

But, in the manner of provincial theatres, from crisis to crisis, the Regent continued to totter on.

Incidentally, those who care about that sort of thing would feel cheated not to be informed that the suicide of Miss Laycock-Manderley in Act Three of *The Message Is Murder* was a blind. She Did It.

# NOT DEAD, ONLY RESTING

To Chris

"With respect to the extravagance of actors, as a traditional character, it is not to be wondered at. They live from hand to mouth: they plunge from want into luxury; they have no means of making money breed, and all professions that do not live by turning money into money, or have not a certainty of accumulating it in the end by parsimony, spend it. Uncertain of the future, they make sure of the present moment. This is not unwise."

WILLIAM HAZLITT (1778–1830)
"On Actors and Acting"

## Chapter One

TRYST WAS NOT Charles Paris's usual scene. It was an expensive restaurant, very fashionable with the most successful members – and, in many cases, the gayest members – of the theatrical profession. Charles Paris was an indigent actor on whom success had rarely smiled, and he was unarguably heterosexual.

But that Saturday evening at the end of August he was the guest of two men who were ideally qualified as clients of Tryst. William Bartlemas and Kevin O'Rourke formed mutually a phenomenon of the British theatre. Though both had, way back in prehistory, been actors, they had long since given up performing in favour of a spreading collection of theatrical memorabilia connected with two great actors, Edmund Kean and William Macready. Fuelled by Bartlemas's substantial private income, they scoured the country for relics of their idols, returning religiously to London for the opening of every show at a West End theatre, where their first night presence in the fifth row of the stalls was regarded by managements with the awe that soothsayers reserve for comets. The couple's habits of dressing identically and talking in an unending shared monologue were just the kind of eccentricities to endear them to the British theatrical establishment, and possibly no one 'in the business' enjoyed greater universal goodwill. Certainly, when a chance meeting the previous week had led to his invitation, Charles Paris had leapt at the opportunity of spending an evening in Bartlemas and O'Rourke's company.

'It's lovely to see them making such a *go* of it...' William Bartlemas was commenting on the success of Tryst.

'Really humming with the right sort of people...' Kevin O'Rourke concurred.

'Sir John over there...'

'Maggie with someone new...'

'And he's so young. I swear that's how she keeps her complexion – melts down young actors for their glands...'

'Hmm. Ooh, and look who Bernard Walton's with...'

'Well, there's a turn-up. And what does her husband say, I wonder...?'

'*Super* fodder for the gossip columns...'

'*Super.* Oh, look, there's Bertram Pride doing his "I am a celebrity' number".'

'Well, after that *Lexton and Sons* series, he is...almost...'

'Who's the pretty girl he's with...?'

'Don't know. A late booking from Rent-A-Tottie, perhaps...'

O'Rourke's sally brought a shriek of laughter from Bartlemas. It ended with a breath-pause, when Charles almost had a chance to say something, but O'Rourke beat him to it. 'Oh yes, dear, *but all* the right people here...'

'Including...' Bartlemas inclined his head towards Charles. 'Including of course our guest...'

Charles Paris grinned wryly. 'Not in the same league as that lot, I'm afraid.'

'Now come on, don't do yourself down...'

'He's so modest, isn't he, Bartlemas...?'

'Far too modest. Always has been...'

'You're a very fine actor, always have been...'

'Never forget your Bassanio, will we...?'

'Lovely Bassanio...'

'Anyway, tell me, Charles...' Bartlemas put on an expression of mock-seriousness. 'What's next for you?'

'What's next?' asked Charles, puzzled.

'Yes, dear. Work. What are you doing at the moment?'

'Ah.' Charles grinned again, this time ruefully. 'At the moment I am "resting".'

'Oh dear...'

'Oh well, sure something'll turn up soon...'

'Been resting long, have you?'

'Except for two days on a radio play last week, it's just coming up for three months.'

'Oh.'

'I am rested to the point of torpor.'

'Bad luck, Charles. Still, it's happened before.'

'Many times.'

'You've had your little patches out of work since you started.'

'It might be more accurate to say, Bartlemas, that I've had my little patches *in* work.'

'Well...Something'll turn up.'

'Oh yes,' Charles agreed. 'Micawberism is the only philosophy for an actor.'

'Who's your agent?' asked O'Rourke. 'Does he beaver away on your behalf?'

'Maurice Skellern,' Charles replied. The faces of the other two fell.

'Oh...'

'Oh dear.'

'Hardly a human dynamo, is he?'

'No,' said Charles.

'And what about that lovely wife of yours...?'

'Dear Frances...'

'You two back together again, are you...'

'I'm afraid not. Frances is having a wild affair with a schools inspector...'

'Oh dear...'

'That sounds serious...'

'I'm afraid it is. When I last spoke to her she was asking about our getting a divorce.'

'What to marry this...?'

Charles nodded, suddenly too emotional for speech. His hosts could not pretend they hadn't noticed the change of mood, and there was an uneasy silence, ended by the timely arrival at their table of Tristram Gowers, who owned the restaurant and whose name had provided its punning title.

'Bartlemas, O'Rourke – *my dears!*'

The flamboyance of his greeting betrayed his background as a professional actor. Indeed, like many actors who go into other professions, Tristram Gowers seemed at times as if he was playing the part of a restaurateur rather than actually *being* one. He dressed invariably in a black velvet suit, with a froth of green silk scarf at his neck. He was a little under six foot, and carried himself as if holding in an unruly stomach. His hands flashed with rings, which, in spite of their value, looked as if they had just been collected from the props cupboard; and his face, too, seemed to have been dressed for the part of an Identikit restaurateur in a revue sketch. Over-large glasses with transparent rims gave him an owlish appearance. His walrus moustache was obviously real, but contrived to look as if it owed its adherence to spirit gum. The silver-grey toupee which crowned his characterization made no pretence at reality. Though it lacked an actual pigtail, it had the air of something devised by Wig Creations for a Restoration drama.

In fact, Charles noted around him three contrasting examples of hairdressing artifice. The wiry remnants of Bartlemas's hair were brushed up into a foam of dyed ginger; O'Rourke's surviving strands were trained across his scalp like piped icing over a birthday cake; but for sheer audacity Tristram Gowers' toupee collected all available awards. Whereas the others still tried to maintain the illusion of natural growth, Tristram had found baldness the stimulus to the creation of a new art form.

The restaurateur clasped Kevin O'Rourke's small face between his large hands. 'O coz, coz, coz, my pretty little coz, how are you?'

Charles would have put down the quotation from *As You Like It* to mere theatrical flamboyance, had not Bartlemas whispered, 'True, you know, they are cousins...'

'Really?'

'Oh yes,' Tristram Gowers and Kevin O'Rourke asserted together.

'Have you met Charles Paris, Trist...?' asked Bartlemas.

The brown eyes behind the owl glasses took Charles in for a moment before saying, 'No, I don't think so. Of course, I know the name.'

If that was the way he wanted to play it, Charles didn't mind. He could understand why Tristram Gowers might be embarrassed about their previous meeting. True, it had been some fifteen years before and the amnesia might be genuine. But Charles suspected that Tristram did not wish to be reminded of the time before he 'came out', the time when he had still been married to the actress, Zoë Fratton, before he met Yves Lafeu and discovered his real nature.

It was as if Charles's thought of Yves prompted Bartlemas's next question. 'And how is Him In The Kitchen, Trist...?'

'Very nice,' Tristram Gowers replied, with a coy smile.

'Being a good boy or a naughty boy...'

Charles recognized this as a reference to Yves Lafeu's occasional promiscuity. Though the restaurateur and his chef were very much a couple, the younger man enjoyed sporadic infidelities. These led to blazing rows between the two, rows which often erupted openly in the restaurant, and which, indeed, were regarded by regulars as one of the attractions of Tryst.

'Goodish,' Tristram replied judiciously. 'Occasional lapses. Picked up a nasty little trollop down at the Sparta couple of weeks back.'

Bartlemas and O'Rourke giggled at this reference. Charles assumed the Sparta must be some sort of gay club.

'Had to put a stop to that very quickly,' Tristram continued in a school-mistressy way. 'Still, all be fine now. For a whole month I'm not going to let him out of my sight.'

'What do you mean?'

'Hols, Bartlemas, hols. *Fermeture annuelle.*'

'Oh?'

'Didn't you know, dear? Didn't you read the notice on the door?'

'No.'

'We close down for September every year. Go away for the whole month. We've got this house near Cahors. Didn't you know? Oh, I tell you, dears, you're very lucky to get seats tonight of all nights. As of tomorrow, poor London has a whole month of being Tryst-less.'

'*Quelle tristesse,*' sighed O'Rourke, and was rewarded by gales of giggles.

'So when are you actually off?' asked Bartlemas, as the hysteria subsided.

'Soon as we've tidied up here,' Tristram Gowers replied. 'What we do every year. Get the restaurant in order, lock up and away we go. Six-thirty ferry from Dover tomorrow morning, then we just drive on from Calais till we get to Mas-de-Pouzard.'

'Which is where you have the house?'

'Uhuh. Eleven kilometres outside Cahors. Wonderful views over the River Lot. Pure heaven.'

'Don't you stop on the way down?'

'No, love, we just press on till we're there. Share the driving. We can't relax until we're actually *there*.'

'You don't even stop for the odd *menu gastronomique*...?'

'No, we're positively monastic in our restraint. I sort out sandwiches which we eat on the way. Mind you, once we're *there*, then we *really* start serious eating.' Tristram smiled in delicious anticipation.

'Does Yves come from that part of France?' asked Bartlemas.

'No, dear. My "in-laws" – whom I have yet to have the pleasure of meeting

– and may that pleasure be eternally deferred – live in Reims. Very solid, I gather. *Petit bourgeois* – with the emphasis on the "petty".'

'So,' asked Charles, 'you close up here, then pack and –?'

'No, dear, no. The whole operation has been organized for *weeks*. Everything's packed already. The Volvo's stuffed to the gills. I've done it all, of course. Yves, the "great chef", is far too *sensitive* to deal with the minutiae of life.' The mockery of the emphasis was not wholly friendly. 'Still, I suppose it makes sense. Though I say it myself, I can state, without unbecoming immodesty, that I am one of the world's great packers. I begin by emptying the car completely, get. it as clean as an operating theatre, and then start the actual packing. It is a work of art when I've finished, you know. I know exactly where everything is. Which is just as well, because I don't get much help from *him* when it comes to unpacking.'

'So what time do you have to leave?'

'Try and get away by half-past three. Should be no problem. The flat's all tidied up; passports, currency, tickets...all sorted out.'

Tristram Gowers' obsessive pride in his organizational skills was beginning to grate on Charles, so he was quite relieved when the restaurateur changed the subject and, prefacing his question with a huge '*Anyway*', asked, 'what are you going to eat tonight?'

'Is Yves...' asked Bartlemas breathlessly, 'doing his *divine....*'

'But *divine...*?'

'Sucking pig?'

Tristram held the pause dramatically, then announced, 'He is.'

'Three sucking pigs, please, Trist...'

While they ate their *pâté en croute*, Bartlemas and O'Rourke regaled Charles with lavish descriptions of the main course, and when it arrived the sucking pig lived up to their Roget's Thesaurus of superlatives. Perhaps because of their conversation with Tristram, they drank the strong black wine of Cahors, and Charles began to feel better.

The ache of his feelings for Frances and the nag of being out of work both dulled. He felt whole, eating and drinking well, with entertaining friends, in pleasant surroundings.

The decor of Tryst was dark red, and the walls were liberally scattered with gilt-framed playbills and old tinted prints of actors long-dead.

'They have got some lovely stuff...' Bartlemas observed, as he mopped up the last juices of sucking pig with bread.

'Divine memorabilia...'

'Nothing to do with Edmund Kean of course...'

'Or William Macready...'

'Of course...'

'I mean, they wouldn't *dare*...'

'Tristram knows we'd scratch his eyes out if he dared buy anything and not offer it to us...'

'Yes. Actually, you know,' said O'Rourke airily, 'Tristram's going to leave all his theatrical stuff to me...'

'Ooh, you big fibber!'

'It's true, Bartlemas, true. Scout's honour. He said if he and Yves both died in a car accident or something, then I could have it...'

'Oh yes?'

'Yes. I am his cousin, you know...'

'Of course...'

'Nearest relative...'

'Hmm...'

Charles looked round the restaurant, as Bartlemas and O'Rourke went through the motions of some formal private squabble. It was strange to see the rich end of the acting profession. As with people in most businesses, Charles tended to mix with actors of about the same eminence and income as himself, but in the theatre the identity of those people changed more quickly than in other areas. Most actors had in them the potential for sudden failure or prosperity. A coincidence, a sudden break, could lift any one of them to stardom; overexposure, one part badly played, or just the lack of suitable jobs, could bring any one of them quickly down to the semi-anonymity of most of their profession.

Charles could see examples of the system at work in that room. Bernard Walton. They'd worked together at the beginning of the younger man's career, and Charles had acted as a kind of mentor to Bernard. But then television sit-coms and the West End had turned Bernard into a household name, earning considerably more in the average month than Charles did in a good year. Charles felt glad that he had his back to the star and could only see a reflection in the glass of one of the playbills. He didn't want to be recognized and drowned in Bernard Walton's patronizing bonhomie.

Bertram Pride – there was another example. He had been a perfectly competent actor in his early thirties, going round the reps dutifully, giving his juve leads in bedroom farces, second leads in Shakespeares – Laertes in *Hamlet*, Sebastian in *Twelfth Night*, Macduff in *Macbeth*, that sort of thing – unbending a little as one of the Ugly Sisters in a pantomime – and then suddenly a lucky break had found him cast as Philip Lexton in the television series, *Lexton and Sons*. This had been one of those unpromising family business sagas, which had turned out to be addictive viewing. The first series had built its audience steadily enough to be followed by a second, then a third, a fourth, a fifth. Gossip said that the sequence had now finally come to an end, but it had done enough to raise Bertram Pride to a kind of stardom.

He had got the money from the original programmes, fees rising as the series' popularity increased. Then the money for the domestic repeats and the foreign sales. On a big success, that could multiply the basic fees by many hundred per cent.

Added to the direct financial benefit from the series, there were the spin-offs. As a well-known television face, he would be invited on to other television shows. He would submit to panel games, unroll anecdotes on chat-shows, be offered feature roles in one-off plays. His face and voice would become disproportionately valuable to advertising companies. He would be paid handsomely for personal appearances to open supermarkets, to host sales conferences. He would, in short, have become a personality. And even though the series that launched him had ended, he had surely by now achieved sufficient momentum to keep him going for the rest of his career.

And all that from one lucky break, Charles thought ruefully. He looked across to where Bertram Pride, conscious that people in the restaurant recognized him, joked with his Rent-A-Tottie. Perhaps the movement of Charles's head caught the 'star's eye, because he suddenly focused on their table and gave a wave of recognition to Bartlemas and O'Rourke. Then, seeming to decide that this acknowledgement was insufficient, he clasped his Rent-A-Tottie by the hand and came across to greet them.

'Bartlemas...O'Rourke...'

'Bertram...'

The effusiveness of the greeting was automatic.

'Have you met Charles Paris?'

'Don't think so. Know the name, *of course.*'

Charles was getting used to that response. It's always a safe reaction when one is introduced to an unknown actor, since it discreetly veils ignorance in the implication that one has followed his career from the very beginnings with unflagging interest.

Bertram waved airily at his Rent-A-Tottie. 'And this is Henry.'

The girl smiled with a little adolescent jerk of her head, and Charles saw how very young she was. Pretty, though. Almost white blond hair that curled in little tendrils at her temples. Blue eyes so widely innocent as to be nearly embarrassing, and skin glowing as softly as if it had just been rubbed with baby powder. Her neat little figure was emphasized by the expensive simplicity of a white pleated cotton dress with lacy collar and cuffs.

'Henry, these are Bartlemas and O'Rourke, who I'm sure you've heard of.'

'Absolutely,' she enthused. immediately placing herself in that area of the upper classes where 'absolutely' is used to mean 'yes'.

'What are you up to at the moment, Bertram?'

'Yes, what are you *doing*...?

'Oh, not a lot. Few things in the air.'

Charles supposed *he* could have answered the question with the same airy nonchalance, but somehow didn't think he'd carry it off. He couldn't have infused the words with the same implications of producers falling over themselves to employ him.

'One interesting thing...change of direction...' Bertram went on. 'Actually got a book coming out next month.'

'Really? What, are you turning into a Frederick Forsyth...?'

'Or a Harold Robbins...'

'Oh God, no. Not fiction. Autobiographical thing, actually. Amazed to be asked. Showman Books are bringing it out.'

'Have you written it yourself?'

'Oh, pretty well, yes. Well, I nattered into a tape recorder for a few days, and then some chap sort of breaks it into chapters and puts in the full stops. Being serialized in the *Sunday Express*, actually.'

'Oh?'

'As I say, I was amazed to be asked, but this chap at Showman Books seems convinced there's a market. *Lexton and Sons* did get such an enormous following.'

'Yes. Is the rumour true...?

'That there aren't going to be any more...'

'Oh yes, I think we really have run that into the ground. All want to go off and do our own things now. You know, very grateful for the success and all that, but can't stand still in this business.'

There were murmurs of agreement. The girl, Henry, looked awkward and a little lost. 'Are you in the business too?' Charles asked.

'Well, yes.' She blushed. 'I mean, sort of. Just out of drama school. Starting out, you know.'

'I see.'

'Frightfully difficult, making a start, you know. You have to get this Equity card. If you haven't got that, it's hopeless.'

Charles was amused at her explaining his profession to him, but didn't comment.

'Never mind, dear,' said Bartlemas. 'I'm sure Bertram can give you a helping hand...'

'The odd tip...' O'Rourke agreed.

'Oh yes, I'll teach her a thing or two. We're going down to my cottage in Kent for the weekend.'

Bertram Pride's abrupt change to undoubted sexual innuendo brought a new blush to Henry's face and an awkward stop to the conversation. It was fortunate that the arrival of the couple's sweet course provided a reason for moving.

'Better get back to our profiteroles,' said Bertram.

Charles watched the 'star' back to his table. Bertram was tall and his brown hair was cropped very short. (Charles wondered idly if that meant he had just been working on another period serial. Television's love-affair with the first three decades of the twentieth century had led to a lot of actors walking around with short-back-and-sides.)

Strange, how someone like Bertram, who had only been thought moderately good-looking before his success, was now, thanks to the mythologizing power of television, accepted as an archetype of masculine beauty. And presumably would have no problem in picking up any number of delicious little Henries.

And what of Bertram Pride's talent? Good, yes. As good as a few thousand other actors who could have done as well, given the same opportunities. Yet again, Charles was struck by the strange values that obtained in his profession.

He did not feel jealous. He had long since accepted the lottery nature of acting.

He wouldn't have minded a bit of Bertram Pride's income, though.

Bartlemas's voice brought him back from his musing. 'No, the one over there on the door. I'm sure it is...'

'The one behind the bar. She looks much more like Yves...'

Charles's quizzical look brought an explanation from O'Rourke. 'Yves's sister. Apparently Yves's sister has started working here. Name of Monique. We were trying to sort out which one she was...'

'I'd *put money* on the one by the door,' asserted Bartlemas.

'Really. I mean, she's got that pout...just like Yves when he's throwing a moody. So tall, though. He's got all the looks...'

'Yes, but really, dear, the colouring. It must be the one behind the bar. Just like Yves. And she's so petite...'

'Go on, Charles love, you must decide...'

'*Arbitrate*, that's the word...'

'Yes, *arbitrate* for us...'

Charles shrugged. 'I'm sorry. I'd love to, but I'm afraid I've never met Yves, so I can't be much help.'

'Never met Yves!' Bartlemas threw his hands to his mouth in mock-amazement. 'But I thought you were bound to have worked together when he was a choreographer...'

'Two left feet, I'm afraid,' said Charles. 'Never had a lot to do with shows that had choreographers.'

'Oh, but you –'

'Never mind.' O'Rourke stilled his partner with a gesture. 'Charles will have the opportunity to meet Yves now.'

The other two followed his outstretched hand towards the figure who issued from the kitchen.

Yves Lafeu was beautiful, and knew it. His colouring was not typically French; the translucent blue eyes and flopping blond hair made him look more Teutonic than anything; only the olivey sheen of his skin, heightened by sweat from the kitchen, gave him a Latin air. He was dressed in the traditional white jacket and checked trousers of a French chef, though a spotted handkerchief knotted round his neck turned the image into something insolent and piratical.

The grace with which he moved showed his dancer's training. His step had a self-mocking tartiness as he moved across the restaurant, waving in acknowledgement of his guests, most of whom applauded his entrance. It was obviously a Tryst ritual for him to appear at the end of the evening's cooking to receive his due of praise.

He came first to Bartlemas and O'Rourke's table, clutching one of their hands in each of his with genuine affection. 'My dears!' His heavy French accent contained the same element of self-parody as his walk. 'Trist said you were in tonight, and I'm just so...*enchanté* to see you both.'

'You're looking younger than ever...' said Bartlemas.

'And more beautiful...' agreed O'Rourke.

Yves made a self-depreciating moue. 'All bridgework and vanishing cream, *mes chéris.*'

'But now you're here, you can settle a dispute for us...'

'Yes, you can...'

'But I did not think you two had *disputations.* I thought you were the perfect couple. I thought it was only Trist and me who –'

'No, not a dispute, just a disagreement...'

'That's all...'

'We just want to know which of these pretty young ladies...'

'Is your sister.'

'Ah, Monique.' Yves nodded lugubriously. '*Ma petite soeur.* Well, she is –'

He turned towards the entrance, confirming Bartlemas's speculation. The tall girl by the door, with the long dark hair, was Monique Lafeu. Around thirty, with a discontented expression.

But what her brother saw when he turned to her stopped him dead. Monique's job was to check the reservations and take the coats of the arriving guests. When they looked at her, she was doing this service for a tall young man with unnaturally blond hair. He wore a blue and white striped shirt and tight beige trousers. A matching jacket was slung over-casually across his shoulders. He appeared to be questioning something about the reservation.

Yves moved across the room, mesmerized by the young man's appearance. 'Gary,' he murmured, opening his arms to welcome him.

The newcomer looked up. The expression on his face was at first one of total surprise; then recognition and pleasure took over. 'Yves.'

But before the two met, a voice from the kitchen entrance stopped them in their tracks. 'Get out!'

Everyone in the restaurant turned to look at Tristram Gowers. His face beneath the toupee was bright red. In his hand he carried a large Sabatier kitchen knife.

He moved across the room towards the two young men, who still stood frozen. 'Get out, you little tart,' he hissed at the boy called Gary.

'But why? I've got a date here.' The young man's defiance was not very convincing. His manner of speech was stagey and elocuted, like a chorus boy from a musical given his first speaking part.

'How dare you –'

'No, I have, I have. My name's Gary Stane and I'm meant to be meeting a Mr Carruthers. For dinner. It was arranged.'

'Get out!' Tristram Gowers gestured with the knife.

'I don't see why I should. I have a perfect right to –'

But the next, closer, gesture of the knife stopped his expostulation. Deciding discretion to be the better part of valour, the boy called Gary turned on his heel and slipped out of the restaurant.

Tristram turned to his lover. 'How you dare...how you have the nerve to invite your nasty, dirty little bit of Sparta rough trade into my restaurant –'

'But I did not. I was not expecting him. He just came. It was not –'

'Get into the kitchen!' Tristram shouted.

Yves pouted his lips as if to reply, but then thought better of it and, with an exaggerated swing of his hips, minced off to the kitchen.

Tristram Gowers moved across to the bar and poured himself a heavy slug of Armagnac from a bottle pivoted in a wrought-iron container. He downed it in one, then let the kitchen knife fall on to the bar in the silent restaurant.

This was the cue for conversation at the tables to restart. The cabaret was over.

'Someone,' said William Bartlemas, in the voice of a long-suffering children's nanny, 'could do with a holiday.'

## Chapter Two

CHARLES'S APPOINTMENT TO sign on at the Unemployment Office that Monday was not until half-past eleven. He always tried to fix the visit so that he could go straight to a lunchtime drink. He could usually guarantee to meet another acting acquaintance in the queue, and rather jolly sessions in the pub often ensued. Charles got to know that pub well. His visits to the office were more regular than those of most unemployed. Once they'd signed on, they'd receive their Giro cheques in the post. Because Charles lived in a house divided into bedsitters, his was reckoned to be an 'unsafe address', so he had to go and collect in person.

The trendiest Unemployment Office for actors is the one in Chadwick Street near Westminster Abbey, but Charles went to the one in Lisson Grove, which was a brisk half-hour walk from his Hereford Road bedsitter. Though it has not got quite the cachet of Chadwick Street, the staff there do at least know about actors, who aren't subjected to the endless questioning about their lack of work which they sometimes experience in provincial offices.

Almost all Equity members have had to sign on at some point or other; it's part of the job. Even so-called 'household names' will get back on the register immediately they finish their current job. In fact stage-struck autograph-hunters would do much better hanging round the entrances at Chadwick Street and Lisson Grove than they would at the stage doors of West End theatres.

But, though he didn't expect any more than a cursory questioning about his job prospects – if even that – Charles decided he'd show willing and ring his agent. He had an hour to kill before he set off for Lisson Grove and...well, you never knew...something might have come up.

It hadn't.

'No,' said Maurice Skellern's voice predictably. 'It really isn't a very good time at the moment.'

'Is it ever?'

'Well, no, Charles, not really. I mean, all the television companies are cuffing back on production, the provincial reps have mostly settled their companies for the autumn season –'

'When we last spoke, you said they hadn't yet started to select their companies for the autumn season.'

'No. Well, they must have done it in the interim since we spoke, Charles. I haven't heard of any auditions coming up, and you know how close I keep my ear to the ground, don't you?'

Yes, about as close as an orbiting space satellite, thought Charles. But he didn't say it.

'I did hear of one open audition coming up, actually.'

'Oh.'

'For a musical, though...'

'Oh. Well...'

'Never been your strong suit, musicals, have they, Charles?'

'I wouldn't say that.' (OLD ACTORS' RULE: Never admit you can't do anything. If the part requires tap-dancing or horse-riding or scuba-diving or deaf-and-dumb language, of course you can do it. Let the truth come out once rehearsals have started and the contract has been signed. Much of an actor's life he spends following the principle enunciated in the old joke:

'Are you Jewish?'

'Not necessarily.'

An actor is not *necessarily* anything; but when the occasion arises, he can be *everything*.)

'Trouble is, Charles, this musical's all kids. No part for anyone over sixteen.'

'Oh.' Charles offered no further opposition. Though actors should think themselves capable of everything, there are moments when it is prudent for them to recognize their limitations.

'Nothing doing on the commercial scene, I suppose, Maurice?'

'Not a lot. Bit iffy, that, at the moment. There's this dispute brewing between Equity and Channel Four over rates for commercials, and a lot of the production companies are holding fire until that's resolved. Presumably it'll be sorted out once Channel Four actually starts in November, but...'

'Yes...'

'Otherwise, doesn't look too wonderful...'

"No...'

'I don't suppose you heard of anything coming up when you did that radio last week...'

'No...'

'No...' The conversation was becoming becalmed in unfinished sentences.

'Ooh, one thing,' said Maurice suddenly.

'Yes?' Charles was instantly alert.

'Did I tell you I was off on holiday next week?'

'No. Somewhere nice?'

'Oh, just the Canaries.'

*Just* the Canaries. It was dismissed as if it had been Littlehampton. Charles tried to remember when he had last had a holiday. How did Maurice manage it? Certainly not on ten per cent of Charles Paris's earnings. Not even on fifteen per cent, thought Charles, remembering ruefully that his agent had recently raised his commission rate. So where did Maurice get his money from? He mentioned occasional other clients, but none of them were much more successful than Charles. Perhaps Maurice had one huge international star on his books, whose earnings subsidized all the rest...? It seemed unlikely that that could be kept a secret. Nor would it be in Maurice's nature to want to keep it a secret. No, he must have some other source of income. Inherited wealth seemed improbable, so what was it? A string of launderettes? A hamburger franchise? White slave traffic? Charles somehow knew he would never find out the real answer.

He also felt a kind of emptiness at the prospect of Maurice being away. His agent never *did* ring with amazing offers of work, but the fantasy that he *might* remained intact; when he was away, even that possibility was gone.

'How long are you away?'

'Just the fortnight.'

Again the casual 'just'.

'Well, have a good time.'

'I'll try to. Could certainly do with a break.'

From what? Charles restrained himself from asking the question.

'Fine. Yes, well, Maurice, if anything does come up in the next few days, be sure and let me know.'

'Charles, you know me.'

'Yes, I do. That's why I said "be sure and let me know".'

'Ooh, one thing.'

Again the words commanded Charles's full attention. 'Yes?'

'Do you know a Casting Director at West End Television called Dana Wilson?'

'No.'

'Oh well, I might be meeting her socially tomorrow. I'll put in a word.'

'Thanks.'

'Maybe set up a general interview for you.'

'That'd be nice.'

'Yes. Not that they're casting anything at the moment, though.'

As he always did when he put the phone down after talking to Maurice Skellern, Charles wondered whether he ought to change his agent. It's a common feeling among unemployed actors, their special version of the unsuccessful workman blaming his tools. Some greet every bout of 'resting' as an invitation to start ringing round other agents to set up interviews.

But they all come up against the same Catch-22. They go in to see the new agent, explaining that they're currently out of work, reeling off lists of credits, possibly showing portfolios of press cuttings and photographs, and saying that their current agent just doesn't seem to be trying to get anything for them. The new agent is very nice, very sympathetic, says yes it does seem amazing that someone with credits like that isn't working, and yes he hasn't heard very good reports of the other agent, and certainly he might consider taking the actor on. At this point the actor beams. Then the agent says that of course he couldn't commit himself finally until he's seen the potential client work. Is there a chance of seeing something he's in? Well, no, there isn't, that's the whole point, he's out of work. Oh dear. But there was that television series earlier in the year, I had a good part in that, says the actor. Kicking himself for the omission, the agent regrets that somehow he failed to see a single episode. (At this point, a clued-up actor may try to call the agent's bluff by producing a video cassette of the show. Only momentarily fazed, the agent will be very grateful for the idea, but regret that the office video is on the blink, or that he's only got one at home and he wouldn't want to run the risk of losing such a precious record, so he doesn't feel it would be fair on the potential client for him to take it.) Then, apologetic that he really must get on with some work, the agent ushers his visitor out of the office, suggesting that maybe the actor and some friends should get together a lunchtime fringe show. He'd love to come and see that. End of interview.

(The few who do actually make the effort to put on a fringe show encounter a new twist to the storyline. They write to or ring up the apparently interested agent well in advance of the performances and receive copious assurances that he will move heaven and earth to witness the actor working. Other agents, notified of the show, are equally grateful for the golden opportunity they are being offered. The week of performance comes, and the cast play their hearts out every lunchtime to a small audience composed entirely of loyal unemployed actor friends.)

So, as he had many times before, Charles Paris decided he would stick with Maurice Skellern.

He thought of ringing his wife. Frances, headmistress of a girls' school, would still be on holiday. She had been away to Wales for a fortnight with their daughter Juliet, son-in-law Miles and grandsons, Damian, Julian and Sebastian. Charles couldn't remember exactly when they were returning, but reckoned they must be back by now. Frances would need a few days to prepare for the new term. And, no doubt, to see her schools inspector.

The thought of this unknown figure, this David, hurt again. Most of the time he could shut it from his mind, just close off the part of his brain that controlled jealousy. But every now and then the pain seeped through.

He knew little about his 'rival' – if that was the right word for his deserted wife's lover. He knew that David was married, and he knew that the affair was being conducted with elaborate secrecy. Indeed, its clandestine nature had provided a point of contact between Charles and Frances. They could laugh together at the ironies of the situation and he, more experienced in such deceits, could even give points of advice to his wife. So long as the relationship remained like that, so long as David remained firmly married, Charles could cope with it, contain it, shut out of his mind the details he did not want to know about.

But at their last meeting, for the first time since he had walked out on her, Frances had mentioned divorce. She had been unwilling to be pinned down to specifics, but the implication was clear that David finally intended to leave his wife and marry his mistress. After more than a year, the relationship had reached a new level of seriousness. And, for Charles, a new level of pain. While Frances was involved in the indignities and deceptions of an affair, he had not lost her; when she was actually married to someone else, he could no longer fool himself that he owned any part of her.

He wanted to talk to her, but was afraid to hear of any further advance in her plans to remarry, so he didn't dial the number of her Highgate flat.

For once Charles didn't meet any actors he recognized at the Unemployment Office, but he didn't let a detail like that stop him from going to the pub. After he had collected a pint, he saw a man along the bar who had been two ahead of him in the queue. He was in his thirties, dressed in a smart suit, very pale, and quickly downing a double scotch. Charles raised his glass amiably in salute and moved along the bar.

'Your first time, was it, signing on?' The man gave a brief nod.

'Not an actor, are you?'

A slightly shocked shake of the head. 'What do you do then?'

'Until I was made redundant,' the man said bitterly, 'I was a sales manager for a firm making industrial plastics.'

'Oh,' said Charles.

'Now,' the man continued dramatically, 'I am nothing.'

'Oh, don't take it so hard,' said Charles. 'Lots of people in the same boat.'

'Oh yes,' the man agreed, his voice thick with emotion, '...but the shame.'

Charles provided further appropriate soothing. The encounter interested him. The recession had perhaps brought actors nearer to other workers, as more and more experienced the uncertainties of unemployment. In a world where nobody's job was secure, actors were no more vagabonds than anyone else.

That afternoon, as he dozed in his bedsitter, the payphone on the landing rang. It was a call he had been waiting for, not daring to hope for.

'Hello, Charles, it's Stan Fogden.' The voice at the other end of the line was raucously Cockney.

'Yes?'

'Listen, you know we talked about you stepping in if someone dropped out?'

'Yes?'

'Well, it's happened. Phil suddenly got a telly.'

'You mean –?'

'Yes, Charlie. The understudy's dream. You're on!'

They met in the Patisserie Valerie in Old Compton Street. Set in the middle of London's theatreland, it's a popular haunt of actors and actresses, who sit crowded on creaking wooden chairs, drink endless pots of tea, wolf cream cakes, browse through scripts, and gossip. Charles and Stan arrived around five o'clock, a busy time, as people working in the local theatres drop in for a snack before their day's duties start. There was a ten-minute wait before a table was free.

Stan eased his huge bulk down on to a defenceless chair. He was a Cockney actor in his forties, whose set of chins and matching stomach earned him a fairly regular living as television heavies, barmen, delivery men, taxi-drivers, bodyguards, removal men and so on. He had black hair that stuck out at odd angles and enormous good nature. If he had a fault, it was a tendency to overplay his role of lovable Cockney.

They ordered tea and eyed the plate of pastries. Stan picked up a large cream-filled slice and took a gargantuan bite.

'So,' asked Charles, 'what's the job?'

'Sure you can 'andle it?'

'Yes.' (Never admit you can't do anything.)

'Well, look, set-up we got is this: the kind of A-Team is Bill Timmis and Phil, but Bill's got this three weeks on a feature in the Bahamas – all right for some, eh? – so I'm in for him, and now Phil's landed this telly. So, since the job's meant to start Wednesday, leaves me in a Loch.'

One of Stan Fogden's supposedly endearing Cockney qualities was his constant use of rhyming slang. Some of it was familiar, but most was totally incomprehensible. Charles had a strong suspicion that Stan made it up, and had got used to asking patiently for glosses on the more obscure usages.

'Loch?'

'Loch Ness, Charlie – Mess.'

'I see.'

'So anyway, you'd be free? Haven't had the call from the Casting Directors at the National Theatre? Rachel Grant hasn't rung and asked you to give your King Lear?'

'Not this week, Stan.'

'It'll come, it'll come.'

'So what is the job?'

'It's a flat. Bloke wants a flat done.'

The casual eavesdropper might have interpreted this as the planning of a burglary, but that was not the case. Nor was the job to which Stan referred a theatrical engagement. He, like many actors; dealt with his inevitable periods of 'resting' by developing a sideline. In his case it was decorating.

'Is it complicated?' asked Charles, getting slightly cold feet about his skills as a decorator.

'Well, yes and no. I mean, there's quite a bit of paperhanging, but don't worry, that's my specialty. I'm hot stuff with the old pot of paste. All I'll want you to do is the Diana and the Jetpro.'

'The what, Stan?' asked Charles patiently.

'Diana Ross – Gloss. Jet Propulsion – Emulsion.'

'You do make them up, Stan.'

'Absolute cobblers!' (Charles did know that one.) 'Learnt 'em all at my mother's knee. Anyway, so I do the paperhanging, you do the paintwork, you know, and help out as and when. Reckon you can manage?'

'I think so. But what about… er…?'

'Ah, you want to know about the Beesmake.'

Charles wasn't sure whether or not that one was authentic, but he reckoned he could work it out. Bees Make Honey – Money.

'Well, yes.'

'Right, the job's five hundred. We'll split fifty/fifty.'

'That's very generous.'

'Only way to do business, Charlie. Oh, one thing…'

'Yes?'

'Stumm about the money, okay?'

'Right.'

'Don't want to make extra work for the taxman or the old DHSS, do we?'

'No. Don't worry. No one will ever know.'

'Right.'

'How long do you reckon the job'll take?'

'Hard to say, really. It's only basically four rooms. And the owner's away, so we can go at our own pace and move the stuff around. Don't know, week maybe…'

Two hundred and fifty quid for a week's work. Not a bad rate of pay for an actor. Many appearing on West End stages got less.

'And where is it?'

'Sort of Notting Hillish…'Olland Park. The flat's over a restaurant. Called Tryst or something. D'you know it?'

'Yes,' said Charles. 'I do.'

## *Chapter Three*

ON THE TUESDAY evening, flushed with the confidence that he would soon have something coming in apart from his Unemployment Benefit, Charles decided to indulge in a little light drinking. Not too much, of course – he must have a steady hand for the gloss and emulsion in the morning – but just enough to make him feel comfortable.

The Montrose was a drinking club tucked away in a basement behind the Haymarket. The conversation that greeted anyone who pushed through its battered grey door left no doubt as to the profession of the majority of the club's clientele.

'...I looked at Gemma and I could see, the line had just gone...'

'...and the director says I must cut my hair, says it makes too much of a statement like this...'

'...I said, "For God's sake, Nigel, I'm through with playing funny vicars..."'

'...I tell you, she couldn't direct a bicycle up a one-way street...'

Charles moved through the chorus of 'I's up to the bar and ordered a large Bell's whisky. When he was only going to have a couple of drinks he'd have beer; when he intended to have more, he'd concentrate on the scotch. He drank more scotch than beer. Simply a matter of bladder-control, he told himself.

'How're things?' he asked the barman, whose name he could never remember.

'Pretty grim,' came the lugubrious reply.

'Why?'

'Lease is coming up.'

'What, the lease here? On the Montrose?'

The barman nodded. 'And the block's been bought up by a new company who want us out.'

'So the Montrose'll be closing.'

'That's right.'

'When?'

'End of the year.'

'And isn't there any hope that...?' Charles' words petered out as the barman shook his head.

The shock emptied the first large Bell's and another was quickly ordered. Holding it, Charles moved slowly across the crowded room.

It had been quite a body-blow. To lose the Montrose would upset his internal gyroscope. He'd been using the club for...how long? With a shock he realized it must be over fifteen years.

He had had too many such blows recently. Frances selling the family house in Muswell Hill and buying the flat. Frances taking up with her schools inspector. And now the Montrose...Next thing he'd be evicted from his Hereford Road bedsitter. Charles's world seemed to be crumbling around him. He felt every one of his fifty-five years. And, God, he was nearly fifty-six. He took a long, shuddering pull at the whisky.

'Charles Paris, isn't it?'

He focused on the woman from whom the voice came. Once before a chance encounter in the Montrose had started him on a bizarre adventure, the investigation of the death of Marius Steen. But that had been ten years earlier, and Jacqui, the girl he had met then, had been considerably younger than the woman who now confronted him.

This one was not unattractive, though the pinkish tinge to her brown eyes and the dark circles around them suggested he was not seeing her at her best. She was tall, almost Charles's height. Her brown hair had been cut short and not all its streaks of grey were due to the hairdresser's art. She was dressed in well-cut jeans and a floppy smock, but there was an air of untidiness about her, as if she had fallen asleep in a chair and just woken, dishevelled.

'Yes, you are Charles Paris,' she repeated. 'And you don't remember me.'

It was embarrassingly true. She looked familiar, he was sure he had been thinking about her recently, but he couldn't put a name to her.

'Zoë Fratton,' she said, without malice. 'Don't you remember, we did a *Doctor Who* together.'

She swayed. Charles realized that he was talking to someone very drunk.

'That's right. Of course. Zoë Fratton. And we met when...' He changed the subject abruptly. 'Let's sit down.'

They squeezed their way on to one of the Montrose's tattily upholstered benches, but the move had not sufficiently obscured Charles's *faux pas*.

'I know what you were about to say,' Zoë slurred. 'You were about to say that we met a long time ago, while I was still married to that shit, Tristram Gowers.'

Charles could not deny it.

'Before he went off with his pretty little bum-boy and left me stranded on the shore.'

'Well –'

'That's what he did – just threw me over like I was something nasty his spade had turned up in the garden.'

'I don't know the ins and outs of –'

'There are no ins and outs to know. That little French shit ruined a perfectly good marriage – that's all there is to it. Still...' A thought seemed to calm her. 'Still, forget them. They're nothing. Finished. Out of my life. I've got new friends now. Friends who bring me bottles of gin.' She held out her glass. 'Have I got friends who'll buy me glasses of gin...'

She'd obviously had enough, but Charles didn't have the courage to refuse her. 'Make it a large one,' she called to his back as he went to the bar.

She looked shame-faced when he returned. 'You're very kind, Charles. I'm sorry. I drink too much. Since Tristram went off, I...I'm sorry.'

'Don't worry. I often feel the same. Cheers.'

They clinked glasses.

'It's just so petty,' said Zoë. 'I feel myself getting old and embittered and alcoholic. Sometimes I'm frightened about the way I can behave. I do awful things, just awful...' She put a hand across her eyes, as if to wipe away some painful inner vision. 'It's so horrible to feel yourself just eaten up with hatred. Not really hatred for Yves – he's not worth it, just a little tart. It's hatred for Tristram. And I know hate is the other side of love. I think I still love him.'

'It takes a long time for –'

'Yes, yes. You're being very kind, Charles. You're kind to listen to me. I know I'm behaving appallingly.'

He could see the pain in her brown eyes, and feel the effort as she tried to claw her way back to self-respect.

'I'm not normally like this, Charles. It's just the weekend, knowing they were going off together yet again. The thought sort of made me mad. I just didn't feel responsible for myself at the weekend. I feel terrible about it.'

Suddenly the tears came. Charles's proffered handkerchief was accepted and applied to her eyes. She shook her head firmly to demonstrate the return of control.

'I'm sorry about that. I'll stop now. Really.' Her voice was firmer; there was even a hint of humour as she said, 'It's just so pathetic – a grown woman torn apart by such a childish emotion as jealousy. That's all it is. I suppose I'm jealous of their money too, their success, the fact that they've made such a success of Tryst. Perhaps I could have coped better if things had been going well for me.'

'Work?' asked Charles, seizing on a non-contentious subject of conversation.

'Yes.'

'Nothing doing?'

'Nothing at all on the –' She stopped herself. 'Do you know I'm so used to saying that, it's instinctive. As a matter of fact, a chance did come up this afternoon. Long chance, though. I'm sure I won't get it.'

'What was it?'

'My agent rang after lunch. That's an event in itself.'

'Same with mine.'

'She'd been trying to get through all morning but –'

'Were you out?'

'What?' She paused. 'No, I, er...the phone. The phone had just got knocked off, you know, the receiver...I didn't notice till after lunch.'

'Ah. Well, what was the job?'

'Oh, be nice,' she said wistfully. 'Won't get it, though.'

'Don't be so defeatist.'

'No. Must think positive, mustn't I? The job is a week on a feature film in

Tunisia.'

'Starting when?'

'Next Monday. I am free, would you believe? But you know how last-minute features are. I rushed along to an interview this afternoon.'

'How was it?'

She shook her head gloomily. 'Don't think I did too well. There was another girl waiting who looked very glam. Sure she'll have got it. Still, nice to dream.' She shook her head ruefully. 'No, I'm sure I'll get the call tomorrow and I'll still be "resting". I wouldn't mind if "resting" wasn't so bloody exhausting.'

'We've all done our share.'

'I think I've done more than my share. A bit of "resting" out of drama school. "Too tall," they all said, "you're too tall." "What about Vanessa Redgrave?" I said. "She's tall. She's done all right." "Oh yes," they said. "Trouble is she's cornered the market in tall girls' parts. But don't worry, dear, you'll come into your own when you're older. Character parts, they'll be your forte." So a few more years of resting'.

'Then, suddenly, it came right. Suddenly there were parts for me. In my early thirties I blossomed. I played principal boys, I did Noel Cowards, Shakespeares – I played Viola, Portia, Rosalind...And then it just seemed to go again. I was back to "resting". The fact that that coincided with the break-up of my marriage didn't help.'

'And since then it's been – what? Bits and pieces, the odd day here, day there, nothing lasting. This should be my great time, showing off my forte in my forties. Where are all those wonderful character parts they promised me? No, I'm washed up. No doubt I've got a reputation for the booze, too. "Thinking of booking Zoë Fratton? Och, I wouldn't, love. She's no good after lunch." And that's all there is left of me.'

She was silent and looked down into her glass. As if symbolically, it was empty. A slice of lemon clung precariously to the side.

'I'm sorry, Charles. I'm not always like this.'

'I know.' He believed her. Through all the maudlin self-hatred, there was something appealing about Zoë Fratton.

'It's just sometimes I feel so dreadful, as if I've done something awful. I feel so alone.'

'We all do, Zoë.' He rose. He had lost his taste for drinking. 'I must go.'

'Meet me here again, Charles,' she pleaded urgently.

'All right,' he said. 'Thursday?'

'Okay.'

Stan Fogden had all the gear – brushes, ladders, pasting tables, lining paper, old newspapers, dust sheets. He kept it all in his 'little Charlie' ('Charlie Chan – Van. Geddit, Charles?'), in which they drew up in the mews behind Tryst just before eight the next morning. It was an early hour for Charles, but Stan was a great believer in working 'just like the professionals–because that's what we are, mate.'

Charles had given some thought to what he should wear that morning. Obviously he needed old clothes for painting, but he was too much of an actor to wear just any old clothes. He had finally settled on a grey flannel shirt and a pair of shapeless tweed trousers. It was the costume he had worn in the role of a Communist poet in a play about the Spanish Civil War ('I would have welcomed the assassination of a President or anything else that curtailed this tedious piece' – *Huddersfield Daily Examiner*).

Since, as soon as they arrived, Stan handed Charles a huge pair of overalls that would cover everything, this attention to costume was rather wasted.

Tryst was set in that little hinterland of streets north of Holland Park Avenue. At the back it was made up of two mews cottages. The kitchen was in the garage part of one, with additional restaurant seating above. The other garage was used for Tristram Gowers' car, and above it was the flat in which he and Yves lived.

Both decorators were loaded with buckets and dust-sheets as they walked towards the entrance. One door led up to the flat; the other was the back way into the kitchen. Outside the flat door, propped against the wall, lay a plastic bag with the name of a Swiss Cottage butcher printed on the side. A rather nasty smell emanated from it.

Stan took a look inside. 'Phew. Load of liver going off. Someone got the delivery wrong. Didn't know they was going away. That'll be pretty niffy by the time they get back, won't it?' He reached through the side of his overalls into his trouser pocket. 'Now, out with the old fiddle.'

'Don't tell me...Fiddle-dee-dee – Key?'

'You're learning, Charles my son. You most certainly are learning.' Stan opened the door to the tiny hall. On the left another door led to the garage. Straight ahead was a staircase, carpeted in soft beige. 'Up we go then. See what's to do. They was going to leave all the wallpaper and paint. They'd bought it. Be very pretty, I imagine. Did you know these two was a pair of soups?'

From the context Charles was pretty sure he knew what was meant, but he couldn't work it out. 'Go on. I give up.'

'Charles, I am disappointed in you. Soup Tureen – Queen.'

They arrived on the landing and opened the door into the sitting-room. It was beautifully furnished and as spotless as Tristram's high standards would demand. Neatly in the middle of the carpet was a pile of paint tins and rolls of paper.

Stan knelt down. 'I'll take a shufti at this lot. You go and see what's what in the Max.'

'Sorry?'

Stan Fogden grinned triumphantly, 'Maximum Headroom – Bedroom.'

'Oh God,' said Charles in mock exasperation as he crossed the landing and opened the door of the Max.

'Oh God,' he said again, but this time it was a whisper of horror. Splayed across the white bedspread lay the naked body of Yves Lafeu. Black blood had dried from the wounds in his throat and his mutilated genitals.

He was at least three days dead.

# Chapter Four

WHILE STAN WAS phoning for the police, Charles hurried down the stairs of the mews cottage, seized with the thought of a new horror. The sight of Yves's bloody body had raised immediate and unsettling suspicions about the contents of the plastic bag outside the front door.

A cloud of flies dispersed as he approached it, seeming to lift the smell of decay up with them. As carefully as he dared, without making his inspection too apparent to any subsequent forensic investigator, Charles poked around in the nauseous contents of the bag.

With some relief he saw that it was only calves' liver. Three days in the sun hadn't made it a particularly salubrious package, but at least it did not contain any human remains.

Back in the mews, he was about to go upstairs when he thought of the garage. The door was not locked. He switched on the light to reveal emptiness.

Tristram Gowers' meticulously packed Volvo had gone.

The first of the police arrived in two squad cars with blue lights whirling, but by the end of the morning the mews yard was full of further marked and unmarked cars and vans. The predictable crowd of gawpers gathered on the periphery of the scene. Yves Lafeu's private moment of dying had suddenly become public property.

Charles and Stan were politely asked to wait in the restaurant until there was someone free to take statements from them. The sight of the slashed body had subdued even the Cockney's usual ebullience. He produced no rhyming formulae for murder. They sat in silence, Stan apparently engrossed in one of the old newspapers he had brought with him.

Charles looked around Tryst. Empty, and in daylight, the restaurant was drab and dusty, as if it had been closed for six months rather than three days. It was hard to remember how much life had been contained there on the Saturday evening. The atmosphere was as dead as that of a theatre the morning after a triumphant first night.

Charles looked across to the counter by the entrance and tried to visualize Monique Lafeu letting in the young man with blonded hair. He tried to see her brother swanning across the room to greet his friend, and Tristram appearing like an avenging fury from the kitchen. But the memory he raised was intellectual rather than cinematic. The only part of the scene he could recreate in his mind with clarity was the sound of Tristram's kitchen knife clattering down on to the bar counter.

He looked across there wistfully, but decided that swigging the Armagnac might not be the sort of thing the police would appreciate.

He felt uneasy and rather sick. The nausea arose partly from the recent shock of discovering Yves's body, but it had another cause as well. There were certain logical connections about the death which he was as yet unwilling to make. He didn't want to follow them through to their conclusion.

Stan stolidly did not look up from his paper as Charles rose and went up the brass-railed staircase to the upper dining-room. From there the whole mews could be seen except for its cul-de-sac end. Through the arch which provided the only access another police van was arriving as Charles looked. Tapes had been stretched between cones to provide a barrier and uniformed police opened these to admit the new vehicle, before returning to the job of convincing the curious crowd that there would be nothing to see and that they must have better things to do with their morning.

The side of the mews yard Charles faced backed on to a shopping parade. On street level were all the back-doors and delivery gates; above, a few windows, through which piles of boxes could be seen, suggesting that the first floors were store-rooms and offices rather than flats. The residential property was on Tryst's side of the mews, tarted-up and overpriced little cottages. On the previous Saturday night the shop premises would have presumably been empty. If there had been any witnesses of comings and goings to the mews in the early hours, they would have been Tristram and Yves's neighbours...or lovers sitting in parked cars in the mews...or passing vagrants...

Charles knew it was wishful thinking. After Tryst's diners and staff had left on the Saturday night, he felt fairly sure there was only one other significant event to witness – the departure from the garage of a Volvo containing one person.

The vast majority of murders, after all, are committed within the narrow confines of a close relationship.

'The police seem to have forgotten us,' Charles observed, once again eyeing the well-stocked bar with yearning.

He only got a grunt from Stan, which was a measure of how deeply the Cockney had been shocked by what they had seen.

'Mind if I look at one of the papers?'

This was rewarded by a 'Please yourself' shrug. Charles reached down and picked up one of the tabloids. Its news was sufficiently familiar for him to check the date. That Monday, two days previously. He settled down to pass the time.

Strange, he thought as he flicked through, how little news really stands the test of time. The initial shock of disasters fades, and increasingly the bulk of column space is filled with forecast and speculation, which are quickly rendered obsolete as real events overtake them. After two days, there was hardly anything left in the paper he was reading that seemed to have any relevance.

The exception he found in the gossip column. And that was only relevant because it added extra poignancy to the circumstances in which he found himself.

What caught his eye initially was a photograph of an extremely pretty girl. She was wearing a large hat, suggesting that perhaps the picture had been taken at a wedding, and her hair was longer, but Charles had no difficulty in recognizing the girl who had been introduced to him in that very room as 'Henry'.

The report confirmed it.

TV smoothie *Bertram Pride*, known to millions of adoring matrons as Philip Lexton, seems to have a new love in his life. The ageing juvenile obviously believes in the rejuvenating properties of youth (and maybe money), because he's gone for *Henrietta Rawsleigh*, 18-year-old daughter of 'Bring Back The Rope' Tory MP, Sir Timothy Rawsleigh. Henry, as she's known to her Sloane Ranger chums, is apparently set on becoming an actress, so maybe the back-scratching with Bertram won't be completely one-sided. The couple, who've been seen together a few times in the last two weeks at London's night-spots, including Froggie's and Tryst, are keeping quiet about the connection. Neither was available for comment over the weekend, though there were strong rumours that they spent it together in Bertie's love-nest cottage in Kent, scene of many of his other conquests.

And since the subject of Tryst has come up, I'm afraid I have to report that Saturday night witnessed yet another of the public rows between the proprietors which contribute so much to the restaurant's unique ambience.

The snide tone of the piece seemed doubly inappropriate to Charles as he sat in the melancholy silence of Tryst.

It was nearly mid-day when a plain-clothes Inspector and a uniformed constable finally came to take their statements. The Inspector was very apologetic for the delay, and, once he had started, very efficient in getting the details from them. Needless to say, he passed no comment on the murder, but something in his tone seemed to categorize it as a case that was finished, a case where the main outline had been defined and all that remained was the formal filling-in of the details.

Within an hour Charles and Stan were allowed to leave warned that they might be required for supplementary questioning and that their appearance at an inquest might be necessary. They were thanked for their patience and assistance, and dismissed.

Stan's decorating equipment was neatly piled outside the front door of the mews cottage, and they were granted permission to take it away. The tapes were drawn back to allow the van to pass through, and they drove the gauntlet of curious stares of onlookers, who were no doubt fantasizing wildly about Charles and Stan's role in the proceedings.

Without asking, Stan drove back towards Hereford Road. He had turned left at the Notting Hill traffic lights before he spoke directly to Charles.

'Well,' he said, 'there's our five hundred quid up the sauer.'

'Sauerkraut – Spout?' asked Charles automatically. Stan nodded grimly. 'If he's topped his boyfriend, I somehow don't see him wanting the flat decorated no more.'

Charles didn't comment. He could hear the tension in Stan's voice. The apparent callousness was just his way of coping with the shock.

'I was glad that copper didn't ask nothing about how we was doing the job …you know, whether we was going to declare the loot or not.'

'Oh, come on, Stan. He had more important crimes to think about than a little modest fiddling of the taxman.'

'Yes, I suppose so. They unsettle me, though, any officials. It's their attitude of mind. Maybe they do all work for different organizations, but I reckon they're all hand in heavens.'

Heavens Above – Glove. Charles had no problem with that one. The van turned off Westbourne Grove into Hereford Road. 'This is you, isn't it, Charlie?'

'That's right. Just up there on the right. Beyond the Volkswagen.'

The van stopped outside the flaking frontage of what had once been a prosperous family house, but was now segmented into bedsitters. 'Come in for a drink?' asked Charles. 'I've got half a bottle of Bell's, if you –'

'No. Thanks all the same, Charles. Get back to the missus, I think. Feel quite shaken after that lot.'

'Me too.'

'Yeah. Well, look, if another decorating job comes up, I'll get in touch. Mel Ponting said he might want something doing – do you know Mel?'

'I seem to remember seeing credits for him a few years back, but not for some time.'

'Ooh, Mel's not in the business any more. He's no fool. He's got a much better racket going.'

But before Charles could ask what this 'much better racket' was, Stan continued, 'Anyway, I'll give him a bell and let you know. See you, Charlie. Sorry your introduction to the decorating business was a bit messy. Let's hope next time we don't find a lover's.'

Charles was half-way up the stairs before he found a satisfactory explanation for it. Lover's Tiff – Stiff.

And he didn't feel very sure about that.


By the payphone on the landing there was a message scrawled by one of the interchangeable Swedish girls who occupied the other bedsitters in the house. Charles sometimes wondered why it was that every new tenant always turned out to be under thirty, female and Swedish (and, incidentally, built like a docker). He wove fantasies of an accommodation agency in somewhere unpronounceable like Jönköping, whose sole business was to stock this one house in Hereford Road. He awaited the day, without much hope, when a Swedish man in a suit would knock on his door, offering him millions of kronor to move out and make the Scandinavian monopoly absolute. In more realistic moods he concluded that news of forthcoming vacancies was circulated by word of mouth from wench to strapping wench.

The messages they left for him contained such regular ambiguities that he thought they must be the result of perverseness rather than just unfamiliarity with the language. The current one read: 'WRING WET DIANA VILSON', which a moment of thought translated into 'RING WEST END TELEVISION – DANA WILSON.'

No actor can contain the little surge of excitement which comes with a message to ring a Producer or Casting Director. This always could be it, the Big One, the call that sets everything else in motion. Presumably Bertram Pride received such a call when he heard he'd got the part of Philip Lexton. Presumably every major success has started from one small call.

Dana Wilson's voice was so relaxed as to be almost inert. 'Oh yes, Charles Paris. I met your agent at some reception. What was his name? Marcus Scotton…?'

'Maurice Skellern.'

'That's right. He was singing your praises like nobody's business.'

'Was he?' That sounded most unlike Maurice. Charles found it difficult to imagine his agent as anything other than a voice at the end of a telephone, and even when he could give this image flesh, the idea of it going round lavishing praise on its client seemed mildly incongruous.

'Well, perhaps not that. He did say you'd done a couple of decent bits in your career.'

Yes, that sounded much more like the Maurice Charles could visualize – reducing thirty-two years of work to 'a couple of decent bits'.

'Anyway, he seemed very keen on the idea of you coming along for a chat.'

'Yes, fine.'

'How's your availability at the moment?'

Trick question. Charles knew he must hold back the instinctive response. ('Not another solitary booking between here and the grave, so far as I can see. Even my promising sideline as a decorator has just been prematurely cut short by murder.') No, the skill was to imply interest, but not desperation; and to suggest that, by careful juggling, a few hours could be prised out of a busy schedule. He remembered with gratitude the line he had heard from Bertram Pride.

'Oh, a few things in the air,' he replied casually, adding, 'but can probably be shuffled around.'

'How's this Friday for you?'

'Um…' Charles left a pause long enough for someone to summon up the image of a crowded diary before asking, 'What sort of time?'

'Well…' Dana Wilson sounded less as if she were speaking than yawning. 'There's a lunchtime fringe show I ought to get to, so I'd have to leave round twelve...then the afternoon looks a bit gummed up...got a half-past ten interview in the morning...how would round eleven do...?'

'Ah.' Charles's tone of voice implied a snag. 'On the other hand...' No, the snag was perhaps not insuperable. 'Yes, I shouldn't think he'd mind...' The 'he' was meant to be some mythical American film producer. 'Yes, I should think...A moment's doubt cut this optimism short. 'Hmm.' The snag reared its head again. 'Look, could we make it quarter past eleven? Then I'll be sure of making it.' This suggested some early morning meeting of enormous significance. The fact that all Charles would have to deal with on the Friday morning was the hurdle of getting out of bed did not matter; the 'availability' game must be played according to the proper rules.

Dana Wilson bought it, anyway. 'Yes, I think that'll be okay.' And then, to ensure that she didn't lose any points and to reassert the enormous demands on her own time, she qualified her assent. 'Might have to go to an outside rehearsal Friday morning, if the schedule on a drama we're doing gets changed. Long chance, but might happen, thought I should warn you. Anyway, I've got your number, so I'll let you know in good time if I have to cancel.'

Honour was now satisfied on both sides.

'Oh, by the way,' asked Charles, 'is the interview for anything specific?'

'No, no, just general,' drawled Dana and, after appropriate goodbyes, rang off.

Charles's question had not been unimportant. Actors like to know what part they're being considered for, simply so that they can choose their wardrobe and demeanour for the forthcoming interview. Young aspirants have turned up in spats and monocles to auditions for P. G. Wodehouse dramatizations. Casting for plays set in dockland brings out heavy denims and steel-toecapped boots. First World War dramas keep barbers busy doing the statutory short-back-and-sides. Beards and moustaches sprout and vanish on rumour of forthcoming parts; heads were shaved when a play about Buddhism was announced.

There is even a (surely apocryphal) story about the auditions for a new drama on the life of Abraham Lincoln. An actor who bore a slight likeness to the President read in *Stage* that the auditions would be held at a certain theatre a month from that date. He decided he would go all out for the part, growing the right sort of beard, hiring the right sort of costume, and reading so much about the character that by the day of the auditions he thought he *was* Abraham Lincoln. When he arrived at the theatre, he was assassinated.

Charles Paris adjusted his appearance according to the part for which he was being considered, but nowadays he did not make his metamorphoses too extreme. On one occasion he had gone to an audition for Jean Anouilh's play about the martyred Archbishop of Canterbury, *Becket*. Due to a misunderstanding by Maurice Skellern, Charles had arrived expecting to read for Samuel Beckett's *Waiting for Godot*, and had therefore dressed as a tramp.

He still felt shaken by the morning's events and it was with difficulty that he restrained himself from hitting the whisky bottle until half-past five. The fact that the pubs were then open made him feel almost righteous about pouring a couple of inches into a tumbler. But just as he raised the drink to his lips, the telephone on the landing rang.

It was Kevin O'Rourke.

'Charles. Have you heard about Yves?'

Charles explained the harsh circumstances in which the news had been broken to him.

'Oh, my God. Listen, Bartlemas and I are in a terrible state about it. And about Tristram... Where on earth is Tristram?'

'His car had gone from the garage.'

'Oh, no. Charles, do you think you could come round?'

Bartlemas and O'Rourke lived in Ideal Road, Islington, in a four-story Victorian house, which inside was a shrine to their two idols, Kean and Macready. The walls were hung with prints and playbills; on every horizontal surface clustered statuettes, hats, swords, rings and other props; bookcases were tight with leather-bound volumes of biographies and memoirs.

Charles had been to the house for a good few convivial evenings over the years, but on this occasion the atmosphere was subdued. William Bartlemas and Kevin O'Rourke were, as ever, dressed alike, but the sober black trousers and charcoal pullovers did not draw attention to their livery. Bartlemas was sympathetic to his friend, but O'Rourke was clearly the one who was suffering most.

'It's terrible, Charles...'

'Terrible...' Bartlemas echoed supportively.

'We only saw it in the paper this afternoon...'

'And at first we just couldn't believe it...'

'To think of Yves being dead...'

'I mean, he was so beautiful, and so alive...'

'Yes, wicked sometimes, but so alive...'

'The paper implied it was murder...'

'There weren't many details, but...'

'Do you think they could be wrong? Do you think perhaps it wasn't murder...'

Charles shook his head sadly. 'I'm sorry. I'm afraid there is no question about it.'

He was glad they accepted that. He could have elaborated, but would rather have spared their feelings, and his own, by not recreating the bloody tableau he had seen that morning.

'They're bound to blame Tristram,' said O'Rourke with sudden bitterness.

'Bound to...' Bartlemas agreed.

'Well, you can see their point.' Charles made his voice as level and reasonable as he could. 'In any murder case the first suspect is always the victim's cohabitant. And we all witnessed Tristram threatening Yves with the knife.'

'Yes, but that was just part of their relationship. Yves was always a bit of a tart, always being unfaithful, always hurting Tristram, but that was part of his charm. Tristram would never have killed him.'

'Not just for *that*, no...'

'We don't know the full background,' said Charles judiciously. 'The arrival of that boy at the restaurant on Saturday night may have been the culmination of a quarrel. Perhaps it was the final straw. It made Tristram see red and –'

'Oh, for God's sake!' O'Rourke broke in with uncharacteristic anger. 'Tristram wasn't like that. He was quite sane. Everyone seems to think just because a person's gay, he lives life on a permanent emotional knife-edge.'

'Now, I didn't say –'

'No, you didn't, but you were moving in that direction. And I'm sure that's what the police are thinking. "Oh well, if it's a gay couple, they must be at each other's throats all the time. It must be the lover who did it."'

Charles didn't mention the attitude of the Inspector who had taken his statement, though it might very well have reflected the sort of views O'Rourke described. 'Listen, I know you're fond of Tristram –'

'Of course I'm fond of him. He's my nearest relative, apart from anything else. And round the time that he "came out", when he was very confused, we saw a lot of each other and got very close.'

'I'm sure you did,' said Charles gently. 'But you must see, just from the point of view of ordinary logic, that Tristram is the obvious suspect.'

O'Rourke's silence conceded this point.

'I mean, it'd be different if he was around to defend himself. But the fact that both he and his car are missing does look like an admission of guilt.'

'That's certainly how the police are taking it.' The new bitterness in O'Rourke's voice seemed temporarily to have silenced Bartlemas's echoes.

'Have you spoken to the police?' asked Charles.

'Yes, of course I have. Tristram's my cousin. I have a right to know what's going on.'

'What did they say?'

'They were pretty non-committal. They confirmed that Yves was dead and "foul play" was suspected. They also confirmed that Tristram was missing.'

'Nothing else?'

'They said that enquiries were under way, and they would keep me informed of appropriate developments.'

'Meaning?'

'Meaning very little, I imagine. Meaning that, so far as they're concerned, another pooftah's done in his lover and the world is probably a better place without him.'

The depth of resentment in O'Rourke's tone spoke of a long history of persecution. Charles was a little surprised to hear it. He had known Bartlemas and O'Rourke for so long that he had almost forgotten they were gay.

He maintained his tone of moderation. 'I don't know whether they are as prejudiced as you think or not, but suspecting Tristram of the murder is a fairly natural reaction. I mean, do you have any alternative thesis to put forward?'

O'Rourke gave a short shake of his head.

'Well, I'm afraid, until Tristram turns up to clear his name, he's bound to remain the Number One suspect.'

Tristram Gowers didn't turn up. But his car did.

To Charles's surprise, the police were as good as their word to Kevin O'Rourke. They did ring to keep him informed of appropriate developments.

The enquiry had taken on an international aspect. The French police, at the request of Scotland Yard, had investigated the house at Mas-de-Pouzard.

Outside it they had found Tristram Gowers' Volvo, all packed up for the holiday.

Of the vehicle's owner there was, as yet, no trace.

## *Chapter Five*

'THE THING I want to know, Stan, is how was the job set up?'

'What – decorating Tryst?'

'That's right.'

'Well, the owner set it up. One who's disappeared. Him with the Irish.'

Irish Jig – Wig. Charles knew that one; it was authentic, traditional rhyming slang, not one of Stan's more dubious comings.

'What, he rang you?'

'No, no. Remember, I'm only Bill Timmis's understudy. Someone must've recommended Bill to him, but Bill couldn't do it because of his Bahamas job, so he put the bloke on to Phil, but Phil'd just heard about his telly, so Phil put him on to me.'

'I see. When were the arrangements made?'

'Ooh, two weeks back, I reckon.'

'You see, I was wondering why the job was set up to start on the Wednesday. Tristram and Yves were meant to leave on the Sunday morning, so the decorators could have moved in on the Monday...unless Tristram actually wanted the delay...unless he didn't want Yves's body to be discovered for three days, which would give him time to make his getaway.'

Charles sat back, rather pleased with the way he had worked that out, but looked up to see Stan shaking his head with pity.

'Doesn't work, Charlie. Number One: I asked for it to start on the Wednesday. I was doing a job down at Teddington.'

'What – with Thames Television?'

'No, no. Vinyl wallpaper on a kitchen, bathroom and toilet. And I reckoned it'd take me longer than it did. I worked evenings and finished end of last week.'

'So why didn't you start doing Tryst on Monday?'

'Two reasons. I hadn't got you set up for a start.'

'Oh, that's true.'

'*And* I didn't know when old Tristram and his mate was actually leaving. I'd said I couldn't start till the Wednesday and he said, "Oh, fine, we'll be away by then".'

'I see.'

'But, Charlie,' Stan continued inexorably, 'there is another flaw in your logic. If you're trying to work out some theory that Tristram Whatnot set this whole murder up in advance, then you're way off beam.'

'Why?'

'Oh, come on, Charles. Use your Michael.'

'Er?'

'Michael Caine – Brain. Look, if Tristram was planning to top the Frog, he chose a pretty peculiar way of doing it. Immediately he makes himself the main suspect and pisses off to France. Now there's no way he can come back here after that, is there?'

'No.'

'So, if he knew he wasn't coming back, why the hell did he arrange to have the restaurant redecorated?'

Charles couldn't answer that. He had occasionally prided himself on some ability as a detective, but now he felt he was being given a lesson in the basics.

'What it means is,' Stan continued, making Charles feel even smaller, 'that, if you think old Tristram done it, then it has to be a spur-of-the-moment job. Sudden blaze of anger, out with the old knife –' he drew a finger across his throat with an unpleasantly guttural sound '– and get the hell away as soon as possible.'

'What it also means,' said Charles slowly, 'is that if you think somebody else did it –'

'And you'd have to be a bit of a loony to think that.'

'Maybe,' Charles conceded. 'But, if somebody else did do it, they might not have known about the decorating, and they might have thought it would be a month before anyone would go into the flat and find the body.'

Once again his optimistic look was met by a pitying gaze from Stan.

'And what, meanwhile, does this other bloke who done it do with Tristram?'

'Ah,' said Charles. 'I hadn't thought of that.'

'Charlie, my son, you're really a bit of a prat.'

That wasn't rhyming slang, but Charles knew exactly what it meant. 'Another beer, Stan?' he asked, picking up their two glasses.

When Charles came back from the bar, Stan had been joined by a thin man with a sharp face, who, in spite of his greying hair, managed to look like a naughty schoolboy, a sort of grown-up Artful Dodger.

'Charlie – this is Mel Ponting, who I told you about.'

'Hi. What can I get you to drink?'

'Oh, vodka Campari, please.'

'It only took me a couple of years in the business,' Mel Ponting announced when they were all supplied with drinks and sitting round the table, 'to realize that acting was a mug's game. I mean, I done all right, got a few good tellies, that sort of thing, but I got this feeling I wasn't maximizing my potential. I mean, it doesn't take many weeks of "resting" for you to twig that you ain't got any money coming in.'

Charles and Stan smiled condescendingly at this truism. 'But that's just part of the business,' said Charles.

'Well, that was the part I wasn't going to put up with. I grew up in the East

End, and all my mates, they was earning money. When they hadn't got work, they made work. As an actor you can't do that – you got to wait till some berk employs you. Well, I'm not good at waiting.

'So, anyway, I looked around at all the actors I knew and almost everywhere I saw the same thing – people being under-used, spare capacity going to waste. Now any businessman'll tell you what you got to do is make sure that you're using everything you got all the time – that's the way to productivity. So I saw all these actors, and I knew they had a lot of potential, I just had to harness that potential. I had to find a market for all the energy they was wasting while they wasn't in work.'

'So what did you do?'

'Well, my first thought was to make more work for them, actually get things going myself, go into production. I did that for a few years, put on a few shows, made a few bob, but it wasn't what I was after. All risks and hassles, that business. As a producer, you're damned nearly as exposed as an actor. So I give that up.

'Then I tried agency. All right, one actor on his own can't keep in work all the time, but if you're drawing on a whole stable of actors, well, you spread your risk and you ought to be able to survive. All right, I proved you can. Survive. Wouldn't put it a lot higher than that. Shall I tell you what the trouble is? As an agent, you're only on ten per cent. Okay, you can push it up to fifteen, but it still ain't princely. You see, you're still dependent on the same berks who wouldn't employ you as an actor, and at any given time, half your stock – you know, the actors you got on your books – are doing bugger all.

'And then it come to me. I realized where I was going wrong. I saw the light – like Paul on the road to Singapore…or was it Bob Hope on the road to Morocco? I realized that in a profession where most of the people are out of work most of the time, it's daft to try and make money out of that small slice of their time while they're actually working. What you got to do is make your money out of the time they aren't working. And that's how Actors Anonymous was born.'

'I'm afraid I've never heard of it,' Charles confessed.

'Well, of course you haven't. That's why they're Anonymous – no one knows who they are. Anyway, I like to keep a kind of low profile, publicity-wise, because I don't want to draw the Inland Revenue's attention to what I'm doing.'

'So what are you doing?'

'Basically, I supply actors wherever they're needed. That is, wherever they're needed outside of show-business. You'd be surprised how often someone's glad of an actor round the house or in the office.'

"But what sort of things do they *do*?'

'Well, all right, the basic stuff's domestic.'

'What, you mean the old charring?'

'Yes. Domestic cleaning, waiting, serving behind bars – that's the basic turnover of the business. It's also the official bit – that's the stuff that goes through the books. Davenport Domestics that side's called. But it's only the tip of the iceberg, you know. Lots of other things Actors Anonymous do.'

'Like?'

'Well, sticking with the domestic, we can do the Rolls-Royce service. That's really butlers and parlour-maids. Surprising how popular they are to add a bit of snob value to the old suburban dinner party.'

'But I thought butlers had years of training and –'

'Listen, Charles, how many actors do you know who haven't played a butler at one time or another in their career? Go on, how many?'

'Well...'

'Anyone who's done rep has been in God knows how many tatty old thrillers in which the butler at least might have done it. There's butlers and maids in hundreds of plays. And, as long as television keeps churning out all these Victorian and Edwardian series, new butlers are being trained every day. A series like *Upstairs, Downstairs* is like a blooming university course.'

'But do they really know enough to convince the –'

'For one evening, Charles, they can busk it. Go on, how many actors have you known go on stage without knowing their lines?'

'A good few.'

'Right. And yet they don't dry, do they? They keep going, they get through. Any actor worth his salt can be a totally convincing butler for one evening.'

Charles laughed. 'You said it wasn't just domestic stuff.'

'No. Once you get the idea, all kinds of other things follow. I mean, back to our suburban dinner party. All right, you got the staff sorted out, trouble is the hosts have the most unbelievably boring friends. But if you throw in a couple of actors, playing a...what shall we say?...a Detective-Inspector and a poet, well, things may start to hum a little.'

'It'd never work. They'd never sustain it.'

'It has been done, Charles. You take my word, it has been done. Not often, but it worked.'

'But you'd have to know so much about –'

'You don't need a lot for an evening. And every actor's played a Detective-Inspector at some stage or other – in all the thrillers where he wasn't playing the butler.

'But now I get more exotic requests, you know. Had a few bookings for blokes to appear as long-lost boy-friends to break up affairs that weren't working. Well, saves a 'Dear John' letter. Then I had a good one last year from a bloke who was in the Scrubs doing seven years for his part in a mail-snatch. He'd got this boy at public school and he wanted me to provide a respectable pair of parents for Speech Day, you know, to keep up his son's image. I found a couple who did that lovely – just played the same parts in *The Browning Version* in rep.

'Had another good one recently. Bit different. Request from a fairly big firm that was getting worried about productivity levels. You know, they thought the staff was getting lazy, taking too long lunch-breaks, that sort of number…So they come to me and ask if I've got a couple of actors who can spend a week in the place pretending to be Management Consultants. No problem. I give them a good briefing, tell them how they've got to keep asking everyone how many people there are in each department, and use a lot of phrases like "staff redeployment", "redundancy levels" and "early retirement" and that's all there is to it. Worked a treat. The firm was delighted. Everyone pulled their socks up, productivity soared. And, of course, the firm saved thousands. I mean, I charged plenty for the two actors, but that's about one per cent of what real Management Consultants would have cost. No, Actors Anonymous is really booming, and you know I get the feeling I'm only scraping the surface of the market.'

'And you take an agency fee for all this?'

'That's right. Twenty per cent because I've got the contacts.'

'But surely some of the actors get recognized?'

'Very rarely, Charles. Trouble with all you Thespians is you think the world has only got eyes for you, think no one notices anyone else in the room. Not true, I'm afraid, my son. Anyway, it's a matter of context. If you go to a party and someone's pointed out to you as the butler, you tend to accept that at face value. You don't go staring at him and thinking, "Didn't I once see you giving your Malvolio at Hornchurch?" Even if the bloke does look vaguely familiar, so what? There's enough actors who've given up the unequal struggle and gone into other businesses, aren't there?'

'True enough.'

Mel Ponting grinned. 'I reckon old Stan here's sometimes in two minds about giving it all up and concentrating on the decorating.'

'Do sometimes think about it, yeah. I mean, if I've just spent a couple of days on a telly with one of those young directors who thinks he's Cecil B. De Mille, I'd give anything to get back to the old wallpaper brush.'

'Yes, but, Mel,' Charles insisted, 'what happens if one of your domestics really gets a big break, suddenly becomes a household name? You can't send him out charring then, can you?'

'Well, no, but no successes happen like literally overnight. There's always a bit of a time-lag. Anyway, with that sort of break, the bloke probably doesn't need the money from the charring, so he gives it up naturally. Mind you,' Mel added, with a shrewd tap of the finger to his nose, 'I don't lose out that way. A lot of them, when they become big stars, they want staff themselves. They're loyal, they know me, so I get bookings for other actors to go and clean for them. I mean, I done that for Bernard Walton.'

'What, he used to char for you?'

'You bet. Don't mention it when you see him – bit sensitive about it – but he did. And Bertram Pride, and all. Whole lot of them. And now they've made it, I provide their staff. It's a nice self-generating business I got going, Charles.'

'Sounds like it. But don't you ever hanker to get back on the stage?'

This suggestion got a derisive snort. 'You have got to be joking.' Then Mel Ponting's tone became brisk and businesslike. 'Anyway, do you want to get on the books, Charles?'

'Well...'

'That's why Stan fixed up this introduction.'

'Yes.'

'I gather the old decorating's a bit quiet right now. Last job came to a bit of a sticky end, didn't it?'

'You could say that.' Charles winced at the memory. 'Well, yes, I'd like to have a go. I just wonder whether I've got the abilities to –'

'Charles,' asked Mel patiently, 'have you ever played a butler?'

'Of course. Lots of times. The *Eastern Daily Press* described my butler in *Arsenic For Two* as "to the manner born".'

'See. What about barmen?'

'God. Story of my television career, barmen. I even played one for a whole series called *The Strutters*...well, the series was never completed, but...And then, when I was a barman in some incomprehensible *Play For Today*, the *Observer* said I was "lugubriously efficient".'

'Well, that's all you need to be, isn't it?'

'Mind you, I've never played a char. Those parts are always monopolized by lovable Cockney ladies.'

'Yes, but everyone knows how to hoover and dust.'

'Hmm. Don't think my bedsitter would be much of an advertisement for my talents.'

'I didn't say everyone *did* it; I said everyone *knows how* to do it. Anyway, you can do most things when you're being paid for them.'

Charles nodded, in full agreement with that sentiment.

'Right. You're on the books of Actors Anonymous, as of today.'

'Great.'

'Can't promise anything straight away, but things will come up, you take my word.' Mel suddenly looked cautious. 'Oh, and...'

'Yes?'

'I can trust your discretion in not mentioning any of our mutual activities to the taxman, can't I?'

Charles's expression was deeply pained. 'Mel, what do you take me for?'

'Fine. Sorry. Had to ask. Do come across the odd nut in this business, you know. Right, so that's it.' Mel Ponting drained the last of his vodka Campari and rose. 'Back to the office. Thanks for the drink. Oh, and, Charles...'

'Yes?'

'Don't ring me, I'll ring you. Okay?'

Charles had been in two minds about going to the Montrose on the Thursday evening. After the collapse of his financial hopes from the decorating job at

Tryst, he knew that he shouldn't really afford another evening's drinking. But, though that particular door had closed, Mel Ponting had opened another at least a little, and Charles felt he could take the risk. His attitude to money always hovered between two extremes. When he had no prospects of anything coming in, he felt despairingly poor; but it only needed a hint of a rumour of a prospect for him to imagine the money already in the bank. And to spend it accordingly.

He had not forgotten his vague arrangement to meet Zoë Fratton at the club, but, after the events at Tryst, he had discounted the possibility of her turning up. However inimical her relationship was with her ex-husband, she was bound to be affected by his disappearance after apparently committing a murder. And, apart from her emotional state, she was likely to be occupied with questioning, as the police tried to establish Tristram's whereabouts.

He was therefore surprised to see Zoë ensconced in a corner when he eased his way through the theatrical crush at the Montrose at nine o'clock that evening. He was almost more surprised to see that sitting beside her was Bertram Pride.

'Can I get you a drink?' asked Charles, gesturing with his own large Bell's.

'No, thanks. Bertram's just got us one.' As on the last occasion, her voice was slurred, suggesting that the gin and tonic she clutched was not her first of the evening. 'Do you two know each other?'

'We met...recently...'

'Yes, Saturday, wasn't it?' Neither of them wanted to mention where they had met.

But Zoë herself brought up the fateful word. 'You heard about events at Tryst, Charles?'

'Yes.' He didn't elaborate. If she didn't know about his discovery of the body, there was no need to draw her attention to it. She looked in a very tense state; he didn't want to do anything to aggravate her condition.

She appeared not to know of his involvement; at any rate, she didn't mention it. 'I'm lucky,' she said, 'to have good friends. Bertram came round when he heard. He knew I'd be upset.'

Bertram Pride gave a self-depreciating dip of his head at the compliment. 'Just glad if I can be any help.'

'Oh, but you *were*,' asserted Zoë. 'He brought me another bottle of gin, Charles. Certainly knows the way to a girl's heart.'

She let out a little giggle, but there wasn't a lot of humour in it. 'Good to have friends who're loyal, when things are bad. Bertram and I worked together in rep...Bromley. He knew I'd be upset. Doesn't forget his old friends, just because he's a big star.'

Bertram Pride gave a little, embarrassed grin, as Zoë continued, 'And I've got you too, Charles, you coming to support me in my hour of need.' Her voice gave a little, hiccoughing lurch. 'Or do I mean my hour of triumph?'

She smiled at their blank expressions. 'Don't you understand, Yves Lafeu is dead. And, so far as the world's concerned, Tristram killed him. Wouldn't you call that two birds with one stone?'

'What do you mean – "as far as the world's concerned"?' asked Charles gently.

Zoë looked flustered. 'Well, I don't mean anything. I mean, Tristram must have done it, mustn't he? There isn't anything else to think, is there?'

'No,' said Bertram soothingly. He was watching her very carefully, as if worried about her mental state.

'Have you had long sessions with the police?' asked Charles.

'Long? Yes, long, long sessions. I have had long sessions with the police. Their view is...' Her voice was suddenly more sober, 'that I will not see Tristram again.'

'You mean they think he's committed suicide?'

She nodded with too much emphasis. 'That is exactly what they think. They've sent a team to France to investigate. Their view is,' she repeated the words with fastidious care, 'that dear Tristram's body is likely to turn up in the River Lot.'

'Well, I suppose that might be a logical conclusion,' said Bertram.

'Oh yes. For years I've wanted both of them dead, dreamed about it, been obsessed by the idea, and now it's happened...' her voice broke, 'I can't cope.'

Both men leaned forward to take her hands, and murmur reassurances about it just being shock and her soon feeling better and all the other insufficient platitudes that are produced in times of stress.

'I know it's difficult,' said Charles, 'but you've really got to try to think beyond this, think of the rest of your life.' Then, remembering something that might cheer her, he asked, 'Oh, what happened about that job in Tunisia? You never told me about that.'

Unfortunately, that subject was not calculated to improve her mood. 'I heard from the Casting Director. No. It's gone to the other girl.'

'I'm sorry.'

'Was that the job you mentioned when I rang you Wednesday morning?' asked Bertram.

'Yes. I was all excited about it then. Ten minutes later I heard I hadn't got it.'

'Bad luck.' Bertram looked genuinely upset by the news. Charles decided he would have to revise his opinion of the star. He had been inclined to dismiss Bertram as just another smoothie, but was impressed by the depth of sympathy Zoë was receiving.

'Wednesday,' she went on bitterly, 'was not a good day. First that news, and in the afternoon the police.'

'I'm sorry,' Charles repeated, again inadequately.

Bertram Pride looked at his watch. 'I'm afraid I've got to be off. I really just dropped by to the flat for a quick chat, Zoë, and I'm running a bit behind.'

'Of course. No, I'm very grateful. Sorry to have kept you. I do appreciate what you've done.' Zoë Fratton rose with surprising grace to embrace her friend. She was almost as tall as he was and they made an impressive couple. 'You have been most provident in peril.'

Bertram smiled at some private joke. Charles thought the reference was probably a quotation, but he couldn't identify it. The conversation of actors who have worked together is frequently littered with incomprehensible allusions to productions long forgotten.

'You'll be all right with Charles,' said Bertram reassuringly, passing over the baton of responsibility.

Charles discharged his duty well. After a couple more drinks, he steered Zoë out to a taxi, and accompanied her to her flat in a rather grim block round the back of John Barnes department store off the Finchley Road.

Inside her dark hall, she suddenly put her arms round him. 'You've been so kind to me, Charles. I don't deserve it.'

'Of course you do,' he said, as if patting a dog.

'I've done awful things. I've thought awful things. I'm not a good person.'

The tensions in her body squeezed him closer to her. His own body, with its usual appalling sense of timing, responded physically.

Zoë observed this, and looked at him closely, with a half-smile. 'No, I don't think it's quite the moment for me to expose my varicose veins to you.'

'No, I didn't mean...' Charles gently disengaged himself.

'Oh, you probably did. Quite flattering, you know, when you get to my age.' Charles blushed.

'And who knows,' Zoë continued, giving him a little ginny kiss, 'the day may come...' Her mood darkened suddenly. 'But not now. Not till all this is sorted out, till the police have consigned the file to their archives. At the moment there's too much tension, too much suspicion.'

Charles moved to the door. 'Are you sure you'll be all right here on your own?' he asked, wishing as soon as the words were out of his mouth that he'd rephrased them. The question sounded too much as if he were suggesting he should stay.

But fortunately Zoë didn't take it that way. 'No, I'll be all right,' she assured him.

Charles said his goodbyes. Just before the door closed behind him, he heard Zoë, with a strange, cracked laugh in her voice, announce, 'I wanted the pair of them dead. And now I've got what I wanted.'

## Chapter Six

THE LANGUOR OF Dana Wilson in the flesh matched that of her telephone manner. She was small, with hooded sleepy blue eyes which were surrounded by shiny reddish make-up. She had that good grooming which seems to be obligatory for women in television – hair recently styled with a couple of pinkish streaks, loose flowered blouse and revivalist miniskirt. She seemed to be having difficulty in summoning up much interest in Charles Paris.

'Of course, we haven't got a great deal in production at the moment,' she admitted drowsily.

'Yes, Maurice said this would just be a general interview.'

'Maurice?'

'My agent.'

'Oh yes. Of course, we have done some wonderful productions. Some of the casting in our big series has been just inspired.'

'Yes,' Charles agreed patiently. It came back to him that everyone in television always attributed success to the contribution of their own particular department. Failure was, of course, due to the shortcomings of all the other departments.

'I mean, I myself actually cast *Lexton and Sons*.'

She left a pause which Charles filled with an appropriately impressed 'Really?'

'One of my first big assignments. Before that I was secretary to Tilly Lake. Do you know Tilly?'

'Yes, she cast *The Strutters*, which I was in.'

'Oh, you've worked for W.E.T., have you?'

'Yes.' God, she hadn't even made the effort to check in the company index to see whether Charles had a record card or not.

'Of course, Tilly's mostly Light Ent.,' said Dana, with the contempt all Drama Departments always demonstrate for their more frivolous and popular rival.

'Yes.'

There was a languid pause. Charles decided he had better volunteer some of the information he would have expected her to ask for. 'I didn't bring any photographs or cuttings, because I never think they mean a lot.'

'Oh, don't you?' This idea seemed to elicit a tiny spark of interest.

'No. Do you?'

'No, not really.' She slumped back into inertia.

'But perhaps you'd like me to tell you some of the things I've done...?'

'Oh, I don't think so,' Dana replied, as if he were suggesting some enormous imposition. 'No, I'm very much a *face* person.'

'Oh.'

'I see a face, and I lock it away in my mind – I have a photographic memory, you know – and then, maybe weeks, maybe months, maybe years later, I see a script and I see apart, and a face rises to the surface of my mind.'

'I see,' said Charles with proper awe for this mystic approach to the business of casting. 'But perhaps if I were to tell you the sort of parts I've played in the past, you might –'

'Oh, I don't think that'll be necessary. I've got your face locked in my mind.'

Charles felt tempted to ask whether he should leave, since the important part of the interview seemed to have been achieved, but he held back. That seemed to suit Dana well; she wanted a passive audience for her monologue of self-congratulation.

'When I saw the first scripts for *Lexton and Sons*, I just knew their faces instinctively. It's a knack, you know' She condescended this information to Charles as a mere mortal. 'I knew that Millicent had to be Rita Lexton, and of course George was born to play Walter. Then Hilary was a natural for Gilda.'

'And Bertram Pride for Philip,' Charles supplied, in the hope of speeding up her somewhat torpid delivery.

Her face clouded. 'Well, yes. Actually, someone else suggested Bertram. I had another idea, but, well...' She shrugged. 'Sometimes we all have to bow to *force majeur*, don't we?'

'Yes.' Charles made another attempt to bring the conversation round to his own work. 'I have done television drama, you know. It hasn't all been Light Ent.'

'Oh.' Dana spoke dreamily, not hearing him. 'I have discovered some very major stars, you know, or people who could have been. Do you know Wally Gammons...?

'Know the name.'

'I gave him his start.'

'Really?'

'And Frank Stillman – such a sweetie, Frank...And Martin Sabine – do you know him?'

'Again, the name...'

'Of course, he just does radio now. Tragic, that. And then there's Valeta Chambers...'

As the catalogue continued, Charles remembered another fact about people in television – *they all discovered everyone*. Any successful name that's mentioned immediately prompts a sequence of claims from those who 'gave him his first break'.

Charles wondered why the interview with Dana Wilson had been set up. Then, on reflection, he realized that it was absolutely typical of Maurice Skellern. His agent's eternal instinct was to do nothing, but every now and then he would sense the client's unease was building to the point of separation, and he would make a gesture. He would be seen to do something on his client's behalf. The fact that these gestures were invariably useless did not matter. The client felt obscurely reassured, convinced that in his own special way Maurice really was rooting for him. Charles's current interview at W.E.T., he reflected, was a perfect demonstration of the Skellern technique.

He was getting bored with Dana Wilson's listing of her discoveries, but he didn't feel he should interrupt. Though the prospects didn't at the moment seem promising, there might come a day when he would be glad of the Casting Director's goodwill. An optimist, after all, might conclude that his face was already locked in the filing cabinet of her mind, just waiting to be matched with the right script, after which the name of Charles Paris would join the roll of honour Dana Wilson was so laboriously reciting. But Charles Paris was not an optimist.

Relief came when the phone on Dana's desk rang. Apparently it was her secretary ringing from the outer office.

'Yes. All right. Could you ask her to wait? I'm nearly through.'

The Casting Director put the phone down and smiled wearily at Charles. 'Well, it's been most interesting to hear about your work...'

What? But I haven't told you anything.

'And I do assure you that I will bear you in mind, and when the right sort of part comes up...'

Oh yes, heard that before.

'I've got all the details of your agent...Marcus –'

'Maurice Skellern.'

'Yes.' The weariness of her smile was now melting into long-suffering.

Charles decided he could risk a straight question. 'Are you actually casting anything at the moment?'

Dana Wilson looked pained by this lapse of etiquette. 'Well, there have been production cutbacks...I mean, with the funding of Channel Four, the company's resources are stretched and – '

Having breached the wall of good manners, Charles felt he had nothing to lose by pressing on. 'Yes, but are you actually casting anything?'

'Well, there is a big new drama series currently under consideration, in which I would almost certainly be involved...'

'And when's that scheduled in the studio?'

This did unsettle her torpor a little. 'Well, it's not confirmed yet, but it's hoped that December...certainly early next year...'

Good God, and until then she would have no work, just come into the offices, sit through any number of tedious interviews of the kind she had just conducted, go to a few theatres in the evenings, chat with her colleagues... Not for the first time, Charles was aware of the huge gulf between himself and people in full-time employment. When they had nothing to do, they still got paid; when he had nothing to do, he didn't. On the other hand, when he thought of the idea of killing time for six months in W.E.T. House, he knew he wouldn't have changed places.

He instantly recognized the girl who sat in Dana Wilson's outer office. Not only had he been introduced to her within the last week, he had also seen her photograph in the newspaper. 'It's Henry, isn't it?'

The huge blue eyes widened even further as she struggled for a second to place him. Fortunately she got to his name before he had to prompt her. 'Charles Paris?'

'Yes.'

'We met at Tryst, where that frightful...thing happened.'

'Yes. With Bertram.'

She blushed. 'That's right.'

They stood awkwardly in silence. The phone on the secretary's desk rang.

'Look' said Charles abruptly, 'I'm going to the pub opposite. The Green Man. If you fancied a drink after your interview...'

'Oh...er...well...' She looked confused, like a small child, in spite of her adult clothes. She was dressed in the style of that summer, a sort of punk-with-the-rough-edges-smoothed-off, skin-tight black and white striped trousers and a fluorescent purple shirt with a black snake-skin tie.

'Dana will see you now, Miss Rawsleigh,' said the secretary in a voice which disapproved of middle-aged men trying to pick up nubile teenagers.

'Yes. Well, er, fine...Yes, well, I might see you...' And Henry bobbed off into Dana's office.

Charles caught the secretary's eye and felt stupid. For once he hadn't been making an advance. He just wanted to talk to anyone who had a connection, however distant, with events at Tryst on the Saturday night.

He was drawing to the end of his second pint and thinking it was about time he got back to Hereford Road when, to his surprise, Henry appeared. She gave him a slightly self-conscious little wave, and then went across to a table where another girl was sitting. The two immediately broke into animated conversation.

Oh dear, thought Charles, this really is embarrassing. I just mention meeting in the pub and she's already fixed to see her friend here. Cue for Paris to down remainder of pint and make hasty getaway.

But before he could complete this plan of action the two girls were standing in front of him.

'Mr Paris,' said Henry with great politeness, 'could I introduce my sister Honoria. Hobby, this is Charles Paris.'

'How do you do?'

The second girl gave him a firm handshake. She was probably some five years older than her sister, and in the distribution of family looks she had been the loser. The hair, blond in Henry, was a duller mouse colour in Hobby.

The eyes, still blue, were smaller, and set either side of a determinedly large nose. Henry's ample curves contrasted with Hobby's almost boy-like flatness.

But she was not unattractive. There was life and humour in the face as she said to Charles, 'I gather you've just been to see Dana Wilson too.'

'Yes. I'm afraid I don't think mine was a very profitable interview. What about yours, Henry?'

The girl's brow wrinkled childishly. 'Well, I don't know. I mean, perhaps I didn't know what to expect – I haven't done many of those sort of interviews – but I'm afraid I just couldn't work out what she was talking about.'

'Not much, if she said the same to you as she did to me.'

'No. I mean, a friend gave me the introduction to her...'

Probably without her blush Charles could have made the connection, through *Lexton and Sons*, of Dana Wilson and Bertram Pride.

'And he didn't really tell me what it'd be like, but I suppose I vaguely thought she'd talk about, you know, prospects for work and what sort of stuff I'd done, but all she did seem to talk about was all the things she'd done in the past.'

'You did have exactly the same interview as me.'

'It was very strange.'

'It's a very strange business you've got yourself into,' said Hobby, in a tone of humorous reproach.

'I gather you're not in the theatre.'

'God, no.' The elder girl shuddered at the thought. 'No, I have a nice, respectable, sensible job as a secretary at Conservative Central Office. Henry's the stage-struck idiot in our family.' But it was not said without affection.

'Actually...' Henry giggled, 'I'm quite glad that Dana didn't ask me what work I'd done, because I'm afraid there isn't that much to tell.'

'We all had to start somewhere,' Charles comforted.

'Yes, but really mine's all just school and, you know, college. Hardly, you know, much to write home about.'

'Not that Daddy'd be very interested if you did.'

'Your father doesn't approve of the theatre?'

'Well, I don't think he minds the theatre a*s such.*' Henry's brow wrinkled again. 'But Daddy's a businessman, and I don't think he thinks the theatre is a very good *investment.*'

'He is one hundred per cent right. Anyone who's looking for an investment shouldn't touch the theatre with a barge-pole.'

'Anyway,' Henry continued, 'I suppose he is being quite decent about it. He says he'll support me for a year while I try to get started, and if I'm not on my own two feet by the end of that, then he wants me to do something else.'

'So I think you'd better start thinking about what you're going to do next year,' Hobby remarked rather tartly.

'Don't you be a pig!' Henry was instantly back to the nursery. 'I am jolly well going to make a go of it, just you wait and see.'

Charles intervened before Hobby could come back with a riposte. 'I'm sure you will, Henry. If you work at it, and if you're really determined, you'll get there.'

He wasn't sure to what extent he believed these platitudes, but they were obviously the right things to say to Henry, who positively glowed as she heard them.

'Yes, that's what I think. I'm sure it's just a matter of making the right contacts. I've heard it said that in the theatre it's not *what* you know, it's *who* you know.' This was pronounced with great gravity, as if it was an observation of profound originality.

'I'm sure that's true,' Charles agreed, equally gravely.

'But the trouble is, I don't really know many people "in the business".' The phrase was put into quotation marks with some daring. 'I mean, I've got lots of friends, you know, from home and school, but they're mostly doing dreary things like Cordon Bleu courses and they don't seem to know the right sort of people. Not for the theatre. Not the sort of people who are going to be of help to me. And Daddy's friends are all useless – they're sort of Chairmen of ICI and frightfully draggy things like that.'

She must have misinterpreted Charles's expression, because she added hastily, 'You mustn't think I just want to get into the theatre through other people. I really am prepared to work hard...I mean, all the hours there are. Really. And I do go and work out at the Dance Centre and that sort of thing. It's just I'm sure I do need to meet people "in the business".'

'Hence,' said Hobby, again with some asperity, 'the attraction of Bertram Pride.'

Predictably this produced a blush from her younger sister, as Hobby went on, 'Have you heard about this bit of cradle-snatching, Charles?'

'Well, yes,' he replied awkwardly. 'I did in fact meet Henry with Bertram last Saturday.'

'Of course. Just before they went off for their dirty weekend.'

'Hobby, it wasn't like that.'

'What, the gossip columnists got it wrong?'

'No, it's...just...' Henry looked even more confused.

'According to the *Mail*, Bertram took you to Tryst and then spirited you away to his Bluebeard's Castle in Kent.'

'I know you don't approve of my seeing Bertram.'

'It's up to you who you do rude things with, Henry. I just think it would have been more sensible to choose someone nearer your own age than Daddy's.'

'I'm old enough to choose for myself who I go out with.'

'Of course, dear. Eighteen. A great age. I just can't imagine that a certain person from Gloucestershire can be too happy about the Bertram Pride connection.'

'You mean your father wouldn't approve?' Charles elbowed his way back into the conversation.

'I can't think Daddy'd be over the moon about it. But he wasn't the person I was referring to,' said Hobby with a hard look at her sister.

Henry looked close to tears; clearly she was finding the emotional strain of her affair with an older man hard to cope with. Charles came to the rescue with a blatant change of subject.

'Erm…any other interviews or auditions on the horizon, Henry?'

Hobby gave him an ironical look, well aware of what he was doing, but was content to withdraw from the sisterly bickering.

'Not a huge amount, no.' Henry was relieved by the change of direction. 'In fact, nothing, really. There's an agent I got an introduction to from… someone, but he's away on holiday at the moment.'

Not Maurice Skellern, surely, thought Charles. He wouldn't wish that fate on any young aspirant in the theatre.

But Henry quickly defused that idea. 'Chap called Freddie Winston…don't know if you've heard of him…?'

Bertram Pride's agent, as it happened. 'Oh yes. He's quite big in the business. Lot of famous clients.'

'Yes. Don't know what chance there is of his taking one on…'

Absolutely none, if one were making the approach as just any would-be actress without an Equity card. As Bertram Pride's bit of stuff, though, one might meet a different reaction.

'Otherwise, not a lot happening?'

'No, actually the scene's a bit draggy at the moment. Lots of people away, no one seems to be casting much…'

'You don't have to tell me.'

Hobby, who felt she had been silent too long, snorted. 'Can't understand why you voluntarily go through all this agony. You ought to both get nice jobs in the Civil Service.'

'Don't be silly, Hobby. As you say, you just don't understand.' Henry turned her back dramatically on her sister and faced Charles. He suddenly realized his attraction for her. He was 'someone in the business', perhaps a potential interpreter of the vagaries of the theatrical profession.

'I did see one thing coming up,' Henry continued, looking closely at him with disconcerting earnestness. 'It was advertised in *Stage*. A general audition for a musical.'

'Oh yes.' Charles spoke without enthusiasm.

'I mean, do you think it'd be worth one going along?'

He grimaced. The straight answer was of course that there was absolutely no point in someone of her limited experience and lack of union card going within a million miles of that sort of audition, but he didn't want to depress her too much.

'Well, Henry, there are always hundreds, thousands even, who do go along, and they tend to be pretty grim occasions…'

'Yes, I'm sure. I'm not thinking one might get a part or anything like that, I just think it could be frightfully good experience – the sort of thing one ought to *have done.*'

'That is a point of view, yes.'

'The audition's next Wednesday morning at the King's Theatre.'

'Oh yes.'

'The trouble is...' Henry paused. 'I am frightfully weedy about that sort of thing. You know, not knowing exactly where to go, what to do...'

'There's not much to it.'

'No, but I'd feel so much happier going along with someone who knew the ropes, someone who'd done that sort of thing before...'

'Oh yes.' Charles looked up, suddenly aware of the direction her speech was taking. The appeal in the huge blue eyes would have melted the Colossus of Rhodes. 'You mean you'd like me to go along to this audition with you?'

'Oh, Charles!' She clapped her hands delightedly. 'I'd be frightfully chuffed if you would.'


That evening Charles sat in his bedsitter, trying to read and trying to pretend he'd never thought of the idea of going to the pub or the Montrose. Two evenings in the latter with Zoë had made quite a hole in the old finances and if he was reduced to living on just what he got from the Unemployment Office, a bit of serious back-pedalling was called for.

He ignored the house-bell when it rang, assuming that the visitor must be for one of the Swedish girls. A series of thin Swedish youths with spots and glasses appeared fairly regularly for the various wenches. Or perhaps it was always the same youth, who was working quietly through the occupants of the other bedsitters. Charles couldn't tell, but, if it was, he didn't envy the young man his task.

The bell went on ringing. All the Swedish girls must be out, probably with their Swedish youths or youth, engaged in some Swedish recreation. Charles went downstairs and opened the front door.

Kevin O'Rourke was standing there. Charles realized with a shock that this was the first time he had ever seen the man without his partner. O'Rourke without Bartlemas was an incomplete and disturbing sight.

Charles could not suppress the instinctive question. 'Where's Bartlemas? Is he all right?'

'Yes, he's gone to a first night at Wyndhams.'

'And you haven't gone with him?'

'No. I'm afraid I'm in no state for the theatre. May I come in?'

'Of course.'

Few visitors ever came to Charles's bedsitter, but Kevin O'Rourke did not pass comment on the dusty piles of books and unmade bed. He was too upset for his customary fastidiousness to assert itself.

Before Charles had time to offer coffee (without milk – he never seemed to get round to buying any) or the scant remains of his last emergency half-bottle of Bell's, O'Rourke said, 'I've heard more from the police.'

'About Tristram? Have they found his –'Charles stopped himself just in time from saying 'body', and finished lamely, 'him?'

'No. But they've checked his movements as far as they can on the night Yves was killed. He certainly caught the six-thirty ferry on the Sunday morning, because one of the officials remembered him being very flustered and saying he'd had to change his plans and his friend couldn't come. Then he must have driven fairly flat out for the house at Mas-de-Pouzard, because a local farmer saw the Volvo parked outside early on the Monday morning.'

'In other words he followed exactly the plan that he and Yves had made. Except he was on his own and Yves...'

O'Rourke winced.

Charles shook his head slowly. 'So I suppose the police view of suicide is the most likely explanation. If he was going to do a bunk, why did he leave the car at the house? Why not drive on further or hide himself somewhere totally different? The police were bound to look at Mas-de-Pouzard, weren't they?'

'On the other hand...' O'Rourke's voice was hard. On his own he seemed much more serious and positive than he did in the company of Bartlemas. 'If he was planning to commit suicide, why did he bother to go all that way? He could kill himself anywhere. Why didn't he do it in the flat?'

'I don't know. But he must have been in shock. I mean...after what happened. And I think it's quite common for people in shock just to get on with whatever they were doing, follow arrangements that they've made. It gives them something to do, shuts off what's happened from their minds. So I suppose, after he'd killed Yves, he just went through the motions of driving down to France, as they'd arranged...and it was only when he got to the house, when he actually stopped, that the full horror hit him and...'

'That's your solution, is it?' asked O'Rourke as Charles tailed off.

'Well, what other solution could there be?' Charles shrugged. 'All right, he might still be alive. We mustn't assume suicide...at least until his body's found. But it does seem likely. Tristram was a pretty emotional guy. He's not the sort to take committing a murder in his stride.'

In the silence that followed O'Rourke shook his head wearily. 'So you're convinced that Tristram killed Yves?'

Charles gazed at his visitor in amazement. 'Well, yes. I mean, that does seem to be the one certainty in this case. We and a whole restaurantful of people saw Tristram threaten Yves with a knife, we know that he was unhappy about Yves's promiscuity...And then the way the murder was done ...I mean, with Yves naked...and the way he had been slashed around the genitals...There was no reason for that, not to kill him. That must have been sexual jealousy.' Charles paused. 'I'm sorry, O'Rourke. I know he was your cousin and you're fond of him, but I really don't think there is any other way of looking at the case.'

The next words were spoken with slow intensity. 'Charles, I want you to think of other ways of looking at it.'

'What do you mean?'

'Ten years ago you found out how Marius Steen died. I want you to do the same now with Yves Lafeu.'

'But, O'Rourke, in the case of Marius Steen, there was at least a mystery. Here, to think of any solution other than the obvious one involves incredible mental contortions.'

'I want you to go through those mental contortions, Charles.'

'But –'

'Please. Just think about it, just bring your mind to bear on it. Look, I know I'm being illogical, but I just cannot believe that Tristram would have killed Yves. He would be annoyed with him, furious with him, but he just wouldn't have done that. I'm sure.'

'Hmm. What's your alternative explanation?'

'I don't know. That's why I've come to you. You're good at this sort of thing.'

'Not very, I'm afraid.'

'Oh, please, Charles. Just think it through with me.'

'Sure, I'll do that, but I don't think we'll get far.'

'I'll pay you. For your time. For your services.'

Charles shook his head wryly. 'I'm not a detective, O'Rourke. I'm an actor. Still, I'll play along. Let's have a drink.'

He shared out the remains of his emergency Bell's into two glasses, one slightly chipped, which had been given away with soap powder.

'Right, let's start from the premise that Tristram didn't murder Yves, unlikely though it is. Under those circumstances, who did? Do you have any suspicions?'

O'Rourke shook his balding head dolefully.

'Well, Zoë certainly hated them both. She's in a pretty strange emotional state, so I suppose she might have done something stupid. Who else is there? Monique, Yves's sister. Don't know anything about her, but maybe she nursed some grudge from childhood against her brother. Jealous of his beauty, perhaps. Or what about the blond boy, the one who came to the restaurant and caused all the fuss? Perhaps he had some reason to hate Yves or…I'm sorry, O'Rourke, I'm really clutching at straws. And I don't think I'm getting anywhere. I mean, just thinking of that boy…Gary…brings it all back. We saw it. He was the cause of their quarrel. His arrival set the whole thing in motion, didn't it?'

'Yes. Very neatly. Rather too neatly, to my mind.'

'What do you mean by that?'

'I've been thinking about it. Why did the boy, Gary, arrive at that moment?'

"He said he'd come to meet someone."

'Yes, but it was after eleven o'clock. The restaurant wouldn't have taken a booking for that time. Yves was already doing his lap of honour.'

'Which was why he saw the boy.'

'Yes, half an hour earlier and they wouldn't have met.'

'That's true.'

'And I thought the boy looked genuinely surprised to see Yves. The chances are that if they'd met through the Sparta or somewhere like that, the previous encounter would have been purely physical. Yves certainly wouldn't have talked about what he did for a living. Probably wouldn't even have used his real name.'

'Hmm.'

'And Yves also seemed to be surprised. He said the boy hadn't come by arrangement.'

'Yes, he said, but –'

'All right. He may have been lying. He was certainly quite capable of it. But there was something odd about it. The boy said he had a date to meet a Mr Carruthers. Well, there certainly wasn't anyone sitting alone at a table, waiting. Everyone was in couples, or parties.'

'Maybe he lied.'

'Yes. Just seems a very specific lie. Why "Mr Carruthers"? Is that the sort of name you think up on the spur of the moment?'

'It could be.'

'All right. But there was another thing that was odd.'

'What?'

'Monique was on the door to check the reservations, take coats, give them back to people as they left, and so on.'

'Yes.'

'Well, she knew how the restaurant worked. She knew when last orders were. Why did she let Gary in? Why didn't she just tell him that Tryst was closed and he must have got the wrong end of the stick about there being a reservation?'

Charles was silent, as he ran the scene through his mind. Yes, now O'Rourke mentioned it, the sequence of events had been odd. 'What do you want me to do?'

'I want you to talk to Monique. And I want you to track down that boy Gary.'

Charles grunted a laugh. 'Just that?'

'For the moment, yes. Will you? Please.'

He agreed. Just as he had agreed to accompany Henry to the general audition. Dear oh dear, he thought, I'm becoming a soft touch.

## *Chapter Seven*

TALKING TO MONIQUE and tracking down Gary proved not to be easy. Charles had airily agreed to help O'Rourke without actually thinking how he was going to make contact with either of them, and when he did think about the problem, on the Saturday morning, he realized that he had no idea of what his approach should be.

Except for the fact that the girl was called Monique Lafeu, he knew nothing about her. The only people he knew who might be able to give him an address, her brother and Tristram Gowers, were unavailable to be asked. O'Rourke, whom he rang, didn't have any ideas. Charles had hoped O'Rourke might know some of the other waiters or staff at Tryst, but this was not the case. He and Bartlemas, like Charles, had known only the proprietor and chef.

Charles tried ringing Zoë, but was quite relieved that she was out. He didn't think she'd be very pleased to be asked about the sister of Yves Lafeu. Nor did he think it likely that she would know where the girl lived.

Of course it was quite possible that Monique was not in the country. Tryst, after all, was to have been closed completely for four weeks, so it was likely that all of the staff would be taking their holidays at the same time. Monique might well have returned to family or friends in France. But if that had happened, she would probably have been summoned back by the police after her brother's murder...

Charles had to admit he just did not know. And he couldn't think of any way of finding out. He tried looking up 'Lafeu, Monique' in the telephone directory, but was unsurprised to find no such entry. Not for the first time in his dabblings in investigation, he felt envious of the police's resources in research and information. The odds, he reflected, are very much stacked against the amateur detective.

The phone-book was no more helpful in his search for Gary Stane. He hadn't really thought it would be; an entry in the directory implies a permanence of address which did not match the boy's manner and appearance. Charles could remember Gary's camp theatricality well, and was sure he would recognize the boy again. The question was, where to start looking.

Of course, Tristram had referred to Gary as Yves's 'bit of Sparta rough trade', so perhaps investigation should start at the Sparta Club, wherever that might be.

It was not a lead Charles relished following up. He was not prejudiced against gays; he had worked in the theatre so long that he no longer particularly noticed people's sexual proclivities; but he felt a kind of social unease about the prospect of entering a gay club. He was not worried about being seen there or being the subject of unwelcome advances; he just didn't feel confident about doing the right things at the right time, like an Anglican going to a Catholic Mass. But he realized he might have to overcome his shyness and make the attempt.

Before he did that, he thought of another approach. Gary, he remembered, on arriving at Tryst, had said he was expecting to meet '*a* Mr Carruthers'. The use of the article suggested that he had yet to meet the Mr Carruthers in question. He had also said, 'It's been arranged.'

The two facts could be interpreted, as O'Rourke had suggested, to mean that the boy's appearance had been set up, deliberately stage-managed to precipitate a public row between Tristram and Yves, and provide an apparent motive for the murder to come.

If that had been the case, what would be the simplest way of arranging it? And what sort of person finds nothing unusual in the idea of turning up at a restaurant to meet an unknown man?

It didn't take Charles long to think of an escort agency. A few actors and actresses of his acquaintance eked out their incomes during lean patches by doing escort work (and had provided him with some hilarious and pathetic stories from their experiences). His friends had worked for heterosexual agencies, but he felt sure that there were parallel set-ups for gays.

He decided he needed to do a bit of background reading.

Westbourne Grove is a good place for shopping if you're interested in either overpriced one-bedroom flats, cheap air-tickets, Islam, or sex. For the last-named there are a few specialist shops, but all the newsagents carry a large and varied stock of hardish pornography and contact magazines. Charles had never taken much notice of this display in the paper shop where he bought his *Times* every morning, and was surprised at the range of material available. Since most of the magazines were sealed in transparent plastic, he found it difficult to make his selection. He knew that what he wanted was homosexual, but he did not want to end up with an album of posing boys. After all, an agency whose clients booked into Tryst was not down the meat-rack end of the market; it would be likely to advertise in a journal bought by the more sophisticated and discriminating gay.

'Can I help you, sir?' asked the impassive Pakistani from whom he bought his paper every morning.

'Yes. Thank you. I'll have a *Times*, please, and…er…I wanted a magazine…'

'Yes, sir. What magazine?'

'A sort of…specialist magazine.'

'Computing, is it you want? Video games? Hang-gliding?'

'Er, no. It's…um…I want a magazine which has advertisements in it for gay escort agencies.'

'Certainly, sir.' The shopkeeper reached across into the rack and instantly picked out a yellow-covered publication called *Patroclus*. He certainly knew his stock. 'This is what you want, sir.'

As Charles reached into his pocket for the rather large amount of money that was required, he heard a disgusted snort behind him.

One of the Swedish girls from the Hereford Road house was staring at him with frosty Scandinavian disapproval.

*Patroclus* was quite a revelation for Charles. He did not find anything to shock him in it, but he was surprised by what a well-organized and detailed culture the magazine revealed. No doubt he would have had the same reaction had he bought the publications on computers, video games or hang-gliding which the newsagent had recommended.

Still, in the back pages he found the information he required. A large number of escort agencies offered discreet and efficient service. In fact, he was daunted by the number of them. Presumably they represented only a fraction of those that existed in the capital. The odds against tracking down Gary Stane by that method lengthened.

Still, his only other lead was the Sparta Club. It was worth trying a few agencies first.

For no very good reason he felt coy about using his own voice for his enquiries. He wondered what identity he should use instead. For an actor the voice is everything. Who should he be?

He had played his share of mincing queens in his time. He'd done Gorringe in Peter Shaffer's *Black Comedy* at Birmingham ('I have always thought this play was actor-proof; last night's cast proved me wrong' – *Birmingham Post*). Then he'd appeared in the very, very short run of a play set backstage at a drag beauty contest ('I should think Gay Lib will ask the author of this awful little piece to go back in again' – *The Listener*). But he didn't think either voice was right for the task in hand. The sort of people who used the services of gay escort agencies would, he felt sure, not be flamboyant effeminates but serious businessmen down in London for a meeting or conference.

That gave him a bit of a lead. He tried to think of the characters of that sort that he had played. There had been a carpet salesman in a rather awful thriller at Worthing ('Charles Paris seemed to be acting in a different play from the rest of the cast – and who could blame him?' – *Worthing Gazette*). That had been a sort of indeterminate Midlands accent. Then he'd used Bristolian as a purser in an episode of an interminable series about a cruise liner ('What Charles Paris was doing in the cast I could not fathom' – *Sunday Telegraph*). Trouble was…Bristolian always sounded slightly funny, as if the speaker was sending himself up.

Yes. He got it. The South London twang he had used as an insurance assessor in another thriller, *Dead To The World*, at Worthing ('I have been more thrilled by a cup of cold tea' – *Worthing Gazette*).

He dialled the first number on the page.

'Hello, One-Off Escort Services.'

It was a girl's voice. He was relieved to find someone there on a Saturday, though when he thought about it, that was only logical. The weekend must be the busiest time for that sort of service, as the lonely desperately try to avoid spending Saturday night alone in the city.

'Er, yes. Good morning. I am, er, down in London on business.' It struck Charles that he should have used a more provincial accent. His voice placed him somewhere in mid-Croydon, which hardly justified staying in town after meetings. Never mind, he couldn't change accent now. And no doubt the girl at the other end of the phone had heard a good few lies in the course of her work. He pressed on. 'Yes, and I, er, seem to find myself at a loose end this evening, and thought it would be rather nice to, er, have some...'

'Company?'

'Yes. Exactly.' Then, following the instincts of Charles Paris rather than those of the character he was playing, he hastened to add, 'I mean, just for a drink, or dinner or...I wasn't thinking of anything more, er, you know...'

'Just as well,' the girl said frostily. 'Ours is purely a service to provide escorts. We are not a sexual contact agency.'

'No, no, of course not.'

'That would be illegal,' she averred primly.

'Yes, yes, I understand that.'

He was trying to sound properly chastened, but she obviously took his tone for disappointment. 'On the other hand...' she began more cheerily, 'we have effected introductions which have led to more romantic associations. It often happens that good friendships are formed through meetings we arrange. And, of course,' she concluded, removing any vestigial ambiguity from her speech, 'what our escorts do in their own time is their own business. But for the fee you pay us all you are buying is a pleasant companion for the evening.'

Charles got the picture. 'Yes, well, as I say, it is, er, company that I'm after.'

'Well, we have a very charming selection of young men on our books. I take it you would like someone in the younger age-bracket?'

'Oh yes. I think I would like a young man. In his twenties, say...And tall and blond.'

'I'm sure we'll be able to accommodate you, Mr Smith.'

'I didn't say my name was Smith.'

'Oh, didn't you?' Charles could feel her stopping herself from saying, 'Everyone else does.' Instead, she just apologized.

'I'm really looking for a boy called Gary,' said Charles.

'Ah, well, I'm sure one of our escorts wouldn't mind being called Gary if that's what you want.'

'No. I mean a specific boy called Gary. I'm trying to make contact with a young man called Gary Stane.'

'We have no escort of that name on our books.' The voice was all frosty again.

'But I'm just trying to find this boy...tallish, as I say, blond. good-looking...'

'We have plenty of other escorts quite as good-looking.'

'It's not just looks I'm after. I just want this one boy.'

'I'm afraid we're not a Missing Persons Bureau.'

With that the girl rang off. Charles sighed and replaced the receiver on the payphone.

'You are an old filthy perversion.'

He turned round, to find himself staring into the baleful eyes of the Swede from the newsagents. He didn't know how long she had been standing on the landing listening.

He tried ringing a few more agencies, but with diminishing confidence. The services that they offered were disguised in phrases of varying subtlety, but none of them had heard of Gary Stane. And all of them clammed up when they realized that he was searching for one specific person rather than a nameless stranger. Charles decided that he could spend months ringing round all the available agencies, and still have no certainty of finding his quarry.

So that left the Sparta Club...

*Patroclus* provided the address in its comprehensive clubs listings. Charles had been expecting somewhere in Soho and was surprised to find that the club was in Leominster Terrace, in that hinterland of hotels, flat conversions and private clinics between Queensway and Paddington.

Nor did he find the club's frontage as he had expected it when he presented himself there at half-past nine that Saturday evening. His mental projection had been of something Soho and shoddy, with garish neons and thumping music like a strip club. He had not been prepared for the white portico and huge black door, nor the discreet brass plate beside it, reading 'Sparta Club – Members Only'. The impression was of the embassy of a small but prosperous foreign power.

Charles had delayed his visit till half-past nine for a very simple reason, which he was almost ashamed to admit to himself. It was just that he knew it would be dark by then, and though he was not a man who had any reputation or image to lose, he still felt a degree of embarrassment about his mission.

The man behind the table in the entrance hall had the air of the *maître d'hôtel* in an expensive restaurant and his first appraising look made Charles feel perhaps he should have excavated his one suit from his wardrobe for the occasion.

'Good evening, sir. Can I help you?'

Two middle-aged men and a young one, all dressed in suits, entered from the street. While the young man was being signed into the visitors' book, Charles had a moment to decide his approach.

But the diversion didn't last long. Again Charles found himself looking into the sceptical eyes of the man behind the desk.

'Yes?'

Oh well, direct approach was as good as any.

'Er, good evening.' He had been intending to stick with the Croydon insurance assessor persona, but found himself instinctively upgrading his accent to the one he had used as Major Petkoff in *Arms And The Man* ('Surely crustier than Shaw intended' – *Western Evening Record*). 'I'm trying to make contact with a young man called Gary Stane.'

'Really, sir? May I ask if you're a member of the Sparta Club?'

'No, I'm not.'

'Then I'm afraid I can't help you.' The man turned back to some bills he was studying on the desk.

'But all I want is an address or telephone number for him.'

The man looked up again, scepticism giving way now to anger. 'I'm sure that's all you want, sir. That's all a lot of people want. To invade privacy. And our club is set up to guard the privacy of its members.'

'But I...Can't you even tell me if Gary Stane is a member?'

'No.'

'I suppose I couldn't join?' asked Charles in some desperation.

'I think you could safely suppose that. Unless, of course, you could find two members to propose and second you. Then your name would in due course be put up to the selection committee.'

'And what is the membership fee?'

The man told him. Charles reeled out in shock. He felt as if he'd just been blackballed for the Garrick Club.

He rang O'Rourke mid-morning on the Sunday to report progress. Since he had made none, that didn't take long. O'Rourke had managed to contact one of Tryst's waiters, but got no lead on finding Monique Lafeu. However, the older man seemed anxious to talk further about the murder and invited Charles out to Islington for lunch. The actor had, as usual, not made any other plans, so he accepted the offer gratefully.

Sundays he'd never really sorted out. Throughout his childhood they had been days of ritual tedium, punctuated rather than enlivened by church, days when sneaking upstairs to do homework had been a welcome alternative to genteel conversation and helping in the garden. Anything was better than that kind of regime, so he had quite welcomed National Service, when duties didn't often coincide with the normal working week and Sunday was just another in an interminable sweep of undistinguishable days, church parades seeming to Charles not that different from any other sort of parade. Then had come Oxford, when Sundays suddenly came into their own. With guaranteed freedom from lectures and tutorials, without even the tiny feeling of guilt that the Bodleian was open, Charles and his friends had lazed and chatted. It was during that period that he had first begun to concentrate on what was to be a lifetime hobby for him – drinking. At the same time his interest in the theatre was developing and Sunday afternoons would often be amiably mopped up by rehearsal for OUDS or college productions.

And when he started working in the professional theatre Sundays again conveniently merged, camouflaged, into the rest of the calendar. In weekly rep, of which he had a few years, Sunday was the busiest day of the week. They would start to clear the previous week's set as soon as the curtain went down on the Saturday night, and then, often working through, erect the new one. In those days the demarcations between actors and backstage staff had been less rigidly defined, with the result that everyone did a bit of everything. Sundays were days of convivial panic, one minute supporting a flat, the next painting it, knocking props together, mending fuses in the lighting-box, donning unfamiliar costumes and negotiating unfamiliar sets in hysterically unprepared dress-rehearsals, trying every minute to cram the words of the new play into a mind which hadn't quite flushed out the lines of the last, and all working towards what most of the time seemed to be the impossible aim of opening the show before a paying audience on the Monday night.

But all that had changed. Now, on the occasions when he was in work, Charles hardly ever worked on a Sunday. Equity, ever protective of its members' interests, had finally managed to impose some regulation on the number of hours that could be demanded of actors, and brought such modern concepts as overtime into a business where for so long the work ethics of nineteenth century cotton-mills had operated. The result had been a change in the pattern of production in repertory theatres. Weekly rep had given way to fortnightly; and then three-weekly, or even longer, intervals between new productions became the norm. And the costs of overtime meant that most actors got their Sundays off, and the new shows would most likely open on Wednesdays rather than Mondays.

Charles knew the changes were a Good Thing, a very belated improvement in working conditions. But he couldn't help feeling a bit of nostalgia for the old days. In weekly rep there had never been time for anything except doing the current show and getting the next one on. He knew he had been less depressed in those days than he had since; there just hadn't been the time.

And in the midst of that manic activity, when he wasn't working, when he had the odd day off, there had been little oases of married Sundays with Frances. Before Juliet, their daughter, was born, these had been days of Sunday papers and sex, late rising and pub, with often an afternoon return to bed for more Sunday papers and sex. With the advent of Juliet, and the purchase of the Muswell Hill house, this occasional pattern had changed. Less time for the Sunday papers and the sex (though neither was ignored completely), more 'doing things in the house', 'pottering in the garden' and eating too much of traditional roasts and two vegetables. Their Sundays together had become, in fact, a parody of the childhood Sundays Charles had spent with his parents. The difference was that he enjoyed the times with Frances and Juliet. He was away a lot, working, and so those days retained their rarity value. He had no opportunity to get bored with them, and even felt the actor's satisfaction from having given a good performance in his role as conventional husband, father and rate-payer.

But then he and Frances had drifted apart...

He realized on that Sunday morning that he should ring her. Thinking back made him nostalgic for her. He even had a flash of his much-discredited fantasy that they might get back together again. Sometimes, just intellectually, it could seem so simple. But he knew that all of their attempts to live together again had failed, not in scenes of violence and anger, just in the rueful recognition that neither of them had changed and that the differences in their priorities which had led Charles to leave Frances in 1961 remained, more than twenty years later, a continuing source of mutual exasperation. The affection survived, but their ability to cohabit decreased with each passing year.

And now of course there was David. Now Frances was talking of a divorce. Now she was going to start a new life with her schools inspector.

Or probably was.

Charles couldn't summon up the nerve to ring her for a precise definition of her plans. At least ignorance left the possibility of hope.

'And are you two actually members of the Sparta Club?'

O'Rourke shook his head. The strands of hair, apparently glued across its baldness, did not stir. 'No, not quite our scene. We've got a lot of chums who are members, though.'

'Perhaps some of them might have a lead on Gary Stane?'

'Possibly. Certainly worth asking. Though I doubt if we'll get anywhere.'

'Why not?'

'Well, you see, I'm sure that a boy like Gary Stane wouldn't actually be a *member*. Too young, for one thing. And I wouldn't have thought he could afford the membership.'

'No,' said Charles, remembering the figure he had been quoted.

'So it's most likely that he'd gone along as someone's guest.'

'And met Yves?'

'Yes. And they'd got on together...or got off together, if you prefer, but it's quite possible that that was the only occasion when Gary went to the club.'

'Hmm. Anyway, if you could ask...'

'I will.'

'And I'll try to think of some other approach.'

Charles sipped at his glass of icy *kir*. O'Rourke seemed more relaxed than he had on the Friday evening. At that time the surprise of seeing him without Bartlemas had made Charles fear that there might be some rift in the relationship, but that was obviously not the case. William Bartlemas, realizing how deeply O'Rourke was taking Yves's death and the suspicions of Tristram, though unable himself to take them so to heart, was showing great care and solicitude for his friend. He was in the kitchen, discreetly preparing lunch, leaving O'Rourke and Charles the opportunity to talk.

'I suppose,' Charles asked diffidently, 'you haven't had any other thoughts as to who might have killed Yves? As always, assuming it wasn't Tristram.'

O'Rourke shook his head again. 'Sorry.'

'We talked a bit about motive, and we only came up with Zoë, who certainly hated them both, and Monique, for reasons we cannot begin to imagine, and Gary Stane...I don't know, because of some sort of sexual jealousy?'

'It's not a lot, is it?'

'No, but suppose we approach it from the other end – opportunity.'

'What, you mean who could have got into the flat and killed Yves?'

'Not just that. I mean, if you are thinking of a planned murder, then you have to think of a murderer who knew Tristram and Yves well enough to have heard the details of their holiday plans.'

'Why?'

'The choice of that night to kill Yves wouldn't have been random. I was talking this through with Stan Fogden, you know, the bloke who was with me when we found the body. Now if the murderer did know about the holiday, but didn't know that Tristram had arranged to have the flat decorated, then he might safely assume that Yves's body would not be found for a full month.'

'Yes, I see what you mean.' O'Rourke looked excited; then saw a snag. 'What about Tristram?'

'Well, this bit is pure conjecture, but let's just imagine for a moment that our murderer breaks into the flat – no, no signs of forcible entry – is *let* into the flat...which again suggests that he or she was known to Tristram and Yves...and draws a gun on them.'

'But Yves was killed with a knife,' O'Rourke objected.

'Wait till I've finished. He – or she – holds them both at gun point, gets Yves to strip naked and kills him with the knife, mutilating his body in a way that will suggest sexual jealousy and turn the suspicion on to Tristram...'

'And Tristram's watched all this?'

'Maybe. I don't know. Anyway, then the murderer turns his gun on Tristram and threatens to kill him too, unless he gets into the car and drives it, according to plan, down to France.'

'But how does our murderer get on to the ferry? Or through passport control?'

'I don't know. Maybe he or she hides in the back of the Volvo, hidden under the luggage. Maybe goes on the ferry as a passenger. Let's not worry about the details for the moment. Okay, so the murderer gets Tristram to drive all the way down to Mas-de-Pouzard and then kills him. Kills him in a way that looks like suicide, and does it somewhere where the body is unlikely to be discovered for some time.

'So, so far as anyone in this country is concerned, Tristram and Yves are away for a month. No search-parties will be sent out till that month is over. I don't know what the house is like in France, how many friends they've got out there, but if the place is fairly remote, it's quite possible that none of the locals would be particularly interested in whether they were there or not.

'In that way, the murderer would have achieved a self-sealing crime. Yves's body is found at the end of September; then they start looking for Tristram's body – perhaps find it, perhaps don't – and the police think Tristram killed his lover in a mad fit of jealousy, drove off to France, thinking he might get away with it, realized the hopelessness of his position, and then killed himself.'

'Which is exactly what they appear to think at the moment.'

'Yes. A perfect crime, as far as someone who wanted to kill Tristram and Yves is concerned.'

'Hmm.' O'Rourke looked torn. He desperately wanted to believe any alternative to the idea of Tristram having killed Yves, but he was quite as aware as Charles of gaping holes and implausibilities in the storyline Charles had just outlined.

'I'm sorry, O'Rourke. But you did ask me to try and think of other ways of looking at the crime, and I've just produced one.'

'Yes,' O'Rourke said slowly. 'And I'm very grateful to you. You never know, there might be something in it. But who? Who would do that?'

'Well, let's go back to the fact that there was no sign of a break-in. Tristram and Yves must have let in anyone who arrived to kill them.'

'Unless the person was already there.'

'You mean Monique?'

'Yes. Or someone who had been having dinner in the restaurant.'

'What?' Charles laughed. 'Sir John? Bernard Walton? Bertram Pride?'

'They all knew Tristram and Yves well.'

'Yes, but what are we going to do – check through all the reservations for that evening and find out where all the people went when they left the restaurant? I think that might be difficult to do.' He remembered something. 'Though one, in fact, I've already done.'

'Who?'

'Dear Bertram. Straight after he'd finished he spirited off his Rent-A-Tottie for a naughty weekend at his country cottage. I have that not only from the newspaper gossip columns, but from Rent-A-Tottie herself.'

'You've met her since?'

'Yes. Sweet kid. Aspiring actress.'

'What's she like?'

'Hmm. I think the word I would have to use is "naive".'

The phone rang in another room. O'Rourke did not react, confident that Bartlemas would take it.

'In terms of thinking of our murderer, Charles, we must presumably pick on someone who wanted both Tristram and Yves out of the way'.

'I don't know. If Tristram was a witness of the killing of Yves...'

'Someone capable of the kind of tortuous planning you've devised would surely have only done it that way to get rid of them both. If he just wanted Yves out of the way, there would have been much simpler ways of doing it.'

'Yes, you're right. We need someone with a motive against both. I wonder if –'

He was interrupted by the appearance at the door of Bartlemas. His shirt-sleeves were rolled up and he was wearing his favourite apron, with an advertisement for 'Camp Coffee' on it.

'O'Rourke, telephone for you...'

'What a time of day to call...'

'People just don't think, do they...'

'Just before Sunday lunch...'

'Meant to be a day of rest...'

'I don't know...'

Charles was amused to see how instantly O'Rourke dropped back into stereo conversation when his partner appeared.

O'Rourke rose from his chair. 'Who is it then?'

'It's Monique Lafeu,' said Bartlemas.

O'Rourke was gone some time. Bartlemas had apologized that he must 'rush back to the kitchen and flagellate my mayonnaise', so Charles was left on his own.

The sitting-room, like the rest of the house, was filled with memorabilia of Kean and Macready. The dominant feature was a large gilt-framed painting over the fireplace. Experts at various museums and galleries had disputed the claim, but Bartlemas was in no doubt that the work was of Edmund Kean in one of his most famous parts, Sir Giles Overreach in *New Way To Pay Old Debts*. It was very different from Clint's version in the Garrick Club, but the eyes were certainly demonic enough to justify the identification, and Charles always regarded the picture as a symbol of concentrated, but theatrical, evil.

The bookshelves contained a predictable collection. Barry Cornwall's *Life of Kean*, Lady Pollock's *Macready As I Knew Him*, Thomas Colley Grattan's *Beaten Paths And Those Who Trod Them*, Genest's *Account Of The English Stage*, and so on. But amongst the props of idol-worship were some more modern reference works. A complete set of *Who's Who In The Theatre*, going right back to the first edition of 1912. And the four volumes of the current *Spotlight*.

*Spotlight* is the producer's and casting director's bible, in which every actor and actress who can afford the fee (and a good few who can't) insert their photographs, agent's name and possibly details of recent work. The entries are telling. The height of panache is just to put in the name without a photograph, but that is a practice only indulged in by the hugest stars, totally confident of their universal recognition. The next step down is a half-page photograph in the 'Leading' section; here extremely well known faces mix with vaguely well known faces and a few extremely optimistic faces. After comes 'Character', a section into which some surprisingly famous actors and actresses put their half-page photographs, shrewdly aware that there are more character than leading parts around. Next comes 'Younger Character', a section which, particularly in the 'Actresses' volume, covers a remarkably wide age-range. (Actresses' photographs are also inclined to be a little misleading. It is usually safe to add ten years to what their *Spotlight* pictures look like.) Finally comes the 'Young' section, though even that can provide a few surprises.

Charles could never see a set of *Spotlight* without reaching down the 'Actors L-Z' volume and stealing a look at his entry. He knew it was pure self-indulgence, rather like an author looking himself up in a library catalogue, but it did give him reassurance that he existed. The fact that so many producers and casting directors must see his picture looking out at them as they flicked through the book made it only the more remarkable that his telephone rang so rarely.

Perhaps, he wondered as he looked at his photograph, it was a matter of expression. His face seemed to him to have a defeated air, like an unwanted puppy at Battersea Dogs' Home; it seemed to say to the prospective employer, 'Oh, come on, I'm sure you can find someone better than *me*.' Which, all too often, his prospective employers did.

'Maurice Skellern Artistes' didn't inspire confidence either. Once again Charles wondered whether he should try to join a better-known agency.

Nor did his list of credits change the image a lot. 'RECENT TELEVISION: Barman in *The Strutters* (WET series)' was hardly going to send a Hollywood producer into paroxysms of enthusiasm.

Charles wondered if it would make any difference if next year he got himself categorized as 'Leading' rather than 'Character'. Somehow he doubted it.

He was about to return the volume to the shelf when an idle thought struck him. Turning to the index at the front, he looked up under the 'S's.

And there it was. 'STANE, Gary' and a page reference.

He was in the 'Young' section, right at the back, where most of the hopefuls can only afford quarter-page pictures.

Though the hair was darker and longer, Charles recognized the pretty face with its defensive petulance.

'Maxine Ruttemann Agency', it said, with an address and phone number.

At that moment O'Rourke came bubbling back into the room. 'Monique,' he announced, 'she wants to meet and talk.'

Things were beginning to move.

## *Chapter Eight*

'MAXINE RUTTEMANN AGENCY,' said a nasal female voice at the end of the telephone when Charles rang through on the Monday morning.

'Hello. I believe you have an actor called Gary Stane on your books.'

'Yes.'

'Oh, good. I'm trying to make contact with him.'

'Is this theatrical work you're talking about?'

'Well...' An electric typewriter hummed over the line as Charles tried to frame his approach.

'I mean, is it an acting or a dancing job?' the girl's voice clarified.

'It isn't exactly a job,' Charles confessed. 'I just want to make contact with him.'

'I see.' The nasal voice took on a new scepticism. 'I think perhaps you've come through to the wrong agency. I book Gary as an actor and dancer.'

'Yes. But you must have a phone number for him. I'm sure you could –'

'His escort work,' she continued, riding above his voice, 'is handled by Intro/Outro.'

She gave him the number and rang off abruptly.

Charles dialled the new number.

'Intro/Outro Agency.' Again it was a female voice; again nasal; but this time it was American. Charles wondered. He was sure he could hear the same electric typewriter working away.

'Was I talking to you a moment ago?'

'Sorry?' asked the American voice.

'I was just talking to the Maxine Ruttemann Agency.'

'This is the Intro/Outro Agency,' the American voice repeated blandly. If she was the same girl, she certainly wasn't giving anything away.

'Yes. Of course. Listen, do you have a young man called Gary Stane on your books?'

'We have a lot of very charming escorts, sir, and I'm sure if you were looking for company, we could provide someone with whom you would have a most enjoyable evening.'

'Yes. It's actually Gary Stane I want to meet.'

'Have you spent an evening with him before?'

Her reply was incautious, implying that Gary Stane definitely was on the agency's books. Charles decided it was time for a little tactical lying. He wished he had started the conversation in his Croydon insurance assessor's voice, but pressed on in his own.

'Er, yes. Some months ago. Had a most pleasant time. And at the end of the evening I did say how...er, pleasant it would be if we could meet up again when I was next in London.' There was a pause. The girl had not yet risen to the bait. 'I come down on business from time to time,' he went on.

'Yes.' The girl spoke slowly, thinking. Her American accent sounded weaker. Charles was almost certain it was the girl from the Maxine Ruttemann Agency. 'Well, listen, I think it might be possible to arrange another meeting with Gary.'

'I would be most grateful.'

'Presumably if you're only down on a brief trip, you'd like to meet soon.'

'Please.'

'This evening?'

'That would be ideal.'

'Well, look, I'll have to speak to Gary and see if he's free. Is there a number where I can reach you?'

Charles felt disinclined to give the Hereford Road one. 'Erm, no. I'm rather in transit at the moment. Between meetings. You know, I'm down for an insurance conference.'

He tried to restrain the Croydon twang from creeping into his voice, but the image of the insurance assessor was becoming stronger by the minute. A hazard of acting is the tendency to build up a full background to every funny voice. Already Charles could visualize the young man with his guilty secret, the wife and two children secure on the Barratt estate in Milton Keynes, the occasional guilt-ridden indulgences (while on trips to London) in the 'other side of his nature'.

Mustn't let the fantasy get out of hand. 'Perhaps I could ring you back in a couple of hours,' he suggested, firmly sticking to his own voice.

'Yes, that'd be fine. Presumably,' the American voice went on (she too seemed to have done a bit of mental sock-pulling-up and the accent was more assured), 'since you've used the agency before, you know about our rates and arrangements.'

'Remind me,' said Charles, playing safe.

He reeled a bit at the figures mentioned. The investigation was going to prove rather expensive. Perhaps he should have taken up O'Rourke's offer of payment. Expenses, anyway. Yes, expenses. The word had a nice Philip Marlowe ring to it.


It occurred to him after he rang off that he needn't have followed this laborious and costly method of contacting Gary Stane. When he got through to the Maxine Ruttemann Agency, he could just have pretended to be a producer or casting director, said he had a part for which he thought Gary might be ideal, and fixed to meet and talk about it.

No actor would have refused that bait.

But, equally, no actor who had himself suffered the agony of disappointed hopes could stoop so low as to play that sort of trick on a fellow-member of his profession.

When he rang back an hour later, it was confirmed that Gary Stane would be free that evening. He would meet Charles for a pre-dinner drink in the bar of the St Nicholas Hotel near Oxford Circus. Charles was to tell the barman when he arrived, 'just in case Gary didn't recognize him'.

Charles felt extremely self-conscious sitting in the bar at eight o'clock that evening. The large Bell's in front of him was not having its customary calming effect. He had exhumed his one suit for the occasion, even brushed it, and its unaccustomed stiffness added to his unease. He had also gone to the lengths of digging out a tie, a paisley silk number whose colours had been rather subdued by removal with greasepainty fingers every night he wore it in *Rookery Nook* ('The production showed as much sense of humour as a cremation' – *Coventry Evening Telegraph*).

Charles felt ridiculously nervous. It wasn't like stage fright; with that, through all the anguish, you always have the confidence that the author's lines are there to fall back on (if you can remember them). It wasn't even like doing an impersonation, being in disguise as someone else, an exercise that Charles had undertaken a good few times in his career. No, on this occasion he had to be himself, and he had no idea how the evening would have to be played.

Gary Stane soon put him at his ease. Charles recognized the tall young man as he entered the characterless bar-room. The unlikely blondness of the hair stood out, and to make identification simpler, Gary was wearing exactly the same clothes as he had been on Charles's previous sighting of him. Maybe the blue and white striped shirt and the beige suit were his standard costume for dates. Maybe its colour or style had some particular significance to his usual hosts. Charles felt horribly out of his depth.

But Gary came across from the bar and gave him a firm handshake. 'Mr Paris?'

'Oh, er, yes.' Charles half-rose from his seat, then wondered whether that was the proper form for the circumstances. He sat back down again.

The young man sat opposite and looked at him expectantly. Gary was undoubtedly very beautiful. His skin was carefully tanned; the shirt was opened far enough down to show a long triangle of hairless brown chest. Only the unrealistic hair and a slight dullness in the blue eyes spoiled the image.

The silence had gone on some time before Charles realized his duty and waved for a waiter. 'What will you have to drink, Gary?'

'Oh, a Campari soda would be very nice, Mr Paris.' The boy smiled, revealing an orthodontist's dream of white teeth.

At least Charles felt financially secure for the evening. He had explained his problem to O'Rourke, who had instantly paid two hundred pounds into his account, so Charles had dared to draw out half of that. (Had he withdrawn a hundred without the subsidy, he would have worried about giving his bank manager a coronary.)

'It's very nice to see you again, Mr Paris,' said Gary. He spoke with flat but punctilious elocution, like the Head Girl proposing a vote of thanks to the visiting speaker.

'You remember me?'

'Of course. How could I forget?'

This was said with an edge of automatic flirtatiousness. Just part of the job, Charles assumed. He felt certain Gary hadn't seen him at Tryst the night before Yves died, so the recognition must be pretended. Still, if the Intro/Outro Agency had reported his claim to have been out with Gary before, then Gary wasn't going to argue. If that was what the client wanted...It was quite possible that he spent so many such evenings, anyway, chaffing away on automatic pilot, that he really didn't notice who he was with.

'Down in London on business, are you, Mr Paris?' Gary was doing his job well, not letting the pauses sag too long, keeping the conversation going. No doubt a lot of genuine lonely businessmen had been glad of his services.

'Yes, yes,' said Charles. 'Insurance conferences, meetings, that sort of thing.'

'Must be interesting,' Gary lied brightly.

Charles was having difficulty with his persona. As soon as he mentioned 'insurance' the Croydon voice threatened. He really should have done a bit more preparation. He felt as if he were in the early days of rehearsal of a new play and he hadn't yet worked out which way to play his part.

'Yes, well, you know...Interesting some of the time. Every now and then. Most of the time dead boring. Like most jobs.'

'Yes,' Gary agreed, but without ironic comment on his own work. 'That's why it's so nice to get out and have a fling, isn't it, Mr Paris?'

'Oh, yes.'

'Actually...' Gary lowered his long eyelashes over his lifeless blue eyes, 'I do feel a bit formal calling you Mr Paris. I'm sure you've got a Christian name...?'

Charles found this flirtatiousness a little unnerving. 'Charles. Er, Charles.'

'Oh, that's a nice name.'

Charles winced. The line was too mechanical. It reminded him uncomfortably of the few sad occasions in his life when he had resorted to prostitutes, the minimal, soulless dialogue which exposed the routine tedium of the transaction. He didn't think that he could face a whole evening of fencing innuendo with Gary, and decided it was time to own up to his real purpose in arranging the encounter.

'Listen,' he began suddenly, 'I didn't really fix to meet you this evening for a lot of small talk over dinner.'

'No?' Gary Stane arched an eyebrow quizzically.

'No. I set up this meeting merely as a means to an end.'

'Did you? I wonder why.'

'Well, it's –'

'You don't have to tell me.' Gary raised a hand to quiet Charles, and began to recite a well-known rubric. 'The Intro/Outro Agency merely provides companions for social evenings. A drink, dinner, theatre, that sort of thing. That is all that the fee you pay secures, and at the end of the evening, when I have discharged my duties as your companion, we part, having both, I hope, had a good night out.'

'I didn't mean –'

Again the hand was raised, and this time the voice was lowered. 'Mind you, Charles, if we were to get on particularly well...'

Charles felt a pressure against his shin. He realized it came from Gary's leg and sat back, disguising the suddenness of his movement with a manufactured sneeze.

'Particularly well,' Gary repeated, 'then maybe the evening could continue in our own time. My own time, that is, outside my working hours. Of course, we'd have to negotiate a separate fee for that. But I'm sure we could come to some...arrangement. What hotel are you staying in?'

Charles took a deep breath. 'I'm afraid that wasn't what I meant.'

Gary's eyes narrowed. 'Anything...unusual comes extra.'

'No, listen. I've got you here under false pretences.'

'What do you –'

'No, not under false pretences. I'm paying for your company and your conversation, and what I've paid entitles me to choose what that conversation is about.'

'Ye-es,' the boy conceded cautiously. A new understanding came into his eyes. 'What sort of things does it excite you to talk about?'

'I want to talk about the Saturday before last, the evening before Yves Lafeu was murdered.'

This at last brought some animation into Gary Stane's eyes. First came shock, then resentment, finally petulance.

'Are you a cop too?'

'You've talked to them?'

'They've talked to me.'

'Well, I'm not one of them.'

'Why should I believe that?'

'Because it's the truth. I am an actor called Charles Paris.'

'Suppose I should be grateful that at least you used your own name,' said Gary sarcastically. 'What's your interest in it, anyway?'

'A friend of mine is Tristram Gowers' cousin. He doesn't believe that Tristram killed Yves, and he wants me to prove his cousin's innocence.'

'Well...' Gary said. 'No, I don't think you are a policeman.'

'Meaning?'

'Meaning that they're all convinced that Yves was killed by Tristram.'

'And what do you think?'

Gary shrugged without great interest. 'It seems the obvious solution.'

'Look, do you mind talking to me about all this?'

The boy shrugged again. 'As you say, you've paid your money, so you can choose the subject.'

'How well did you know Yves?'

'Hardly at all. Met him twice.'

'The second occasion being the evening before he died?'

'Right.'

'And the first being at the Sparta Club?'

'Done your homework, haven't you? Yes, I met him at the Sparta Club.'

'Of which you are not a member.'

'God, no. Way out of my league financially. No, a 'gentleman' took me there. Through the agency. He booked me. And when we were there, Yves came up and started chaffing me up outrageously. I'm afraid the guy I was with got rather pissed off.'

'Was Tristram there?'

'Yes. He wasn't in a wonderful mood either.'

Charles felt embarrassed. 'Did you and Yves, er, go off together?'

Gary smiled, enjoying his discomfiture. 'Off to do naughty things together?'

'Yes.'

'No. We just danced. It was a bit of fun. He was only behaving like that to get Tristram angry. I know the sort. Flirt like mad – they get some kind of charge out of it. Make the boyfriend furious and then have a lot of fun making it up. That must have been how their relationship worked.' He stopped. 'Until it went wrong.'

'And that was really all that happened between you?'

'Really. I couldn't have gone off with him, anyway. I was with my client. Shouldn't really have danced like that, but I couldn't resist it.' His face turned glum. 'Had to pay for it.'

'From the agency?'

'No, Maxine didn't get to hear about it.'

So Charles had been right. The Maxine Ruttemann Agency and Intro/Outro were the same girl. But he didn't say anything, as Gary elaborated.

'But I had to pay for my client's silence. Go back with him to quite the vilest hotel in Paddington, where he insisted on doing things that...Well, some people have got the nastiest tastes.'

'But, Gary, if your acquaintance with Yves was as slight as you say, why did he make such a fuss of you when you arrived at Tryst – greeting you like a long-lost lover and all that?'

Gary tutted with exasperation. 'Don't you see? He was doing the same thing again – teasing Tristram, flirting, getting him furious. That sort of thing stimulated them, both of them.'

Charles reached for his whisky glass, but it was empty. Gary was out of

Campari too. Charles waved at the waiter and re-ordered.

'Tell me, Gary, how did you come to be at Tryst? Why did you go there?'

'Just a booking through the agency.'

'To meet Mr Carruthers?'

'That's right. At eleven o'clock.'

'You'd never heard of Mr Carruthers?'

'No.' Gary Stane gave a twisted smile. 'Very few of my clients use their real names.'

'And you didn't know that Tryst would have stopped serving dinner by eleven o'clock?'

'Like the Sparta, love, Tryst is outside my usual range.'

'And you didn't know that Yves worked there?'

'God, no. I knew nothing about him.'

'And were you surprised when there was no Mr Carruthers waiting for you?'

'I wouldn't have been. Quite often turn up and find I'm alone. People make the booking and then lose their nerve. But in this case, I didn't know he wasn't there.'

'What do you mean?'

'Well, the girl on the door said she'd check the book, and before she'd done that, Yves appeared...and then Tristram...and the furies were unleashed.'

'Hmm.' Charles picked his words carefully. 'I don't suppose you know –'

Gary smiled triumphantly. 'I know what you're going to ask.'

'How?'

'You forget, I've been through all this with the police. You want to know the voice of the person who made the booking.'

'That's right. Do you know?'

'Oh yes. Maxine took it. Very reliable memory, Maxine.'

'Ah.'

Gary smiled, a gentler smile than before. 'Good girl, Maxine. We're getting married in the spring.'

Charles's mouth fell open. 'What?'

'God, you don't think I do it with men because I like it, do you? If there were the acting work about, or the dancing, I'd do that. As it is...well, we're saving up the deposit on a house.'

Charles looked bewildered.

'Yes, I know, Charles, terrible, isn't it – the things people will do to make money.'

'Oh, I don't know. I've recently been talking to someone about the chances of getting work charring.'

'Hmm.' Gary grimaced. 'At least you can wear rubber gloves for that.'

'But back to the booking,' urged Charles.

'Yes. Of course. Well, Maxine remembered because it was such an unusual voice to be using the name 'Mr Carruthers'.'

'What sort of voice – male or female?'

'Oh, male. And with a strong French accent.'

'Oh. But I –'

'Don't you see? It must have been Yves himself. He set it up. Part of his teasing of Tristram. I mean, if you think about it, it was rather a coincidence that he should appear just as I arrived. But if he knew I was coming...'

'I hadn't thought of that.'

'No. But that must have been it. That's what the police reckon, anyway. Just another of Yves's little games at Tristram's expense – only this one misfired.'

They had their second drink and talked a little longer, but Gary had no more information to give. Eventually, with some awkwardness, Charles suggested that maybe they didn't bother with the rest of the planned evening.

Gary said that, so long as the agency fee was paid, he was quite happy to forego his dinner.

He looked more animated than he had all evening as he pocketed his twenty pounds and rose to leave. 'Thanks. It's like being given a half-day off school,' he said skittishly. Then he winked. 'Maxine and I could do with an early night.'

## Chapter Nine

MONIQUE LAFEU WAS strangely unfeminine. It was as if her brother had appropriated the family ration of femininity and left her drained of sexuality. She was not ugly, but there seemed about her a coldness, a dullness even, that did not invite intimacy.

She was tall and big-boned, but there was no angularity or awkwardness in her movements. She walked, as she did everything, with short-tempered efficiency. The distinctive Gallic pout of her lips carried no message of passion, merely one of slight resentment, as if every external contact of her life was an imposition. Seeing her again, and remembering her at the reception counter of Tryst, Charles could visualize her in a few years in charge of a French restaurant, a looming presence at the cash-desk, keeping an unsmiling spider-watch over her diners.

Her manner was already proprietorial when they met that Tuesday morning at Tryst. She had suggested the venue, so presumably she had a key and had either sought or not bothered to seek police permission to use the premises.

Her resentful pout was marked, implying, even though she had set up the meeting, that Charles and O'Rourke's appearance was an intrusion. 'Things will be a lot simpler,' she began, after minimal formal greetings had been exchanged, 'now they are both dead.'

Her English was heavily accented, but fluent and easy to understand.

'This is a good setting for a restaurant,' she went on, 'and I think it should do very well. There is no need for all of the…what's the word you use?… campness which Yves brought to it.'

Charles did not agree with that view. To his mind, much of the appeal of Tryst had been in the outrageousness of its owners. But he did not interrupt Monique.

'What makes a restaurant is not all of the…what do you call it?…set-dressing? It is just good food and efficient service.'

'Were your parents in the restaurant business?' asked O'Rourke politely.

'Why do you ask?'

'Well, I just thought with Yves and you both going into –'

'No. My father is *épicier*… he owns a grocery store in Reims.'

'So have they been here?'

Monique's eyes clouded with incredulity. 'No. But if we may get on with our business…'

Though the nature of what she regarded as their business had not yet been defined, O'Rourke showed no curiosity about it. Indeed, he seemed unwilling to move the subject on, anxious for delay. Charles did not interfere, sensing that his friend had some plan of campaign.

'It must have been a terrible shock for you, Miss Lafeu.' O'Rourke said formally. 'To hear of the death of your brother.'

She shrugged. 'Of course. But people who live that sort of life are always at risk of such things. It is perhaps a punishment for what they do.'

O'Rourke did not visibly bridle at this, though Charles knew it must have caused him annoyance. Instead, he went on, 'How did you hear the news?'

'From the police.'

'Here in England?'

'No, I was in Reims. I went for my vacation on the day after the restaurant closed. And then three days later I have to come back.' She tutted and tossed her head back at the inconvenience.

'And did your parents come over too?'

'It was not necessary. There is no need for them to see...this place.' The disapproval was undisguised. 'They do not need to know everything. When the police release Yves's body, he will be buried in France. A terrible accident, a misfortune, the murder by a madman – that is all they need to know.'

'You mean they didn't know that Yves lived with Tristram?'

'There was no need,' Monique snapped.

'But if the police talk to them, it may come out.'

'I hope the police will not talk to them. That is why I am here – to stop such talkings.'

'But surely –'

'Anyway, this is not why we are here,' Monique cut in abruptly.

'No. Why are we here?' asked Charles. He knew why he and O'Rourke were there, but he was interested to know why Monique had instigated the encounter.

She was not amused by his interruption and turned her cold eyes on him. 'I do not know why you are here. Mr O'Rourke is here because I invited him to come and talk to me.'

'Mr Paris is a friend and adviser to me. I wished him to be present.'

O'Rourke's intervention received another toss of the head. 'I will tell you why I wished you here. I heard you were trying to make contact with me. You telephoned one of the waiters, Mr O'Rourke.'

'Yes.'

'He told me. He told me some of the questions you asked him. He gave me the idea you were also investigating my brother's murder.'

'Well...'

'There is nothing to investigate. The police have all the facts. Yves was killed by Tristram.'

'But until Tristram's found –'

'Yves was killed by Tristram!' she repeated with surprising vehemence. 'There is nothing else to think. And it is not good for the memory of the dead to investigate further.'

'But when there are suspicious circumstances –'

'There are no suspicious circumstances, Mr O'Rourke. Tristram killed my brother, drove to Mas-de-Pouzard, and killed himself. This is not suspicious. It is wicked, yes, it is cruel, but it is very simple and straightforward.'

O'Rourke was temporarily silenced by the vigour of her assault, so Charles decided it might be the moment for him to say something. 'I'm sorry, I can't agree, Miss Lafeu. Until Tristram's body is found, there are many suspicious circumstances. And, unless he delivers a confession (if he is still alive) or confesses in a suicide note, those suspicions will remain.'

'They will not! Frequently the bodies of *suicidés* are not found for many years. It is quite enough for my family to have had its tragedy and to have the police interfering, without having other people busying themselves in our affairs.'

'I am afraid,' said Charles gently, 'when people are murdered, that is the kind of thing that happens. You speak of the tragedy of your family,' and, he reflected, without much emotion, 'but there are other families too. Tristram Gowers was – is – O'Rourke's cousin.'

'This is no reason to interfere in –'

'Oh, but it is.' His interruption took the wind out of her sails, so Charles pressed on. 'On the night Yves died, what time did you leave the restaurant?'

She was so surprised at the directness of the questioning that she replied with automatic docility. 'I left with the rest of the staff...about two o'clock.'

'No one stayed?'

'Only Yves and Tristram. We tidied up quickly. It was the beginning of the *vacances*.' By now she had had time to feel affronted. 'I do not know how you have the nerve to question me like this. I –'

'Listen,' said Charles. 'According to you, there were no suspicious circumstances that evening. But there were.'

'For example?'

'All right. The young man, Gary Stane...You remember him?'

Monique nodded curtly.

'When he came into this room at eleven o'clock that Saturday night, were you expecting him?'

'Of course not. Why should I?'

'If Yves had arranged for the boy to come, he might have told you so that you wouldn't turn him out. Did Yves tell you the boy was coming?'

Monique was silent, as if weighing up the advantages of various answers to this question. Charles was equally concerned. If Yves had warned his sister about Gary's expected arrival, then all had been as the police believed – the boy had been set up by Yves to antagonize his lover. And if that had happened, the case for any alternative interpretation of the murder was much weakened.

'No, Yves said nothing,' Monique replied at last.

'In that case,' Charles interposed quickly, 'why did you let Gary in? He had no booking. You knew last orders had been given hours before. The kitchen was virtually closed. Why did you let him in?'

For the first time that morning, Monique looked confused. Perhaps she was wishing she had said that Yves had arranged the encounter. That would have tied up the loose ends neatly; whereas now she appeared to be getting into an uncomfortable area of questioning.

'Come on – why?' Charles demanded. 'You knew how the restaurant worked. If anyone else had walked in at that time of night, you would have said, "Sorry, sir, we're closed". Why didn't you do that with Gary Stane?'

'I did, but he still walked in.'

Charles shook his head. 'I was here that night. So was O'Rourke. We both saw exactly what happened.'

Monique shrugged. 'This is a waste of time. I have nothing to say.'

'What a pity. If you told us your reason, we might get off your back. If you don't, well...' Charles decided it was his turn to have a shrug '...we're just going to get that much more suspicious, aren't we?'

'All right,' Monique conceded petulantly. 'I will tell you. I did not know this Gary...whatever it is? I had never seen him before, but when he came in, I could tell...what he was.'

You'd have been wrong, thought Charles, in response to the contempt of her tone.

'So I knew what might happen if Tristram and Yves met him, so I just let him in.'

'You let him in deliberately to make trouble?'

'If you like.'

'But why? Did you hate Yves?'

'No, I did not hate Yves.' Now she spoke with more animation, perhaps more passion, than before. 'I loved Yves as he was. When I was a child, when he was my big brother, then I loved him. But not after he met this Tristram. Then he is not my brother, he becomes something else.'

'So it's Tristram you hate?'

'Perhaps. Tristram and what he made of Yves. They were wicked. It is good they are dead.'

Monique did not seem embarrassed by what she had said. Her hard eyes took on a dreamy quality as she went on, 'The restaurant will be better without them. It will be simple, ordinary French cuisine, but it will be very good. The best. It will be a place I will be proud for my parents to come to.'

'This is assuming that you would be running it?' asked O'Rourke, who had been silent for some time.

'But of course. That is what I will do. I know enough now about the business. I am a good administrator. I will do well.'

'And what makes you think it will be yours to run?'

'The restaurant?' She looked bewildered at O'Rourke's stupidity. 'But of course it will be mine. My parents have no interests in England. They will let me run it.'

'Suppose Tristram is still alive. What then?'

'Tristram is dead,' she announced with uncontradictable assurance.

'If he is, then presumably his Will will be obeyed.'

'I suppose so.' She did not seem very interested in this. 'If there is a Will. But Tristram had no family, anyway. So it will all come to us.'

'No,' said O'Rourke, suddenly forceful. 'Tristram did make a Will, and he left everything to me.'

Monique Lafeu gaped. When, finally, she could find speech, it was only a whisper. 'No. No. But if that were true, then there was no reason for them to die.'

Charles and O'Rourke sat over a second carafe of red wine in a Notting Hill Italian restaurant. 'Difficult to say,' said Charles. 'She's an unusual woman.'

'Well, she certainly seemed to hate her brother.'

'And Tristram even more so.'

'And she was very put out at the idea of my inheriting the restaurant.'

'Yes, I don't think she believed you. I bet she's talked to a solicitor by now.'

'Yes, I bet she has, Charles.' O'Rourke ran his fingers across the dome of his head, flattening the few hairs into place. 'Certainly big enough.'

'What, you mean big enough, strong enough, to have committed the murder?'

'Yes. Cold-blooded enough, too.'

'Apparently. But you can't always judge –'

'She also went to France the day after Yves was killed.'

'That was pre-arranged. Going to her parents.'

'Oh yes. But if we're following your thesis of someone making Tristram drive down through France at gunpoint...'

'Hardly a thesis, more a random speculation.'

'That's about all we can hope for at the moment in this case.'

'Yes. Either random speculation...or the obvious solution.'

'When Tristram is found and confesses, then I'll believe the obvious solution.'

Charles sighed. O'Rourke looked troubled. 'You are still with me, aren't you?'

'Oh yes. For what I'm worth, you have my full attention.'

'Hmm.' The collector circled a finger round the top of his wine-glass. 'What are you doing for the next few days?'

'Nothing. Oh, well, I promised to take someone to an open audition tomorrow morning. Otherwise...'

'The "rest" continues?'

'That's about it. Why do you ask?'

'Well, Charles, the thing that's stopping this investigation from progressing anywhere is the fact that Tristram has still not been found.'

'Yes.'

'But he is known to have driven all the way down to Mas-de-Pouzard, which is presumably where he was last seen. I want to go and look for him, Charles.'

'What? You mean –'

'Yes. How do you fancy a trip to France?'

## Chapter Ten

CHARLES MET HENRY on the Wednesday morning, outside the Shaftesbury Avenue exit from Piccadilly Circus Tube Station, as they had arranged. The open audition was not scheduled to start until ten, but, knowing how queues built up for that kind of occasion, he had suggested a nine o'clock meeting.

She looked as succulent as ever. Her hair was scraped back into a strict ballet-dancer's bun, which only accentuated the rounded youth of her face. She wore a yellow and black horizontally striped mini-dress over what presumably, from the matching sleeves and tights, was a purple leotard. Little gold boots completed the ensemble of what the television series *Fame* had told her a working actress would wear.

'Oh, hello, Charles. It's frightfully nice of you to turn up. I thought you might have forgotten.'

'I said I'd be here.' His voice was mildly aggrieved.

'Yes, I know. I'm sorry. It's just...well, some people say things and don't do them.'

As they walked along Shaftesbury Avenue, she confessed that she felt 'absolutely ghastly'.

'Nerves?'

'Yes.'

'Well, don't get it out of proportion. Remember, you're just going for the experience. Put out of your mind any thought that you might get a part.'

'Yes, yes, of course.' But there was a note of wistfulness in her voice. Her fantasies had clearly been working overtime, building images of the great producer out front recognizing her unique star quality, casting her in the lead, and setting her on a path of hitherto-unequalled success. It is every actor's dream, the dream of which none of them are ever quite cured. Even Charles, through his layers of cynicism, could still occasionally relapse into it.

So, if he was going to let her down, he knew it would have to be done gently. 'I mean, these auditions won't be for the principals. Those will have been sorted out. They'll just be looking for boys and girls for the chorus. A lot of those may have been sorted out already too. These open auditions are often just a nod in the direction of democracy. I'm afraid real life is very rarely like *Chorusline*.'

'No, no, of course not.' But he had not eradicated the little fantasy bloom of hope in Henry's voice.

'Did Bertram tell you roughly what the form is?' asked Charles, leaving dream-demolition aside for a moment.

'No.' Again the glow that Bertram Pride's name seemed always to bring came, on cue, to her cheeks. 'No, no, I haven't actually seen much of Bertram this week. He doesn't even know I'm going to this.'

Charles made no more comment than an 'Oh', then continued, 'Well, basically what happens is you go and join the queue at the stage door. Then when you get backstage, someone'll take your name and agent's name – oh, you haven't got one.'

'No.'

'Well, never mind. Then they'll probably ask if you're Equity – did it specify Equity in the ad.?'

'It said "Equity preferred".'

'Well, that's better than "Equity only". It means they might take on a beginner who was exceptionally good. Depends whether it's for West End or a tour. And again whether it's a Number One tour or not...'

Henry looked puzzled, but Charles decided not to depress her further with the complexities of his union's regulations. 'Anyway, if they ask about Equity, say you've nearly got your full card. That'll imply you've only got a few more weeks to do.'

'But what if I'm actually offered a part?'

Oh dear, the fantasies were tenacious. 'Cross that bridge when you come to it,' said Charles kindly.

'And then what happens?'

'When you finally get on stage?'

'Yes.'

'Well, you do your bit – or at least as much of it as they'll let you. They're always running way behind time, and they always apologize that they have to be brief, but usually you're allowed to get a few words out before they stop you. You have got something prepared, I assume?'

'Oh yes.'

'Good.'

'I've done a Portia speech.'

'What!' Charles stopped dead in the middle of the pavement.

'You know, Portia, *Merchant of Venice*.'

'Yes, I know Portia.'

'"The quality of mercy is not strain'd", that one.'

'Henry, you can't do that.'

'What?' She looked distressed. 'But I do do it well – really. I played Portia in the school play, and then when I was at college my Drama Tutor said it was a frightfully good audition piece.'

'Where were you at college?'

'A place in Bath. You probably wouldn't have heard of it,' Henry replied, slightly evasively.

'What, a drama school?'

'Well, we did a lot of drama.' Her little chin was set defiantly.

'Hmm.' Charles got the picture. Some kind of high-class finishing school, offering its own totally worthless diploma in performing arts. Henry was even less qualified to be an actress than he had thought. But she looked so vulnerable that he could not restrain his benevolence. 'They really should have taught you about auditions. The important thing is always to have something suitable prepared. I mean, this is for a musical – no one's going to want to hear your favourite gems from Shakespeare.'

In spite of his gentle tone, Henry looked crushed.

'I'm sorry, love, but you did ask me to give you a few tips, and this is exactly the sort of thing you ought to know. At least I've saved you the embarrassment of going up onstage and making a fool of yourself.'

'Yes, Charles. Thank you. I just thought, you know, they'd hear the speech and then, if they thought I was good enough, they'd sort of ask me about singing and that sort of thing.'

'They don't have time. I'm afraid it's straight on and off. Some'll get recalled, but they'll have had to show basic dancing and singing skills first. Incidentally, another tip. If you are recalled, make sure the request is made vaguely publicly. If the director suggests discussing the part further at his flat later in the evening, be wary.'

'Oh. You mean...?' Obviously it wasn't just the mention of Bertram Pride; it was anything connected with sex that made Henry blush. 'So what should I have prepared for this audition?' she asked contritely.

'A song. Do you have any music?' She shook her head.

'But you can sing?'

'Oh yes. I was taught music for ages and ages.'

'So you can sight-read?'

'Yes.'

'Then all is not lost. Come on, let's find a music shop and get you something you can sing.'

In the music shop it turned out that she had once been in a school production of *South Pacific*, so they homed in on *I'm Gonna Wash That Man Right Out Of My Hair*. It wasn't as up to date as it might have been, but at least she was familiar with the tune.

'And what else will happen?' Henry asked, as they neared the King's Theatre.

'There'll probably be a choreographer there. He may take you through a few steps, probably in groups. Or perhaps they'll hear you sing first and only select a few for the dancing. It depends.'

'Gosh, what are all these people doing?' asked Henry.

'I've a horrible feeling they're the queue,' said Charles.

'But we're nowhere near the stage door of the King's.'

'No. Look, you join the queue in case. I'll go and reconnoitre.'

It was the queue. The youth of those waiting, the leotards, the wild clothes, the heightened quality of the conversation all gave Charles the message long before he had rounded the fourth corner to see the 'Stage Door' sign ahead.

It was going to be a long wait.

So it proved. The queue moved with agonizing slowness. Lunchtime passed. Charles snuck off and bought himself a ham roll, but Henry said she didn't feel hungry. She didn't feel thirsty either, and Charles spent opening hours in agony filing slowly past a pub, feeling that in some obscure way it would be unchivalrous to leave her and go inside for a few pints. He had said he would look after Henry and that was what he was going to do.

By three-thirty they were inside the building, and then the queue seemed to stop completely for an hour. Charles wondered what the reason might be – the discovery of a new star, somebody throwing a scene, or the producer and director taking a late lunch-break. He looked anxiously ahead, trying to gauge how many there were to go before Henry. Auditions of that sort were often badly mismanaged and, if it were to happen, it wouldn't have been the first time that people who had been queuing for eight hours were told to come back the next day.

But the log-jam was sorted out and the slow forward progress recommenced. A harassed-looking young man took Henry's details. He had too much on his mind to be worried by her lack of experience, and so that hurdle was passed.

Soon they were in earshot of the stage, and could hear what was being sung. As Charles had feared, audition pieces were keeping well up with fashion. A lot of the hopefuls would have recently been in work and tended to perform items from shows they had just finished. Stephen Sondheim and *Chorusline* were favourites; and a lot had clearly been studying Andrew Lloyd-Webber LPs. But Henry wouldn't sound completely on her own. So many reps had been playing safe and reviving old musicals in the last few years that there was a sprinkling of Rodgers & Hammerstein, even smatterings of Franz Lehar, Rudolf Friml and Sigmund Romberg.

Eventually they could see the stage, and Charles felt Henry's tension grow. The boys and girls who auditioned had all worked professionally before. Their notes might wobble, their vowels lurch transatlantically, their movements betray mannerism rather than rhythm, but they all had the minimal gloss that comes from having worked before a paying audience. Charles, who knew nothing of Henry's performing abilities, felt anxious for her.

Mind you, even the professionals weren't getting long to show their paces. The very good ones were allowed to get through a verse and chorus; the less competent were chopped off after their verse by the anonymous shout from the auditorium. It was like a parody of a Nazi death camp, seeing how long each aspirant could survive before being led meekly off to execution.

At last Henry was next. The young man preceding her had the nerve to object to being cut short. The voice from the auditorium apologized that they had to be brief. The young man said they wouldn't recognize talent if it came and peed over them. He added that the accompanist had as much sense of rhythm as a bag of sick, and, snatching his music from the piano, stormed off the stage.

Whether this prelude would help Henry or not, Charles couldn't judge. Certainly she looked very pretty as she walked onstage. And, considering the circumstances, very assured. Her background and finishing school may not have given her much drama training, but it had given her poise.

She handed her music to the accompanist, who looked at her with the weary expression of a man who has already played the beginning of *Don't Cry For Me, Argentina* over fifty times that day and has just been compared to a bag of sick. He sat at the piano and, without preamble, launched into the opening bars of *I'm Gonna Wash That Man Right Out Of My Hair*.

Henry looked thrown, as if she had expected to make some announcement, or to be greeted by the faceless voices out front. Charles peered through the curtain. Under the lip of the Circle he could see nothing, except for the little glow of a light over an improvised table set on two rows of seats. The faces of producer, director, perhaps choreographer, secretary and casting director, were invisible in the shadow.

But Henry came in on her note. She had a clear, pure voice, and sang very simply, without the mannered emphases of the previous auditionees. Hers was really a drawing-room voice, rather than a stage voice, but it seemed to fill the auditorium.

And she did look so pretty.

For a moment Charles wondered if the miracle was about to happen, if her dream was about to be fulfilled, if she was to be spotted and rocketed to stardom.

She had just started on the chorus when her sentence was pronounced.

'Thank you,' called the nameless voice from the stalls. 'Sorry, love. We have to be brief.'

Charles was worried that she might have been depressed by the experience. She was preoccupied as they left the theatre, dawdled as if waiting for something. (The something in question, Charles feared, was the Hollywood scene of a boyishly handsome producer rushing after her and saying, 'I can't let a girl like you go. You gotta work for me.')

But no such scenario developed and, once they were out of sight of the theatre, Henry seemed to relax. 'Gosh,' she said, 'I'm absolutely ravenous. Always feel like that after a performance – it must be release of tension.'

Charles didn't argue with her definition of a performance, but suggested that they wander down to Covent Garden and have a cup of tea somewhere. (It was still an hour until the pubs opened.)

'No, no, you must come back to the flat,' urged Henry. 'You've been so kind to me, Charles, really. Come back and have a drink and a bit of fodder.'

Then she hailed a cab with a style and readiness that few unemployed actresses of her age would have commanded, and gave an address in Sloane Street.

Inside the cab, Charles dared to ask her what she had thought of the audition.

'Oh it was really A1. I mean v.g., absolutely.'

'You weren't disappointed?'

'Gosh, no. It was just frightfully nice being, you know, with actors, in a really professional situation. I mean, it sort of gave me a feeling of it. You know, the experience will help. I must be ready to go through any number of disappointments before I get where I want to be.' Then, turning her wonderful wide eyes on Charles, she said, 'The Theatre's a cruel mistress, you know.'

'Yes,' agreed Charles, desperately controlling a twitching at the corners of his mouth.

The cab drew up outside an expensive block of flats in Sloane Street and Henry paid off the driver as if by instinct. Charles passed no comment on the elegance of the facade, or the wide hall with its uniformed commissionaire, or the plushly carpeted lift. He said nothing until they were inside the flat itself, whose punctiliously designed interior matched the luxury of the block. He looked out over the highly-priced roofs of Kensington, and allowed himself a 'Very nice.'

'Yes, not bad, is it? Of course, it's not mine.'

'No?'

'Oh gosh, no. Hobby and I are really just squatters here.'

'Squatters?'

'Yes. Well, I mean Daddy owns it, but we're just squatters.'

'I see.'

'Could you fancy a drink?'

Charles admitted that he probably, at a pinch, could.

'Great. After a day like today, I wouldn't mind getting a bit chateaued. Got some fizz in the fridge, that be okay?'

'Fine,' said Charles, not quite sure what the 'fizz' would be.

'And if I rustle up the odd smoked salmon sarnie, be okay?'

'Fine.'

Soon they were sitting over the sandwiches, neat in fresh brown bread, and the 'fizz', which proved to be a very acceptable non-vintage champagne, and Henry was enthusing about how grateful she was to Charles and what she planned to do next to further her career and how she was really prepared to work amazingly hard and wouldn't mind reverses and was really prepared to stick at it until she made it. Charles supplied the relevant agreements and encouragements and drank and thought how amazingly pretty she was.

Their idyll was rudely interrupted. The door to the living room was flung open and, framed in it, stood a stocky young man in his mid-twenties. He wore a blazer and regimental tie, had very short hair and a very red face.

Henry's sandwich plate crashed to the floor as she stood up, aghast. 'James!'

'Yes, James,' the young man confirmed. His voice carried the authority of many generations' shouting at grouse-beaters. 'And what have you to say for yourself eh?'

'How on earth did you get in?' asked Henry weakly.

'Met Hobby in the hall. She waited for the lift. I came up by the stairs. Thought I'd give you a little surprise. And I jolly well did, didn't I? I never thought I'd actually burst in and find you here with your elderly lover.'

Charles cleared his throat. 'I think you're getting the wrong end of the stick.'

'Oh, you mean you're not an actor?' asked the young man pugnaciously.

'Well, yes, I am, but —'

'See!' The young man looked round the flat, as if to support his case. 'And do you deny that your name is Bertram Pride?'

'Yes, I do. My name's Charles Paris.'

The red brow wrinkled as this piece of information was digested. Then a new roar burst out. 'Good God, Henry! You mean there's more than one of them?'

'No, James, Charles is just a friend.'

'Huh! Come on, give me credit for something between the ears. That's the oldest line in the book. I told your father you'd go to the bad if you came up to London. You know, you should never have left Gloucestershire, young lady.'

'Look, could I explain...?' Charles began.

'You keep out of this! Now listen, Henry, I want to know what's what. I'd have come sooner, but I've been on a training course. And let me tell you, it hasn't been much fun having my girl-friend's name plastered all over the gossip columns. Some pretty nasty remarks passed in the mess let me tell you. Honestly, I turn my back for a fortnight and find you've turned into some backstage groupie!'

'No, it's not like that, James. Let me explain —'

'Don't need your explanations! I'd just like to know what this succession of ageing matinée idols think they're doing seducing my girl left, right and centre and —'

'If I'm meant to be one of the succession,' Charles interposed firmly, 'you are way off target. I have just been giving Henry some advice on her career.'

'Huh!' snorted James.

'It's true,' said a new voice. Hobby, a sardonic smile on her face, had appeared in the doorway behind the young officer.

'Oh.' James, momentarily discomfitted, stepped aside to let her come into the room. She put down her brief case, kicked off her shoes, and flopped into a chair, whence she watched the proceedings with enthusiasm.

'Well, I'm sorry if I've slandered you,' James said grudgingly to Charles. Then he rounded on Henry again. 'But what about this Bertram Pride? Do you deny that you've been going around with him?'

'No, I don't. But I've only been out with him for a few meals, discotheques, that sort of thing. It was part of our agreement, James. We did say we should both be free to go out with other people.'

'Go out, okay!' stormed the young officer. 'But not sneak off for dirty weekends at country cottages! There was nothing about that in our agreement!'

'It wasn't like that, James. Really.'

'What, so the gossip column got it wrong?'

'Yes.'

'What, there never was any idea of you going off to this louse's cottage?'

'Well, yes, there was an idea. I mean, we had discussed it. We had intended to.'

'Exactly as the gossip column said.'

'Yes. But...' Henry looked torn, embarrassed. She glanced at her sister, as if wishing that Hobby were out of the room. But she couldn't avoid the truth. James's bristling fury had to be answered.

'We had planned to go...' Henry's voice was very small. 'But, when it came to it, we didn't.'

'James is all right, really,' said Henry. 'You didn't see him at his best. He can be frightfully good company.'

She and Charles were sitting outside a Covent Garden wine bar the next day. She had agreed readily when he had suggested meeting to talk. She wanted to apologize for the haste with which James had hurried him out of the flat.

'You've known him a long time?'

'Since we were tinies, yes. Well, since I was tiny. He's six years older than me. And, you know, our parents are great friends and...oh, I dare say I'll end up marrying him.'

'But not yet.'

'No. You see, one of the great things about coming up to London, I mean, apart from getting into the theatre, was, you know, to meet a few people other than James.'

'You didn't have a big split-up?'

'No. It was just...he was the only boy I'd ever been out with and, you know, I sort of felt I ought to meet some other people rather than going straight into marriage.'

'Reasonable.'

'Yes. Anyway, James said, okay, if that's what I really wanted, then I should do it. I mean, he's in the army, based in Scotland. I don't see that much of him, anyway, so it wouldn't make a great deal of difference to him.'

'So you agreed that you could both go out with other people, so long as nothing got serious?'

'Yes. So long as...well...there was nothing, you know...' She blushed, so Charles knew she was talking about sex.

'I understand.'

'Anyway, James thought the same about my coming up to London as Daddy did. Neither of them think I'll stick it. They both think I'll be back in Gloucestershire – and probably married to James – before the year's out.'

'And will you?'

'No.' Henry jutted her chin out with determination.

'Which brings us to...Bertram Pride,' said Charles lightly.

'Yes.' Henry paused, mustering her ideas. 'It's complicated. I met him at a party, and, you know, he was jolly nice to me, and, well, I was flattered. I mean, he is a famous face. And, you know, him being older than me...well, I never thought someone of that age would be interested in someone like me.'

Then you are genuinely unaware of just how attractive you are, thought Charles. Really, it would be sad to see something so pretty and so charming wasted on an upper-class blusterer like James.

'So, anyway, Bertram started taking me out and, you know, he's good company. He knew the right places to go and everyone recognized him, and we had a good time. And at that stage there wasn't anything, you know...' Her blush told Charles exactly what she meant. 'But then he started talking about this country cottage, and how he must take me down there, and well, I knew exactly what he meant.'

'Yes. So how did you react?'

'Well, part of me was drawn to the idea. I mean, I wasn't in love with him, but, you know, he was attractive and he seemed kind. And also I suppose I was swayed by him being famous and liking the idea of having an affair with someone famous...And perhaps even, selfishly, thinking he could help me in the theatre. So I sort of...didn't say no.'

'Which he interpreted as meaning yes?'

She nodded. 'And then, before I knew it, other people seemed to know we were going to the cottage and I thought, well, why not? And then there was Hobby...'

She tailed off.

'What had Hobby got to do with it?'

'Well, Hobby's a bit strait-laced, and I...told her I was going off with Bertram.'

'To shock her?'

Henry looked full in his face, appreciative of his understanding. 'Yes. A bit of that, yes. But, having told Hobby, having sort of made a stand about it, I thought I had to go through with it.'

'But, in the event you didn't?'

'No. I lost my nerve. You see, Bertram and I were meant to be going straight down in my car after that dinner at Tryst...you know, when I first met you.'

Charles nodded.

'And I felt sort of okay about it, because Bertram had said that, you know, there wouldn't be any...' She blushed furiously, but managed to bring out the word, 'sex.'

'But then, in the car, after we'd left the restaurant, well, it was clear that I had misunderstood him.'

'Ah. So he *was* planning to spirit you off for a dirty weekend?'

Henry nodded. 'And I sort of thought of James, and I knew that I didn't love Bertram, and I thought, well, I was scared.'

'You mean it wasn't the sort of thing you'd done very often.'

She looked very shame-faced, and Charles could only just hear her say, 'Ever.'

'I see.' He looked at her and felt pity, pity for the pressures on a young girl which made her apologize for her virginity. 'So what happened?'

'I'm afraid we had a row. Bertram was pretty angry. After a time he just left me.'

'What do you mean?'

'He stormed out of the car and said he was going to get a cab home.'

'So what did you do?'

'Well...' She looked even more miserable. 'This sounds daft, but in fact I didn't dare go back to the flat. You see, having told Hobby, having made such an issue of it with Hobby, I just couldn't go back.'

Having witnessed the competitive edge between the two sisters, Charles could understand this.

'So what did you do?'

'I drove around for a bit, just aimlessly, trying to decide where I should go. There are various chums whose floors I could have crashed out on, but, well, they all know each other and...'

'And you didn't want to lose face? You wanted to maintain the illusion that you had gone off with Bertram.'

'Yes.' She was nearly crying. 'I thought it'd give me some sort of cachet with them. I don't know why. Whereas all it has got me is the most frightful row with James.'

'Is he still furious with you?'

'Well, not quite so bad. He took me out to dinner last night and we got things a bit sorted out. But he's very hurt.'

Charles pulled the subject back to what interested him. 'So where did you spend that night?'

'In the car. I know, daft, but I did.'

'Where?'

'Well, that was even dafter. I drove round in circles, and found that I'd ended up near Tryst again. I suppose I was vaguely looking for Bertram, thinking he might still be hanging around there for me.'

'And was he?'

'No, of course not. So I parked there and spent an extremely uncomfortable night, dozing intermittently. The next day I drove down into the country and came back on the Sunday evening, pretending to Hobby that I'd actually spent the weekend with Bertram Pride.'

Charles felt excitement welling inside him. 'So in fact you spent the entire night parked outside Tryst?'

'Well, not exactly outside. Round the corner. Just by the entrance to the mews at the back.'

Even better. 'And you say you didn't sleep well?'

'On and off. Not much.'

'And did you see any comings and goings from the mews?'

'Yes, I saw a few cars and things.'

She spoke with her usual innocence, unaware of the importance of her words.

'Tell me what you saw?' asked Charles, trying to contain the agitation in his voice.

'Well, I think by the time I got there, all of the people eating dinner must have gone. But then there were a few cars and motor-bikes and a few people on foot who all came out of the mews about the same time. They woke me, they were calling out goodbyes to each other.'

'Would that have been about two o'clock?'

'Round then, yes.'

The staff, as Monique had said.

'Anything else?'

'I was woken up later by a car going out. It was going fast, the tyres screeched.'

'What make was it?'

'A Volvo.'

'Did you see the driver?'

'Only got an impression. Sort of lots of silver hair. I thought it was probably the proprietor...'

'Tristram Gowers?'

'That's right.'

'You couldn't see whether there was anyone else in the car?'

Henry shook her head. 'It was very loaded up in the back.'

'Any idea what time that was?'

'I seem to remember looking at my watch and seeing it was just after half-past three.'

Right on schedule for the six-thirty ferry at Dover.

Charles felt weary. He had built up so many different pictures of what had happened, and now he had a witness to confirm the police's reconstruction of events. Tristram Gowers had driven off at three-thirty. The idea that he was doing so while held at gunpoint by some hidden murderer in the back of the car now seemed fanciful.

'Thanks, Henry,' he said wryly. 'Don't suppose you saw anything else?'

'No cars, no.'

'I was afraid that would be the answer.'

'But I did see someone on foot.'

'What!' Charles sat bolt upright. 'Who? When?'

'Just before three it must have been. I saw someone walk into the mews.'

'Did you see them come out?'

Henry shook her head. 'I think I dozed off, though. They may have come out.'

'And who was it?' asked Charles.

'I couldn't see the face,' Henry replied, 'but it was a woman. A tall woman.'

## Chapter Eleven

CONTINENTAL TRAVEL IN the company of Bartlemas and O'Rourke was conducted in some style. They drove in Bartlemas's vintage Lagonda, a silver monster which drew admiring glances on the road and seemed to ensure an obsequious welcome at the château-hotels they favoured with their custom.

They also ate on the way. In spite of the serious nature of their mission, they allowed the trip to be a little *tour gastronomique*, and it was a long time since Charles had eaten so much delectable food or drunk so much fine wine. Philip Marlowe, working on expenses, never had it so good.

They did not travel by the same route that the Volvo had taken. Their aim was not a reconstruction of that particular journey; for them the interest lay at the destination, in the house at Mas-de-Pouzard. So, rather than taking the Dover–Calais crossing, they had gone Southampton–Cherbourg and driven down (with detours in the cause of gastronomy) through Tours, Poitiers and Limoges.

When Charles looked at the map of France, he wondered why Tristram had chosen the other route. It seemed to involve more driving through less attractive countryside. He also noted, and wondered whether there was any significance in the fact, that it passed nearer to Reims. There was something important, he felt, in the relationship between Yves and his parents. Or, if not that, in the relationship between Monique and her parents.

But, when he raised the question of the route, O'Rourke explained it away instantly. Tristram had always been an exceptionally bad sailor, and so they always crossed by the shortest way. He would rather spend more time at the wheel than more time on the sea.

The countryside glowed with hazy warmth as they moved further south. Though it was mid-September, and the evening chill set in earlier, the sun at noon was still blisteringly hot. After a summer in London, where the sun is rarely more than a dusty inconvenience, Charles felt his body begin to relax with the therapy of the warm air.

But as they neared their destination, as the domesticated, anglicized scenery of the Dordogne gave way to the wilder, more ragged contours of the Lot-et-Garonne, the mood of the party sobered. Yves's death and the unknown fate of Tristram began to preoccupy them.

And, as so often happened, Charles's mood became dislocated from its immediate cause, and he found himself thinking of Frances. Partly it was being in France. The last time had been with her, many years before, when their marriage was first beginning to show signs of splitting. They had had four days of eating, drinking and sex along the Loire, four days when, removed from the humdrum daily life which their relationship could not tolerate, it had seemed that they might, after all, stay together forever. Back in England, reality had marched back in and they had been separated within a month.

But, in France again, Charles felt himself manipulated by the cheating regrets of nostalgia, went through the pointless circle of "if only's", and speculated, worrying at the idea like a hangnail, whether Frances had been to the Loire with David.

The gastronomic dilatoriness of their progress meant that it was the evening of the third night when they passed through the medieval walls of Cahors. They checked in to a Michelin-recommended hotel in the town and settled down to yet another memorable meal. But they were all subdued. The next day they would go out to Mas-de-Pouzard. And, now that they were so close, they did not know what they were looking for there, or how they would set about finding it.

The next day summer gave a sudden late spurt and it promised to be hotter than ever.

Mas-de-Pouzard reminded Charles of the old schoolboy joke:

'What is the strangest town in England?'

'Diss.'

'Why?'

'Because, when you get near it, the town Diss appears.'

Mas-de-Pouzard also seemed to disappear as they came close to it. It was marked on the Michelin map, and they followed signposts along increasingly narrow tracks towards it, but then the signposts seemed to run out and they found themselves coming back to more major roads. A few kilometres further on there were signposts pointing back to 'Mas-de-Pouzard'.

'Well, we seem to have missed it...' said O'Rourke.

'But there was nothing there...' objected Bartlemas.

'No church...'

'No sign by the roadside...'

'No bar...'

'Nothing...'

'Still, we'd better go back...'

'No alternative...'

This time they stopped on the winding road in the middle of the hills at a point they reckoned to be equidistant between the nearest signposts in either direction. They had passed no road wider than a cart track and the only sign of human habitation was a small shack with scraps of blue fertilizer sacks hanging at its windows. There was no one in sight, but a few chickens scratching around suggested that it might be occupied.

'I'll see if there's anyone there.' Charles got out of the car and walked towards the shack. Although the Lagonda was open-topped, it was only when they stopped that he could feel the full strength of the sun. He was sweating by the time he reached the paintless front door.

Knocking produced no reaction, but, wandering round the back, he found an old man tending a vegetable patch without great urgency.

Charles greeted him. The actor's French had once been quite good, and he found that a few days back in France had sharpened it considerably.

The old man straightened up and looked at Charles without curiosity. He wore blue overalls which had faded almost to brown; his face had the texture and colour of a walnut shell, and his teeth were reduced to three nicotine-stained stumps.

Yes, he confirmed, this was Mas-de-Pouzard.

Charles said he was looking for the house of Tristram Gowers. The old man shook his head. Or Yves Lafeu? Another dubious shake.

The English people, said Charles. Ah, the English. The old man gave a strange little limp-wristed gesture. Yes, said Charles.

'You are police?' asked the old man.

'No.'

'But you want to find the house?'

'Yes.'

The old man digested this for a moment. 'I have the key,' he announced at length. 'You want me to let you in?'

'Well, yes, that would be wonderful. Wouldn't the police mind?'

The old man spat in the dust, but not vindictively. It was just a conversational gesture. 'The police do not care. One of these men kills the other in England, comes here, kills himself. They are English, the police do not care.'

The old man collected the key from inside his shack and accompanied Charles to the car. He found the Lagonda very funny. He found Bartlemas and O'Rourke, in matching Hawaiian shirts, powder blue slacks and espadrilles, even funnier. Every time they spoke, as he directed them along a cart track to the brow of a hill, the old man laughed out loud. But again there was no offence in his laughter.

As they came over the top of the hill, the first thing they saw was the river. The suddenness of the view was breathtaking. Cliffs fell away beneath them to the wide expanse of water reflecting the blue of the sky. Dark green trees mirrored themselves along the bank. On the far side a plain ran through the haze to the dark bulk of further hills.

Next they saw the house. It was an old farm-house built in pale grey stone, its low-pitched roofs covered in curved pinkish tiles. In front was a small covered courtyard from which stone steps mounted to a first-floor door. Under the eaves a row of black holes opened into the pigeon-loft. The building gave a Roman impression, like an illustration from a children's history book.

And in front of it still stood parked Tristram Gowers' Volvo.

The old man let them in through double doors on the courtyard level. Inside the house was cool, but it did not have the mustiness of a building that has been long unoccupied. It was beautifully decorated. Even a quick glance showed that no expense had been spared to bring the interior design up to the standard of the London flat.

'Is it rented out when the owners are not here?' asked Charles.

The old man nodded assent.

'We can't thank you enough for letting us in...' said Bartlemas in his acceptable French.

'No, it's so kind...' said O'Rourke in his almost acceptable French.

The old man roared with laughter. Then, asking them to drop the key in to him when they left, and refusing offers of a lift back to the road, he trudged out into the blinding sunlight. As he dwindled in the brightness, they could still hear him laughing. It was obviously a long time since he had had such a good laugh.

'Well, we've got here...' said Bartlemas.

'Yes, we've got here...' agreed O'Rourke. 'The question is...'

'What do we do now?'

'Now,' said Charles Paris, 'we search the place.'

They were not the first to have done the job. The contents of the house were not disordered, but some items had been moved and replaced in a slightly illogical way. This must have been the work of the French police, who, although, according to the old man, they had little interest in a murder in London, had gone through the motions of a search. Or maybe the Scotland Yard men who had been out had done the job more seriously.

The fact of the earlier searches made it unlikely that Charles's party was going to find much. The chances of coming across Tristram's body strung up from a beam in the pigeon-loft were slender. But they still felt it was worth going through everything. There might be some clue to what Tristram had done when he reached the house and before he disappeared.

The Volvo had been emptied, and it didn't look as if this had been the result of Tristram's meticulous unpacking. The way the contents were spread out on the floor of the dining-room suggested that this had been the work of the French or English police. The suitcases had been opened and their contents riffled through, and the other items were arranged in little piles according to the categorizing instincts of some bureaucratic mind. While Bartlemas and O'Rourke searched the upper storey and the outbuildings, Charles went through this equipment for the holiday that never happened.

On the table were the couple's travel documents and passports. Charles looked inside both of the latter. Yves's was French, and the photograph was a good one, capturing both the beauty and the mischievous insolence of its original. Tristram's was also a good likeness, though his face, with its props of silver toupee, moustache and large glasses, as usual just looked like that of an Identikit restaurateur.

Charles checked both passports. There were no recent stamps for entry into France. But, as he knew from his own experience of a few days previously, passports very rarely get stamped for people crossing the Channel.

He looked at the rest of the luggage.

The most interesting pile was made up largely of books of pornographic pictures. These were not private blackmail photographs, but professionally produced books for specialized tastes. Needless to say, the speciality in this case proved to be homosexual.

But it was the other items on the pile that attracted Charles's attention. There were a pot of Vaseline and two battery-operated vibrators.

And a woman's lipstick.

He called Bartlemas and O'Rourke into the dining-room and showed what he had found.

'Well, the Vaseline, obviously. And the books, well...'

'I mean, if that's what Tristram and Yves *enjoyed*...'

'As they say over here, *chacun à son goût*...'

'And far be it from us to criticize the tastes of...'

'Anyone. Oh, far be it...'

'And the vibrators...well, again...'

'If that's what turned them on...'

'Well, exactly...'

'It wasn't really those I was interested in. It was this.' Charles held up the lipstick between finger and thumb. He knew he shouldn't really be puffing fingerprints on anything, but he had the feeling that the police investigation, certainly from the French side, and probably from the English too, was all sewn up, bar the formalities. 'Now, the cop who sorted through this lot had a tidy mind, and I reckon all the stuff he put in this pile was...what shall I call it?...homosexual impedimenta?'

'What a charming phrase...'

'Enchanting...'

'And so *tasteful*, Charles...'

'And he obviously thought, in the simple way of policemen – homosexual equals transvestite, therefore they had the lipstick for their own uses.'

The two heads shook as one.

'Not Tristram and Yves, no...'

'Not in a...'

'Million years...'

'No...'

'The general public does have very bizarre ides of what gay people get up to...'

'Totally bizarre...'

'I mean of course there are the ones who're effeminate and who dress up in women's clothes, but not Tris and Yves.'

'Never...'

"No...'

'Good,' said Charles. 'Now all this stuff came out of the Volvo. We know how neat Tristram was. There is no way this lipstick would have been lying in the car before he packed. So if it didn't belong to him or to Yves, it must have belonged to someone else who travelled in the car after the murder.'

'Yes,' said O'Rourke. 'And, at the risk of stating the obvious, presumably that someone was a woman.'

Bartlemas and O'Rourke had reached the hardly surprising conclusion that Tristram's body was not on the premises. They had even lifted the metal cover off the old well, but found a metal grille set into the walls that would have prevented the passage of a corpse.

In spite of this, Charles continued to prowl round the house. While the others went off to the nearest town to buy bread, pâté and wine, he continued his search. Buoyed up by the discovery of the lipstick, he was now confidant that he would find something else, some other clue that would explain the mysteries of Yves's death and Tristram's disappearance.

Their bedroom was the best room in the house. Glass doors opened on to a balcony, from which it felt that one could dive straight down into the waters of the Lot.

The bed was made, but the formality of its clean sheets had not been disturbed. They had presumably been put on by the maid who looked after the house between lets, perhaps the wife or daughter of the old man who had let them in.

There was no sign in the room that Tristram had entered it. Indeed, except for the signs of police activity, there was no indication that anyone had been in any part of the house since the last let. Maybe Tristram, after his long drive to Mas-de-Pouzard, had never made it inside.

This thought fed the theory that was beginning to take shape in Charles's mind.

In a drawer of the dressing-table he found a photograph album. It contained a selection of pictures from Tristram's and Yves's lives, mostly from their separate lives, before they became a couple. Many of the photographs shoved haphazardly behind the transparent film were of theatrical productions, showing a younger, pre-toupee Tristram in a variety of costumes, or Yves frozen in a series of dances. Mixed with these were childhood photographs of both of them, family groups, holiday snaps. It seemed like an attempt to marry the lives both had led before they met

There was even, to Charles's surprise, a picture of Tristram with Zoë. The clothes and the poses gave away that it was from a production of Shakespeare. Zoë stood with page-boy haircut, dressed in a tunic and high boots, while beside her a balding Tristram crouched in motley, carrying the zany of a Shakespearean clown.

Charles felt fairly confident he could identify the scene. *Twelfth Night.* Beginning of Act Three.

*Enter Viola, and Clown with a tabor.*
VIOLA:  Save thee, friend, and thy music. Dost thou live by the tabor?
CLOWN:  No, sir, I live by the church…

The desperate unfunniness of the Clown's jokes was seared into Charles's memory. He had once had the misfortune to play the part. He always tried to avoid Shakespeare's funny men, knowing just how excruciatingly their humour fails with a modern audience. But on this particular occasion he had failed to duck it. To compound his agony, the director had been of the school that thought if the cast laughed enough at the jokes, the audience would eventually prove suggestible and join in. He was horribly wrong, and Charles had had to spend a miserable time roaring his head off about cheveril gloves and pilchards, while the audience shuffled in embarrassed silence. It had been a very lonely experience. And it hadn't impressed the critics much either. The *Bristol Evening Post* had found it 'a performance in need of immediate sedation, followed by a very long rest.'

And poor Tristram, thought Charles wryly, had been through just the same comedic hoops.

But why had he kept the photograph? Sentimentality for his estranged wife? No, Charles had a feeling it was just the eternal actor's ego, which needs bolstering by every reproduction of the subject's image, regardless of the company in which it is taken.

He looked at the other photographs on the page, and found what he was looking for. At the bottom was a posed family group in black and white. It was the Lafeus.

The picture must have been at least fifteen years old. Yves looked younger and was dressed in a conventional suit and tie, but his face still showed a gleam of insolence and mischief. His father stood next to him, face tight with the meanness and self-importance of the bourgeoisie. Beside him Yves's mother looked pale and nervy.

And next to them stood Monique. A slightly gawky girl at the end of her teens, but still unmistakably the ill-tempered pouting woman from Tryst.

Charles took the album downstairs with him, and continued his detailed search in the sitting-room.

On the mantelpiece he found a letter, addressed to 'M. Yves Lafeu' at Mas-de-Pouzard. It was postmarked 'Reims' and the envelope had been slit open, presumably by some policeman's hand.

Charles took out the sheet inside and read the copybook French of the letter.

My dear son,
I write to confirm that your mother and I will come to stay with you for the

week beginning the 20th September. I am writing to Mas-de-Pouzard because the price of postage abroad is so ridiculous.

Your mother has had another attack with her liver recently, and it is important that she has a quiet time.

It will be good to see you after all these years. We only know what we hear from Monique. I wish you would be in touch more. I know your mother would like it, but I understand how expensive postage is, and the telephone is so much it is not worth thinking of it.

Armand Lafeu

'Suppose it was Monique,' said Charles.

He was sitting with Bartlemas and O'Rourke round the back of the house, on a terrace overlooking the Lot. They ate slices of rough country pâté with hunks of baguette, and drank the black local wine. The sun was so powerful that they were glad of the shade of the umbrella that rose from the garden table. The setting was so idyllic that talk of murder seemed incongruous.

'You mean suppose she killed Yves?' asked O'Rourke.

'Yes.'

'Well, I suppose if she reckoned she would inherit the restaurant, she had a motive.'

'Not just the financial one. There was also her deep, deep disapproval of Yves's way of life.'

'Yes, but would that have been enough for her to kill him? And why suddenly now?'

'Look at this letter.' Charles handed it over. 'It looks to me as if Yves's parents knew nothing about his life-style. Monique certainly said she told them nothing about it. So, if they were about to arrive down here to stay with Yves and Tristram, they were in for a bit of a shock.'

'And you think she might have killed him to prevent that shock?' asked O'Rourke. In discussion of the murder, Bartlemas seemed content to let his partner do the talking.

'It's possible. Yves might have invited his parents down out of pure mischief and Monique might have killed him to save their feelings.'

'So what do you reckon happened?'

'Monique left the restaurant at two, as she said, with the rest of the staff. But my little friend Henry saw a woman going back into the mews round three o'clock. Tristram or Yves would have let her in, of course. Then she killed Yves and forced Tristram to drive the car down here.'

'At gunpoint?'

'Presumably.'

'Hmm. What, she was hidden in the back of the car?'

'Again – presumably.'

'I'm still worried about the risks of going on the boat and –'

'Yes, I agree. That does raise problems. But let's assume that somehow she managed it. They got down here – out of the car – Monique not realizing she's left her lipstick in there. Then she shoots Tristram and hides his body.'

'So we're back to finding Tristram's body.'

'Yes. Mind you, having seen what the countryside's like round here, I wouldn't give much for our chances. There's the river, lots of cliffs, caves, woods...'

'So we're no further advanced? It's still all just speculation.'

'Yes, except that if Monique came down here in the Volvo, she must have used some other method of getting back to Reims.'

It was at the third car rental agency in Cahors that he struck lucky. Probably he was most lucky in the approach that he took.

'Excuse me,' he said in French to the rather plain girl with large glasses who sat behind the desk. 'I am trying to trace the movements of a woman.'

'Ah. A woman,' breathed the girl, infusing the words with deep romance.

'Yes. I'm trying to find where she went, and I believe she may have rented a car from you the Monday before last.'

'That was when you last saw her?'

'Well, er – '

'Did you have a bad fight?'

'It wasn't exactly –'

'And now you are full of regrets and wish to find her again,' the girl pronounced, not as a question but as a statement. Her fingers were already flicking through a suspended file in her desk drawer.

'Well, yes, that's more or less it,' said Charles, seeing no point in disappointing the girl.

'And the woman you are looking for, she is English like you?'

'No, I think French.'

'You *think*?'

'French.'

The girl extracted a handful of documents from the file. 'The Monday, yes. Three cars were rented by women on that day.'

'And was one of them called Monique Lafeu?'

'No, Monsieur.'

Of course, there was no chance she'd use her real name. Charles produced Tristram's photograph album. 'I have a picture of her here. Perhaps .

He opened the book and held it across to the girl.

She looked at the page and gave him a huge smile of complicity. 'Yes, Monsieur. That is what she looked like. Yes, your lover did rent a car from us.'

## *Chapter Twelve*

EVEN AFTER ONLY a week's break, autumn seemed to have accelerated in England, and Charles felt that he should have worn an overcoat as he walked down from Hereford Road to Tryst.

He wasn't sure yet how to play the scene ahead of him. Monique had sounded frosty on the telephone, but she had not refused to see him. In fact, considering her former manner, she had sounded subdued, as if she was aware of some shift in the balance of power between them, as if she now knew that Charles would be calling the shots.

She sat waiting for him in the stillness of the empty restaurant. Her pout was now less pugnacious, more resigned, and her large body had lost its combative rigidity as she lolled on one of the plush upholstered chairs. The impression that Tryst had been closed down for years was even stronger.

The front door was on the latch and Monique hardly stirred as Charles entered. Inside, he still felt chilly.

'So,' said Monique flatly, 'you were right.'

'Right in some ways. There are still a lot of details to be sorted out.'

She looked at him with mild puzzlement. 'Right about the restaurant, I meant. Right about the Will. If Yves and Tristram both died, everything was to go to...your friend.'

'Ah. Yes. Of course, it has not yet been proved that Tristram is dead.'

'No.' She dismissed this detail with a petulant wave. 'So I shouldn't really be here. But I still have the key. And it's somewhere to meet. I did not want you at my apartment.'

'So long as the police don't mind you being here.'

'They don't seem to mind anything now. They gave me permission to go into the apartment upstairs and sort through Yves's belongings. I think they have lost interest in the case.'

'It's the same in France. Though there I don't think they had that much interest in the first place.'

'You have been to France?'

'Yes. To Mas-de-Pouzard. I got back yesterday morning.' Monique was silent as she took in this information. Charles waited till she spoke again. 'So what do you want from me?'

'I just want to know a little more about the events of the night of your brother's death.'

'What?'

'You say you left here at about two?'

'Yes.'

'And the next day you went to France?'

'To my parents in Reims, yes. I went by train.'

'And after you left the restaurant, you went straight to your flat?'

'Of course.'

'You didn't forget anything? You didn't come back to the restaurant for anything?'

'No.' She looked sulkier than ever. 'Why do you ask?'

'Because I have a witness who saw a woman going into the mews behind here at three o'clock that morning.'

'Ah.'

'So I'm interested to see if anyone can corroborate that.' There was a pause. 'I'm sorry, Mr Paris. I can't help you. As I said, I went straight home.'

'I see.' Charles changed tack. 'Can you think of any reason why anyone would want to kill your brother, Miss Lafeu?'

She shrugged. 'In the gay world there is a lot of violence.'

'Putting that on one side. Any other reason?'

'No.' She hesitated. 'Well...'

'What?'

'There was something I found. Going through his letters. Just a scrap of paper. It looked like a draft, like a letter he had started and then abandoned.'

'What sort of letter?'

'It read like blackmail.'

'Do you have the letter?'

'Yes. I found it tucked between the covers of Yves's writing-case.' She reached into her handbag. 'Here.'

It was just a fragment. The writing was similar to that of Yves's father. The paper had been torn across the top, and the writing ended, amid crossings-out, in mid-sentence. What remained was written in English.

...written them a letter about a chapter from your life-story that may have been forgotten. I refer to what happened to Martin Sabine, an event that I witnessed. I kept quiet at the time, but now I feel they might like to hear about it. The letter will not raise any suspicions at this stage, but will show you that I am serious. Of course, the right sort of financial offer might make me change my mind, but it would have to be...

'Yes' said Charles. 'It does read like a blackmail letter. There was nothing else? You've no idea who it was addressed to or...?'

Monique shook her head. 'I just found it and thought you might be interested. After all, it is you who is always looking for "suspicious circumstances".'

'Yes.'

'Are you finding many?'

'More by the minute.'

'And, Mr Paris...' Monique leant forward earnestly. 'Do any of these suspicions attach themselves to me?'

'No, Miss Lafeu,' said Charles. 'None at all.'

Tracking down Martin Sabine proved not to be difficult. Charles knew the name as a fellow-actor, although they had never met. *Spotlight* proved unhelpful. Martin had no entry in there, because most of his work was in radio and voice-overs, but, through a friend who did a lot of commercials, Charles got the name of an agent. The agent said that Martin was at the BBC that day doing a radio play. Charles went at five-thirty to the old Langham Hotel in Portland Place, where he waited until he saw an actor he knew going into the BBC Club Bar. He soon met one who was working for the organization now known rather poshly as 'the BBC Drama Company', but which Charles still thought of by its old name, 'the Rep'. This friend obligingly signed Charles in, and at five past six they were each armed with a large Bell's and well-placed to see the arrival of the cast who had been working in the studio all day.

'That's Martin,' said the 'Rep' actor.

He pointed out a tall, well-built man of about forty, who had his back to them as he approached the bar with a group of other actors. It was only when he came back with his drink and turned his face towards them that Charles knew why Martin Sabine worked mainly in radio and voice-overs.

The actor's face was scored across with old scars, edged with the puckering of stitches. The shape of the face was that of a handsome man, but it was disfigured like something out of a horror film.

The introductions were easily effected, but it took a bit of time and a few drinks before Charles could get Martin on his own and start asking the questions he wanted to.

'Did you know Tristram Gowers and Yves Lafeu?'

'What, the stars of the recent murder mystery?' Martin, when not using one of his remarkable range of professional voices, spoke languidly, slightly effetely. 'Hadn't seen them for ages. Tryst wasn't really my scene. But I met them a few times years back.'

'Where? Were you in a show with them?'

'No. We were members of the same club.' Martin's hand went gently to his face. 'A club that I have cause to remember.'

'That was where...'

Martin nodded. 'Outside it, yes.'

'Do you mind telling me what happened?'

The scarred face made a wry grimace. 'Why not? It hardly worries me at all now. I've come to accept it as part of my life. Just one of those things that happened. Divided my life in two. Before, I was poised, as the papers put it, 'on the brink of stardom'. Before, I was even rather beautiful. As beautiful as Yves himself, if you could believe it. Everyone said so. I looked rather like him, too. And now...' He shrugged. 'Still, I'm very fortunate in having a lot of chums who've stuck by me and, well... could be worse.'

Charles bided his time, waiting patiently.

'But you want to know what happened. God knows I've told the story enough times, another won't hurt. A face like this really is a conversation-piece. At least it is with the people who dare to mention It. Half of them just gaze appalled, and try to pretend they're ignoring it. Still, on with the story – what there is of it. I'm afraid my narrative is a little slender, but I was unconscious for a good bit of the action.

'Basically, what happened was that I had been in this club we mentioned, round Notting Hill way – it's gone now, been replaced by a video rental shop, but that's by the way. So I had had a pleasant evening, a few drinks, a few dances...'

'Do you know if Tristram and Yves were there that night?'

'Quite honestly I can't remember. They could have been. I think it was round that time that Yves started bringing Tristram to the club. They were working on a show quite close to London...Bromley or somewhere? I can't remember.'

'Sorry to have interrupted.'

'Don't worry. So, anyway, I had had a good evening, but I didn't get lucky, so I left the club on my own. Which, as it turned out, was a silly thing to do. The club was set back at the end of an alley, and I'm afraid in that alley, someone was waiting for me – well, perhaps not for me specifically, but I was the one who got the treatment.'

'Which was...?'

'I was hit on the head from behind. That pretty well put me out. And when I came to, I found someone had been practising engraving on my face with a broken bottle.'

'God.'

'Yes, not nice.' Martin Sabine sighed. 'Still, be thankful for small mercies – at least they didn't touch my eyes.'

'So what happened then? Were the police called?'

'Oh, you bet.'

'But they didn't catch your attacker?'

'No. But they got me to hospital, and when I was stitched up they came and chatted to me.'

'What did they say?'

'Oh, words of infinite comfort. Told me that the attack probably wasn't personal, just – as they charmingly put it – 'another case of queer-bashing'. They were sympathetic, but basically they seemed to imply that it was my own fault.'

'Your fault?'

'For going to that sort of club, for choosing that sort of company. The old biblical view that "he that toucheth pitch shall be defiled therewith".'

Charles nodded. It was the same reaction that he had sensed in the police after Yves's death. There had certainly been advances in tolerance of homosexual activity, but much residual prejudice remained.

'And I suppose...you didn't get even a glimpse of your attacker?' Martin laughed, showing his straight, white teeth. The laugh for a moment took attention off his scars, and Charles could see how very good-looking he must once have been.

'If you knew how many times I've been asked that.'

'And what answer do you always give?'

'That I didn't see my attacker. That all I got, if anything, was the vaguest of vague impressions.'

'And what was that impression?'

Martin laughed again. 'Ah, well, this is what makes me realize that one should never trust vague impressions, because they're bound to be misleading.'

'Why?'

'Because the impression I got was that my attacker was a woman.'

## Chapter Thirteen

ZOE FRATTON WAS in when Charles rang the doorbell of her Swiss Cottage flat. He had contemplated telephoning her to check, but had not wished to put her on her guard.

She seemed pleased to see him. She looked better than she had at their previous meeting, her short hair newly trimmed, but there was still the smell of gin on her breath. She replenished her glass when they reached her living-room and provided Charles with a substantial Scotch.

'Good to see you, Charles. Got any work?'

He shook his head. 'The "rest" continues.'

'Never mind. One day the phone will ring and it'll be Rachel Grant or another of those Casting Directors at the National.'

'Oh yes. Of course.' Then, knowing he was only puffing off the evil moment, he asked, 'You got anything coming up?'

'Not a sausage. Beginning to wonder how long I can keep on the flat.'

'Something will happen.'

'Oh yes,' she said with automatic optimism.

They were silent. She looked at him expectantly, and with a sickening feeling Charles realized that she thought he was there because he fancied her. He remembered they had talked idly of sleeping together when they last met. 'The day may come...' Zoë had said. And perhaps, under other circumstances, he would not have been averse to the idea. But, as things were, it seemed incongruous and tasteless.

He plunged in. 'Zoë, I want to talk about Yves's death.'

Before she had time to express the surprise that showed in her face, he pressed on. 'I want to talk about the night he died. I have a witness who saw who went in and out of the mews that night.'

'Ah.' Her expression of surprise gave way to one of trapped anxiety.

'A woman was seen entering the mews just before three o'clock. A tall woman.'

She looked at him defiantly. 'I'm not the only tall woman in the world!'

'No. But I think you were the one who was seen.'

She prepared for another defiant reply, but then crumpled. 'Oh, why deny it? Who cares? Yes, it was me.'

'And what were you intending to do when you went there?'

'It was stupid. Vicious and petty. I just wanted revenge on them. I'd been drinking and was feeling poor and abandoned, and thinking of them about to go off on this wonderful holiday, and I just couldn't stand it. So I planned this petty revenge.'

'What did you do?'

'I'll tell you what I planned to do, though, God, when I think about it, I can't believe how small-minded it seems. I just wanted something to disrupt them, to make a mess of their infinitely tidy little lives.'

'So...'

'I bought some meat from my local butcher. Liver. Bought it on the Saturday afternoon. I was drunk. I had this idea that straight after they'd gone away, I'd shove it through their letter-box. Just leave it there for a month, for the flies to get at, so that it would smell and so that when they returned, this vile mess would be there waiting for them. As I say, it sounds pathetic, but I've felt such bitterness towards them.'

'What happened when you got to the mews?'

'I saw the lights were still on. I thought they would have already gone, but they hadn't. And suddenly I realized how ridiculously I was behaving, and that doing things like that wouldn't help at all, just make me feel more pathetic than ever. So I left the meat by the door and went home.'

It was plausible. Certainly it explained the carrier bag of liver from a Swiss Cottage butcher that Charles had found outside the door of the mews. But, although it dealt with that detail, there were a great many others that it left unexplained.

'I think that may have been your intention, Zoë, and what you have told me may be true. Except for the end. I don't think you went straight home after you had left the meat. In fact, I don't really know why you took the meat. I think, as you said, you were planning revenge. But the revenge you planned was more than a tasteless practical joke. You planned to kill both the man who had taken your husband from you and your husband himself.'

Zoë gaped speechless, as Charles went on:

'I think you knocked on the door of the mews and were admitted. I think you killed Yves and then forced Tristram to drive down to the house in France. There you killed him and disposed of his body. Then you rented a car in Cahors and drove back to Calais. You arrived back in England the day when I met you for the first time in the Montrose.'

Finally Zoë found speech. 'But, Charles, that's ridiculous! Preposterous! It's not true!'

'Zoë, these are the facts. You have never made any secret of how much you hated Yves, and the more time Tristram spent with him, the more you came to hate Tristram too. You were seen entering the mews at three o'clock on the night Yves was murdered. You left a lipstick in Tristram's car. A girl in the car rental agency in Cahors identified you from a photograph. Not only that, the car was rented in your own name. You showed your passport and driving licence as identification. And the car you rented was left for the agency to collect at Calais.'

Zoë's head moved from side to side in disbelief. 'No, Charles, no. I don't know how you've found all that out, but it's wrong. It just didn't happen. I spent the weekend here.'

'Did anyone see you?'

'Well, no...I...I was drinking. A real bender. I just drank. That's why I was in such a bad state when I saw you at the Montrose.'

'It's not the most wonderful alibi in the world, Zoë.'

'But it's true. You've got to believe me.'

'I wish I could.'

'Oh, how can I convince you?' Her despair had that stagey quality that actresses can never quite keep out of their voices.

'Have you got your passport?'

'Yes. I was looking at it recently. Now it should be in this drawer.' She moved across to a small bureau.

Charles, who had seen something on top of some books on a shelf, also moved.

'It doesn't seem to be here,' said Zoë. When she turned back, Charles was holding her passport. 'How on earth did it get there?'

'Do you mind if I look?'

'Go ahead.'

He let out a sigh of disappointment.

'What were you hoping to find, Charles?'

'A stamp, a customs stamp. But, of course, they very rarely do stamp them when you're crossing the Channel nowadays.'

'No. Charles, I wish I could persuade you how wrong –'

'Ah. Your hairstyle was the same.'

'What?'

He held across to her the passport, open at the photograph. It was a younger Zoë, with a page-boy haircut.

'Yes. I had it like that for a show.'

'I know.'

'*Twelfth Night*. At Bromley.'

'Yes. It was from a production photograph of that that the girl in Cahors identified you.'

'But how did you –'

'Tristram had kept one. With him as the Clown.'

'Oh God...' Her voice was now dull and lifeless.

'It was round the time that you got the passport that the marriage broke up, wasn't it?'

'Yes.'

'Yves was also in the cast, wasn't he?'

'He was choreographer.'

'Yes. It was then that he started flirting with Tristram, that Tristram started getting interested, that the affair started.'

Zoë nodded bleakly.

'And it was then that you made your first attack on Yves.'

Her head shot up. 'What do you mean?'

'What I say.'

'We had rows. There were scenes. Not an attack.'

Charles's voice remained level as he made the accusation. 'I'm talking about the time you waited for Yves outside a gay club in Notting Hill. The time when you thought you'd slashed his face. The time when you got the wrong person and ruined the career of Martin Sabine.'

'Martin Sabine?' she echoed.

'Don't pretend you don't know who I mean.'

'I do know who you mean. Radio actor. But I've never met him. Charles, I don't understand. Why are you saying all this?'

'Because I don't believe that people should be allowed to get away with murder.'

'But I haven't murdered anyone, Charles.' She was weeping now, huge tears of frustration or disbelief. 'Really. I haven't. I couldn't.'

'There's a lot of evidence against you, Zoë. The girl in Cahors identified you immediately.'

Zoë Fratton went suddenly limp. All resistance seemed to have drained out of her. 'What do you propose to do, Charles?'

'I think we go to the police.'

'And...'

'And you confess.'

'Yes. Why not?' she asked with sudden recklessness. 'That really would be the ultimate irony of my career, wouldn't it? At least someone would be giving me the chance to play a big scene for once. Oh, God, that show in Bromley. Everything was all right until that show in Bromley. I was really set to go places. Playing Viola – huh, next stop the West End. And then it all started to crumble. Tristram...that's when I started drinking heavily. That's when it all fell apart.'

'I'm sorry, Zoë. Perhaps I ought to phone the police.'

'Oh yes,' she said cynically. 'At least you don't have to pay rent in prison. And it's a good excuse for not having a job.'

'Yes,' said Charles gently, and moved across to the telephone.

'It was a good production, though, the *Twelfth Night*. Press loved it. Even talk of a transfer at one stage, though of course that was nonsense – RSC's got the West End sewn up so far as Shakespeare's concerned. But we got some good notices. First time some of the critics had understood Orsino's love-sickness, first time Malvolio had taken on genuine tragic stature, first time the twins had actually looked like twins – all that kind of stuff. Oh, only local press, I know, but you can't help believing that sort of praise, at least at the time. I was the great new discovery – after twelve years in the business I was finally being discovered. And what did it lead to? Nothing. Nothing for any of us. Huh, the only one who went anywhere after that show was my dear brother.'

'Brother?'

'Twin. Sebastian. You know, "One face, one voice, one habit, and two persons".'

Charles continued Orsino's speech automatically. '"A natural perspective, that is, and is not!"'

'That's the one.'

'And who played Sebastian?'

'Bertram Pride.'

'Oh, my God,' said Charles Paris.

## Chapter Fourteen

DANA WILSON'S VOICE sounded as languorous and put-upon as ever. To those who have nothing to do, even the smallest demand on their time becomes an imposition.

'It's Charles Paris.'

'Who?'

'An actor. We met the Friday before last.'

'Oh.' She sounded doubtful of his claim.

'We were introduced through my agent.'

'Oh, Marcus Scrotton, yes. I remember.'

It was near enough. Charles didn't bother to correct her. But so much for your photographic memory, he thought. A chap could die locked away in your mind and you'd never notice.

'I'm afraid nothing's come up,' said Dana. 'And I'd really rather you didn't ring me. As soon as there is anything suitable I will be in touch with your agent'

'Yes, it wasn't work that I was ringing about.'

'Oh.' This was a monosyllable of pure surprise. What else could an actor be ringing about? She followed it with another 'Oh', this one registering mild interest.

'No. If I remember rightly, you said that you cast *Lexton and Sons*.'

'Oh yes,' she replied in a new tone of gratification. 'Well, when I saw the first scripts I just knew their faces instinctively. I knew that Millicent had to be Rita Lexton, and of course George was born to play –'

'Yes.' Charles cut into the orgy of self-congratulation. 'It's the part of Philip I'm interested in.'

'Well, that was Bertram Pride. I thought everyone knew that –'

'I know Bertram Pride actually *played* the part, but I thought you said he wasn't your first choice.'

'Well, we had a lot of interviews for the part. A lot of actors were considered. In the end we cut them down to two.'

'Bertram Pride and your first choice?'

'Yes. An actor called Martin Sabine. Don't know if you know him. Does mostly radio now.'

'I know him.' Charles's voice was thick with relief.

'Well, it had been decided that he should play the part. Very clever actor he was. And extraordinarily good-looking.'

Her emphasis on the last words made Charles reflect that she would have been barking up the wrong tree if she had hoped for a little dalliance with Martin as one of the perks of her profession.

'But then he had this terrible accident. Don't know if you heard – he was beaten up. Horrible. And I'm afraid he looked such a mess afterwards, there was no way he could be Philip. Thank God it happened before the contracts had actually been signed or before any publicity had gone out.' Then, in case that sounded too callous, she added, 'I mean, the company did make him some sort of ex gratia payment, though they weren't under any obligation to do so.'

'So you went ahead with Bertram?'

'Yes. And he was frightfully good. Another of my little moments of inspiration. And did you know that I discovered Wally Gammons...and Frank Stillman...and –'

'Thank you,' said Charles, and rang off.

'So you reckon,' asked Zoë, 'that Bertram took my passport when he came round the few days before Yves died.'

Charles nodded. 'I would think so. Did the subject of passports come up?'

'It did, actually. He started talking about publicity photographs and saying how impossible it was to get a good likeness. Then he got on to passport photographs and asked to see mine. I hadn't had my passport out for ages. Took me some time to find it. But I did. And he must have just palmed it.'

'You'd had a few drinks, hadn't you?' She nodded. 'So you probably weren't watching him too closely.'

'And I thought,' she said bitterly, 'he'd just come round out of friendship, just brought me the gin for old times' sake.'

'I'm rather afraid the gin was part of his plan.'

'What, you mean he knew I was likely to go on a bender and...'

'Set yourself up with a lost weekend, yes.'

'Oh God. Is that the reputation I've got now? I really will give it up, you know. I really will stop.'

'Yes,' he said soothingly. 'I often say that.'

'And then Bertram must have put the passport back the next week when he turned up with another bottle of gin. I can't actually see why he bothered about that. I'd never have noticed the passport was gone for ages, and he was just drawing attention to the connection between us.'

'Ah, but you forget. You got the possibility of that job on the feature film in Tunisia. You told Bertram about it when he rang you on the Wednesday morning. Must've given him a nasty shock. If you'd got it, you would suddenly have needed your passport in a hurry.'

'So he came round full of more gin and sympathy and deposited it on my bookshelves.'

'Where I found it, yes.'

'My God. The sod. He'd got it all worked out. But why?'

'Because of the blackmail. Yves had been at the club the night Martin Sabine was attacked. He saw what happened.'

'And you mean Bertram was dressed as me that night too?'

'He was wearing the wig he wore in *Twelfth Night*, and he was dressed in women's clothes. On that occasion his aim wasn't to look like you, just not to look like himself. But that must have been what gave him the idea for the later crime.'

'But Yves saw the attack on Martin?'

'That's what this letter says.' Charles produced the sheet that Monique had given him.

'Can you prove any of this, Charles?'

He shook his head lugubriously. 'Not yet. I haven't got any solid proof. But this time I'm convinced I'm right.'

'You sounded pretty convinced you were right when you were accusing me of everything under the sun,' Zoë chided him gently.

'No, but this time...' He grinned and stopped himself. 'I will prove it. There's something in this blackmail letter. I'm assuming the final draft was sent to Bertram, but it also refers to Yves's having "written them a letter about a chapter from your life-story that may have been forgotten".'

'And who do you think "them" is? The police?'

'No,' said Charles. 'Not the police.'


He decided that a journalistic approach was best. Showman Books seemed to be a company whose success was based solely on immediate publicity, and he reckoned the Editorial Director would be likely to give an interview to anyone who promised him more of the same. His guess proved correct.

Showman Books produced paperback originals about show business. They were brought out quickly, in large quantities, in the wake of any established media success and, for a very short period, they sold well. Much of the list was 'stories of the making of' various films and television series. It also included quiz-books, cook-books and gardening books compiled by hacks and sold under the name of the star whose face beamed from the front cover. And, of course, they sold autobiographies, ghosted autobiographies, picture biographies and 'as told to' life-stories of all the flavour-of-the-month stars. These had titles like *One Green Light*, *Mr Thwaite*, *We'll Have To Lose the Hippo*, and *Not In These Knickers I Won't*: they got serialized in the less serious newspapers, were the subject of many plugging media interviews, and sold in their thousands during their bursts of publicity.

The operation of Showman Books was, as a director of an older-established, more conventional and less financially stable publishing house put it, 'media-mushroom-farming'.

Charles had selected his journalist's voice with care. He decided that he would do better to claim to represent a foreign publication, as this meant that his credentials were less likely to be checked. He thought of being American,

Hank Bergheimer perhaps, European Correspondent of the *Pennsylvania Falls Gazette-Tribune* or something. Then he could use the voice he'd had in *The Front Page* ('Until last night I didn't think this play *could* drag' – *Leicester Mercury*). But he concluded that that might sound a bit 'over the top' after more than five minutes and so settled for the Australian twang he had developed for what the play's author had described as 'a *commedia del arte* interpretation of the Ned Kelly story' ('The knowledge that Arts Council money helped to put on this production is enough to make any taxpayer's blood boil' – *Romford Recorder*) . Somehow the Australian voice suited the crassly insensitive style of questioning that Charles was planning.

When he rang through to fix the interview Charles hit his first snag. Not that the Editorial Director was unwilling to talk. No, according to his secretary, Frank Clayton would be delighted to give up half an hour to the *Perth Examiner*. The catch came in the next sentence, 'He's always happy to do a favour to a fellow-Aussie.'

Still, the interview was set up and Charles didn't want to risk losing it by starting again in another persona. Great, he would look forward to meeting Mr Clayton at four-thirty that afternoon.

Showman Books' editorial offices were two floors over a dubbing theatre in Berwick Street. As Charles entered the building, he felt anxious. It wasn't the first time that he had chosen the wrong accent and been confronted with one of its native speakers. And he knew the situation could become awkward. He tried hastily to fabricate a background for Bill Bunyan, his chosen name, which would explain how far away he had come from his roots.

The offices were small and untidy. Manuscripts and books were piled everywhere; on the walls old jacket proofs, artwork and signed stars' publicity photographs were pinned haphazardly. The visible staff of Showman Books appeared to be two harassed girls, busy over typewriters in the outer office, and Frank Clayton himself an oversize man in shirtsleeves with a little beard like a paintbrush stuck on the point of his chin.

Clayton greeted him effusively. 'Always great to see another exile, sport. You just come over for a trip, have you?'

'No, I'm based in Europe. Paris. Seventeen years since I was actually in the old country.'

'Yes, I've been based here over twenty, but I get back most winters – that is, winter here, I hasten to add, summer back home. I still got family out there. You say you're on the *Perth Examiner*?'

'That's right.'

'Perth where you come from?'

'Yes,' said Charles, taking a chance.

'Oh, I'm from Brisbane.'

Charles heaved a sigh of relief. He had hoped that by choosing Perth as a birthplace and Paris as a base he would avoid embarrassing questions about mutual friends or well-loved places, and the gamble appeared to have paid off. And, so far, Frank Clayton was showing no suspicion of the accent.

'Was it anything specific that you wanted to ask me about, Bill?'

Charles lied. 'No, just general publication plans. Any big tides you got coming up, that sort of thing.'

'Yes, well, we've got some goodies coming for Christmas, let me tell you. So those'll mostly be published in Australia say six months hence. When were you planning to do your piece for the paper?'

'I have a fairly flexible brief. And obviously, if there's anything where we can tie in publication with a television series re-run back home, then all to the good.'

'Now you're talking,' said Clayton, going in exactly the direction that Charles wanted to push him. 'You know that *Lexton and Sons* is as big in Australia as it is here – even bigger, I reckon. Well, they're supposed to be running the last series on Channel 9 – you never know with television scheduling, they keep changing it – but we've got a book coming that's really going to sell, if it ties in with that. You know Bertram Pride, who plays Philip?'

Charles nodded.

'Well, we're doing a very nice autobiography with him. Good story. All the 'How I Became An Overnight Success' bit. And the heartache too, you know, times out of work – even a big star like him had his patches of "resting". Then there's the marriage, break-up of the marriage, girl-friends – you know, he's had affairs with some really good names. It's all in there. Really going to sell, that book. It's called *A Pride of Lextons*. Not bad, eh? Like a Pride of Lions, you know. Gets his name and the series name in the title. No, that book's really going to move in the best-seller lists.'

'That's great,' said Charles. 'Just the sort of thing I need for my article. Was it a difficult book to get together?'

'No, not really. Well, W.E.T. wanted a ridiculous amount for the use of stills from the series – they don't seem to realize that it's free publicity for them. But we sorted that out. Had to give them an arm and a leg, but it got settled. Bertram himself was easy. Charming fellow, you know.'

Bill Bunyan agreed with this opinion. Charles Paris didn't.

'As a matter of fact, Frank, I did meet Bertram recently at a party and he was talking about the book. That's really why I wanted to see you. I mean, interested in the other titles as well, of course, but *A Pride of Lextons* sounds to be the big one.'

'Say that again. Comes out in two weeks here. Just peak for Christmas. Have you had a copy yet?'

Charles shook his head. Frank Clayton reached round to a shelf behind him and handed one over. The cover was a close-up of Bertram. The lettering of the title covered his hair, and all Charles was aware of was how strikingly like Zoë Fratton's the bone-structure was. He felt sure that this time he was on the right track.

This certainty gave him courage and inspiration for his next line of questioning. 'When I met Bertram, he said you were getting a lot of media interest in the book.'

'Too right. He'll be doing *Wogan, Start the Week, Pebble Mill,* signings, the whole works.'

'He also said you'd even had letters about the book before publication...'

'What?' Frank Clayton looked puzzled, and Charles feared that he had taken a wrong turning and wouldn't get the information he required.

'Bertram said you'd had letters from fans about the book,' he amplified hopefully.

'Oh yes, one or two, certainly,' said Clayton, and Charles breathed again.

'He was very encouraged by that, said it was unusual, promised well for the book...'

'Certainly does.'

'And he said I should ask you to let me see the letters, just to show how the whole thing was building up...'

'Oh.'

Charles pressed home his advantage. 'I want to get as full a background for my article as possible. I mean, when it's syndicated all over Australia, that's going to be a good few potential book-buyers who –'

'Yes, yes, of course,' said Frank Clayton, and reached up for a file behind him.

There were half a dozen letters looking forward to the publication of *A Pride of Lextons.* They all appeared to be from gushing middle-aged housewives, the backbone of Philip Lexton's fans.

But one of them was in handwriting that Charles Paris recognized.

'I wonder...would it be possible to have copies of these? It's just, you know, a different angle on the celebrity bit...And, of course, would bring in a little more about the publisher. You know, mention the name of Showman Books a few more times...'

One of the harassed-looking girls was summoned to take photocopies.

To maintain his alias, Charles then had to listen to three-quarters of an hour on the amazing sales potential of Christopher Milton's *Guide for Gormless Gardeners, The Bernard Walton Book of Car Games for Kids* and George Birkitt's no-punches-pulled autobiography, *No Llamas in the Dressing-Room.*

But he didn't mind. He had got what he had come for. The writing on the letter was the same as that on the paper which Monique had given him. The text was short.

Dear Mr Clayton,

I can't wait to get hold of a copy of Bertram Pride's book. I have followed his career closely right from the start and am longing to read all the details, particularly of his work with Martin Sabine. I am sure the press are going to be interested in the whole story. Lots of luck with the book.

Yours faithfully,

Eve Fire (Mrs)

To Frank Clayton it was just another letter, an effusion from one of Bertram's blue-rinsed fans who perhaps hadn't got her facts right.

But to Bertram Pride it must have been something very different. Its message was unambiguous. The apparently irrelevant mention of Martin Sabine was loaded with meaning, and the transparent pseudonym, so typical of Yves's mischievous method, left no room for doubt.

Perhaps Bertram had been unworried by the letter that Yves had sent to him. Perhaps he thought he could charm his way out of it. But when Yves started writing to his publisher, it was clear that the threat was genuine. Yves really would expose the criminal origins of Bertram Pride's 'overnight success'.

Which meant, so far as the star of *Lexton and Sons* was concerned, that Yves Lafeu had to be killed.

## Chapter Fifteen

'I DON'T KNOW whether Mel'd wear it, Charles. He's got a business to run, and if he starts doing that sort of thing, well, if it gets around, he could lose a lot of contraceptive.'

'Translate, Stan,' said Charles, resigned.

'Contraceptive pill – Goodwill.'

'You do make them up.'

'Never.'

They were sitting in Stan's 'little Charlie' (Charlie Chan – van – remember?) outside the Hereford Road house.

'Look, I've got to get inside Bertram Pride's flat and I can't see any other way of doing it. We know Mel supplies cleaners for him, so he must have a key.'

'Yeah, but the whole basis of a domestic agency is that it's, like, secure. No one's going to get stuff nicked or anything. Once Mel starts letting people in to his client's gaffs, well he ceases to be reliable, dunnee?'

'Stan, this is really important.'

'Why?'

'It's to do with Yves's murder.'

'Oh yes. How?'

'I'll tell you. But, Stan, you must swear not to tell a soul, because the kind of allegations I'm making are certainly slanderous until I've got some more proof.'

'You can trust me, Charlie. I'll be as quiet as the permanent.'

Permanent wave – Grave. It had to be.

So Charles went through his complete reconstruction of the case, of all Bertram Pride's crimes from the sabotage of Martin Sabine, which had given him the part of Philip Lexton, right up to the presumed murder of Tristram Gowers at Mas-de-Pouzard.

'Hmm,' Stan grunted after a long pause. 'And none of it can be proved until Tristram's body's found in France.'

'Perhaps not even then. The whole plan depended on making that death look like suicide. I'm sure if his body is found it'll be with a gunshot wound through his mouth or at the bottom of the Lot with a stone tied round his neck.'

Stan grunted again. 'But the French cops are looking for him?'

'Without great enthusiasm. It's difficult country to search there. Bartlemas, O'Rourke and I tried a day's driving round and looking, but there are so many thousands of places where a body could be hidden. I suppose he will be found eventually. Probably not as a result of a search, just dug up by wild animals, found by picnickers, you know, the usual story.'

Stan nodded slowly. 'There's one bit I don't get, though. Bertram came back from Cahors or whatever you said, disguised as Zoë.'

'On her passport, yes.'

'Did he go down disguised as her, an' all?'

'I suppose he must have done. Certainly if he went through customs, he did. If he was hidden in the back of the Volvo, perhaps he didn't.'

'Hmm. That's the bit that seems odd. I mean, Tristram driving all that way with Bertram keeping a gun on him all the time. You'd have thought Tristram could have got away. Bertram must have got out to do a pee or something, you'd think Tristram'd just have driven off.'

'Well, obviously he didn't.'

'No.' Stan didn't sound totally convinced. 'Bloody elaborate crime.'

'Yes. But if it had worked, it would have been perfect. It would have got rid of Yves and provided an explanation of his murder. And you forget, the body was discovered so much earlier than had been intended. If we hadn't been doing the decorating, it would have been a month after the murder and most of the trails would have gone cold.'

'Seem to have gone pretty cold as it is. Still, as you say, no bloody proof.'

'No. Which is all the more reason why I need to get inside Bernard's flat.'

'Yeah. We'll go and see Mel.'

And Stan turned the key in the ignition of his 'Charlie'.

An hour later he emerged from the door of Mel Ponting's Fulham Road office, jauntily swinging a key-ring from his little finger, and came towards Charles waiting in the van.

'Right, we're on. Tomorrow morning.'

'What did you tell him?'

'Nothing, really. Just that we needed to do it. He wasn't keen, but he owes me an electric.'

'Electric tea urn – Good turn?' suggested Charles hopefully.

'No, you great berk. Electric shaver – Favour.'

'Oh.'

'Mel was very reasonable about it. Only conditions he made – it's got to be both of us goes in…and if anything gets broken or goes missing, he'll string us up by our balls from the nearest light-fitting.'

'Sounds fair enough.'

'Like I say, reasonable man, Mel. He also said there could be some real charring coming up for you in the not-too-distant.'

'Good.'

'And he's been recommending us round like mad on the old decorating.'

'Excellent. The money scene doesn't get any better.'

'No. He says the cleaner goes into the flat at nine, and Bertram's usually out at some health club or something. He's not usually back till after the cleaner finishes at twelve.'

'I don't think the search'll take anything like three hours.'

'Ah, that was another of Mel's conditions.'

'What?'

'We do actually have to clean the bloody flat.'

Bertram Pride's flat in Hans Place was like the set for a coffee commercial. It was so neat, so consciously 'designed' as to be completely without character. There seemed no necessity to clean its immaculate surfaces.

The setting reflected the man. Charles had observed that many actors who became successful took on the trappings of their new wealth like a new set of stage props, objects with which they could work convincingly, with which they could appear at ease, but which did not ultimately belong to them. Many of the most skilful actors, who can slip with facility into other characters like well-tailored suits, have but the sketchiest sense of their own identity. It is this quality that is their strength, that gives them the ability to be more real onstage than in their daily lives. It was also this quality, Charles reflected, that had enabled Bertram to think himself into the role of Zoë Fratton, to dress like her, to walk like her, during the time of his necessity to become her.

In spite of the flat's immaculate appearance, Stan insisted that they should keep Mel Ponting's condition and actually clean it. Grudgingly, he agreed that he should do the work, while Charles made his search.

'Though I wish I knew what you was looking for, Charlie,' he said as he donned a flowered apron and extracted the Hoover from a cupboard.

'So do I,' said Charles. 'I just can't think of anywhere else to look. I'm sure I'm going to find something.'

He looked across at Stan, who had now donned a flowered headscarf as well, and giggled.

'Now watch it!' Stan shook a finger at him. 'And listen, if you ever tell my missus about this, I'll bloody murder you.'

'Why?'

'Our marriage is based on her belief that I have a physiological incapacity to do housework. If she ever found out I'd been seen hoovering I'd never have no peace no more.'

Charles searched methodically. Any search where you don't know what you're looking for is difficult, but at least in this case the anonymous neatness of the flat left few corners where secrets could lie undiscovered.

While Stan hoovered, dusted and polished with a delicacy surprising in one so large, Charles went through the drawers and bookshelves of the living-room. The only item he found that had any relevance to his quest was a new Michelin road map, Number 79, which covered the area round Cahors. And, though that gratifyingly fed his suspicions, in no way could it have been regarded as evidence of any mis-doing.

He moved to the small hall and searched its one coat-cupboard, but that revealed nothing untoward. The contents of the bathroom and kitchen were equally predictable and unhelpful.

While Stan whistled cheerfully as he scrubbed the kitchen floor, Charles progressed to the bedroom. This again was out of television-commercial-land, a splendid room with exclusive Knightsbridge views, dominated by a huge suede-covered double bed set into the wall between two fitted cupboards.

The dressing-table yielded nothing.

The right-hand wardrobe revealed only the very extensive selection of clothes required by the suave celebrity-about-town. The pockets of all of the suits and trousers had been meticulously emptied. Serried rows of shirts rose, crisply packaged from the laundry. Underwear, socks and shoes were arranged with the same punctiliousness. Again Charles had the impression of emptiness, of a void where the owner's character should be.

It was the second cupboard that proved interesting.

Its contents were all women's clothes. Most of them were dressing-gowns and night-dresses. Presumably, since it was some time since Bertram had had a live-in girl-friend, these were just part of the professional seducer's kit, comforts to be offered to Rent-A-Totties who unexpectedly stayed overnight, just like something out of the movies.

But it was the day-clothes that interested Charles. Perhaps they had been left by the last girl who had been more than a one-night stand, but that did not conform with the obsessive tidiness of the rest of the flat. Surely, as soon as the woman had gone, someone like Bertram would remove all traces of her.

Also, Charles realized as he pulled out the hangers and looked at them, the clothes were remarkably large.

About Zoë Fratton's size.

About Bertram Pride's size.

He examined the suits and dresses for...what? Bloodstains?

There was nothing. All had recently been cleaned. They still bore the labels and wore their polythene shrouds. If they ever had showed evidence of murder, all such traces had been removed.

In the corner of the cupboard was a pile of light brown boxes. Charles recognized them instantly; he had had enough false hair from Wig Creations in his time to know them at a glance.

With mounting excitement, he reached towards the top box. It contained a blond wig and matching beard.

The second held a similar set in black.

The others contained more, in a variety of hair colours.

Charles knew that the very famous often resorted to disguise when they wished to go out unnoticed. Bertram Pride's television face would have ensured constant interruptions to his social life by ill-disguised stares and requests for autographs. And, though often he might have revelled in these attentions, there must have been times when he sought anonymity and found it through this selection of camouflage.

Charles reached for the bottom box and opened it.

A warm glow filled and relaxed him. He had been right, after all. Now he had evidence.

What was more, he could now explain every detail of Bertram Pride's crime.

Gingerly, he picked the wig out of its nest of tissue paper and held it on his upturned hand. It was beautifully made, a page-boy cut exactly reproducing the one Zoë had worn in *Twelfth Night*. Yes, Viola and Sebastian must have looked identical – no wonder the critics had commented on the fact.

And this hairstyle, too, was exactly the one that appeared in the photograph in Zoë Fratton's passport.

He reached into the tissue paper for the second item. The more important item.

It was a moustache. A grey, gauze-backed walrus moustache. Exactly like that worn by Tristram Gowers.

Charles walked into the sitting-room, holding one of his trophies in each hand. Stan heard him and came in from the kitchen.

'Got something?'

'And how,' said Charles.

At that moment they heard the key in the front-door lock, and Bertram Pride walked in. He was wearing a smartly-cut pale grey track-suit, and still glowed from his exercise at the health club.

He took in Stan in his apron and headscarf first. 'Ah, you're new,' he said amiably, extending a hand. 'I'm Bertram Pride.'

Then he saw Charles. And what Charles was carrying.

'What the hell are you doing?'

'I'm holding your disguises, Bertram.' He raised one hand. 'The wig you wore when you came back from Cahors as Zoë Fratton.' He raised the other hand. 'And the moustache you wore, together with his toupee and glasses, when you drove down to Mas-de-Pouzard, disguised as Tristram Gowers!'

Bertram Pride said nothing. He just turned and rushed out of the flat.

Stan and Charles felt the room shake as the door slammed.

## Chapter Sixteen

'SHALL I GO after him?' asked Stan, stripping off his flowered apron.

'No point in chasing him from here,' said Charles. 'We'll meet him at his destination.'

'But how do you know where he's going to be?'

'I think there's a strong chance he'll be with Tristram Gowers' body.'

'What, down in bleeding France?'

'No. That's the whole point. I've been trying desperately to work out where the second person went in the Volvo, and all the time I should only have been thinking of one person. Tristram Gowers was an easy person to impersonate. His face was all props rather than features. Anyone with brown eyes who was tall enough could put on a false moustache and, with the wig and glasses, he'd pass – certainly well enough for a busy official comparing a passport photograph.'

'So you mean he drove down to the house in France dressed as Tristram and came back as Zoë?'

'Exactly.'

'But you don't think Tristram's still alive?'

Charles shook his head. 'I'm afraid not. But it's no wonder the French police had no luck finding his body, since the body never even went to France. And the English police, who might have found it here, had no reason to start looking.'

'So where do you reckon it is?'

Charles was already dialling on the telephone as he answered. 'I have only one idea. If I'm wrong, we're virtually back to square one. But, thinking about it, on the night Bertram killed Yves and Tristram, he didn't have much time. He left the mews at half past three, and he caught the six-thirty ferry at Dover. He couldn't afford a major detour and he couldn't risk just dumping the body. He had to put it somewhere safe and then probably move it to a final resting-place once interest in the case had died down.'

'But where would –'

Finally the telephone was answered at the other end. 'Henry,' said Charles, interrupting Stan.

'Sorry, I was in the bath,' her Kensington vowels replied.

'Listen, Henry, this is important. You remember the great dirty weekend which didn't take place...'

'With Bertram? Yes.' Her voice sounded small.

'Don't feel bad about it. You were set up, I'm afraid. He planned to fix the weekend and then stage a row with you so that it didn't happen.'

'But I don't see what –'

'I can't explain now. Tell me, did you ever find out the address of his cottage in Kent?'

When he was in a hurry, Stan Fogden's style of driving the 'Charlie' was hair-raising. After a particularly spine-jarring corner, Charles remonstrated, 'Hey, look, nothing's going to be gained if we don't get there in one piece.'

'Don't worry, mate. I know what I'm doing. Every other telly I get I'm driving the getaway jam-jar. I done more drives like this than you've had hot saintsands.'

Saints and sinners – Dinners, Charles translated for himself; as he clung grimly to the door-handle of the van and prayed that his idea about Bertram's movements was correct.

The address Henry had given was in a little village outside Canterbury. Going there would have involved only the smallest detour on the route from London to Dover, and that fact fuelled the hope in Charles's mind.

As they approached the cottage and saw its remoteness from the village of its postal address, Charles also felt hope. It was an ideal place for a temporary morgue. If the cottage had a cellar…or an outhouse…Even a temporary grave in the garden might be possible. You don't have to be over-elaborate in your concealment of a body when the search for it is centred in another country.

Stan parked just to the side of the closed gate. The cottage, like all the accoutrements of Bertram Pride's life, had the heightened reality of a commercial. Its thatch was too neat, its beams too black, its paintwork too white.

There appeared to be no sign of life. The garage door, like the front gate, was closed. There was no car in evidence.

'I hope to God we aren't too late,' Charles muttered. 'If he's off hiding the body somewhere really secure, bang goes our evidence.'

'Assuming of course,' said Stan cheerfully, 'that it ever was here in the first place…'

'Thank *you*,' said Charles. 'Wait in the van. I'll just go and have a snoop around.'

'Sure you don't want me to come? Like I say, I have played a few heavies in my time.'

'No, you watch the gate, in case he tries to get out this way. And if I'm not back in half an hour, get the police.'

'Yeah,' said Stan ruefully. 'That's the line that always gets said to me in tellies. Means I've had my little scene and now the camera's going to follow the bleeding 'ero into the bleeding 'ouse.'

Charles grinned and got out of the van. He tapped it on the roof; glad of Stan's presence, as he moved towards the gate.

There were tyre-marks on the gravel and an arc scraped by the opening gate, but he could not tell how recently the marks had been made. As he clicked the latch and pushed the gate, he felt an awful emptiness. If Bertram Pride wasn't there, if Bertram Pride had not been there that day, then Charles's whole theory was wrong.

Although the cottage itself was fairly small, it was set fifty yards back from the road, so the drive was long. Charles moved forward slowly. Over the garage door he could see a video camera fixed, trained on the gate. Another of the celebrity props, a way of vetting visitors, no doubt keeping away the fans.

Though the camera was trained on him, Charles got no feeling of being watched. The emptiness within him grew more hollow.

What happened happened very suddenly.

Remotely controlled, the garage door slid up and over.

The Range Rover inside must have been already started and revving, because it leapt forward like a race-horse out of the stalls.

Charles just had time to register Bertram Pride's face, expressionless, behind the windscreen, as the car rushed, in a fusillade of gravel, towards him.

He urged his body to the side, but, as in a dream of running in sand, it responded with agonizing slowness.

The Range Rover's bumper caught him on the hip, lifting him, spinning him like a child's toy before throwing him down in a flower-bed.

Winded as he lay there, Charles turned his head to the car's back, and saw it disappearing through the gate which he had so obligingly left open. Bertram Pride had got away.

But Charles had reckoned without Stan Fogden. There was a sudden screech and earth-shaking impact as the little 'Charlie' was driven into the Range Rover's path.

Bertram Pride was out of his vehicle first. Stan's driving-side door was smashed in and he had to get out the other side. As Charles hobbled up to the gate, Bertram had set off down the lane, with Stan a good ten yards behind.

But, despite his bulk, and despite Bertram's fitness programme, Stan moved the faster. He launched himself into an untidy tackle which brought Bertram crashing down on to the tarmac.

Stan was first up. And, as Bertram rose, a fist with some eighteen stones' weight behind it caught him neatly on the point of the jaw. Like a figure from a *Tom and Jerry* cartoon, his body stiffened and he went back down on to the road like a board.

'Bit of rope in the back of the van,' Stan shouted to Charles. 'Bring it along. We'll truss him up.'

As Charles approached, Stan was flexing and unflexing his right hand with evident pain.

'Cor blimey. I've swung that punch in so many tellies, but I'm used to the bloke ducking back before I hit him. Bloody hurts when you actually make contact.'

Bertram groaned as his arms and legs were pinioned, but he was out to the world.

'That was quite amazing, Stan, the way you stopped the car and caught him. It was like something out of *The Sweeney*.'

The fat actor shrugged. 'First time I done it *was* actually on a *Sweeney*. But I've played the scene in a good few other tellies too. Shows the benefit of rehearsal, Charles my old son. Had to get this right first time. 'Cause there's no retakes in real have-you-met-the, is there?'

The context gave that one away. Have-you-met-the-wife?—Life.

Their next task was grimmer.

Charles opened the Range Rover's hatchback.

The smell that came from the huge sealed black polythene bag was not too strong. But when they cut the adhesive tape that held it, the stench suddenly flooded up like gas, invading their mouths and nostrils.

Gagging, they stayed only long enough to confirm that the bag did contain a corpse, and then called the police.

The latter's investigations confirmed that the bag contained, as well as a bloody razor and bloodstained gloves and clothes, the body of Tristram Gowers.

Although after so long it was difficult to fix the precise time of death, it seemed likely that he had been strangled the night Tryst had been closed for its annual holiday.

Charles only hoped that Tristram had died before he saw what Bertram did to his lover.

# Chapter Seventeen

'HE WAS AMBITIOUS,' said Charles. 'He had been out of work, and he was determined it wasn't going to happen again. Martin Sabine stood between him and that part, and he was determined to get it. That was where Bertram went wrong. If he hadn't attacked Martin, he wouldn't have needed to commit the other two murders.'

'He very nearly got away with them...' said O'Rourke.

'Very nearly...' Bartlemas agreed.

They were sitting over one of Bartlemas's 'divine' French meals, drinking the black wine of Cahors. The face that might have been Edmund Kean as Sir Giles Overreach beamed malevolently down on them.

'I wonder why Yves waited so long before he started blackmailing Bertram...?'

'I don't know,' said Charles. 'Sheer mischief, perhaps. Perhaps he needed money for his other activities, for conducting the affairs Tristram wasn't meant to know about.'

'It's quite possible...'

'He was a very naughty boy...'

'But he did love Tristram...'

'Oh yes, in his way he loved him...'

'And presumably,' said Charles, 'just paying Yves off was too risky. So long as Yves was alive, there would be the constant danger of exposure. And if Tristram knew about the attack too...'

'Do you think he did?'

'There was a risk that he might. Also Bertram's plan depended on an absent Tristram on whom Yves's death could be blamed.'

'Yes. Poor Tris...'

'Poor dear Tris...'

'Bertram planned it for a long time. He set up Gary Stane, using a French accent to throw suspicion on to Yves. He set up poor little Henry, planning the row with her all the time.'

'Cynical...'

'And cold-blooded...'

'Yes. But, you know, he was at a very dangerous time in his career.'

'Oh, surely not...'

'*Lexton and Sons* had made him a star, surely...'

'Yes, but the last series of *Lexton and Sons* was over. There was still money coming in – foreign repeats, that sort of thing – but Bertram had a very high standard of living to maintain. He was "resting" too, you know – had been since the last series finished. And it's much more difficult for a "star" – he has to select what he does with great care, wait for the right property. That's why the book was so important to him. *A Pride of Lextons*, with all its attendant promotion, was going to bring Bertram Pride back into the public eye, remind them that he was a star.'

'Hmm. I suppose the book will be withdrawn.'

'Pulped, I expect...'

'Having met its publisher, I wouldn't be surprised if he doubled the print order. All this is going to give him more free publicity than he ever dreamed of.'

There was a silence. Bartlemas served their *digestif*: brandy-soaked prunes from Agen, part of the loot from the French trip.

'Are you going to have these on the menu in Tryst when you take it over, O'Rourke?' asked Charles.

'Not a bad idea.'

'O'Rourke talked to the solicitors today.'

'Yes, it's confirmed...'

'He does get the lot...'

'And are you going to keep it on?'

'I had a rather bizarre idea about that.' O'Rourke smoothed his residue of hair across his scalp. 'I thought I'd get Monique Lafeu in to manage it.'

'She seemed to be a pretty tough businesswoman.'

'Exactly. No great sense of humour, but she'd run it well. In a strange way, I feel that Yves might have approved.'

'I think you're tight, O'Rourke.'

'I'm also going to make over some of the money to Zoë. God knows, we don't need it, and she got a very rough deal out of the divorce...'

'Very rough...' Bartlemas echoed.

'That's an extremely kind thought,' said Charles. 'And it'd really be appreciated. She's desperately hard-up. Mind you, you'd better put a condition to the gift.'

'What?'

'That she's not allowed to spend any of it on gin.'

Bartlemas and O'Rourke shook their heads sadly.

'Heard she was going a bit that way...'

'Such a pity...Lovely girl...'

'Yes. All she needs is a few good jobs. If she had the work, she wouldn't feel the need to drink.'

'No...'

'No...'

'How about you, Charles? Anything on the horizon?'

He grunted a little laugh. 'Stan Fogden thinks there might be some more decorating coming up. Let's hope we manage next time without finding a body.'

'But no acting work?'

'No. No. 'Fraid not. The "rest" continues.'

'Sorry, Charles. Bad time. There doesn't seem to be a lot around at the moment.'

'No, Maurice.' Charles looked at the receiver with resignation. 'And how was your holiday? How were the Canaries?'

'Well...' Maurice's voice made the word long with reservations. 'I suppose it was all right. The trouble is, when you've just got a fortnight, you spend the first week untwitching and by the time you start to feel relaxed, you've got to start thinking about coming back again.'

'Must be hell,' Charles murmured.

'By the way, did you get to see Dana Wilson?'

'Yes.'

'Oh, good. Glad I was able to set that up for you, Charles.'

'But she's not casting anything in the foreseeable future.'

'Oh no, I know *that*. But don't ever say I don't try for you, Charles.'

'No. Goodbye, Maurice.'

He rang Henry to explain the reasons for his sudden call about the cottage and to fill her in on the details of the case. She listened dutifully, but did not seem very interested. Her mind was elsewhere, and when he had finished the recitation of Bertram Pride's mis-doings, the reason became apparent.

'Actually, I'm going back to Gloucestershire next week.'

'What, you're giving up the theatre?'

'Well, for a year or two, yes.'

'What's suddenly prompted this?'

'Well, you see...' She giggled. Charles could imagine the blush spreading over her perfect skin. 'James p'd the old q.'

'I beg your pardon?'

'Popped the question. Proposed.'

'Oh. Er. Congratulations.'

'Thanks. Needless to say, I'm chuffed to bits. But we want to get married before Christmas because James has got a tour of duty out in the Falklands coming up, so me and the aged p.s are going to be absolutely flat out with preparations and what-have-you.'

'Yes.'

'Anyway, sweet of you to ring. V.g. to hear you. We must invite you to the wedding.'

But somehow he knew they wouldn't. And, if they had, he somehow didn't think it'd be his scene.

So much for Henry's theatrical career. Her background had reclaimed her. She would lose her virginity to her husband on her wedding night and devote the rest of her life to bringing up squat, doughty little facsimiles of James.

She would be happy, she would relate to her children how nearly she became an actress. And her father and sister would say, 'I told you so.'

Somehow it seemed right.

That evening Charles had an unexpected call.

'It's Frances. Your wife. Remember?'

'It comes back. How are you?'

'Bad.'

'David?'

'Yes.'

'What?'

'Well, you know we were talking of getting married?'

'Mm.'

'And he was going to tell his wife about us while they were on holiday and ask for a divorce?'

'Yes.'

'Well, he didn't. And so far as I can tell, he never will. He wants us both. And I think, if he were ever forced into the position of having to make a decision, I'd be the one who went.'

'Men are pigs,' said Charles automatically. 'So what's your relationship now?'

'I don't know.' Her voice was tight with emotion. 'Charles, can I see you?'

'Yes.'

It was a month after the murders at Tryst. Charles Paris had a slight headache as he walked through the underpass beneath the Westway. The previous night he had made yet another valedictory visit to the Montrose.

He was on his way to the Unemployment Office in Lisson Grove to collect his Giro once again.

He needed some cash. He was taking his wife out to dinner that evening.

He met a couple of fellow actors in the queue. A very convivial session in the pub ensued, and Charles's headache dissolved.

None of the other actors had heard of any jobs coming up. The 'rest' looked set fair to continue for ever.

It was after four when he got back to Hereford Road. There was a message for him by the payphone on the landing.

For once the female Swede who had taken it had produced a piece of writing without misleading errors. The message was quite clear.

CHARLES PARIS — PLEASE RING RACHEL GRANT, CASTING DIRECTOR AT THE NATIONAL THEATRE.

His hands were sweaty as he fumbled in the directory for the number. His fingers slipped and he had to redial.

But he got through. He asked the voice on the switchboard for Rachel Grant.

'Hello. Rachel Grant.'

'Ah, this is Charles Paris. I had a message to call you.'

'Yes, yes, of course. Thank you very much for getting back to me so quickly.' There was a silence. 'No problem,' said Charles fatuously, filling the space. 'The fact is, you were recommended to me, Mr Paris.'

'Yes?'

'For a job I need doing.'

'Yes?'

'It's the sitting-room of my flat. Just emulsion on the walls and gloss on the paintwork. I wonder, would you be free to do it?'

'Yes,' said Charles Paris. 'I'd be free.'

Lightning Source UK Ltd.
Milton Keynes UK
UKOW041126031212

203110UK00001B/182/A